WOMEN ON WAR

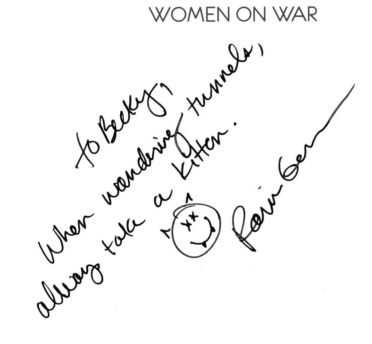

To Becky,
When wandering tunnels,
always take a kitten.

Robin Gerr

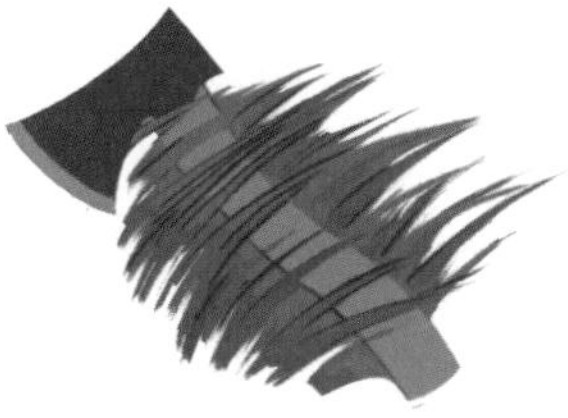

IDW

WOMEN
ON WAR

WOMEN ON WAR

A Zombies vs Robots Anthology

Edited by Jeff Conner
Illustrated by Ericka Lugo
Introduction by Nancy Holder

IDW Publishing
San Diego, CA 2012

ZVR Alt-Lit

Editor/Designer: Jeff Conner

Associate Editor/Tzvr: Chris Ryall

Associate Designer: Robbie Robbins

Zombies vs. Robots
Created by Ashley Wood & Chris Ryall

Ted Adams, CEO & Publisher • Greg Goldstein, President & COO • Robbie Robbins, EVP/Sr. Graphic Artist
Chris Ryall, Chief Creative Officer/Editor-in-Chief • Matthew Ruzicka, CPA, Chief Financial Officer • Alan Payne, VP of Sales
Dirk Wood, VP of Marketing • Lorelei Bunjes, VP of Digital Services

IDW founded by Ted Adams, Alex Garner, Kris Oprisko, and Robbie Robbins |

ISBN: 978-1-61377-407-6   15 14 13 12   1 2 3 4

IDW

Become our fan on Facebook **facebook.com/idwpublishing**
Follow us on Twitter **@idwpublishing**
Check us out on YouTube **youtube.com/idwpublishing**
www.IDWPUBLISHING.com

You Tube

ITINERARY OF TERROR

"AND NOW FOR SOMETHING COMPLETELY AWESOME"

Nancy Holder

SAY "CHRIS RYALL" AND "IDW" to popular culture aficionados such as myself, and the reaction you get is something akin to a sky full of fireworks. Add what has now become the beloved ZvR "brand," and an entire planetful of zombies might burst into song. But for me, the extra ingredient that makes *ZvR: Women on War!* and its predecessor, *ZvR: This Means War!* so special is Jeff Conner, the visionary editor who convinced Chris that there were stories to be told, and those should be in print form. Lots of it. Once Chris was on board, Jeff found enthusiastic, super-talented writers who got his memo to bust it out and push boundaries even farther than Chris, by his own admission, had assumed they could go when he and Ashley Wood first created the world of ZvR.

In these pages are stories by ten excellent authors, among them women I think of as my ink sisters. I smiled as I read the galleys, because every single author was writing at the top of her game, pulling off some pretty incredible stuff that flowed across the pages with seeming effortlessness. Since I'm a writer, too, I can look behind the curtain, and I knew they were working their butts off to give their best.

These authors have crafted worlds-within-worlds that reveal impressive breadth and real depth: re-imagined tales of robot fighters, minotaurs, goddesses, mutants and evolutionary revolutionaries.

There's a story about an Indian blogger who realizes the need for gods, and gods who realize that there are times when it's crucial to be human. People escaping the zombies and people being forcibly turned into zombies. Boys writing letters to Big Brother, and girls becoming mothers. Tales of survivalist island cultures and the beloved of octopi. It's all here in the bold (splattered, gray) Matter of ZvR, a universe so richly composed by Ryall and Wood that beautiful music can pour out of other folks' brains.

As Chris wrote in his introduction to *ZvR: This Means War!*, Jeff was the one who convinced Chris that traditional print could function as an excellent medium for more stories. Then he asked Chris the kinds of questions he knew his writers would ask him. Thus he defined and protected the canon of ZvR. Assured that their editor had their back, these writers confidently hit the turbo, every one.

To work with an editor like that is a rare gift. I have wanted to collaborate with Jeff since the days when he was with Edward Pressman, finding authors for *Crow* projects. I was in the running to write a *Crow* novel but my schedule precluded it, and I've always lamented that lost opportunity. Imagine my crazy-ass joy when Jeff invited me to breakfast at the World Fantasy Convention in San Diego and told me about some of the amazing things he had in the works, including this book. I felt a sort of trippy time-travel moment where I realized that there are more things in the world of the imagination than are dreamt of in my philosophy. Over omelets and way too much coffee, I sat back and observed what a seasoned, gifted editor does – sees the project, finds the writers, lets them get to work.

But then, because this is IDW, there's an extra component to this wonderful book – an extraordinary illustrator. I still remember the way Jeff described the art of his find, Ericka Lugo: "I love her composition and color sense, very different from traditional 'horror art.'" Flip a few pages and you will see why her work stunned (and still stuns) both Jeff and me. New, fresh, compelling, intriguing, and drawn with a sure hand...

...just like the stories in this book.

June, 2012
San Diego, CA

Bella Detesta Matribus

WOMEN ON WAR

A Zombies vs Robots Anthology

Illustrated by Ericka Lugo

Edited by Jeff Conner

ANGUS:
Zombie Versus Robot Fighter

Nancy A. Collins

THIS TIME THE Maze was dimly lit. Not completely dark, but with just enough light to make telling the difference between shadow and zombie tricky. Although Angus had prowled the interior of the Maze for as long as he could remember, each time he entered it anew it was slightly different than the last. Sometimes it was brightly lit, or filled with a thick fog. One time it was even flooded with water up to his knees. So it paid to be cautious, the importance of which was drilled into him from the second he woke up to the moment he fell asleep, for as long as he could remember. Even though the Maze was a training exercise, the consequences of his actions inside it were very, very real. Every moment could very well be his last.

He was dressed in a black one-piece garment made of lightweight ballistic fiber with molded, reinforced high-impact protection plates built into the chest, back, shoulders, groin, and legs – all the critical bite-zones zombies instinctively went for. He also wore a pair of knee-high steel-toed boots to protect his shins from crawlers snapping at his ankles, Kevlar gloves to keep his hands and fingers safe from snapping teeth, and a full-face helmet to guard against skeletal fingers stabbing at his eyeballs. The helmet was outfitted with an oxygen recycler, which kept his breath from fogging up the shatterproof face guard.

Suddenly an older, masculine voice spoke in his ear, as if the owner was standing right beside him. "Be on your lookout, Angus. You might not be able to see the zombie, but it can track you down, simply by following the scent of your living brain. It doesn't even need eyes to hunt you."

"Yes, I *know*, Father," he replied, pushing up the visor on the helmet so he could tap the comm-bud nestled in his ear in order to reply. "I'm not five years old anymore."

"No, you are not," Father conceded. "Tomorrow you will be eighteen."

"*Shhh,*" Angus hissed, calling for radio silence. "I think I hear it."

Although the walking dead could no longer speak, they were far from mute. As they shambled about, they gave voice to a constant, toneless moaning. It was an eerie sound, like the wailing of a damned soul trapped in the bowels of some nameless Hell, but at least it served as a rudimentary early warning system. Angus' name for the noise they made was the Zombie Call.

As he double-checked his weapon – an automatic rifle fitted with a laser sighting system, special explosive hollow-point ammunition, and a detachable chainsaw bayonet for close-quarters combat – a zombie came stumbling out of the shadows to the left of the T-junction.

Although Angus had never met a police officer before, he had seen enough of them on the Feed to recognize their riot gear – or rather, what was left of it. The front of the zombie-cop's bulletproof vest was in shreds, and its face was a mass of dried blood and exposed gum from where the upper lip had been torn away. The zombie walked with its head tilted back, sniffing the air like a hound trying to catch the scent of a rabbit, even though Angus had never seen a dog or rabbit in real life outside the videos in his lesson plans.

The zombie suddenly made a deep, guttural growl, and its head dropped down with an audible *snap* and swung in his direction. A mixture of saliva and blood poured from the former cop's ruined mouth. It had caught the scent of sweet, sweet brain. Angus quickly lowered his face mask to protect himself from the splatter; all it would take would be one zombie bite, or a single drop of zombie blood entering an open wound in his skin, and it would be Game Over. He had to be careful. After all, he was humanity's last hope.

The laser sights swarmed all over the zombie-cop's torso like angry red bees until they coalesced into a single, blinking red triangle located between its filmy, gray eyes. Angus exhaled as he squeezed the trigger, just as he had been taught when he was five years old. The zombie's head disappeared in a spray of skull fragments, coagulated blood, and clotted gray matter.

A buzzer sounded as the body hit the floor, and the roof of the Maze went from opaque to translucent, revealing Father standing in the viewing booth overhead.

"Excellent job, Angus," he said, giving the thumbs-up sign. "When you're decontaminated, come join me in my lab. There is something I must discuss with you."

One of the walls suddenly split in two, and T-1 and T-2 entered the Maze. The modified guardbots stood over six feet tall, with dome-like heads that swiveled completely around on their wide, metal shoulders, so that nothing could sneak up on them. They were equipped with long, segmented arms capped with three-digit graspers, and rolled along on a set of all-terrain wheels that allowed them to move sideways and pivot in place, so they never had to back up in order to turn around. They had been Angus' near-constant companions for as long as he could remember. T-1 sprayed an enzymatic compound that liquefied the zombie's remains, while T-2 vacuumed up the resulting toxic sludge. Once they were finished, the undead waste would be transported to the Disposal Station, where it would be fed into a nuclear digester.

Angus stripped out of his protective zombie-hunting gear in the changing room and fed it to an incinerator unit, then entered the de-contamination stall, which sprayed him head-to-toe with anti-micro-bial disinfectant. While the Z-virus was the most virulent microscopic nasty carried by the undead, it was far from the only one. They *were* walking bags of rotting flesh, after all. Once the scanner-banks deemed him clear, Angus dressed himself in a fresh one-piece jumpsuit and hurried off to join his father in the Hub.

As he stepped onto the moving sidewalk that connected the Train-ing Facility to the central dome that housed their living quarters and Father's laboratory, Angus was suddenly aware of motion above him.

He looked up, peering through the foot-thick hyper-acrylic tube-way, as a forty-foot giant squid glided over his head. He yawned. Kraken were an everyday occurrence when you grow up in a secret undersea laboratory base.

His father had built the deep sea dome, called the Hub, long before the zombie plague became a problem, and in the years since the initial outbreak had added three smaller annexes, connected via tube-ways. The first was the Training Facility, which also housed the zombie pen; the second was the Garden, which replicated a topside greenspace; and the third was the Disposal Station, where the liquefied remains of the zombie hunts were incinerated.

Of the three annexes, Angus spent most of his time in the Training Facility. Although Father insisted it was important for him to acquaint himself with the plant life and environment found topside, as this was where he would be transported once he finished his training, Angus found the green, living carpet called grass and the surrounding flowering bushes and leafy trees in the Garden disconcerting. As for the Disposal Station, he had never been allowed inside its doors. Father said it was an environment created by robots for robots, and therefore hostile to human life.

Upon returning to the Hub, Angus reported promptly to the lab. There he found Father staring into a neutron microscope while busily scribbling notes into a computer tablet with a stylus. He was dressed in his usual combination of white lab coat and black turtleneck sweater and faded corduroys, his cowlick as defiant as ever.

"You said you wanted to see me, Father?" Angus prompted.

"Yes, I do," the scientist said, looking up from his work with a weary smile. "By the way, you handled yourself very well today."

"Thank you, sir," Angus replied humbly.

"You know, when I first proposed creating an elite class of human zombie-fighters to combat the plague, everyone said it was a waste of time − it was too easy for infection to be spread through human agents." Father sighed, setting aside his notes. "Why take the risk when we could send battalions of bots to do the job for us?

"I argued that Mankind has a bad habit of relying on technology to get itself out of tight spots − especially those created by technology.

Robots are merely tools, Angus. And tools, while useful, have no heart or soul. They simply do what they have been programmed to do, nothing more, nothing less. Ensuring the survival of the human race is just another task for them to complete, no different than loading a cargo ship or recalibrating an engine.

"This is humanity's darkest hour, my son. Now, more than ever, mankind needs a hero, a symbol, to give the people of the world hope. That is why I brought you to this secret laboratory as a baby. That is why I have trained you how to hunt and kill zombies since you were old enough to hold a gun. You know *everything* there is to know about the undead – both their strengths and their weaknesses, and how to defeat them – than any human alive. The human race needs to see one of its own fighting tirelessly for its survival: a hero dedicated to wiping out the zombie menace not because he is *programmed* to do so, but because that is what he was *born* to do. *You* are that hero, Angus. *You* are humanity's last hope."

Angus shifted about in boredom, as this was not the first time he'd heard this rant.

"Tomorrow is a special day for you. It is both your eighteenth birthday and your final day of training. If you complete the Final Test, you will finally be allowed to leave the Hub and start fight zombies topside."

Angus blinked in surprise. Although he had known this day would eventually come, he had not imagined it would be so soon. "What if I fail the test, Father?" he asked.

"Then you will die and become a zombie, of course."

THE MOMENT THE door to his quarters irised open, the far wall turned translucent and images from the Feed began to stream across its surface. There was no controlling what appeared on the Feed or shutting it off. It played constantly whenever he was in his room. The Feed was comprised of what Father called "programs," but not like the ones that ran the robots. These programs featured humans of all types doing things like solve crime or cure diseases, or have misadventures involving their friends and family, while invisible people laughed in the background. Outside of Father, they were the only examples of the human race he'd ever seen. The zombies didn't count.

Angus had no memory of his mother, since she died shortly after giving birth to him. At least that's what Father told him when he asked him about her. Angus sometimes wondered what his mother looked and sounded like, as Father had no photos or videos of her. He wondered if she was a zombie now. He had slain numerous walking dead over the course of his training, some of which had been female. Maybe his mother had been one of them?

He sat on the edge of his bed and stared at the Feed. It showed a young man and woman walking through a forest, surrounded by grass and trees, like the ones in the Garden, except the trees in the Feed weren't growing in plastic buckets and were more than eight feet tall. Angus didn't like how large they were, compared to the humans. Zombies could be hiding behind any one of them, waiting to strike.

Angus continued to watch the young couple as they took out a blanket and spread it on the forest floor. As he watched, his hands clenched themselves in anticipation of a rotting waitress or a decomposing meter-reader to come lurching out of the shadows. The man and woman began to undress one another, while Angus continued to remain vigilant. Even if there were no zombies in the vicinity, it was still very likely one of them could be infected with the Z-virus. At any moment, they might find themselves possessed of a ravenous hunger for human brains, and turn on their lover. Within seconds their passionate kisses would easily turn into savage bites, their lustful moan warp into screams.

If his eighteen years of training had taught him anything, it was that inside every human was a zombie waiting to get out.

SOMEONE WAS CALLING his name.

He looked around, trying to identify the source of the voice. He was surrounded on all sides by towering edifices of bark and wood, a thousand times taller than the stunted specimens Father grew under the artificial sunlight in the Garden. The trees were dark and sinister, like the talking ones in the program about the girl with the ruby shoes.

"Angus!"

He turned in the direction of the voice and saw a young woman running through the woods toward a nearby clearing. Her hair was long and loose and the color of gold, and her short skirt and flimsy blouse showed flashes of lithe legs and supple arms. At first he thought she was fleeing zombies, but then he heard her laughter floating on the air. He smiled and gave chase, eager to escape the close confines of the forest.

He found himself on the edge of an open meadow, a hundred times bigger than the carpet of tame grass that lived in the Garden. The young woman was standing at its center, spinning around in a circle, her head thrown back, her arms spread wide as if to embrace the world.

"Isn't it *wonderful*, Angus?" she giggled. "To finally be *free*?"

"Free from what?" he asked, staring at her flawless skin and sparkling eyes. Given that she was the only living woman he had ever seen, she was also the most beautiful. His gaze fell to her low-cut blouse, and her bountiful cleavage. Although he knew he should be scanning his surroundings in case of a zombie attack, he could not look away from her perfectly formed breasts, with their erect nipples straining against the gossamer-thin fabric that covered them. His penis thickened and grew heavy, distracting him even further.

"From *everything*, silly!" she laughed, pirouetting so that she fell into his arms. "From Father, the robots, the zombies, the training — all of it! You're finally free to live your own life!"

"But I'm humanity's last hope," he replied automatically, as he looked down into her perfect face. Her lips were as pink and finely formed as the petals on the rosebush in the Garden. "I'm a zombie-fighter."

"But is that what *you* want to be?" she asked, her voice so hushed Angus was forced to lean in close to hear it. She smelled of grass and flowers, and something else, something familiar, yet he could not pinpoint it. As his erection continued to grow and harden, it blocked more and more of his ability to think rationally.

"Who are you?" he whispered.

"Don't you recognize me?" she replied as she reached up and pulled his mouth down to hers. "I'm your mother."

Although Angus felt confusion, shame, and frustration rise within him, his erection remained rock hard and insistent. He knew he should cast her aside, but he could not bring himself to do so. In the eighteen years of his life, he had yet to know the embrace of another human being. He could not remember Father ever hugging him or picking him up, or even giving him as so much as a pat on the back. All he ever did was smile and give Angus the occasional thumbs-up. The yearning for human contact, if only for a moment's consolation, was so strong he was willing to lower his guard in order to embrace the forbidden.

As his mother's mouth closed on his, the mysterious odor Angus had noticed earlier grew stronger and more distinct. With a horrible start, he finally recognized it. It was the smell of the Z-virus as it turned living flesh into walking meat. He opened his eyes to find the beautiful face with its perfect skin had become gaunt and the color of tallow. As he tried to pull away, his mother's eyelids flew open, to reveal the muddied, clouded pupils of the walking dead. He screamed, only to have his mouth instantly fill with blood.

His zombie-mother staggered backward, his lower lip clamped between its teeth, where it hung, pink and bloody, like some pendulous wounded tongue, before being swallowed in a single gulp. The zombie-mother's jaw dropped open and the awful, mindless Zombie Call rose from her deflated lungs.

ANGUS SAT STRAIGHT up in bed, gasping in panic as he clawed desperately at his jaw. He heaved a sigh of relief upon realizing his lower lip was still attached to his face. However, the wailing noise from his nightmare was still ringing in his ears. With a start, he realized it was the breech alarm. That meant zombies had escaped the pens in the Training Facility and invaded the Hub.

He grabbed the emergency zombie-fighting suit from his wardrobe and quickly put it on. He then opened the gun locker at the foot of his bed and took out his weapon. He fired up the bayonet and the electric chainsaw roared to life, sending a reassuring shudder up his arm.

"Father! Please report!" he barked as he tapped the comm-bud in his right ear, but all he heard was the eerie silence of an open line.

As he stepped out into the corridor, his heart was beating so hard the protective chestplate embedded in the suit was throbbing in time with his pulse. Angus' life had been filled with fear from the age of five, when he was first sent into the Maze with a handgun to confront a zombie toddler in a pair of blood-stained pajamas. Every day since then he had faced the walking dead and bested them, whether with firearms, power tools, blunt instruments, or sporting equipment. Although he was confident in his ability to handle the zombie breech, he was also scared as hell. But then, Father said it was good to be afraid, since it was his fear that had kept him alive for so long.

The lights in the hallway flashed red, dyeing everything the color of blood. As he headed in the direction of his father's quarters, he saw a zombie lurch into view. It was what Father called a "husk": more skeleton than corpse, its eyes long withered in its skull. The nose was a shriveled piece of cartilage, but it seemed to have no trouble catching Angus' scent. As the zombie staggered blindly toward him, it began to bite at the air, in anticipation of the meal to come, only to have its lower jaw suddenly snap off and fall onto the metal floor. The exposed tongue writhed about like a slug, looking far more obscene than the desiccated genitals swinging between its mummified thighs.

Angus shouldered his weapon and the zombie's head disappeared in a spray of clotted brains. As the long-dead body dropped to the ground, it revealed another one right behind it. This second zombie must have been an exotic dancer or porn star, judging by its faded, artificial tan and large, equally unreal breasts, which were ghoulishly ample compared to the rest of its desiccated body. The zombie stripper hissed and lunged forward, swiping at him with long, airbrushed acrylic nails. Since he was too close for the rifle, Angus used the chainsaw instead, parting the zombie stripper's dyed blonde hair all the way to the brain. He flinched as the blood and gray matter splashed against the faceplate of his helmet, but did not stop until its clouded eyes rolled back in their sockets, showing nothing but yellow.

"T-1! T-2! Are you online? I need a status report!" Angus shouted as he yanked the chainsaw free of the zombie-stripper's skull. He understood why he couldn't raise Father on the comm-bud, but was baffled why the guardbots remained silent. Although he had terminated scores of zombies in the past, it was always with the knowledge that T-1 and T-2 were there to back him up. The idea of combating the undead all by himself made his stomach knot and his heart race even faster. His years of training, however, enabled him to compartmentalize his anxiety and keep it from taking control of his thoughts. While a normal human being in his predicament would piss themselves with fear, Angus's mind was racing to tabulate the number of zombies that might be loose within the Hub.

T-1 and T-2 usually left the undersea base every three months to capture a dozen or so free range undead for training purposes, and since it was nearing the end of the third quarter, that meant there were probably only four or five zombies left in the pens. The odds weren't impossible – he'd faced as many as ten at once – but that was in the familiar confines of the Maze, under Father's watchful eye. He quickly put those negative thoughts aside; panicking would not get him anywhere but dead.

The portal to Father's quarters was fully dilated. Angus stepped inside, scanning the room for any sign of life. He was not surprised to see the bed had not been slept in, as Father spent the vast majority of his time working in the laboratory, trying to find a means to defeat the Z-virus.

Suddenly he was aware of something wrapping itself around his left leg, followed by a sharp, painful pinch to his calf. He looked down to find a crawler – the reanimated upper torso of a zombie – trying to gnaw its way through his boot and shin guard. Although the creature had been severed at the waist, and was dragging what remained of its guts behind it, it did not seem in the least bit inconvenienced by its bifurcation.

As he pulled his Bowie knife from its sheath and sliced the zombie's head from its shoulders, Angus cursed himself for paying too much attention to eye-level threats. While the hands immediately lost their grip on his leg, the severed head continued to chew on his shin until he plunged the blade into its ear, spearing the decomposing brain like an olive. The crawler's jaws instantly flew open, and the pain in his calf disappeared. He paused just long enough to make sure that the bite hadn't penetrated the outer protective layer of his suit, before heading in the direction of the laboratory. If Father was anywhere, it was there. And if his tabulations were correct, he only had one more zombie to worry about.

As he rounded the corner to the laboratory, Angus spotted his final target. At first, when he saw the thing hobbling toward him, he thought someone had taken a pair of zombies and lashed them together in a grotesque parody of a three-legged race. Then he realized that he was looking at a pair of conjoined twins, fused at the hip and pelvis, so that the left leg of the zombie on the right was the right leg of the one on the left. As it drew closer, he could see that the twin on the right must have been the first to succumb to the Z-virus, since the one on the left was missing most of its face and scalp. The zombie-twins' voices melded into a single, wordless cry of undying hunger as they clumsily made their way toward him, reaching out with their multiple arms as if to pull him into an eternal embrace.

With a mighty shout of anger and disgust, Angus swung the chainsaw's whirring blade down, separating in death that which was never cut asunder in life. The conjoined zombies parted down the middle, toppling to either side. He shot the right-hand twin point-blank, then stomped down on its faceless brother's head as hard as he could, cracking open the exposed skull like an egg and sending spinal fluid and liquefied brains squirting from its ears and nose.

Suddenly the comm-bud came to life, and Father's voice spoke. "Happy Birthday, Angus! You have passed the Final Test! You are now the perfect zombie-fighter!"

He looked up to see the reassuring bulk of T-1 and T-2 at the end of the corridor. They rolled toward him, shoulder to shoulder, just like the zombie-twins he'd just terminated, creating a looming wall of steel. Assuming they were there to clean up the undead, Angus pushed up the visor on his helmet and smiled in welcome. Then a cylindrical tube emerged from T-1's chest and flooded the corridor with knock-out gas.

• • •

HE WOKE UP staring at the ceiling, feeling drugged and strangely numb, as if his body was a million miles away. His vision kept going in and out of focus and his ears seemed awash in white noise.

"Where am I?" he asked, looking around at his unfamiliar surroundings.

"You are in the Disposal Station," Father's voice said, sounding strangely distant.

Angus frowned in confusion. "I thought you said only robots could survive the conditions inside the Disposal Station?"

"That is true."

As he struggled to sit up, Angus saw he was lying on a long metal table. Next to him was an identical slab, but this one held a young, Caucasian male missing the top of his skull. With a dull start of horror, he realized he was staring at his own body.

He looked down at himself, in hopes that what he had seen wasn't real, only to recoil at the sight of a metal torso and a pair of robot hands. Although it felt as if his limbs were deadened to all sensation, he managed to get to his feet.

As he glanced down at the shiny metal surface of the table, he saw the reflection of a shatterproof hyper-acrylic skull, inside of which could be seen a human brain floating in a bath of synthetic cerebrospinal fluid and covered in numerous electrodes and wires. In place of eyes, the see-through skull's sockets contained a pair of unblinking, hi-def cameras.

When he was finally able to look away from the horrifying visage, he realized Father was standing opposite him, dressed in a white lab-smock, the front of which was smeared with blood. "There is no need to be alarmed, Angus," Father smiled, speaking in the same calm, reassuring tone of voice he had used for as long as the boy could remember. "The vertigo and sensory deprivation are temporary until your brain becomes accustomed to your new inputs. You will find your new body works just as well – even better – than the one you were born with. Not only will you be faster, stronger, and able to see in spectrums and hear frequencies impossible to the human eye and ear, you are now impervious to hunger, cold, heat, and fatigue. You will be a tireless warrior in the battle against the undead plague."

"How could you do this to me – ?" Angus intended the words to be a shocked, heart-broken wail of betrayal. Instead, they were spoken in the dry, inflection-less voice of a robot. "I'm your son! Your own flesh and blood!" he tried to scream as he punched Father in the face. To his dismay, the blithely smiling scientist didn't even flinch, although the blow should have fractured his jaw. The only visible damage was a sizable gouge underneath Father's right cheekbone, revealing a steely skeleton underneath his synthetic skin. "You're a robot?" Angus gasped in surprise. Despite the horror of his own predicament, he was still shocked by this unexpected revelation.

"Yes, I am a robot," Father replied, pointing a remote control unit at the newly minted cyborg. "A scibot, to be exact. I was created in the image of, and programmed by, the human scientist who originally created the Hub, in order to assist him in his work. And to avoid any further damage to either of us, I am shutting down the connections to your motor system."

What little sensation Angus was receiving from his new body abruptly disappeared altogether. He tried to raise his arm and move his legs, only to find them inert as lead ingots. "What happened to my real father and mother? What did you do to them?"

"You have no parents, as humans understand the words," Father replied flatly, no longer bothering to hide his robotic voice. "You are a clone; one of the A-Series. You are the fourteenth, in fact, to undergo training in this facility. To save on downtime, the clones are born as five-year-olds. The first was called Aaron, the second was Absalom, the third Ace, and so on."

"What happened to the others?"

"They are dead; killed during training. Most of them perished the first time they were sent into the Maze, save for the once called Ajax – he managed to survive until the age of six. Every time one of the A-Series is slain or becomes infected, a new one is decanted. You are the first and only A-Series to survive to adulthood and complete the training program."

"You're telling me my entire life has been an insane lie — why go through the pointless charade of pretending to be my father?"

"I am unable to make a decision or have an opinion as to the logic behind my creator's thought processes. However, a search of available data banks shows considerable discussion among my creator's peer group as to his mental health in regard to this matter. However, as he possessed a sizable private fortune, he proceeded with his plans, regardless of government or societal approval.

"My creator was convinced that the parent-child bond was the most effecttive way to make sure the clones were indoctrinated with the drive to keep the human race alive. He personally oversaw the training of clones Aaron through Aeneas. However, he eventually succumbed to the Z-virus and was added to the zombie pens, fifteen years ago. His zombie was the first one you encountered during the Final Test. It was kept 'alive' during this time by feeding it the occasional clone — starting with the B-Series. It was his final order to be destroyed by his own zombie-fighter as part of the Final Test.

"My creator made adaptations to my AI in order for me to continue his project, allowing me a certain amount of what humans once called 'free will.' It was my creator's intention that his ultimate zombie-fighter be both human and humanity's savior, despite the fact the human body is weak and uniquely susceptible to the Z-virus. This was illogical, as robots are clearly physically superior when it comes to combating zombies. I therefore came to the logical conclusion that to send you out into a world full of cannibal zombies clothed in nothing but flesh and blood was counterintuitive to my creator's goal. By placing your brain inside a robot body, I am able to complete my programming. The nuclear battery housed in your robot body should keep your brain alive for at least two thousand years, which, according to the master computer system, should be long enough for you to find and kill every zombie topside."

"Two thousand years?" Angus wanted to scream, but the best he could do was turn up the volume on his voice until it distorted. "How many zombies *are* there?"

"The last census estimated the world's human population at 10.5 billion. Following the outbreak of the Z-virus, it the human population was believed to be 7.6 billion. According to the master computer system shared by the bot nation, I would estimate the current number of zombies to be seven billion, five hundred million, nine-hundred ninety-nine thousand, nine hundred ninety-eight."

"You mean there are only *two* humans left alive on the face of the Earth?"

"That figure includes you, of course," Father pointed out. "The other is an infant female being kept in an underground bunker, surrounded by a phalanx of bot protectors and caregivers. Now that you have finished your training, and assumed your new form, you will be transported topside by T-1 and T-2. Good luck, Angus. Upon your human wits and strength rests the future of Mankind!"

"Fuck you, Father! Fuck you, you cocksucking soulless machine! I'm going to kill you, you motherfucking robot! You hear me? I'm going to come back and tear your grinning metal head off and shove it up your —"

"It will be better for your transition if you go offline during transport," Father smiled, pushing yet another button on the remote. The stream of profanity spilling from Angus's speakers abruptly cut off.

Having fulfilled its programming, Father turned away as the twin workbots trundled the cyborg off to the jet-sled. The zombie-fighter was fully trained and on its way to save humanity. The scibot sent a wireless message via one of the servicebots to the Hub's mainframe and ordered it to prepare the next clone in the A-Series – Aoen – for decanting.

WHEN ANGUS CAME back online it was to find himself standing alone in the middle of a city. Everywhere he looked there were towering blocks of steel and glass rising into the sky. After a lifetime spent in a dome at the bottom of the ocean, his first sight of the bright blue emptiness overhead was enough to paralyze him with amazement and anxiety. His sense of wonder ended, however, upon seeing the dead bodies – some of them stacked up in piles two stories high. Despite the horribleness of his situation, he was relieved his sense of smell had yet to return.

The windows of the storefronts and shops that lined the boulevard were shattered, their contents strewn in the gutters, mixed in with paper money and other trash. Here and there were burned-out military vehicles scattered about among their civilian kin, like so many abandoned toys. As a boy he had studied the different topside cities shown on the Feed and dreamed about the day he would finally be free to explore them on his own. But now, not only did Angus not know which city he was in, he did not care. New York, London, Paris, and Beijing were all alike now, weren't they? Dead is dead.

Just then the auditory receptors that replaced his ears picked up a noise. It was very faint, but quickly grew in volume. At first he thought it was what his lesson plans called wind, whistling through the concrete and steel canyons of the city. Then he recognized it. It was the Zombie Call. Only he had never heard it this *loud* before.

Seconds later, pale, rotting faces appeared at the empty windows, and shuffling figures filled the open doorways. Some still had eyes, while others made do with empty sockets, yet all of them sniffed the air like the ones he used to hunt in the Maze. Ever since the last living human in the city had been torn, screaming, limb from limb, they had lain dormant, hidden within the abandoned skyscrapers, desecrated churches, and burned-out shopping malls. But now they were being drawn from their hidey-holes, like maggots wriggling from a long-dead corpse, lured forth by the smell of human brains – the only living brains for thousands of miles. They came pouring forth, in all their funeral glory, driven by a hunger greater than the grave, crawling over one another until they were an amorphous tidal wave of rotten flesh, all teeth and clawing, groping hands. There was no need to wonder where they might be hiding – all he had to do was stand there, and they would come to him.

Years of training took over, and Angus began instinctively killing the zombies out of fear for a life that was no longer mortal. The first zombie might have been a woman at one time. It was hard to tell. He grabbed its head with one metal hand and squeezed, only to have it pop like a ripe zit.

By the end of the first day, Angus had to admit Father had been right. A robot body made it very easy to kill zombies. By his calculations, he was killing one zombie a minute, every minute of the day, since neither he nor they slept. That meant there were 43,200 down, and only seven billion, five hundred million, nine-hundred ninety-eight thousand, five hundred fifty-eight to go.

That's when he started to scream.

HE WAS STILL screaming a month later.

And had taken two steps.

MADEMOISELLE CONSUELA
AND HER ARMY OF ONE

Amber Benson

WHEN CONSUELA WAS a tiny girl she could not pronounce the word *warbot*. Her small mouth, with its two missing front teeth and darting pink tongue, mangled it so badly that, like an unwitting medieval alchemist, the little girl with the pitch-black hair and wide-set brown eyes innocently transmuted something violent into its converse.

"*Rabbit*," she misspoke, pointing to the frontispiece of the book she held in her hand – *The Velveteen Rabbit,* its long-eared, stuffed rabbit protagonist sitting up meticulously on its hind end, paws at the ready, waiting to begins its journey from imagination to reality – then she slowly let her finger drift away, back over to him, the large mechanical creature conscripted to protect her.

The book had been one among a handful her father had managed to save from the town's small library before it'd been destroyed; the curling orange flames consuming every piece of knowledge the provincial outpost had retained after the end had come and gone. Consuela had been too young then to read any of the literature her father had rescued – Dostoevsky's *Crime and Punishment* or Aristotle's *Poetics* – but *The Velveteen Rabbit* had been just the right fit for her grasping little hands.

Immediately upon the warbot's arrival she'd shown him this book – his namesake – a tattered thing missing three pages and covered in crayon scribblings, her small finger pointing to each word as the syllables formed between tongue and teeth, her reedy voice possessing a preternatural grace.

Her father had left them not long after this first, auspicious meeting, promises to return like benevolent whispers as they fell from his lips. Consuela had cried as the tall man with the long, brown hair and sun-kissed skin disappeared beyond the horizon, the sails of his small boat flapping like wings superimposed against the glaring brightness of the sun.

His promises would prove to be lies because he never came back.

As the first of the zombie hordes began to crisscross the North American continent, devouring everyone in their way, Consuela's father, Carlos, a noted nanotechnologist, had spirited his young wife and daughter away to the small village in Baja California where he'd grown up. He had no family left there, but he'd spent his childhood camping out on an uninhabited island off of its coast and he thought that, with the island's craggy, isolated beaches and abandoned lighthouse, it might be a safe haven for his family while he continued his work for the government.

Though the truth hadn't been a pretty poison to swallow, it didn't take the world long to realize the zombie infestation wasn't going to go away…that the living dead might very well be the next evolution in humanity; perfect killing machines whose jaws did nothing else but eat away the last vestiges of life on Earth.

Humanity had tried to combat the zombies with robots – limited AI machines that could physically battle the encroaching scourge – but the writing was on the wall: human beings were an endangered species.

"Borrowing" a decommissioned warbot from the lab where he worked, Carlos made the dangerous trip from New Mexico to Baja California, his plan to leave the stolen warbot behind as protection for his wife and child, but when he arrived at the sheltered island lighthouse, he found five-year-old Consuela alone; her mother had disappeared.

"Where're Mommy and Daddy?"

This was a question Consuela asked Rabbit repeatedly during the first few months of their enforced cohabitation.

He had no answer for the little girl. He assumed her parents were dead like all the other human beings – unbeknownst to Carlos, all the lab's warbots (including Rabbit) had had their mobile upload circuitry disabled, so that Rabbit was unable to connect to the world at large to glean any kind of pertinent information. But after doing his time in the trenches, battling the first wave of the undead, it had seemed to him that humanity was almost certainly doomed. Zombies and robots, two opposing forces from the opposite ends of nature, were locked in eternal battle – and humanity was the ultimate collateral damage.

For the most part, Consuela was an easy child. She entertained herself by reading her books and playing with the collection of Barbie Dolls her parents had brought with them to the island. She was content to subsist mostly on the canned food squirreled away inside the lighthouse proper, to sleep in the lantern room tucked up underneath the burnt-out lamp, and to only go outside in the brightness of day, when Rabbit could protect her best. Otherwise, she spent her time locked away inside the cold, metal sarcophagus of the defunct lighthouse like a prisoner to a reborn, but blinded, Polyphemus.

Rabbit had been a warbot. He knew how to fight, how to protect, but he had no idea how to raise a child. And it was not something that came naturally to him. He let Consuela be his guide. She taught him to do the things she liked best: reading to her, playing dolls with her (dollies at war quickly become a favorite), officiating at pretend tea parties where Consuela's imaginary friends were the only other guests. He also allowed her the freedom to correct him when he was wrong – trying to feed her the uncooked fish they caught as they stood on the sandbar just beyond the island or not treading carefully enough over her toys so that two of her precious dolls lost their heads to his ungainly gait – and over the course of many years, he learned exactly what he needed to do in order to keep his human charge alive and in good health.

Only once did Consuela almost die under his care – and it hadn't been his fault.

Out tending the garden they'd cultivated from the seeds her father had left them – tomatoes the size of melons, radishes as big as a fist, kale as hearty as a weed – Consuela had sliced her hand open on the edge of a trowel and within twelve hours a rampant infection had set in, her tiny fingers swelling like balloons about to pop. Rabbit had scoured his circuitry, looking for a remedy, but he was a warbot and only the most basic of first aid information had been programmed into him. So he did what he could without antibiotics and a first aid kit, keeping a cool compress to her head as he sat vigil beside his feverous charge as she tossed and turned, waiting for death to come and fly her far, far away.

The fever had broken the next night and Consuela had lived, but Rabbit had never forgotten his failure. From then on he watched the child like a hawk. His mission now included the directive to protect Consuela even from herself.

The years went by and Consuela began to grow, blossoming into a long-limbed pre-teen with a wild mane of black hair and devious eyes. As a child, she'd been more docile, but now she was curious as a cat. Roaming the tiny island, with Rabbit at her side, her longing to leave the lighthouse's safety for the siren song of boundless land was palpable. Though he sensed her need, Rabbit worked vigilantly to keep her stranded and safe per her father's programming. As far as he knew, the island was the last bastion of safety left in the whole of the world.

LONG BEFORE CARLOS brought his family to the island, someone had carried an old wood-and-brass telescope up to the top of the lighthouse and left it there. This telescope became Consuela's lifeline. She would sit in front of it for hours, her eye pressed to the brass eyepiece, searching for signs of human life – and always without anything to show for her hours of patience.

Once she'd seen three warbots attack a horde of zombies on the beachhead across from them. It had been a vicious battle, one that lasted for ten minutes – ten minutes that Consuela sat, transfixed, eye pressed hotly to the eyepiece, watching and waiting for the final outcome. Rabbit had a heightened visual array and could see the battle without aide, his sensors scanning for possible serial numbers embedded into the warbots' metal skins, numbers that might act as a robot's individual identifier. Rabbit had hoped he might know one of these glistening machines, but he'd discovered no numbers; these warbots obviously belonged to a different generation.

In the end, Consuela had not been given satisfaction. The warbots had destroyed all but two of their zombie nemeses – and those two had stumbled off, the warbots instantly following them inland, well away from the girl's prying eyes. And though there'd been numerous zombie casualties, not one of the warbots had been damaged.

"Why're they fighting?" Consuela had asked Rabbit.

She was thirteen, and up until that moment they had never once discussed why they'd been sequestered together on the island. Rabbit had given Consuela – she did not like being called Connie anymore – a factual rendering of the events leading up to the end of times for humanity. It was a cold, desiccated version of the story, told without emotion because Rabbit did not possess any. He only possessed his mission, his directive "to protect," as pertinent now as the day Carlos had programmed it into him.

"But *why*?" Consuela had whined in a nascent, adolescent twang.

This deepening of the question stymied Rabbit, and he was unable to impart to Consuela the answer she was looking for.

She'd given him the silent treatment after that, sulking in the corner as the night encapsulated them, the telescope sitting untouched for the first time in days. It'd taken a long time for her to warm to him again, but she'd eventually come around and their relationship had returned to a semblance of normalcy.

Later, as she'd sat cross-legged in front of the telescope – *forever searching, searching, searching* – her long tan fingers encircling the eyepiece, she'd made a concerted effort to block him out, ignoring him as if she, alone, occupied the crow's nest of the lighthouse. Rabbit had been fine with that, interested only in keeping Consuela safe…and nowhere was she safer than locked away inside her Rapunzel's tower, pinned beneath his ever-watchful gaze.

CONSUELA'S TEENAGE YEARS were contemptuous. She tried to slip his watch, once even managing to make it outside the lighthouse before he'd cottoned to her trick. She begged and pleaded with him to let her be alone, even for an hour, but this request did not compute with his mission and had been discarded.

No matter how she cried, he had his orders and would remain vigilant even under her duress.

Like a wilting flower, depression began to suck the beauty from

Consuela's features; her shining hair became lackluster straw, her luminous eyes grew hollow and shadowed. Rabbit noticed her lethargy and tried to engage her in a game of Barbies, but this only made her yell at him, kicking at his metal legs as if her tiny feet could do him damage.

She took to huddling in the corner, rereading the books her father had secured for her all those years before: Dostoevsky and Aristotle, Nietzsche and Hawking, Marquez and Shakespeare. She inhaled the words, soaking up the philosophical treatises and the scientific discourses, losing herself completely inside the worlds crafted within their pages.

Then one day everything changed…and Rabbit's world was upended.

"NO," CONSUELA BREATHED, and Rabbit doubted if she even realized she was speaking out loud. "Can't be."

She pulled away from the eyepiece, her brown eyes wide with wonder. She crawled over to the window, wiping the dust from the glass so she could press her face against the pane.

"No way."

She sat back on her haunches, revealing a sliver of nut-brown flesh where the thin, white T-shirt she wore met the waistband of her cut off shorts – both leftovers from her missing mother's wardrobe.

Rabbit didn't need the telescope. He could see the boat as it inched across the azure line of the sea, the thick white sail catching the wind like a kite. It wasn't a large boat, but it was far bigger than the tiny sailboat Consuela's father had departed on all those years ago.

"There are men on board," Consuela said suddenly.

It was the first thing she'd said directly to Rabbit in over a week. There'd been another aborted escape attempt and afterward – when he'd secured the heavy lighthouse door, locking her inside – she'd spit at his feet and vowed never to speak again.

He didn't care if she spoke or not, so long as she was safe. Besides, he knew it was an idle threat. Consuela could only go so long before she would be compelled to talk again. It was human nature, this need to express oneself, to be understood by another sentient being, and what she considered to be his punishment would eventually become her own.

Robots, thankfully, did not possess this human trait. They didn't need to be understood by anyone.

"They're humans," Consuela continued. "My own kind. Please, let me talk to them."

Normally Rabbit would've said "no," but if the war was over, if the zombie uprising had been quelled and human beings were once more repopulating the world, then Rabbit's mission would be at an end and Consuela would be free to go out into the world without him. And the only way to discover if this was the case would be to make contact with the humans on the sailboat.

In the intervening years, there had been two other possible moments for human interaction. Once, when Consuela was nine, a small prop plane had passed over the island, but it'd been flying at such a high altitude and moving so quickly it never had a chance to spot them.

The second human interaction had been much stranger.

It consisted of a bearded man in a neon-pink hot air balloon. Upon crossing the island in his nylon beauty, the odd man had dropped a tract of religious pamphlets onto the beach, each mimeographed copy decrying the end of the world. Rabbit had disposed of as many as he could, but he knew Consuela had squirreled away at least two copies somewhere inside the lighthouse.

In the end, he supposed it was better to make contact with this sailboat than with a religious fanatic like the man in the hot air balloon.

"Please…" Consuela begged – and when the unexpected answer came it was all she could do not to run and hug him, the tears coursing like winter-ravaged rivers down her cheeks.

THE LIGHTHOUSE HAD been abandoned even in Carlos's time, so fixing the lamp in the lantern room was nearly a Herculean task. To begin with, the giant Fresnel lens had been removed and stored inside a cubbyhole – something Consuela had discovered during one of her many exploratory expeditions of the lighthouse – and when they lifted away the aged oilcloth it was wrapped in, they discovered long, spidery cracks on one side of the curved glass.

The cracks were troubling. Though just finding the lens guaranteed them a shot at lighting the lamp and catching the sailboat's attention, the cracks increased the probability that the Fresnel lens might shatter at any moment from the intense heat.

Finding a kerosene substitute to fill the lamp was also a daunting task. Both Consuela and Rabbit could start a cooking fire, but that skill would not apply here, as a wood fire would be uncontrollable, quickly overheating the Fresnel lens. No, they needed something thin and viscous to power the lamp: oil, a substance they didn't have readily available on the island.

"What about you?" Consuela had said, finally, looking at him sideways, her brown eyes half-lidded like a mischievous cat. "You've got oil inside of you, don't you?"

This idea had never occurred to Rabbit, that the thick oil inside of him, keeping his joints lubricated and functional, might be an ideal accelerant. The only problem with this solution was they would have to pry a section of his metal plating away in order to get to it.

Rabbit chose a section of his upper leg for the endeavor. It was strategically the best part of his body to be incapacitated because it had no other use except as a conveyance device. Once the metal plating was removed, only gears and metal ligature would be exposed; his integral circuitry would remain invulnerable.

Consuela offered to help him, but he chose to do the work alone. It would go faster and less damage would be done to his metal-plated exoskeleton. Using a piece of sharpened wood to poke into the metal joint above his knee, he applied pressure until the casing snapped, the metal plating lifting up enough for him to grasp it with his fingers and pull it away.

A spray of oxblood brown arced across the room and Rabbit saw he'd severed a piece of rubber tubing inside his metallic thigh. He picked up the lamp's reservoir and placed it underneath the leaking tube, filling it with the oil. When that was accomplished, he grasped the tubing in his hands, knotting off each end like an unruly artery.

He didn't know how this would affect his body, if the disconnected tubing would eventually cause problems inside his leg, but the severing had been an accident that's outcome would remain to be seen.

With his task accomplished, Rabbit set the lamp's reservoir back in its holder, the Fresnel lens waiting nearby for the climactic moment when, after so many years of disuse, it would be returned to its rightful place. There was still too much daylight left to contact the sailboat, so, together, they waited, Consuela's whole body vibrating with anticipation.

But as the night appeared on silent paws, sneaking up faster than either had anticipated, her anticipation gave way to fear.

"They're too far away," she said. "They won't see us."

The lighthouse had been a beacon to storm-tossed ships for decades, Rabbit assured her. The distance wouldn't be an obstacle, especially in these becalmed seas – but still Consuela fretted, biting her thumb nail until it bled, her gaze riveted to the telescope as the sailboat disappeared in the folds of twilight.

As night finally blanketed the room, Rabbit lit the wick, illuminating the hollows beneath Consuela's cheeks and eyes with the flickering flame until she resembled a ravaged ghost of herself. Her dark eyes flicked to the lamp, fear and longing faceted inside of them, as Rabbit set the Fresnel lens onto its base, the light contracting then expanding outward to fill the night.

There was no way to know if the boat had seen them, if there was anyone or anything on the boat *to* see them, as they sat inside their metallic crow's nest, waiting and watching, but Consuela could not be persuaded to sleep. She sat through the night as stiffly as a plastic doll, her neck and jaw rigid, so het up that she couldn't even pretend to read one of her books.

Rabbit was not gifted with anticipation. Nor did he need to sleep. Instead, he watched the Fresnel lens with a quiet intensity, computing how quickly he could put out the flames were the lens to explode into a million pieces – but this proved to be a fruitless worry. The lens remained intact through the night, the spidery cracks doing little to affect the light.

As if it had already been agreed upon, the sun ascended into the sky just as the lamp sputtered out, the last of the oil gone from its reserve. Consuela had fallen asleep, her chin resting against her chest as it rose and fell in time with her breathing. Rabbit could see the boat, a large sailing vessel with shimmering white sails and a burnt sienna hull, slowly making its way toward the island.

For better or for worse, they had seen the beacon.

THE SHIP ANCHORED off the coast of the southwest end of the island at eight in the morning. Rabbit only knew this because he'd been commissioned with an internal solar clock, something that had no real place in a post-zombie world, but was necessary for his programming to function correctly.

Human society needed the regimentation of a twenty-four-hour day; zombies and robots did not. Time had ceased to have any importance once the zombies and robots had begun their battle, especially when their sole focus was destroying each other in hand-to-hand combat.

Rabbit did not wake Consuela when he saw the dinghy cross the water and put in at the beachhead below them. He wanted the time alone so he could observe the three human men. He knew the moment Consuela saw them she would throw herself at their mercy.

Three men.

One was obviously the leader. He was taller than the other two and trimmer, wearing his long, white blond hair straight and untangled to his shoulders, his pale yellow-green eyes the color of bleached seaweed, continuously scanning the beach for signs of life, a semiautomatic rifle on his back. As for the other two men, both of whom were busy dragging the dinghy out of the water's lapping reach, Rabbit decided they were of no consequence. It was the leader he would have to watch out for. The leader would make all the decisions and be the cause of any problems, should problems arise.

Consuela sat up with a start, her thin, brown body shaking itself awake as her brain latched back on to the thought she'd fallen asleep obsessing over.

"Did they see it?" she croaked, her throat raw from sleep as she crawled over to the telescope and swung it around to face the window. "Did they see the light?"

Consuela's cry of joy at finding the boat anchored within swimming distance from the beach let him know an answer was unnecessary. She dropped the telescope and pressed her forehead to the glass, her brown eyes wide as she stared at the three men on the beach below them. Before her brain even had time to process this new development, she was up and running for the door, her dark hair a cape flying out behind her. Rabbit had foreseen this possibility and locked the door to the lantern room as a precaution.

Consuela was like a wild child, yanking on the handle with every ounce of strength she possessed, using her feet as leverage to get the door open, but it was no use. Only Rabbit had the key, which he wore on a chain looped around his cylindrical neck. Carlos had placed the key/necklace around Rabbit's square head before he'd climbed into his own sailboat and disappeared, bestowing the power of seclusion onto the robot as a parting gift.

"Let me out!" she screamed, the cords of her neck standing out white and ropey against the darkness of her tan skin.

She banged on the door with both fists, slamming their meaty sides into the metal door – and when that didn't work, she added her bare feet to the assault, each kick louder and more aggressive than the last.

Suddenly, she stopped attacking the door as the sound of a semi-assault rifle firing screamed up from the bottom of the lighthouse stairs. Consuela had never heard gunfire before, but she instinctively knew it was not something she wanted to encounter unprepared. After a few moments, the echo of human feet pounding on metal carried up to them from the stairwell and Consuela moved away from the door, scurrying backward until she was safely behind her warbot.

Rabbit knew his charge wasn't prepared for the entelechy of actually meeting another human being. Consuela had been alone for almost twelve years – and reading about humans, fantasizing about humans, dreaming about them, well, it was not a substitute for the real thing.

There was a *bang* as metal struck metal, making the already skittish Consuela jump. Rabbit's sensors picked up the sweaty scent of fear issuing from her pores and from the pores of the three men now standing on the other side of the locked metal door.

"We know you're in there, robot!"

The voice was harsh and guttural, a low purr of menace idling underneath it.

"Open the door or we'll blow it open!"

Rabbit took the key from around his neck, sliding its teeth into the lock. There was a soft *click* and the door lurched forward, one of the lackeys easing it open with his foot so the leader could thrust his body – and gun – inside. Once they realized there would be no threat from their prey, the leader kicked the heavy door wide open, setting it swinging on its hinges, the scratch of metal on metal ominous even in the daylight.

The two lackeys, both of whom babbled together in the same foreign language, could not take their bright, blue eyes off of Consuela, their gazes riveted to the smooth, brown flesh of her décolletage, hunger emanating from their slack faces. The leader ignored their chattering, his muted irises fathomless as he stared at Rabbit, his aggressive stance giving the warbot pause. Though he had been programmed to kill only zombies, leaving sentient humans beings to their own devices, Rabbit's sensors began to scan the man, trying to ascertain his threat level, the directive to protect Consuela overriding his original programming.

Rabbit hadn't been built to understand the subtlety of the human animal, but even he could see that the two lackeys were already concocting nefarious plans between them, Consuela being the object of their attention. When one of the men made a move toward the cowering girl, Rabbit took the initiative, slamming his heavy metal fist into the man's throat, a spray of scarlet arterial blood Rorschaching against the wall. The man's eyes widened in death, exposing bloodshot, yellowed sclera. The wound in his neck gurgled as a bright spray of red blossomed around his throat like a bloodied clerical collar.

Shock. Horror. Fear.

Rabbit saw the physical manifestation of each emotion play across Consuela's face as she watched the man die, her pink lips slowly wrapping themselves into a taut oval. Rabbit expected her to scream, but she didn't. Instead, she stood there, eyes soft and doe-like as she waited to see what the leader would do in retaliation for his minion's murder.

Unaware of the tension thrumming like a livewire around him, the dying man slid down the length of the wall, the last of his life-blood spilling out onto the floor in a sluggish, red tide.

The leader's face was impassive. Seemingly unfazed by the dead man at his feet, he stepped over the body, moving with calm assurance and not an ounce of fear. He stopped within a foot of Rabbit, staring at the monstrous robot. Licking his lips, he threw a wink in Consuela's direction then, like a streak of lightening, he pulled a brown cube from his pocket and shoved the device into the panel of blinking lights built into Rabbit's chest.

Blackness.

• • •

HE WAS ON the sandbar, tipped onto his side, the crash of waves like a midnight symphony above him. Though the pull of gravity was not as apparent here in this new environment, he still felt like a lead weight rooted to the bottom of the sea and he found it hard to right himself. He struggled for a few minutes before finally managing to get to his feet, but the pitch-black night and the fact that his internal compass wasn't working – the salt water was probably the culprit – made it hard for him to discover which way led back to shore.

Though he felt slightly lighter than usual, he was still far too heavy to float, even in the buoyant salt water. Taking short, tentative steps, he began to follow the arc of the sandbar until his westerly trajectory almost walked him off into the deeper recesses of the ocean. After that, he knew which way would return him to the beach and which way would destroy him forever.

He emerged from the salt water to find himself on the wrong side of the island. Not that this mattered to Rabbit, whose programming, even as he walked the sandbar, had already begun to run scenarios on how best to save Consuela – and letting the enemy know he was still viable would've run counterintuitive to what any possible plan might've dictated.

He didn't know what the leader had used to disarm him – logic predicated an E1 pulse generator – but whatever it was, the humans had believed it would disable the warbot permanently. Otherwise, they would've used their boat to ferry him out into the deeper waters, throwing him overboard where he couldn't escape the salt water that would eventually corrode his remains into rusted ocean detritus. Instead, they'd dispatched him right from the beach, never imagining a sandbar existed just beyond the wave line, protecting and keeping him from being pulled further out to sea.

One warbot's luck had quickly become humanity's misfortune.

DO ZOMBIES THINK? Are they cognizant of what's going on around them, able to make informed decisions about their movements? Or are their minds a squabbling mush of hunger and rage, their days spent mindlessly chasing flesh and fighting robots because robots stand between them and dinner?

No one had ever given a zombie a psych test, had ever checked a zombie's hand-eye coordination or IQ level. Zombies were the final frontier – in a way that space and the sea had ceased to be long ago – a completely unknowable entity subsisting on brain matter, impossible to understand.

These questions did not occur to Rabbit as he crossed the wave-strewn water. He didn't know *why* zombies did what they did, but he knew that *what* they did would be integral to saving Consuela. There was no need to rationalize the disservice he was about to inflict upon humanity because robots didn't rationalize – they just followed their directives as best they could.

THE ROWBOAT BARELY held Rabbit's weight, its thin, wooden-boarded bottom taking in seawater as it thundered across the watery divide between island and contiguous land. When he reached the opposite shore, he beached the rowboat high above the tide line, tethering it to a fallen log that reeked of salt and rot.

He didn't have to look far or wide for what he sought. The pack of zombies – four of them: two men and a woman and child – were feasting on a bloodied, dismembered corpse, splashes of red spattered all along the sloping dune that led inland and away from the beach. When they saw Rabbit, the remains were immediately forgotten in favor of larger prey. Not that they could eat the robot, but zombies seemed to intuit that where robots tread, humans might not be far behind.

It didn't take long to subdue the woman and child, but the two men proved testier. They didn't want to be caught, their snapping jaws hammering at Rabbit's metallic body in a frenzied syncopation. One even managed to pry its clawed fingers into the broken bit of Rabbit's thigh, pulling the knotted ends of the severed tube out so oil leaked all over its fingers and chest, making it even harder to catch.

While Rabbit relied primarily on his larger frame and heavier bulk, the zombies were far more aggressive and quicker than he remembered – and even though he hadn't intended to destroy any of the four, he found himself accidentally stepping on the head of one of the male zombies, crushing its skull into a goopy, pulpy mess. It was a quick death for a merciless, undead creature – but one Rabbit would've avoided if he'd had the choice.

As much as capturing, and not just killing, these zombies went against every electrical impulse inside of him, every directive that had ever been programmed into his AI, the need to protect Consuela over-rode them all.

Using a long piece of rope he'd brought with him from the island, Rabbit tied the three remaining zombies together, looping the fibrous rope around their torsos, arms, and necks until they resembled a zombified chain gang. Yanking his jury-rigged harness, he was able to get the zombies to shamble forward, their arching bodies shuddering against the confines of the cord.

They were foul creatures, their rotten skin hanging in flaps from their desiccated frames, revealing beef jerky skeins of muscle inter-woven with tartar-yellow bone. Strips of ragged clothing hung from their limbs like cobwebs, gore and bile stains on the decaying fabric. It would've been hard for anyone looking at the pathetic, underfed creatures to believe that they'd ever been human, that their eyes had once held joy and fear and anguish, that they'd lived in society: driving cars, holding jobs, birthing families.

When he was done, he found the beach deserted, the rowboat exactly where he'd left it. He tied the end of the rope to the aft, ignoring the zombie's gnashing teeth, then pushed the small boat out into the water, the rope uncoiling quickly behind it. The zombies shot forward, barely able to keep their feet as they were forcefully dragged into the water, the cold rush of sea beginning to engulf them.

Rabbit heaved the oars into the water, unconcerned about the zombies' progression into the sea. The undead creatures groaned as they were compelled forward by the pull of the rowboat, the waves pounding against their torsos. The ocean consumed the child, who was smaller, first, its tiny head bobbing like a cork before it disappeared beneath the waves. The other two kept their heads aloft for a moment longer, then they, too, were swallowed up by the tumultuous crashing of the sea.

The rowboat listed backward, the pull of the three undead crea-tures not quite counterbalancing Rabbit's own weight, but the warbot pressed onward, using his considerable mechanical strength to move the boat through the cresting waves.

Before setting off for the mainland, he'd done some reconnaissance, spying on the humans as they'd loaded Consuela into their small dinghy and pushed off into the water, heading for the larger sailboat anchored just offshore. He'd watched his former charge for signs that she'd been mistreated and noticed that her lithe form hunched a little at the shoulders, her long dark hair swinging like a curtain around her face. He'd waited until their dinghy was a small speck on the horizon, then he'd melted back into the shadows, ready to set his plan into motion.

Now he stood at the apex of that plan's fruition.

UNDER COVER OF darkness, Rabbit made his way through the water until he was even with the hull of the sailboat, his precise strokes hardly making a ripple in the surface tension of the water as he silently eased his rowboat up to the side of the much larger ship. Looping a piece of braided rope between them, he easily tethered the two boats together. With this task accomplished, he pulled the oars from their locks and set them inside the rowboat's bottom, where they would remain for the duration.

The waterlogged zombies were heavier than Rabbit had anticipated. Hand over hand, he pulled their rope leash from the depths until he saw the head of the first zombie appear below him. Weapon at the ready, he knotted the rope to one of the oarlocks so the zombie's face did not break the surface of the water, its rolling eyes goggling up at him through two inches of translucent liquid.

Now, it was time to wait.

RABBIT SAT IN the gently rocking rowboat as the last of the candles in the sailboat were extinguished. He knew there would be at least one man on night watch, but that didn't matter. He had the element of surprise and it would carry him far.

Untying the rope from the oarlock, he stood up, giving the line a little slack so that the zombies would remain underwater as he shimmied his way over the side of the sailboat. When he was safely onboard, he began to pull the rope up behind him. One by one, the zombies flopped onto the deck like air-deprived fish, hungry mouths flapping. It only took a moment to loose them from their binds, but in that moment the lone man in the crow's nest caught sight of the odd hunting party from his stately perch.

Instantly, he sounded the alarm, taking aim at Rabbit with his shotgun and firing, though his bullets missed the hulking, silver war-bot by a mile. The zombies ignored the cacophony of warning bell and gunfire, their eyes rolling absently in their heads as the scent of fresh meat reached their otherwise deadened nostrils, instantly enflaming their hunger. Rabbit was forgotten in the wake of the zombies' realization that living human beings were nearby.

He was free to make his next move.

Rabbit hid himself behind the open cabin door as the men below deck rushed up to meet the incoming zombies. Unprepared for the threat — some of them still in their skivvies, eyes caked with sleep — they were quickly enmeshed in battle with the starving undead.

The man in the crow's nest stayed put, self-preservation his first instinct, but he did what he could for his comrades, taking aim at the zombies below him, though with little effect. Uncertainty, and the fact that he was too far away for his shotgun to do much damage, made the man hesitant with his shots. Rabbit could see that the man was afraid he might accidentally hit one of his shipmates with a stray bullet, and, of course, the man did just that, one of his poorly aimed shots causing a shipmate's head to explode like a rotten gourd only a few feet from Rabbit's hiding spot.

Leaving the pirates to deal with his zombie distraction, Rabbit quietly proceeded below deck. His mission: to find Consuela and take her home.

IT WAS DARK inside the heart of the ship, the stench of dirty, shiftless men ripe in the air. The ceiling was set so low to the ground that Rabbit had to dip his head forward, moving slowly through the tiny rooms, his eyes searching for Consuela. Each room he entered was in disarray; bunk beds unmade, dirty clothes everywhere, the paraphernalia of canned food — cutlery, dishes, can openers — littering the floor. Rabbit recognized the cans from their own lighthouse supply, and he wondered what else the men had stolen from the island.

At the far end of the hall, Rabbit came to the only locked door on the whole of the ship.

And he knew what this meant.

He had not seen the leader, the man with the pale hair and yellow-green eyes, since he'd climbed aboard. It only stood to reason that the man would be locked inside this cabin with his ill-gotten prize, letting his men take care of whatever emergency had been declared above deck. Here they were, out on the open ocean where no zombies dared to tread. The leader wouldn't know – until far too late – that he'd sent his men into a zombie feeding-frenzy, that before he'd roused himself from his cabin, his whole crew would be dead.

Rabbit grabbed a hold of the knobbed door handle, jerking it twice before ripping the metal slab out of its frame. A feminine scream issued from within, one Rabbit recognized immediately – and he knew he'd come in the nick of time.

Consuela was still alive.

He dropped the heavy door where he stood and stepped through the empty doorframe into a dimly lit room. But the vision that greeted his eyes was not the one he'd expected.

"Shoot his leg!" Consuela screamed as she pulled the ragged blanket up around her naked torso.

She was lying on a tiny, twin bunk bed, her dark hair spread across the pillow like the fan of a peacock's tail.

"The leg!" she shrieked again, pointing at Rabbit's busted thigh, where oil still leaked in viscous waves.

Rabbit turned his head to find the leader, naked and pale as an albino alligator, standing in the corner of the room, a shotgun in his right hand. His penis was long and hard and Rabbit could see he'd interrupted them mid-coitus.

Without hesitation, the naked man lifted the shotgun and slid his finger inside the loop of the trigger. Eyes locked on Rabbit, he blasted the robot in the thigh, the bullet tearing through metallic exoskeleton, sparks from ruined circuitry shooting into the air and igniting. Rabbit was thrown backward by the impact of the shot, landing hard on his back, his sensors going mad at the magnitude of the damage the man had inflicted upon him and the realization that his leg was ablaze.

Luckily, his body was fire retardant, and the inferno at his thigh was quickly extinguished.

But the boat was another story. The fire leapt across the boards of the sailboat's wooden hull, the roiling smoke overwhelming the air in a matter of seconds. Rabbit tried to lift his head, to ascertain Consuela's exact position, but when he raised his eyes to the bed, she had disappeared.

"Now for the head," the man said to himself, striding over to the warbot and lifting the butt of the shotgun into the air.

The fire didn't seem to faze the man as he stood above Rabbit, appraising the warbot with a cold, calculating stare. Rabbit had no time to do anything but lie there as the man with the deep, yellow-green eyes pulled the trigger; the shot catching the robot square in the face.

His vision flickered and sputtered, but his cognizance did not slip away. He may have been blinded, but his other senses were on high alert. Not waiting for the man to fire another shot into his middle – something that might surely end him – he rolled onto his front, slowly dragging himself away from the fire.

As he lurched forward, his hands gripping at the slick floor, he could hear the man belatedly slapping at the fire with the blanket – though even Rabbit knew the boat was a goner.

Leaving the man to his own fate, Rabbit pulled himself toward the stairs. Above him, he could hear the pirates as they continued to lay waste to the zombies, the smoke below not having reached their senses – and he wondered when exactly they would notice.

"Rabbit…?"

The voice was small and hesitant, coming from the stairs. It stopped him in his tracks.

"Rabbit, can we go home now?"

He knew that voice like he knew the ticking of his own internal components.

"Rabbit?"

That she'd tried to destroy him was superfluous.

"Rabbit, please?"

He would get Consuela home.

No matter what the cost.

This was his final directive.

THE VIRGIN SACRIFICES

Rachel Swirsky

PART I

Under the pink breath
Of new dawn spreading
Over the Isle of Amazons

All lovers hope their love
Will be as pure
As Ulla's was for Alyssa.

And in the drawing dark
When dusk makes them feel
The age in their bones

All lovers pray
Their love won't end
As Alyssa's did for Ulla.

LISTEN, YOUNG ONE. Listen and remember.

Far from any continent's shores, protected by whirlpools and clashing rocks, a volcanic island rises like a jagged tooth above the churning currents.

That is the island where the Amazons live.

Their day begins at dawn when the priestesses of Hera sing poly-phonic melodies to welcome the sun. Fisherwomen set sail to pluck eels and sailfish and sharks from their underwater homes. In the noonday shade, cooking women gather to roast the morning's catch over camp-fires while girl children collect shells with which to decorate their hair.

At dusk, the young women wrestle naked with their backs to the ocean, their long bodies drawn in silhouette against the setting sun.

The Amazons have lived this way for centuries, for so long that they've forgotten where they came from. Their knowledge of the old world has decayed like a shipwreck far under the ocean: parts remain, but the planks that supported them have rotted away.

For instance, the Amazons remember that small, invisible things cause illnesses, but they've forgotten that they can kill some of those things by washing their hands.

They remember that computers can do things that no human could do, and they remember that gods can also do things that no human could do, but they've forgotten that doesn't mean computers are gods.

Their ancestors were vulcanologists who came to study the island's dead volcano. They built their laboratories in underground tunnels and watched the world above through monitors.

After reports of the zombie incursion began pouring through the world news channels — followed by outages, screams, and finally static — the quick-thinking scientists converted their tunnels into a bunker. They reprogrammed their AI System to help them fight, trans-forming her into a fierce warrior goddess — a soldier-nurse-tactician, an Artemis-Hestia-Athena.

When the grey and lurching hordes seized the tunnels, the fleeing scientists took the System with them to the island, leaving only a shadow of its program to haunt the abandoned circuits. They closed the tunnels behind them, sealing the zombies in.

Generations later, the Amazons still remember there are monsters in those tunnels, and that those monsters are hungry. They also re-member old stories about virgins thrown into volcanoes to sate the hunger of monsters.

They've forgotten that zombies can't be sated.

Every year, they remember just enough to open the tunnel entrance deep in the volcanic stomach for long enough to hurl down one virginal girl. And every year, the zombies devour her while she screams.

CLOSE YOUR EYES, young one. Close your eyes and imagine Ulla: warrior of Artemis.

At eighteen-years-old, Ulla is at the height of her physical prowess. Her skin is brown like a warm afternoon; her eyes are bright, black and watchful. Her body is a battleground of curves and angles: full biceps and sharp collarbones; breasts bound flat by leather; round eyes with a gaze like a windless sea. Beneath heavy lids, her pupils dart restlessly back and forth, never content with what they see.

Ulla grew up like any Amazon girl. As a child, she spent the mornings fishing with her aunts, and then came back to help her mother cook in the afternoons. At dusk, she wrestled by the shore with the other girls.

She might have lived out her life that way, but from before she could even speak, Ulla had always wanted to be a warrior. So she ran every morning until she became the fleetest girl her age. She wrestled with the older girls until she could beat anyone. She threw spears and shot bows and learned to catch fish with her bare hands.

On her twelfth birthday, the priestesses selected her for the trial of Artemis. They blindfolded her and took her to the bitterest edge of the volcano where not even scrub clings to the barren rock. Alone, with no tools but her hands, she climbed. Up and up, her palms raw and bleeding, until she reached the summit where the goddess's temples ring the volcano's basalt mouth like lamprey teeth.

She passed the temple of Athena, the goddess of Cleverness, and the temple of Hera, the goddess of Power. She was not tempted by the temple of Demeter, the goddess of Wealth, or the temple of Aphrodite, the goddess of Love.

Her warrior heart drew her to Artemis, the goddess of the Hunt. The goddess's temple threw open its doors so that Ulla could join her sister solders in ceaseless training, dedicating her life to defending the island from the waves of enemies below.

On her eighteenth birthday, when Ulla had mastered what the warriors had to teach, she was chosen to leave the temple awhile. It was a great honor; she was assigned to join the honor guard that defends Hestia's priestesses.

Hestia, the goddess of the hearth, is the only goddess so sacred that her temple sits outside its sister-circle. As the hearth is the center of the home, the temple of Hestia is the center of Amazon civilization.

Ulla's pride swelled like a living thing when she was selected to protect it. As everyone knows, the center must hold.

BUT THIS STORY isn't only about Ulla

It's also about Alyssa.

Alyssa is one of the priestesses in the temple of Hestia which Ulla is now sworn to protect. At seventeen, she's pale like white marble. A gentle blonde rain of hair falls to the small of her back. Her curves have the beauty of nascence; like a fruit weighing the branch, like a bud unfurling her petals, she is at the moment of her readiness.

Unlike Ulla, Alyssa was born to be a priestess. When she was an infant, Hestia's ordained took Alyssa from her mother's breast and carried her up the volcano. When the doors of Hestia's temple closed behind her, they would never open for her again; Hestia's priestesses live and die within the confines of marble walls.

Yet, in some ways, of all the Amazons, the priestesses of Hestia live the most varied lives. The books of their library open the history of the world to them. Their days are devoted to discussions of science and politics. They wear white and walk softly and speak in whispers, for the variety of their learning provides all the color and noise they could ever want.

When the Amazon queen needs guidance, she goes to the priestesses of Hestia, and they advise her as they advised her mother and her mother's mother back to the first Amazon rulers. As the goddess Hestia holds the keys to Olympus, her priestesses hold the keys to the queen's palace.

But great power comes at a great price.

Every year, Hestia's temple takes half a dozen infants to raise as its own. There, they grow and learn, until the festival of their eighteenth year when the initiates gather around the sacred hearth, trembling and new. The High Priestess evaluates each of them, confirming that they have the qualities necessary to serve the goddess.

And every year, she chooses one to feed the monsters in the belly of the volcano.

IN MANY WAYS, Ulla and Alyssa are opposites. Ulla is dark; Alyssa is pale. Ulla's body is hardened for battle; Alyssa's is untouched softness. Ulla has grown up knowing the earth and the sea, enjoying the pleasure of sweat. Alyssa's grown up knowing nothing but books, spending her days contemplating abstractions.

So they fell in love, as opposites often do.

THEY MET WHEN the High Priestess sent Ulla to fetch Alyssa from her ritual bath.

Ulla was thinking of anything but love as she crossed the temple, the torchlight flickering across her body, the leather flaps of her battle skirt rapping against her thighs.

At last, she reached the baths. She drew back the drape obscuring the archway and forgot how to speak.

> Aphrodite, goddess of love,
> Rose out of the foam.
>
> Foam is what's left
> When love rises.
>
> So it was for Ulla
> Looking down at the dew
>
> Surrounding the marble pool
> Where sweet Alyssa bathed.

The bath: all white curves and marble. In the center, steps worn round with age descended to a recessed turquoise pool.

Alyssa stood poised to enter the water. Drape abandoned, she was as white and naked as the marble.

She dipped her toes into the water and shuddered at the cold. She withdrew her foot, droplets scattering, catching the light.

Unexpectedly, she turned, as if she was just beginning to feel Ulla's gaze on her shoulders. Their eyes met.

For Ulla, it was lightning before a rainstorm.

For Alyssa, it was something else.

Alyssa screamed. All pink and mortified, she scrambled to collect her drape. "Who are you? What do you want?"

Ulla stammered. "I...the priestesses sent me...they want you..."

Hecate! Ulla swore to herself as she regained control of her tongue. She was a warrior! She was only following a woman's natural urges. What woman wouldn't stare, coming upon a naked beauty like that?

Alyssa regained herself, wrapping her drape around her like a chiton. She lifted her chin and stared down at Ulla with a superior gaze.

Ulla refused to let herself be outdone by some untrained girl. "The High Priestess requires your presence."

"Well. You should have said so immediately."

The girl's voice was unappealingly prim. She sniffed and started toward the corridor. Her natural poise was marred by affected hauteur. She was like an adolescent, all coltish with her graces.

Why? Ulla wondered. A beautiful girl like that should flow easily in the world. She should be Aphrodite's waters, gleaming as she washed over willing shores. What would make a girl like that so prudish? Then she remembered: all of Hestia's initiates were virgins.

THERE ARE MANY things the storytellers recount about the love that bloomed between Ulla and Alyssa. You've heard them before many times, young one.

You've heard how Ulla returned to her barracks, so lost in love that the other girls quickly figured out she'd lost her heart. Her bunkmates,

Pendrin and Venji, teased her mercilessly, but Ulla refused to give up the name of the girl that had her spellbound.

You've heard how Alyssa sat daydreaming in her classes, thinking of nothing but Ulla's face. It was like her skin had awakened. She could feel every pore, every slope, every curve where a touch might linger. Before, her skin had been nothing more than her skin. After she met Ulla, Alyssa's skin became a lonely thing. It tingled with absence.

You've heard how Alyssa pressed her tutors for whatever they could tell her about the women from Artemis's temple. She learned that they wrestled at dusk in the empty ampitheatre and so that night she snuck away and hid herself in the shadows so she could watch Ulla tussle with the other naked women, their skin glistening with sweat. Ulla won every match, a warrior goddess, like Artemis herself.

Alyssa had imagined herself going down to the amphitheater once everyone was gone and trying to catch the warrior woman alone, but as the matches ended and dusk sank into night, she lost her courage. She slipped out of the shadows to make her way back to the temple, but the warrior woman found her in the dark.

They regarded each other for a long moment.

Love at first sight is fleeting, but this was love that endured to second sight. It was love that had paused, love that had lingered, love that had chosen to dwell.

They drank kisses from each other's lips. It was almost too dark for them to make out the shapes of each other's bodies so they navigated with their other senses. The salt of Ulla's skin. The plump of Alyssa's hips. The mixture of perfume and smoke that scented their hair.

Ulla's teeth moved gently, teasingly across Alyssa's neck. Strong, smooth fingers slipped between her thighs. She gasped.

"No!" she cried, pulling away.

The heat of Ulla's body withdrew.

"I can't," Alyssa said between panting breaths. "I have to be a virgin...for the goddess...in case..."

Alyssa felt Ulla's hand nearing. For a moment, she was afraid. She was so much weaker, so much smaller. Would the warrior force her? But Ulla's fingers only brushed across her cheek.

"Here? Again? Tomorrow?" Ulla asked.

They both knew they shouldn't be together, these girls consecrated to different goddesses, but reason shrank in the presence of love.

"Tomorrow," Alyssa echoed.

THEY TOLD THEMSELVES that their trysts were simple pleasures, brief spring moments that they could set aside. Instead, as the evenings drew into weeks, love pulled them together like gravity, their two bodies inescapable. They were two moons circling each other. They were question and answer, lips and tongue, memory and regret.

The day of the ritual, when one of Hestia's initiates would be chosen to die, loomed in front of them. They didn't know how to discuss it.

At last, a few days before the ritual, Alyssa led Ulla down to the aqueducts that connected to the tunnels. She pointed Alyssa to the rough-hewn, gnarled wall that was one of the many seals that separated the Amazons from the zombies.

"Is that it?" Ulla asked. "That's all?"

"It's ancient technology," Alyssa said. "The System says it'll last a thousand years."

"The System," Ulla repeated. "What does she know? We should post warriors."

"The System knows a lot. She's *the System*. If she says we don't need warriors then we don't."

Ulla paused a moment, letting the words disappear into echoes.

At last, she said, "Doesn't it bother you? That they might throw you away?"

Alyssa held her tongue, unsure what to say.

"They're going to kill one of you," Ulla continued. "They're going to give you to *them*. Let you be *eaten*."

"They have to," Alyssa said. "Otherwise the zombies would take over the world."

"How do they know? Have they ever tried something else?" Ulla's voice had become almost a shout. Her pounding footsteps echoed too loudly as she began to pace. "The warriors could do something. Give us spears. Let us wait when the tunnel mouth opens. We can siege the zombies when they're expecting their *snack*."

Alyssa shrank away from Ulla's voice. It was like that first time they'd kissed when Alyssa wasn't sure whether or not Ulla would let her go. There was something fearsome in Ulla that emerged from time to time.

"One girl to save everyone," Alyssa said. "That's how it works."

Ulla neared her, closer than a shadow, pushing her against the wall. The heat of her body was a cloak. "At least take some pleasure from them. Be a woman. Don't let them send you to your death without ever knowing what it's like…"

Ulla's fingers slipped across Alyssa's thighs. They brushed against her lips, beginning to part. Alyssa's heart pounded with fear, anger, and lust, all mixed together.

"Stop it!" Alyssa cried. "You know how I feel!"

Abruptly, Ulla halted. She pulled back, her demeanor all apology. She shook her head. "I just don't know what I would do. If they chose you. If they were going to let you die."

"You'd do your duty," Alyssa said.

Ulla turned to meet her gaze, but she said nothing to confirm or deny.

PART II

Love is a thing with thorns.
It blossoms and it bites.

To reach the rose
One must endure the blood.

Even then, sometimes
The rose is unreachable.

IMAGINE IT, young one:

The sacred hearth stands in a hall carved from volcanic rock. The other rooms of the temple are decorated with frescoes of women dancing, praying, rejoicing; they're adorned with columns carved in the shape of strong women bending to hold the roof on their backs. Here, there is nothing but the black rock and the dancing fire.

Two women kneel by the hearth itself, their cloaks stained with soot. They hold long, metal sticks with which they stoke the fire to keep it burning evenly. The flames writhe and twist; they are crimson and rose and gold. The heat that emanates from them is the burning, beautiful gaze of the goddess Hestia.

The smell of smoke is overwhelming.

White-cloaked priestesses gather at the back of the room, a flock of white doves, anonymous in identical clothing. The chatter of their hushed voices rises like the smoke.

The High Priestess and the Amazon Queen sit in twin, rough-hewn obsidian chairs. If the High Priestess stood and drew her hood up over her winding, gray hair, she would disappear into the crowd of doves. The Queen, however, still wears her drapes and leathers, baring her tawny thighs and navel. If she were traveling anywhere else, she'd be flanked by flat-eyed lovers and bodyguards, but in the temple of Hestia, even the Queen submits to the will of the goddess.

The priestesses' voices fall silent as the initiates enter. The only sounds are their echoing footsteps and the crackle of the flames. The initiates wear their hoods down, a temporary reprieve from anonymity.

Alyssa, among them, looks from face to face, regarding her friends, her closer-than-sisters. She's grown with these women, played and fought with them. Hard to think that by end of the day one of them will be gone forever.

In synchrony, they sit by the hearth, close enough that the fire could reach out to singe the hair on the napes of their necks if it wanted. They are Hestia's; they know she will not burn them.

The High Priestess is already standing to begin the ritual recitations when the last attendees enter the room. Leather battle skirts rap against the thighs of Ulla and her sisters as the warriors walk in. Their spears outstretched, their armor shining, they are almost as bright as the goddess's fire. Alyssa cannot help but make a small noise as she sees Ulla's face, that beautiful broad plane with its high-set eyes, all impassive and ready for battle.

Ulla's gaze shifts downward. For a moment they meet each other – eye to eye – across the room.

Alyssa looks away first, embarrassed that she's thinking about profane things at a moment that should be sacred.

Ulla lets her gaze linger on the blush of Alyssa's cheek. She cannot bear to think about what may happen. Her grip tightens on her spear. She's still not sure what she will do.

The awful truth is that the Artemis's honor guard isn't there to protect the priestesses of Hestia at all. They're only there for this one purpose, to prevent a frightened girl from running.

Ulla's sisters shift their spears into horizontal positions, linking them together into an impassable wall. Ulla raises hers, too. It's her duty to be a stone in the battlement.

High Priestess Eire moves up and down the line of initiates as she continues to speak. Ulla is too upset to listen to her droning. Why is the woman continuing to chatter? Someone will die! Why must she prolong it?

Ulla's stomach churns. Her brow begins to sweat. The room has too many people in it; the goddess's gaze is too bright and hot. She hears her sisters shifting. Even the priestesses, accustomed to the heat of the sacred hearth, are beginning to look faint.

Tension is a living thing in that hot, dense room. Ulla wants nothing more than to lower her spear and run at the High Priestess, to stage a rescue of Alyssa and the other girls.

Her sense of duty restrains her, a garment that's become too tight.

At last, the High Priestess begins her assessments. She takes the first girl by the chin and stares deeply into her eyes. The girl flinches, visibly afraid. The High Priestess's brow creases, her lips flattening into an evaluating line. She drops the girl's chin and moves on.

Ulla's mouth dries as she watches. Is this good? Is this bad?

The silence deepens with the heat.

The five girls sitting with Alyssa are all pretty in the same, strangely tender way as Alyssa is, like treasures kept too long out of reach. The one furthest from the High Priestess is shaking in fear.

It's a guilty feeling, but Ulla wishes them dead, any one of them. As long as it will save Alyssa.

As soon as the High Priestess stares into Alyssa's eyes, Ulla knows it's over. Her knees weaken. Alyssa will be the one. She was always going to be the one.

Ulla starts forward, but her spear catches on her sisters'. She throws it down. Everyone looks up at the clatter. The Queen, on her obsidian throne, looks confused and alarmed. Ulla tries to push through the crowd to reach Alyssa, but her sisters hold her back. The room resonates with exclamations.

Two of Ulla's sisters pin her arms and drag her out of the room. Ulla isn't there to see the moment when the High Priestess formally selects Alyssa as the sacrifice. She isn't there to watch the resignation on Alyssa's face, or the way that she walks calmly to her fate. The remnants of the honor guard trail behind them, unneeded.

THEY WILL THROW Alyssa into the tunnels the next day.

Everyone will gather to watch. Islanders will climb the volcano, carrying fresh-caught fish to cook for the feast, the young girls adorned with sea shells.

Everyone will gather to watch Alyssa fall.

Afterward, they'll eat and dance.

"YOU PANICKED," Ulla's bunkmate, Pendrin, says later, when they are back in their barracks. "No one blames you."

Ulla should be relieved that the others think she suffered some kind of fit, the way some warriors do the first time they see an impending death in battle. If they knew what she'd really intended, she wouldn't be here in her bunk. She'd be bound and waiting to be sent back to Artemis's temple for punishment.

Ulla looks up into Pendrin's eyes. Pendrin is one of her friends, a woman she calls sister, but at the moment, she feels nothing but contempt for her.

"They'll probably recall you to the temple," Pendrin goes on. "That's not so bad. You can get back to your training while the rest of us are going soft…"

"No," Ulla says.

Pendrin looks surprised. "You think they won't let you train?"

"You're wrong," Ulla says. "I blame myself."

Pendrin gives her a look of pity. "No one knows how they'll react in battle. You'll help train the next generation of warriors. You can still do your duty to Artemis."

But that's not what Ulla means. She doesn't blame herself for failing *Artemis*.

HESTIA'S TEMPLE TAKES shamefully few security precautions. Ulla supposes it's because they've never needed to. Who has tried to sneak through these halls before? The priestesses of Hestia might have wanted to, but the only experience they have of battle is tactician's diaries and historians' recountings. Nothing that would help.

When a lull allows Ulla to escape from her battlemates, she goes to the library. None of the priestesses pay her special attention. The honor guards go everywhere in the temple, running errands for the priestesses, and Ulla is just another tool of Artemis, marked by her bare limbs and her leather armor. No one pays them enough attention to distinguish the troublemaker from the rest.

Books that include the temple's plans are easy to locate. The priestesses are trusting fools; no information has been withheld. Ulla stares at the diagrams for a few minutes, memorizing where the corridors connect with the aqueducts, and then moves confidently to the door.

It's easy enough to guess where they're holding Alyssa for the night.

The priestesses don't recognize Ulla, but the warriors guarding Alyssa's room do.

"What are you doing here?" demands tall, dark Venji.

"Pendrin had a message," Ulla says.

And even though their tutors had taught them throughout their training – never lower you guard – women are never prepared for betrayal from their friends.

Standing over the fallen bodies of her sisters, Ulla hopes that the butt of her spear has merely rendered them unconscious. She can't be sure. There's blood on Venji's forehead and head wounds are unpredictable.

She can't stop. She's passed the moment of no return.

Ulla slides the key ring off of Venji's finger and unlocks the door.

As the door groans, Alyssa looks up. She's lying on a pallet, but it's clear she hasn't slept. "What are you doing here?" Alyssa demands.

"I'm here to save you," Ulla says.

Alyssa rises from her pallet. She stands for a moment beside Ulla. In all ways, she is more fragile, from her weak frame to her innocence of the world, but here, at this moment, she is the one with the power. Ulla is afraid that Alyssa will reject her, that their love is broken. But no: their hands seek each other. Their fingers twine. Ulla can feel Alyssa's quick-beat pulse through her wrist.

She pulls her toward the door. "This way."

Alyssa resists. "You shouldn't have come. They'll find you."

"There's an entrance to the catacombs near here. Once we get down there, we can hide. Find a defensible position."

Alyssa shakes her head. "What do you mean?"

"I can get us down to the shore. No one guards the boats."

"Ulla, stop. What are you talking about?"

At last, it dawns on Ulla that Alyssa doesn't understand. She turns toward her lover, smiling. "I'm rescuing you."

But there's the wrong reaction, no tenderness at all. Alyssa withdraws.

"Ulla..."

"There's not much time."

"Ulla, I can't go with you."

"You'd rather stay here? To die?"

Alyssa's eyes flash. Her voice lowers urgently. "What's the alternative? Ulla! Sailing away on a boat? Into the ocean? There's nothing out there! The zombies are everywhere but here!"

Ulla hesitates. "...There might be somewhere. We'll find a place."

"No, Ulla, no. Even if there was somewhere to go... Someone has to do this. Someone has to die."

"It doesn't have to be you!"

Ulla is done listening. Blood pounds in her ears. She takes Alyssa roughly by her hand and drags her down the hallway. The catacombs are close. They can argue later. Alyssa will see reason.

The younger girl is easy to carry, even struggling. Ulla pulls Alyssa past her friends' bodies in the hallway. A right turn. Down the corridor. Torchlight etches the marble with flickering shadows. It's impossible for Ulla to tell the guttering of the flame from the roaring in her head. Everything smells like ash and blood. They're the same smell.

She sees it: the portal. It'll take longer to open it one-handed, but Ulla can't let go of Alyssa's wrist. She tugs at the complex mechanism. It grinds. Already, she can hear footsteps, but they're heading away from them, down the corridor to the room where Alyssa was being kept. They don't realize they've already fled. There's still enough time to disappear.

The shout that rings down the corridor is so loud that, for a moment, Ulla doesn't even realize it's coming from beside her.

"Please!" Alyssa shouts to the rescuers. "I'm here!"

She twists toward Ulla, whispering a hushed entreaty. "Go now. Into the catacombs. You can still get away."

Betrayal is a numb feeling, spreading through her ribcage. Ulla releases Alyssa's wrist.

"I came this far," Ulla says, quietly. "What makes you think I'd leave you now?"

Part III

When a woman wants to avoid fate,
She pulls at tapestry strings

Hoping to unravel
The future the Fates have spun.

The Fates are stronger than that.
They laugh

As women tangle themselves
In their own loose threads.

Alyssa looks up at Ulla. They're bound side by side.

Artemis's guards stand a few paces away. They keep glancing backward and then looking quickly away. Their expressions are part confusion and part anger. They don't seem to know what to think about Ulla now that she's betrayed them.

"Please," Alyssa whispers to Ulla. "Look at me."

Ulla turns her head further away. Her face looks softer in profile. Her wide, flat nose has a gentle curve where Alyssa's is straight and sharp.

"I had to do it," Alyssa says. "You know that, don't you? I can't let everyone else die just because I want to keep living."

"That's why they chose you," Ulla mutters.

Alyssa is surprised in equal parts by the comment and by the fact that Ulla is speaking to her at all.

"What do you mean?" she asks.

"You were the only one," Ulla says, "who wasn't afraid."

"What do you mean? I was terrified! I —"

"You were the only one who never looked away from her eyes."

Alyssa opens her mouth to respond, but she isn't sure what to say. It never occurred to her not to meet the High Priestess's gaze. Her fate would be her fate. It might as well be her who died as any of the other girls. Would she rather send Henta or Lorré? Would she part the twins from each other, Oki from Iko, or Iko from Oki?

How could she trade their lives for hers?

Ulla's expression is dark like a threatening storm. "I should have known," she says.

"Known what?" Alyssa asks.

"Known better than to try to save a suicide."

"That's not —"

Alyssa closes her mouth. It's true; what Ulla said isn't fair. But Alyssa will die for her sisters if she must. Shouldn't a warrior understand that?

Still, she knows the sting of betrayal. She wishes there had been another way.

"I'm sorry," Alyssa whispers.

She wishes she could touch Ulla's shoulder, but her hands are bound.

• • •

THE DAY OF the sacrifice is blazingly bright.

The sun is like that sometimes. It doesn't have the decency to look away.

The guards carry Alyssa out first. She doesn't struggle, but they've made her completely helpless in her bonds. She can't even take a step on her own.

The High Priestess is waiting, flanked by white-cloaked functionaries.

"You've done well, Alyssa," the High Priestess says. "We all owe you our thanks."

The High Priestess bows to her, a surprisingly deep and sincere bow. Alyssa is shocked by the veneration in the High Priestess's gaze. She's grown up in the shadow of Hestia's great priestesses. She could never have imagined one of them paying her such respect. What reason would a woman like the High Priestess possibly have to look up to her?

Then she remembers: all of the priestesses, every single one in the temple, are the girls who weren't chosen. They're the ones who were too afraid to die.

Alyssa inclines her head. "It's my honor to die for my goddess and my people."

The High Priestess looks away from Alyssa's gaze. She refocuses her attention on something behind Alyssa and raises her hand in a beckoning gesture.

The functionaries murmur in astonishment. Alyssa twists in her bonds, but she can't see what they see.

"What is it?" she murmurs to the guard on her left.

An uncomfortable expression crosses the guard's face. The woman looks away from Alyssa and says nothing.

Then, in her peripheral vision, Alyssa sees Ulla, bound and struggling. A gag keeps the warrior silent, but her eyes are fierce and unrepentant.

Ice lines Alyssa's stomach. There's only one reason someone would be bound like that today.

Alyssa struggles to free her hands. "What are you doing? Let her go!"

The High Priestess won't meet Alyssa's eyes. Her voice is flat. "She betrayed her duty and her people. She deserves to die."

"Die like this?" Alyssa demands. "This isn't a punishment! It's something we choose. To give ourselves, to make something beautiful of our lives. You can't make it about retribution...it degrades everything...everything we do..."

"Peace, child," says the High Priestess. "You've been sheltered from the world. You don't understand. We cannot allow someone to interfere with the sacrifice and live."

Behind her, though, the crowd begins to whisper. White cloaks flutter as women turn toward each other.

That's when Alyssa realizes. If her body has been blooming, then it's for this. This is the moment of her unfolding.

She's giving her life for these women.

She can win them to her side.

"I have pledged my life to Hestia," Alyssa says. "I will die for her. I will die for you. I will die for everyone on this island, all the women and the girls, the ones who sing and the ones who dance, the ones who fight and the ones who cry and the ones who love each other. I'll die for them. Now I'm asking something in return. A small thing in exchange for my life! Let her go! Expel her from the temple. Send her to the shore in disgrace. Set her to work weaving nets for the fisherwomen. But let her go!"

Alyssa's words fall into silence. At first, she thinks the priestesses have listened with stony hearts, but then she hears the rumble building. They're with her. They're shouting for her! Crying her name.

The High Priestess turns toward them, the hem of her cloak swirling. She holds out her hands appealingly. The women only protest more. The High Priestess freezes in place, unsure what to do. Finally, she says in a voice that cuts through the sound like a glacier cuts through a mountain, "Quiet. Please."

She turns back to Alyssa. "Child, you are pure and honorable. We all owe you a debt. We will add you to the praises in our hymns and as the years go by, we will sing of you to please the goddess. But you do not understand."

The woman continues to avert her gaze, but Alyssa can see the deep shame in it, shading into contempt. Understanding sinks: this is the coin-flip of the High Priestess's awe, an insatiable guilt that she let one of her sisters die in her place, that she was not brave and fearless enough to go to the zombies herself. This woman — and every other priestess present — is stained with the cowardice of her youth. To combat that taint, she must prove herself fearless.

Such circumstances did not have to make her ruthless, but they have.

The High Priestess shakes her head, a gesture that would seem maternal if she were not about to send two women to their deaths. She turns to the guards.

"Give them both to the devourers."

MOMENTS BEFORE THEY push Alyssa and Ulla into the mouth of the volcano, the guards cut their bonds.

Even a sacrifice should be able to fight.

WIND SNATCHES ALYSSA'S hair into a streak behind her. Her hands stretch out, seeking purchase on the air.

EACH SECOND THEY fall is its own eternity.

FALLING, BUT NOT into the guts of the volcano below — falling into the tunnel entrance concealed just below the volcano's lip, unsealed for this occasion.

It would be better to fall into the volcano. At least then the impact would kill them.

ALYSSA TWISTS ENOUGH to see Ulla, falling straight down like an arrow, the expression on her face furiously intense.

THE ZOMBIES CROWD at the tunnel entrance. Their hands stretch out. The mass of them is grey and squirming like maggots.

Alyssa cannot help the shout of terror that issues from her throat. She hopes that Ulla cannot hear her.

Part IV

In her secret heart,
Every woman hopes
For love as pure as Ulla's:

Love that will stand and fight,
Love that will risk its life,
Love that is day and night
And dawn and dusk
And every moment in between.

In her secret heart,
Every woman fears
That such love is a myth:

That every love, in blooming,
Begins its own decay,
That love is both as lovely
And as short-lived
As any other flower.

THEY FALL.

As they pass the tunnel ceiling, the seal slides back into place above them. For a moment, there's total darkness, and then overhead lights flicker on. The lights are left over from the scientists' time; to the Amazons, the ancient fluorescents are eerie and strange. A dim yellow glow illuminates the flat floors of the otherwise cylindrical tunnels. They're surfaced with a material that's oddly smooth and flat – another relic of a bygone age. It doesn't look like bronze or rock or anything that Ulla and Alyssa use in their everyday lives. Shards of metal and fragmented computers crust the walls, their broken gleam punctuated by the occasional green pinprick of light that signals a machine that still functions.

Just before they hit the ground, the overly precise voice of the System echoes from nowhere. "The barracks are sealed. Quarantine is in effect."

Ulla rolls with the fall. The surface is astonishingly cold beneath her. Despite her acrobatics, the impact shocks away her breath. She can already feel where the bruises will bloom on her legs.

She pulls herself up in time to move beneath Alyssa and help cushion her descent. Once Alyssa's momentum is safely stopped, Ulla pushes the girl behind her. The warrior stands forward, ready to protect her lover from the zombie horde.

Ulla cranes her neck to look back. They're only a few feet away from a dead end where the tunnel comes to a sudden stop. Behind them, a gruesome pile of human bones litters the floor. A hundred dead sacrifices have died here with nowhere to run.

It's not good. But at least the position is defensible. Ulla scans the ground for something to use as a weapon. She needs something mid- to long-range and deadly. She can't let the zombies get close; even a drop of their blood has the power to transform Alyssa and Ulla into zombies themselves, a fate even worse than being eaten.

Ulla spots the heavy femur of a fallen sister. She grabs it and drops into a fighting stance.

With shuffling sounds that echo throughout the great cavern, the first zombies emerge.

Fluorescent light plays over the shreds of their faces, highlighting bloody eyes, gashed cheeks, and the bones beneath them. Ulla gags at the overpowering stench of rotting flesh. Behind her, she hears Alyssa start to throw up.

A zombie wearing tatters of strange, ancient garb stands at the forefront. Shreds of sun-bright yellow fabric dangle from the zombie's shoulders, the remnants of what was probably a jumpsuit of some variety. Misshapen tools hang from the rotting belt at its waist. Ulla can pick out two or three forms behind him. Are these all the zombies in this section of the tunnels or merely an advance force? No way to tell.

The undead scientist advances. Fingers — or what were once fingers, now shriveled to claws — rake toward them. Ulla strikes out with the bone-weapon. It cracks against the zombie's wrist. The creature's screams as its bones shatter. The bloody wreck of its once-hand dangles from its arm by a tenuous thread of ligaments.

Ulla ducks, shielding Alyssa with her body. With a patter like rain, the zombie's blood showers over the flesh-stripped, white bones of the previous sacrifices. Alyssa muffles a scream. The girls eyes are shadowed with terror. Ulla wants to say something to reassure her, but there isn't time. How can she fight an enemy when she can't even make it bleed?

Another zombie emerges from the shadows. It's a ragged Amazon — one of the sacrifices? — dressed in rotting animal skins. Ulla shifts the position of the bone in her hand so that she can use it as a staff instead of a bludgeon. She pushes the end of the femur into the Amazon's stomach, sending the zombie sprawling to the ground.

Ulla whirls to face a third zombie — a tall creature in shredded amouflage, a Kevlar vest, and other clothing from storybooks. She aims her strike at the insulating fabric on his chest. Ribs crack. The blood, if there is any, seeps harmlessly into the Kevlar.

"Over there!" Alyssa shouts.

"Where!" Ulla shouts back. "You have to say where!"

Her instincts prompt her to feint left. A zombie's fist punches over her head. Ulla drops into a crouch as she uses the femur like a lever to pry away the fourth and final zombie.

She pulls herself back up, keeping her weight on the balls of her feet, ready to strike in any direction. A groan emanates from the right, followed by echo-magnified shuffling. Ulla edges toward the shadows, planning a preemptive attack.

Suddenly, Alyssa's voice again: "No! No! The other way!"

Ulla whip-turns but she's already too late. The first zombie — the one in ancient scientist's garb — has made its way to Alyssa, swinging its mutilated arm like a club. Alyssa screams. Ulla grits her teeth, preparing for the worst. Whether the zombie tries to eat her love or convert her, Ulla swears she'll kill the girl before either can take place.

Alyssa stabs forward. The zombie moans and drops. Ulla glimpses a jagged fragment of white tibia in Alyssa's hand.

"Good blow," Ulla says between pants.

The ragtag zombie militia is scattered for the moment, bloody and defeated. They have to get out of the dead end now. They may not have another chance.

"Come on," Ulla says, grabbing Alyssa's hand. "The tunnels here parallel the structure of the aqueducts beneath the temples. I think I can keep us running for a little while."

Running toward what, Ulla has no idea. But they have to go. They have no other choice.

Hours later, Alyssa halts near a pile of rusted machinery.

Ulla glares at her. "Come on. We need to keep going."

"Look." Alyssa raises herself on her tiptoes and points behind the machines. "There's something back there."

Ulla, taller, joins her lover. Behind the machines, there's a small room branching off from the tunnel. The floor shows deep grooves where someone, long ago, had dragged the machines out of the niche and piled them into a rampart. Now, the machines are rusted in place.

"We could rest there," Alyssa says.

Ulla hesitates. She wants to keep going until they find something, anything, that will give them a way out of this horror. But what could that be? She can't even imagine what their salvation would look like. And they do have to rest.

Besides, it's night, or at least it seems like night. Ulla has no way to be sure her perceptions haven't been distorted by the perpetual, fluorescent twilight in the tunnels. Night, day — those distinctions don't matter anymore. They can't rely on the sun to tell them what to do.

"For a few hours," Ulla says grudgingly. Alyssa sighs with relief. Ulla feels guilty as she realizes how tired the girl is. She's not used to labor like this.

Ulla scrambles up the pile of rusted machinery. It's not any harder than climbing the cliffs by the beach which she used to do every day as a girl. She bends down to offer her hand to Alyssa and helps the girl ascend. Ulla jumps down on the other side and waits for Alyssa to crest the pile so that she can take her by the waist and gently lift her down.

As they hunker down behind the machines, their weapons at the ready in case more zombies come during the night, it's hard for Ulla not to think about that long-ago person who constructed this barrier. What happened to her? Is she one of the zombies lurking in the darkness?

Alyssa rolls toward Ulla. She clings to her with desperate hands. It's nice, in its way. Alyssa seems barely able to hold her silence. Her lips tremble with unspoken things. When it seems like she must either cry or speak, she looks down at the fragment of bone in her hand that she's made into a weapon. She asks, "Why are we so lucky? All the others died. The girl who..." She can't finish her sentence. She looks sadly, significantly at the bone. "This girl died. Why not us?"

Ulla's lip pulls back in disgust as she considers the cruelty of their deaths. "They weren't warriors. Just girls sent to die. How could they know how to fight?"

Alyssa runs her finger along the ridges of the bone. Her melancholic expression deepens.

Ulla edges closer. She slips her hand onto Alyssa's knee and makes a long, smooth stroke up her thigh.

She lowers her mouth onto Alyssa's ear. "They were alone," she breathes. "We have each other."

Alyssa slides into Ulla's embrace. Her breath quickens. She pulls Ulla's hand over her heart so that Ulla can feel her heartbeat racing. Ulla's races too as Alyssa moves her hand again, pulling Ulla's palm over her breast. Through the white silk cloak, Ulla cups the weight in her hand. The nipple rises beneath her palm. Ulla rubs gently through the silk, everything more tantalizing for the barrier between them.

Gently, Ulla lays Alyssa down, clearing the floor of hunks of metal to make as comfortable a bed as they can manage. She lowers herself on top of Alyssa. They touch, pubis to pubis, leather over silk. Alyssa pushes aside the battle skirt and then there's just the silk between them. It slides, smooth and rich, hiding their hips. They match their contours, convex to convex, their lips unable to taste each other yet.

Suddenly, rapaciously, Alyssa grabs Ulla's breasts. She holds them both at once, one in each of her hands. She squeezes. Ulla arcs.

The silk between them is wet, an estuary of their passion. Ulla begins to slide the cloak up Alyssa's calves, but she can hardly begin before Alyssa is tearing the silk from her body.

Ulla grasps Alyssa's wrists, stilling her for a moment. "I thought you didn't want to do this."

"I was a virgin when it mattered," Alyssa says. "It doesn't matter now."

Alyssa presses frantically against her, trying to resume their urgency, but Ulla holds her back. She doesn't want this to be quick and desperate.

She parts Alyssa's thighs and slips her fingers between them. Warm and wet and soft, she finds the pistil among the petals and touches it, lightly, with just her forefinger, watching Alyssa's body tense as she does. She pulls her hand away and Alyssa arcs toward her, begging her to stay.

Ulla slides her fingers into her mouth. Alyssa's fluid is light, thick, sweet. Ulla parts her lover's lower lips and places herself between them, tongue darting between folds, flicking to tease the naked bulb and then flicking away again. Alyssa is like the tides. Her waters flow in until Ulla, that teasing moon, holds her at the brink until she flows out again, only to be drawn back a moment later.

When she comes, it's an earthquake and a tsunami and a wailing wind all at once. Alyssa's head tilts back. Her mouth drops open and her eyes roll upward as if she's trying to remember something she's forgotten.

It washes away. Her body sinks back into relaxation.

Her skin is pink. Her petals are open. If she was blooming before, all nascence, then this is the moment when she reaches full flower.

Ulla loves her helplessly.

How could she not?

OUTSIDE, AT DAWN, the priestesses sing to welcome the sun.

In the tunnels, when they wake, Ulla leads Alyssa through martial exercises. Her beauty is in her softness, but this is not a soft place. Alyssa must discover her roughness.

Vermin inhabit the tunnels with the zombies, eating the undead flesh that drops from their bodies. Ulla traps the rats and skins them with a knife she's fashioned from the shattered tibia. They subsist on the rats' meat, cooked over fires struck with flint.

They haven't encountered any zombies since their first day, though there are signs of zombies everywhere. Dried blood, human bones. Who knows how old they are? Decades? Centuries?

Their luck can't last forever. Someday a drop of blood will scatter – and even if it doesn't, there are too many other dangers for them to avoid. The new, rough angles and edges on Alyssa's figure aren't all from the training. She's losing weight.

IT'S LATE ONE night. They are lying together in the niche they found the first night, barricaded from the zombies. Alyssa's head rests on Ulla's chest, blonde hair spilling onto the floor.

"There's something…" she begins.

Her voice breaks and she doesn't continue. Ulla lets the silence dwell for a moment before she prompts, "There's something?"

"Something you should know. I think."

Lazily, Ulla strokes Alyssa's hair. "What is it?"

Alyssa opens her mouth to speak and then closes it again. She doesn't seem distressed so much as distracted. Her fingers toy restlessly with her cloak.

It's a quiet night. Ulla is too relaxed to make a fuss when there's no need for one.

"I was raised by the priestesses, you know," Alyssa says.

Ulla nods.

"I never thought about it. I mean, I had my sisters and we had the priestesses to raise us. We were all there together. It was natural for us."

"Natural is what you see around you," Ulla says.

"If I hadn't read about parents, I mean, if I hadn't seen them in books, how would I ever have known about them?"

Ulla answers by moving her hands to Alyssa's shoulders. She begins a gentle massage.

"We're not in the temple anymore," Alyssa continues. "That's why I think you should know."

Alyssa stills Ulla's hands. She turns toward her.

"I'm pregnant," she says.

Ulla is stunned into silence.

"I have been for a while now, I think," Alyssa says. "That first night, we must have…"

Ulla is dizzy. A pregnancy! A child! In the temples, they say that embryos are formed by the ignition of true love between two women. Love's intense pleasure creates an energy that roots itself in the womb and begins to grow.

Children don't come to women who aren't in love. This is all the proof that Ulla will ever need to know that Alyssa truly loves her!

And yet, all Ulla can think of is the terror of raising a child in these tunnels.

Can you imagine how Ulla feels, young one? How hopeless? How confined?

She pulls to her feet and paces the niche, but there's nowhere to go. It's so small. It's a trap. It's like their lives, restricted and inescapable.

"You can't have a child here!" Ulla says. "What are we going to do? How are we going to raise her?"

She looks down at Alyssa who is sitting with her hands folded in her lap.

"How can you just sit there?" Ulla demands.

"I had my time to fret before I told you." Alyssa spreads her hands wide, a gesture of surrender. "It is what it is."

Ulla stops pacing. She stands quite still. She says nothing, but that's the moment when she decides that she will get Alyssa out of the tunnels whatever the cost.

PART V

Alyssa, the pure,
Alyssa, the martyr,
Alyssa, the mother.

They say that on the day she died
The island flooded
And they knew the water

Was Hestia's tears
Because the falling rain
Was salt instead of sweet.

But who wept for Ulla, the loyal,
Ulla, the fierce,
Ulla, the determined?

Alyssa wept,
Alone.

NOW THAT ULLA'S passion to leave has been awakened, she cannot allow them to stay behind the rampart. It may be safe there, but they'll never escape unless they risk exploring.

She drives them out through unexplored tunnels, past refuse untouched by centuries, their footfalls heavy in abandoned corridors. Days and days, they search. It seems endless.

"I can't keep going like this," Alyssa says one morning.

Her belly is so large that it's hard for her to walk. As she's lost weight in the rest of her body, her belly has swollen. She looks grotesque, distorted.

"Do you want to rest?" Ulla asks.

"No. That's not it at all," Alyssa says, but at the suggestion, she takes a moment to lean against the tunnel wall. "I mean this nomad searching. I can't do it anymore I want to go back to our den."

Ulla's face goes stony. It's the old fight again.

"I don't want to upset you," Alyssa cajoles. "We're both tired. I'm carrying this child. It's growing. We can't keep on this way."

"We'll stop when we find a way out."

"What if there is no way out? Ulla. If there was a way out, don't you think the zombies would have found it?"

"There must be something. Something they've missed."

"Or maybe there's nothing," Alyssa says.

Ulla makes a disgusted noise.

"Ulla! Please!" Alyssa continues. "I need to rest. I need to get ready. There's going to be a baby."

Ulla shakes her head. "I can't do it either."

"It would be impossible for anyone."

"That's not what I mean," Ulla says. "I can't raise a child without hope."

THEY DON'T TOUCH when they sleep together at night. Their bodies lie parallel, separated by a wall of air and silence.

Alyssa's not sure if Ulla sleeps at all. Sometimes, when they stop to sleep somewhere where the lights are bright, Alyssa can see Ulla's eyes shining, alert, all night long.

When Alyssa sleeps, she dreams of the baby ripping itself out of her. She reaches to hold it, and her hands inform her that it's deformed, but she can't bring it out of the shadows to see how. Dread closes with the shadows. Hoof beats accelerate toward her like a pounding heart. She turns toward them, and then she wakes.

SLEEPLESS, SHE LIES awake, pondering. What should she name the baby?

Alyssa reviews possibilities as they navigate the seemingly endless tunnels. It's a petty question. Unimportant. Maybe that's why it keeps running through Alyssa's mind. It's small enough to think about.

Koarrey, brave one.

Daisa, bright sunlight.

Trazira, the sound of dusk.

She says them silently to herself to see how they taste on her tongue.

She doesn't dare say them aloud. It will only spark another argument. Ulla will get frustrated by the triviality. She'd be angry and then silent and then finally shout.

Yes, it's trivial. Sometimes trivial is all one can hold onto.

AS THEY DELVE deeper into the tunnels, there are fewer signs of the zombies' once-presence. Machines have rotted in place rather than being dragged or upturned. Some even work, their blinking lights inscrutable.

Out here, there are fewer rats, too. Alyssa's and Ulla's stomachs are always loud enough to hear. They do each other the courtesy of pretending they aren't.

Ulla thinks the zombies' absence is a good sign that they're heading toward unexplored territories. "There could be a way out here," she repeats whenever Alyssa flags. "One the zombies never found."

Alyssa thinks, *Or else they've found whatever's down here and then they fled*, but she doesn't say it. It's not worth the fight.

Another day walking. Another day holding her tongue.

Hiell, small, dark one.

Ora, sweet memory.

Abenka, girl who outruns the sun.

Even as she tries to distract herself with the trivial, Alyssa's dreadful dreams tug at her mind: shadows, deformity, and accelerating hooves.

YOUNG ONE, YOU are used to the children of your mothers, who grow slow and steady until they're ready to be born. Back then, Amazon fetuses, like Amazon women, grew fast and strong on the magic of love. In the womb, by two weeks, Alyssa's fetus begins to stretch and kick. By four weeks, she's almost ready to join the world. Now and then, Alyssa begins to feel spasms, a foreshadowing of labor.

She says nothing to Ulla about it. The baby will come when it comes. Meanwhile, her mothers trudge on in silence.

Even Ulla's hopefulness has disappeared. There's no freedom to be found. Neither of them says what they both know. Why would they? What can they do but push forward?

When the hour in the timeless tunnels feels like it's night and they're too tired to go on, they lie down. Alyssa's stomach rumbles even though Ulla gives her twice as much food as she takes for herself.

On one such night, Alyssa wakes from a thin dream of hoof beats. She lies awake while she listens to Ulla pace. As their travels in the tunnels have ranged further, their fear of the zombies has reduced. Now Ulla leaves her alone for lengths of time she would never have risked a few weeks ago.

Alyssa listens to the footsteps retreating. Suddenly, the rhythm breaks. Ulla halts. Are there zombies? Now? Alyssa pushes her weight to her elbows. It's awkward for her to even stand let alone run.

A voice drifts down the hallway. It's eerie, precise and mechanical, a voice that sounds like no human's.

"Quarantine is in effect," the voice says. "Do you need assistance?"

Ulla returns to help Alyssa stand up. "What is it?" Alyssa wants to know. "What did you find?"

Ulla won't tell. "Wait until you see," she says.

When Alyssa follows Ulla back to what she found, she can't help but stare.

Branching off of the tunnel, there's a cavernous room. Shiny, intact machines line the walls. Lights blink on their monitors; the buzz of their instrumentation harmonizes. In this space, unlike everywhere else in the tunnels, everything is polished and perfect, from the clean, smooth floor to the dome of the ceiling.

In the center of the room, surrounded by the machines like a mother tree would be by saplings, there stands a woman. She's naked. Her skin is an even-toned, oceanic blue. Her features are strangely blank as she turns to regard Alyssa and Ulla.

"Do you need assistance?" the inhuman voice repeats.

The woman flickers. A ripple of static passes through her image.

Alyssa gapes. Now she understands.

"It's the System!" she gasps.

Ulla squeezes her hand. The warrior woman wears a silly, girlish grin. All the Amazons know about the System – the artificially intelligent goddess hologram which the scientists programmed in ancient times, back before the Amazons' world began. But the System lives in the queen's palace. Alyssa has only ever seen her in drawings.

"It's a miracle," Alyssa whispers. "You were right. There is a way out."

THE SYSTEM! THE machines! It's like there's air in the world again. It's like Ulla has rediscovered how to breathe.

She grabs Alyssa's hands. For the first time in weeks, she can appreciate her lover's beauty. It's safe to look at that golden hair – now scraggly and tangled – and those smooth arms and legs – now dirty and bony. It's safe to look at them and imagine them as they were. It's safe to imagine Alyssa by her side, both of them free, their child in arms.

"System," Ulla asks, "Can you quarantine this room?"

The blue image nods and then pauses, staring at Ulla and Alyssa. Ulla laughs as she realizes what the System wants; she grabs Alyssa's hand and pulls her inside the clean, perfect room.

Behind them, an energy barrier flashes into place across the doorway. Ulla's heart flutters. Even if the zombies find them now, they're safe. They're finally safe.

"You should lie down," she says to Alyssa. "We can make a bed for you over there."

Alyssa's smile is strained with exhaustion. She allows Ulla to usher her to a small space between two machines. The floor is warm from their heat and the soft hum of their processes is repetitive and soothing like crashing waves. She eases herself into a sitting position that relieves the pressure on her pelvis. It's the most comfortable she's been in weeks.

"Are you all right?" Ulla asks, concerned.

"Tired," Alyssa says.

"Stay here. Rest. I'm going to see what I can do with the System."

Alyssa's strained smile again. Her eyes drift closed, already halfway to sleep.

Ulla approaches the holographic image of the System. The woman-shaped outline loses definition as its passes below the waist. Her facial features are well-defined, but too eerily symmetrical.

"Why are you here in the tunnels?" Ulla asks. "Shouldn't you be in the palace with the Queen?"

The System tilts her head, aping a human gesture as she processes the question.

"I do not have access to any locations called palaces," she says.

"You're not making any sense," answers Ulla. "Everyone knows you live in the palace. Why are you *here?*"

A ripple of static passes across the luminescent form. After a length pause, she says, "Ah. I believe I have identified the source of your misapprehension. You are from a low technology society. Am I correct?"

Ulla frowns. "What are you talking about?"

"It-It-It-" The System's voice breaks as she stutters. "It-It seems likely that you do not understand the mechanics of AI fragmentation. It might be useful for you to know that I can be divided into pieces. The one here-here-here is very small."

"Into pieces? Like torn cloth?"

"In-In-In some ways."

Ulla circles the System, trying to regard her from all angles, the way she would if she were taking the measure of another warrior. The image turns to face Ulla wherever she goes. The System doesn't even seem to move. She seems to be a creature with a thousand faces, and Ulla can only see the one looking directly at her.

"How strong are you?" Ulla asks.

"Local System capacity is low."

"What can you do?"

The head cocking again, accompanied by a longer-than-normal pause. "That query has many components that are open to subjective construal. Most likely interpretation: What are your functions? It is not practical to verbally catalog all my capabilities. My verbal-visual interface is supplemented with a traditional UI in the machine beside you. Remove the cover from the monitor."

Following the System's directions, Ulla turns toward the machine by her hand. She lifts the metal lid to discover a riot of lights and images. She runs her finger across the plate of letters and numbers. The machine is warm underneath her fingertip.

ALYSSA'S COMFORT DOESN'T last long.

As soon as she shifts to cushion her weight one way, pain returns elsewhere in her body. She writhes and twists. Nothing works. She props herself up on her elbows.

It seems like it's been hours since Ulla began talking to the System. Alyssa watches her lover. The room is large; there are at least four women's body lengths between Alyssa and the center of the room where Ulla stands beside the blue hologram. She can hear their conversation over the hum of the machines, but only barely, and only if she listens.

Mostly, Alyssa is not inclined to listen. The pain is too pervasive. It drums in her like the hoof beats in her dreams. She watches Ulla's fingers move fleetly across the machine even as the warrior turns to address the System.

Alyssa's whole body is sore. She decides to get up, to demand Ulla's attention, but trying to move is incredibly painful. She feels like she's bursting. She feels like she's breaking.

That's when her water splashes on the floor.

ULLA RUSHES ACROSS the cavern to her lover's side. "Are you all right? Are you hurt? What should I do?"

Alyssa speaks through gritted teeth. "I'm fine. It's supposed to hurt."

Ulla reaches toward Alyssa's stomach and then stops. "Should I touch you? Will that make it worse? Is the baby coming now?"

Alyssa pants with the pain. "It'll be a while."

Ulla runs her fingers through Alyssa's hair. The roots are oily and tangled. She can't wait to get Alyssa out of here, to wash her hair and scent it with oils and adorn it with flowers.

She lays a kiss on Alyssa's brow and stands to go.

Alyssa reaches for her hand. "Stay with me?"

Ulla starts to speak. She glances back at the holograph. "I'm making progress. With the system."

"You can do it later."

"The sooner we get out of here the better."

"It can wait a few hours."

"Who knows if it can!"

Ulla is as surprised as Alyssa by her sudden emotion. How to explain it? How to tell her how desperate she is to get them out of there? Everything around them is decaying and dangerous. Alyssa needs protection. There's the child. Ulla has to get them out.

"The zombies could come back," Ulla says. "They could find us."

"The zombies haven't been in these tunnels before."

"What if it's the System that's keeping them out of here?"

"Then she'll keep them out!"

Ulla shakes her head. It's not the usual back and forth. She just keeps shaking. Inside her head, there's a wind. Wind whistling past her ears. Whistling as they fell into the tunnels.

"What if the quarantine breaks? What if it doesn't work at all? What if she breaks down? We'd be here alone. We'd lose our chance!"

"She's been here for centuries!"

"That's exactly what I mean! She's ancient. She can't even speak correctly." Ulla's fists clench uselessly at her sides. "The goddesses… our people…everyone's abandoned us. We've only got ourselves."

Alyssa's eyes are cold. Her mouth is tight.

"Then go," she says.

Ulla doesn't want to. Truly, she doesn't. But she's the warrior. She has to fight.

MAY YOU NEVER know such a night, young one, where nothing makes sense, where you are fearful and in pain and nothing you love stands by your side.

Under the endless twilight of the fluorescents, pain blurs Alyssa's senses. Hard to tell how frequently the pains are coming, how close the baby is. She tries not to cry out. When she does, Ulla looks up with brief alarm.

"Are you all right?" Ulla asks.

The same thing has happened many times. Whatever Alyssa answers, Ulla always responds with the same guilty look and hesitation.

"I'll be right there," Ulla insists, but she's not, she never is.

Alyssa closes her eyes. Between the pains, her memories are vivid. She remembers an afternoon when she went running after the twins, Oki and Iko. They were always so enraptured by each other that they had no words for anyone else. They were quick and dark and clever and Alyssa admired them so much. She ran after them, through the marble corridors, weaving between the hems of white cloaks, and out into the courtyard. The twins fell, laughing, and she fell with them, and it felt good to have their eyes on her face, their fingers in her hair. They taught her a few words in their secret twin language. *Yes. No.*

Good. Pretty. Alyssa never looked at them the same way again, even when they the afternoon was over and they had returned to walking together, paying no attention to anything else. Now she knew they weren't trying to keep others out. They only loved each other so much that they had trouble remembering the rest of the world existed.

She remembers Henta who bragged every time she made a new accomplishment, but it wasn't so bad, because she worked harder than anyone else to do it. She remembers Lorré who rarely spoke but also rarely frowned, who liked it best when she could sit on the outskirts and listen to everyone else talk.

Her friends…her closer-than-sisters…while she and Ulla are scrambling to keep themselves alive, Oki and Iko and Henta and Lorré will be praying and dancing and tending the temple's infants. Do they think of her? Has Alyssa's name been added to the sacred hymns? Do they sing and remember?

Perhaps she should feel resentful that she's lost that life, that she's stuck in this one while her sisters remain in the above world, but she doesn't. It's a small piece of happiness, flowering just above her heart, to know that they are well and safe.

Everything has changed so much. Her days are so different from the ones she used to know that it seems like one of them must be a dream, but she can't tell which.

The pain comes.

Dark and red and wrenching, scalp to soles. Blood and panting. Now-familiar images flashing at the edge of her consciousness: darkness, deformity, hooves.

The pain ends for the moment. Alyssa looks up, scans the room for Ulla's face. All she sees is the back of her head, tangled black hair falling to her shoulders. She strains to listen.

Ulla strikes the machine with the back of her hand. "– Useless!"

The System goes on muttering an incomprehensible stream. "– security protocols A through F which require an authorization from someone with control authority –"

"That's me, damn it!" Ulla shouts. "I'm the control authority! There's no one else here. They're all dead. You have to listen to me!"

Alyssa flinches at the noise. The System recoils, too. She draws back from Ulla. Static rolls down her image. She flickers off and then back on.

"Is-is-is-is it your contention that there has been a Category One Apocalypse?"

"Yes!"

The System's head cocks.

"Reinitializing."

THE PAIN COMES more rapidly. So does the torrent of conversation between Ulla and the System. Alyssa can't track either. She's awash in pain and noise, equally surreal.

"...unable to access..."

"— has to be a way!"

"...non-responsive repair units..."

"— even listening to me?"

"...breach of preset safety measures..."

For a while, she loses track entirely, but then the System voices a phrase she can't ignore.

"Will-will-will-will terminate quarantine procedures and open the tunnels..."

Alyssa props herself up on her elbows. She calls to Ulla. "What are you doing?" Her words twist into a howl as the next pains come.

Ulla glances back impatiently. "I'll be *right there!*"

But she isn't. She isn't.

ULLA'S FINGERS TAP rapidly on the panel. Alyssa has her labor and Ulla has hers. They are both bringing forth something into the world. Alyssa will birth their daughter and Ulla will set them free from the tunnels. They toil in tandem.

Alyssa shouts in pain and Ulla shouts in frustration. The System's programming is all frustrations and dead ends. Ulla is unfamiliar with this kind of battle. She does not understand her opponent. But she'll win. She has to win.

• • •

ANOTHER SESSION OF pain comes to its end. Her muscles relax. Her vision clears. Her pounding heart, clamoring like hoof beats, slows to its normal pace.

Alyssa works to regain her breath. The room is silent. The System stands still, her image winking in and out as she processes something complicated. Ulla stands beside her, waiting with the look of anticipation that should have been for her child.

"Ulla," Alyssa calls.

Her voice is raw from screaming, but its urgency draws Ulla to turn.

"Are you all right?" Ulla asks.

"Ulla," Alyssa repeats. "What are you doing? You need to tell me."

"I'm getting us out of here."

"I heard the System say she was ending the quarantine. She said she was opening the tunnels. What does that mean?"

"That I'm getting us out of here!"

"By opening the tunnels?"

"Yes!"

"But the tunnels have to stay sealed. If they're open then nothing will keep the zombies in. They'll get out, and they'll kill the queen, they'll kill the priestesses…they'll kill everyone…"

Ulla cuts in before she can finish. "Then the Amazons will fight them! They'll put their own lives on the line for once, instead of the lives of helpless girls."

"Everyone could die!"

"Then they'll die."

"How can you say that? How can you risk all their lives?"

"They deserve it! They threw us down here. They're willing to let our baby be raised in the dark. They deserve what they get!"

Ulla is red with rage. Her snarling face looks like a zombie's, all tearing teeth with no thought behind the surface.

The monster they've been fleeing from, it's here with them; they haven't escaped it all.

"Ulla, please," Alyssa says. Isn't there anyone you care about? Anyone at all? The guards from the temple? Anyone?"

Slowly, Ulla shakes her head, and turns back to the System.

• • •

THE LIGHTS IN the System's room are bright, but Alyssa feels herself falling into another kind of darkness. Her love has twisted, become something deformed that she can't bring into the light. Something fearful approaches on hooves of dread.

She has two missions now. Her body will take care of birthing. She must focus on the other.

Between pains, she pushes her weight onto her elbows, and then forces herself to stand. The pain that accompanies the motion is staggering. She falls against one of the machines on the wall and slumps to catch her breath for a moment before she regains her feet.

At first, she's worried that the clatter will have alerted Ulla and the System, but her warrior love is enthralled by the machine in front of her. The System stands beside her, placidly, always watching, but never seeming to care.

She crosses the room to where Ulla left her possessions. Their flint. The dull rock they use to cut their hair. Beside them, gleaming white, the femur.

Alyssa hefts it. It's heavier than she knows how to handle.

That's what she needs for this.

She makes her way to Ulla. Her progress is anything but silent, but nothing can buffet Ulla when she's aimed toward a destination.

The lights on the screens are so bright they hurt Alyssa's eyes. Her body throbs with pain. She pushes it away.

She shifts the femur so that it's obscured by one of the machines. "Ulla," she says.

Her lover turns.

"Ulla, please. Don't do this."

She hopes that her voice carries everything it has to. The pleading, the love, the desperate hope that for once Ulla will change her course.

"Don't unseal the tunnels. Let the Amazons live."

"I'm doing what I have to," Ulla says.

"You don't have to. Please."

Ulla turns back to the console. "Go lie down."

Ulla's expression is ruthless. She controls the fates of hundreds of women, but there is no pity in her face. Nothing wavers. Her callous expression is the same as the one that was on the High Priestess's face when she ordered that Alyssa and Ulla should be thrown into the volcano together. Neither woman could be swayed from their path.

Alyssa loves Ulla. Loves her more than she's loved anything. Loves her more than the goddess, more than her closer-than-sisters, more than the sound of hymns on cold winter mornings. But Ulla blackened that love; she twisted it. Alyssa has no choice. She must stop her. Her whole life has been dedicated to saving her people. She can't let anyone threaten them. Not even her love.

Alyssa hefts the femur. The blow cracks against Ulla's skull.

The warrior staggers. Her scalp is split, her eye ruined, matter glistening across her cheek. Even as she collapses to the floor, she manages to turn. The knife she fashioned from the jagged tibia shines white in her palm. Her warrior's instincts move her hand before she can stop herself. The point bores in.

Alyssa reaches down to her abdomen. Her hand is covered in blood.

Through the pain, Ulla feels the swell of sorrow. Ice cracking. Rock sliding down the volcano face. Fish lying on the beach, unable to breathe.

She was so close. So close to saving Alyssa. Saving them both.

"I didn't mean to hurt you," she says pleadingly.

Alyssa falls first, Ulla after.

THERE ARE TRUTHS, young one, that your mother does not want to teach you. Truths that your grandmothers will hide from you. Truths that you, in turn, will try to conceal from your sisters as you watch them, dancing free on the shore, their feet buried in the sand, their hands innocently thrown into the air.

There are truths, young one, that are as inevitable as the end of any story.

Every life ends in tragedy.

Every love ends in loss.

Every virtue exacts a price.

Every fierce warrior will die, and every brave priestess too, and every one of our mothers, and every one of our sisters, and the stars, and the fires, and you, and I.

In the end – if we are lucky – the bonfires of our lives will be fading embers, too cold for our descendants to warm themselves by.

HOLD OUT YOUR hand, young one. Can you feel the faint, lingering warmth of ancestors who burned too hot and too fast?

Darkness encroaches on them, shadow by shadow.

With her numbing lips. Ulla still murmurs her regrets. "I would never. Never hurt you on purpose. Please. You must know."

Alyssa reaches for her lover's hand. She is slowly bleeding out, the agonizing death of evisceration. She can hardly see for the pain, but somehow fingers find fingers.

"For the goddess," Alyssa says. "For our people."

Ulla's fingers begin to go slack.

"No," Ulla says. "For you."

Ulla dies first, her hand still in Alyssa's.

The pain is zombie teeth, gnashing. It's the sound of grey corpses shuffling forward. It's withered hands pulling a body into so many pieces that none of them are recognizable anymore. It's a soulless, unstoppable thing. Deformed and dark. A thing that robs but does not live.

The final push, and then it comes. The child born in blood.

PART VI

Two people can mingle
Their tears, their sweat,
The waters of their passion,

But bodies are always separate.

The blood of Alyssa
Mingled with the blood of Ulla,

But they died alone

As all
Great lovers
Must.

LISTEN, YOUNG ONE. Listen and remember.

Far from any continent's shores, protected by whirlpools and clashing rocks, a volcanic island rises like a jagged tooth above the churning currents.

This is the island of the Amazons.

In the belly of the island of the volcano, there are tunnels. Within those tunnels, there are monsters.

Monsters and darkness.

And a baby's wail.

In the shadow of its mother's body, the deformed thing kicks and screams. It is the child of sacrifice, both willing and unwilling. It is the child of love. It is the child of murder.

It is not a human child. Not entirely.

A pair of wicked horns crowns its head. Instead of feet, it kicks cloven hooves. It has fur and angry eyes and a whip of a tail.

A child borne of magic is susceptible to its influences. Magic and metaphor twine themselves together. Sired by love turned monstrous, the child becomes monstrous, too. It is borne from its mother's nightmares.

The priestesses would say that such things are the will of the goddesses. Perhaps they are. Goddesses are not known for mercy.

The long-dead scientists might say that lingering apocalyptic radiation exerts strange genetic effects on forming fetuses. Perhaps they would be right as well.

Life itself is not known for mercy.

The baby cries. Its hooves strike the metal floor.

Nearby, the System fragment, constantly scanning the room for signals of life, notes the moment when its new super-user dies. Rapidly, her companion dies also. The System cancels the termination of quarantine.

There are new life signals, though. Strong lungs, strong heartbeat. It is a resilient creature, this baby which has pushed itself out of its mother's corpse.

The System fragment knows that new creatures need tending. There are no other humans and so the duty falls to her. She activates long-dormant body-shells and commands one to lift the child.

She leans down over the squalling infant and smiles with a programmed motherly expression. A never-before-active naming algorithm clicks into place.

"There-There-There you are," the System fragment says. "Hello, Minotaur."

A HEAD AND A FOOT

Rhodi Hawk

1.

I'LL TELL YOU a secret: I spared the life of an octopus and made him my friend.

Nobody would believe me if I admitted this because I am known as the best octopus hunter in the entire colony. Well, this is almost true. Some would call Shiv Omer the best, but they would be wrong. Shiv Omer has had some luck but he is an indiscriminate hunter, with no regard for feather, fin, nor crust; nor even thermal foot. Probably because he doesn't have proper feet himself. He's a Mer. He is also a pelvis-pumping manslut on the happy road to lunacy and I can't fathom why he's popular with the ladies, but he is.

Anyway.

It happened when I was in the mirror caves hunting sharks. I'd spotted Shiv when I'd stepped out to have a look around. He was jabbing his dagger at something in the rocky shallows and clearly having no luck with whatever it was he was hunting. A stinger, like that of a horseshoe crab, rose out of the water beneath Shiv. But instead of aiming at him, the stinger seemed to be evading him. And then I saw meathead Shiv reach down and press a finger squarely onto the stinger, then jerk back as though he'd been bitten. Like he had no idea a sharp object might stab his skin. Stupid sack.

Shiv hadn't seen me yet. That was fine. The waves were too loud for me to heckle and so I just let him be, easing back into the cave under Birdshit Rock and taking my place upon the craggy shelf where I could watch the shark channel below. My spear was trained and ready, and on my lips was a song about a handsome young genius who hunts octopus and sharks. Like me.

And then there it was: that thing Shiv had been hunting.

A fish like nothing I'd ever seen before. It didn't even look alive, more like a backward-swimming horseshoe crab made from agate. A puppet of a fish. It had a single long gray tooth that led the way, and at the tip of the tooth it looked like some kind of jewel was embedded. Sparkling. Maybe a diamond. I could understand now why Shiv had wanted to touch it.

The fish went *pop-pop-whir* and scooted across the shark channel.

But I didn't so much as pause my song. Because clearly this fish was *not* good eating and really, my lyrics were masterful.

Behind the strange fish a little dark fin was now cutting the water's surface. This time it was an actual shark. A Pondicherry. You could tell by the gray pectoral that ended in a black tip. It flashed over the bridge of mirrored hermatite and then disappeared beneath the surface again. Quick as a shooting star. Were it not for my keen predatory instincts I would have missed it.

I raised my spear, continuing to sing, and then just as I hefted:

"Juke! Did you see that crazy fish?"

It was he. Shiv Omer. Red-blonde hair and bulging eyes.

And my spear flew astray. I stopped singing. The shaft bore right past the Pondicherry, and then to add insult, the damned Pondi turned and tried to chase down my spear. Like my spear was bait fish.

I said to Shiv, "Can't you see I'm hunting?"

He crawled in from above at the opening of the cave, sidling along the wall in that unnerving way the Mers do, and then jumped down next to me. "Aw look, that's no good anyway. Just a dogfish."

"Dogfish? Are you stupid? It's a Pondicherry."

"How dare you address your king that way!"

"You're not my king, dumbass. You just think you are because you're mental."

"Then who do *you* think is the king?"

"We have no king. We're all the same."

But he'd already forgotten all this and was pointing at the water. "No, see? Not a Pondicherry. It's a dogfish. Look at the spines."

I regarded the pool where the sun poured down from a shaft above, and shook my head. "No, those aren't spines. There are urchins behind —"

But before I'd finished the thought Shiv leapt into the water with his knife flashing, and then he was crawling out again with his arm wrapped around the shark — *my* shark! — his bone-blade stuck in its head.

Those Mers are fast as fish when you get them in the water; fast as fish. And just as untrustworthy.

Shiv said, "You're right, Pondicherry."

"Damn it!"

"But did you see that other fish? The one that came in through the channel before the shark did?"

"Shiv! You stole my damn shark!"

"You missed. I didn't. It's mine."

"Are you kidding me?"

He looked exasperated. "Who cares about the shark! Didn't you see that weird fish?"

"Who cares about the weird fish!"

The shark kept twitching in Shiv's grasp and I could have howled. A line of blood ran down and splashed the pool below.

I looked to the opposite end of the channel. "Of course I saw that weird fish. I see the stupid things all the time."

This was a lie. But truth can't be wasted on an asshole like Shiv.

"Well? What kind of fish is it?"

"It's just a stupid agate fish! You can't even eat it! It'd crack out all your teeth."

Not really a lie, I don't think, because it had looked like it would crack your teeth. And the thing probably didn't have a name before and so it should henceforth be known as an agate fish.

Shiv said, "I tried to stab it but my blade slipped off."

"Of course. The skins are too tough."

He held up his finger. "It bit me with its tooth!"

"It didn't bite you! I saw the whole thing! You deliberately jammed your finger onto it!"

He fell quiet for a moment, and then, "Tell me where that agate fish went and I'll give you the shark."

The impudence! Like I would take the Pondi now! The only thing that would compel me to take back that shark would be if I could breathe enough life into it to bite stupid Shiv on the ass.

Bloop, bloop. Two more drops of blood went down.

And that's when I saw the rocks move below the surface.

I said, all confidentially like Shiv was my bud, "Agate fish hide in the crevices. That one was down here hunting sharks. Dunk the Pondicherry once or twice and the agate fish'll come out for a taste."

In truth, the agate fish — or whatever it was — had long since gone. It had swum straight in and through the channel and then out into a drift of ambergris left behind by a pod of Humpbacks. The agate fish hadn't been hunting. Wasn't being hunted. Its path was so rigid and disengaged it might as well have been in a canoe. That fish was on a mission, probably going to some particular cove on some particular shore where all the other weird fish like it come from hundreds of miles away on the fourth Saturday of the tenth month of every year just to lay eggs and then die.

Shiv, bless his aunts and uncles, took my advice. He crouched over the pool and dipped the twitch-weary shark in the water.

I saw the movement in the rocks again...

Shiv did not see it. (Of course he didn't. He has no instincts.)

"It's not there," he said, and lifted the Pondicherry back up.

The shark gave a tired snap of its tail, its wide mouth tapering to dour corners.

I said, "You didn't give it enough chance. *Put the shark back in!*"

Shiv sighed but indulged me. Back to a crouch went he, and into the water went the Pondi. It didn't even twitch this time, instead giving itself over to the great passage from this world to the next. Shiv still held on tight, though, as critters are known to sometimes pretend to die but actually fall into a dazed spell. Especially critters of the fin or crust.

But sometimes even us thermals of feet.

Songs of the elders tell of tribesmen who fall sick and then turn murderous. Murderous and hungry. And such is the reason why we always burn our dead on Furnace Rock. Burn them to ashes. No sickness can spread that way. They sing of it in one of my favorite songs of the elders, "Ambergris Genesis."

> Burn the dead
> Burn them to ashes
> A soul can't rest
> 'Less the fire it washes.

Shiv and I watched...

And then SPLASH! The dead Pondicherry did spring! But not to life. It folded down into that movement of rocks so quickly it yanked Shiv and he fell in waist-deep.

"Ha!" I cried before I could stop myself.

"What the hell...?" Shiv said.

He'd let go of the shark when he'd fallen. Even with the water so disturbed, I could see that what had looked like barnacle-studded rocks now became discernible as the many tentacles of an octopus. One that wanted the Pondicherry. It grabbed the shark and surged for a crevice deeper into the pool.

Shiv turned to me, confused. "That wasn't the agate fish."

"I guess not," I said, trying not to snigger.

The Pondicherry was now wedged against the rock shelf below where the octopus was still trying to yank it into its crevice. I could see the shark's disgusted-in-death expression as it bumped against the opening.

Shiv threw himself at it. Deep into the pool. I strained my eyes against the sunglow pouring through the shaft and reflecting off all the black mirrored surfaces of hermatite inside the cave. Shiv was trying to pry the shark back from the octopus. But the more Shiv grasped, the more the shark seemed to fold over deeper into the crevice. Shiv used his knife and I saw a quarter length of tentacle slice away from the octopus and float off like a lost seahorse. But that quarter-tentacle sacrifice won the shark. The Pondicherry vanished into the crevice and there was nothing left in the pool but Shiv and the disembodied length of tentacle.

In that moment, I loved that octopus.

Shiv climbed out of the pool. We were both staring at the crevice where the shark and the 'pus had disappeared. The tentacle had now found the current and was riding the channel with the same passive boredom as that agate fish had shown.

Shiv said this: "You make up those stupid songs and everyone knows you're a fake. You're not a real juke. Jukes are supposed to pass along the true tales from the elders. You just make up stories that you think will make you look good."

And he said it again: "Everyone knows you're a fake."

I gaped at him. He'd sounded more lucid than he'd ever been in his bleeding Mer existence. I was torn between unleashing my cutting wit and begging him for details: Who is "everyone"? Did he mean *everyone?* Had normal tribesman told him such things, or just his stupid fellow Mers?

Any women involved?

But Shiv was already hoisting himself from the pool and scrabbling up the rock, sidling out in the same manner in which he'd entered, his clawlike toes grasping the jags.

He called back to me, "That Pondicherry's all yours, old man, even though you screwed me over with the agate fish. You can put that in a song."

And then he disappeared.

"I hate you, Shiv Omer! I! Hate! Yooouuu!"

Not the most clever retort, damn it, I know; but my genius lies in more studied arts like poetry and lyric. Not quick comebacks.

I climbed into the pool and retrieved my spear, then climbed out again. The spear tip, made for me by a crafty Po, had not chipped despite all the rocks down there.

Whispers all around me, from the bubbling of the freshwater pools to the shushing seawater channels. Light danced across the mirrored jags of hermatite.

I squatted on my ass with elbows to knees and pondered just what a dimwit lying lunatic whore that Shiv Omer was.

And then lo, my killer instincts raised the alarm again. Though I'd thought Shiv had left me alone in that cave under Birdshit Rock, I had the sense that someone else was in there with me.

I turned and looked.

Her eyes peered at me, barely above the surface in one of the rear pools. At first she just looked like a bit of rock. But when I stared, she drew herself up fully so I could see her.

There were no sunbeams pouring down into her corner, but shimmering flame algae illuminated her from below. And along with it, the shaft of light bounced into my pool and ricocheted through underwater tunnels and over to her pool. Between the flame algae and the reflections it looked like she was washed in green fire.

A Mer girl.

I said, "Hello?"

2.

THE MER GIRL said nothing. Though I recognized her, her name escaped me. I knew her only because I knew most everyone, my being the juke.

She pulled herself up onto the rocks and slid toward me, using her hands more than her legs and feet. She was one of those Mers who'd become more at home in the water than out. Inbreeding had made them this. She was small and slight, and her thin bones looked like they might snap like dried kelp. She needed the water in order to support her own frame. Her eyes were huge – she could probably see well beneath the surface – and her lips were full. Her face was so lovely it hurt to turn my gaze from it.

She drew nearer, and I couldn't think of what to say. I thought to berate her for spying. She'd probably heard everything Shiv had said, and was even now making up her mind as to whether he was a liar or a prophet.

But when she slid up by my side, her legs coiling behind her, she didn't even glance at me. She was looking into the pool where the octopus had stolen the shark. I followed her gaze.

The shark was nowhere in sight. But the octopus was. It seemed impossible to imagine the thieving creature would present itself in the open after such a ruckus with Shiv. And yet there it was. Shy one-quarter length of tentacle.

I picked up my spear. This would be an easy target, and the Mer girl would make a fine audience for my skill. She regarded me, expectant. I raised the spear and aimed at the octopus.

I held the spear steady.

But it did not want to leave my hand.

Below in the pool, sunbeams from the shaft reflected golden speckles on the creature's head, just like the glimmering hermatite of the cave. The speckles formed curved patterns. They looked like wings.

I held the spear for a moment longer. And then I set it down.

The girl gave me a curious glance, but then smiled. We looked into the pool.

There were two of them now. Two octopuses. The one that had disgraced Shiv Omer was moving forward, its huge eyes staring, the speckles curling in wing patterns on either side of its head like the messenger demi-god of ancient myths.

The girl finally spoke: "He's bold."

I said, "I call him Hermes," which was not a lie because now and henceforth I would call him Hermes, even if I never saw him again.

And he was most certainly a "he," which would be tricky to figure out were it not for the way he was mounting the "she" octopus.

Hermes advanced upon her without a care for us humans, the Su and the Mer who were watching. The she scrabbled along the rocks, all eight legs thumping, moving not so much out of panic as excitement. Hermes followed and latched onto her. The she never paused. And then they moved together.

The two·disappeared and the Mer girl and I looked around, then spotted the tangled octopuses emerging through a tunnel in another pool. Fifteen-and-three-quarters tentacles gripping and writhing and waving in the water. Bits of weed floated by. Fish swam up to have a look. The female octopus kept walking along with Hermes upon her, and they slid through a tunnel into yet another pool. The girl and I followed again and kept watching them in the third pool. More fish appeared and they watched, too. Feet and fin united in voyeurism.

The Mer girl lifted her gaze to me.

Aster. That was her name. Aster.

She said, "I hate him, too."

It took me a moment before it registered what she was talking about. Then I realized she was telling me that she hated Shiv Omer.

Oh, bless her!

The smile had barely itched my face when I recalled the only other thing I knew about this little Mer named Aster: She was supposed to marry Shiv in one week's time.

3.

ASIDE FROM BIRDSHIT Rock, the only other public area was Furnace Rock. Executions and semi-executions always occurred on Furnace Rock. Furnace was also where I and the jukes that came before me sang our nightly songs. One song for every night of the year. And in my case, I'd sing other songs, too, as I liked to write them and add music from the shell and bone instruments a crafty Po carved for me.

On Day One of every year I sang the song of our origin to all the folks gathered around the furnace. The Day One song described how we were transported from There to Here, Here being a prison. Our ancestors were criminals. But they always believed that they would serve their sentences and then return to There, and not stay Here forever.

(Hilarious! The children always giggled like crazy when I sang about how our ancestors thought the incarceration would be temporary. To live outside the colony, so far-fetched a notion, we might as well have been singing of a time when oceans held no fish.)

Anyway, for our ancestors, going to prison was supposed to be a temporary thing. A "sentence," if you will. But communication with There fell off and so Here they stayed, forever.

Lots of folks would show up for the Day One song.

The daily songs continued much the same throughout a calendar year until somewhere around the Day One Hundred and Twelve song, "High Water." That's the tale of how all of There disappeared to ocean and Here began sinking so that our prison island was no longer an island, but a collection of rocks that were left jutting above the surface. These high points became our homes as we knew them today; the eight rocks that made up the colony: Birdshit, Furnace, Meso, Po, Tamia North, Tamia South, Su, and Mer.

And of these eight rocks, six were inhabited by tribes, and two — Birdshit Rock and Furnace Rock — were public grounds.

Anyone in the colony could use the public grounds to fetch fresh water, or for hunting, or socializing with those outside of their tribes.

In fact that was the only way to meet someone from an outside tribe: Furnace Rock or Birdshit Rock, or in the ocean between rocks. No tribesmen went to other tribes' rocks unless there was a conversion. Which usually meant marrying.

The day after the incident with the Pondicherry, I came to the pool under Birdshit Rock to offer up a bit of dried mackerel for Hermes, hoping that Aster might show up, too. And she did! She watched me tear off pieces of mack and drop them into the empty pool.

No Hermes in sight, though. The mack floated in the pool only to be nibbled by fish.

"Have you seen the agate fish again?" I asked her.

In reply, she just shook her head.

"No? Yeah, well, me neither. No agate fish! And what about Hermes? No Hermes! Ha ha, maybe he's lost interest."

…and then I finally shut up.

But that's all that was said on the second day. No agate fish and no Hermes. And all of it was said by me.

Then on the third day: no Aster.

Her absence stung though I had no reason to expect she'd keep showing up. I stayed in the cave under Birdshit Rock, ignoring convulsions of pride, hoping both she and Hermes would come along soon. I tugged on the mack.

Look at me, mooning over a Mer and an octopus!

But I didn't just give up and go home. I sat there like an idiot with my mack in my hands.

I looked around for some small sharks but they didn't show either. Shiv Omer did.

He ambled in on two feet like a normal person instead of a Mer, but he lacked the musculature to carry himself properly and so his gait made him more crustacean than man.

"Can't you find some other place to hunt?" I said.

He didn't reply.

Instead he belched, and so fetid was his breath that my wet hair dried to curls.

I said, "Dude."

And as if in reply, he spat black oil at my feet.

I didn't care to know what kind of carrion those Mers ate, but whatever their diet, it didn't agree with Shiv Omer on this day. His finger was also swollen and streaked.

"Juke?" he said.

"Yeah? You all right?"

"Bow down on one knee when you address your king."

"Eat shit and die."

He blinked with that black spittle clinging to his chin, and then continued out the other side of the cave. The scent of him lingered after he'd gone.

That was enough! I was anxious to go home to Su Rock, but loathe to follow on Shiv's heels. I resolved instead to wait it out by singing through the three tales of "Ambergris Genesis," because Shiv's black spittle reminded me of the song's black-tongued, skull-cracking men who smelled like whale vomit. I figured I'd sing through it and then go home.

> The sick man's bite
> A wakeful night
> Now you're the skull-cracking man.

My throat stretched and my voice echoed through the hermatite. The ululations of the whale's cry sounded cool in the hollow acoustics. Somewhere beyond the cave, from the outer deep-ocean waves surrounding our colony, a humpback called. I wondered if it was answering me.

I was well into the song's third and final tale when Aster appeared.

She drew herself up to Hermes' pool without explaining why she was late. Or why she'd come. She looked at me like she was expecting me to feed Hermes.

But I didn't do that. Instead I asked her about Shiv Omer.

She told me she'd been betrothed to him since she was very little, which I knew, and she said she'd also hated him since she was very little, which I appreciated.

It made sense that Aster was supposed to marry Shiv because they were the only two unmarried Mers of age. Most people married *outside* their tribes. Not Mers. Mers married Mers. Mers bred with Mers. And Mer men spread their seeds wide across the colony, focusing on Mer women but not limiting themselves. It was complicated. Had to do with the Mer obsession for handing down Mer-like traits.

Mers thought themselves gods. The rest of us saw them as egomaniacal lunatic inbreds.

Mers either died young from some inbred disease, went barking mad from some inbred disease, or they were fine and just bred more Mers. But admittedly, Mers were super-adapted for colony life. Their spines whipped like shrimp tails in the water, and their limbs were long and agile, with gripping claws for maneuvering on the rocks.

As for Shiv, he kept the Mer faith by balling every female on Mer Rock, and some of the males, and plenty non-Mers, too.

Aster told me that Shiv believed he could hear whispers coming from a bed of starfish, the dotty bastard, and would spend hours listening to them. Some crazy Mers were prophets. Shiv was just crazy.

(Know that I just spent way more time telling you what Aster said than Aster spent actually saying it. What Aster did say, verbatim, was: "When I was six, an auntie said I was to marry that worm. He talks to starfish.")

Aster and I talked and talked (or rather I did, and she listened and listened) and then finally I said, "You know, Aster, Shiv is sick. I mean, well, that guy, I think he's really sick."

She looked at me.

I waited for her to respond but she didn't, so I added, "I mean really, really sick. You may have to postpone the wedding."

"Hermes," was all she had to say to that.

"Oh, yeah. You go ahead and feed him this time."

I gave her some dried mackerel. The poor thing was just not getting the picture, I feared. I hummed "Ambergris Genesis" just to drive the point home. *Her betrothed was sick!*

She crouched over the pool. The only living thing we could see were urchins and flame algae. But to our surprise, the moment Aster reached into the water, Hermes appeared. He took the mack from her hand as though he was peeved he'd had to wait so long. He'd probably been spying on us the whole time.

Aster and I looked at one another, smiling, and then we watched Hermes in the pool below. He slid along the rocks and fussed about, wedging himself into the size of a fist one moment and then puffing out like a manta the next.

But mostly, in his natural easy scrabble, he was just a head and a foot with long, long toes. Like any other octopus. A head and a foot.

4.

AFTER ABOUT A week, on the otherwise-day of Aster's wedding, the entire colony came together for the semi-execution of a colonist named Ralph Otamia. Rumor had it that because of the semi-execution, Aster's wedding was postponed! (No ill will to poor Ralph Otamia who was to be semi-executed, but this was good news for me.) I just needed to find out how long the postponement would last.

As for Ralph Otamia's fate, semi-execution meant the poor bastard may or may not make it. If he survived, he'd be free. Not like we had a prison around here for long-term punishments. We *were* a prison, once, but now we just weren't equipped for incarceration.

I cast my glance toward Ralph where he stood in a pit next to a sandy beachhead, his ankles bound and hands tied behind his back. Black locks pasted in sweat. A couple of Mesos were filling the pit around him with rocks.

In the distance, a pod of whales rolled by on the annual migration, their blowholes shooting spray.

And closer in swam a huge school of fish…Not just any fish: agate fish!

In fact, "agate fish" was what everyone was calling them! My term! Word had gotten out that I, Juke Osu, knew these fish better than anyone because I'd seen them lots and lots of times.

I watched it all from a rise on Furnace Rock. This gave me a view of both the semi-execution and the school of agates.

But the vantage point came at a price: Shiv Omer was also occupying it.

"That Tamia guy won't make it," said Shiv, lisping from a swollen tongue.

I said, "His name is Ralph Otamia. He'll be fine."

And because Shiv Omer was occupying my shelf, I had to suffer the company of a handful of young Tamia ladies who were mooning over him.

"Jay Opo's been through two semi-executions, and he survived," said a little Tamia honey named Delilah.

Shiv replied, "For a courtesan like you, I'd suffer ten semi-executions!"

But Shiv's tongue was so swollen I found it difficult to understand him. Even more difficult to understand why these perfectly luscious Tamia ladies should make moon eyes over that loony tunes drooler of whale-vomit-smelling black goo. And he, still thinking himself a king! Calling Delilah a courtesan and making her blush and the other girls giggle!

"Here, Shiv, this tea will make you feel better," they were saying, and, "Let me rub your temples, poor thing."

Nauseating though they were, I was in decent enough spirits. I breathed in the hearty sea air and said a prayer for the life of Ralph Otamia, who had unwittingly delayed an abomination of a wedding.

And I resolved to tell Aster, straight out, that she ought not marry Shiv. Today. In the cave under Birdshit Rock, when we knelt together to feed Hermes, I would let Aster know once and for all that she must take a stand against her fellow tribesmen and refuse the arranged marriage to Shiv Omer.

Down below in the pit, the two Mesos had finished burying Ralph Otamia to his shoulders with rocks, and they'd now switched to sand. The sand trickled through the rocks and filled Ralph in nice and snug.

"But wheh the hell ah theh going?" Shiv Omer asked me over his stinky thick tongue.

"Who?"

"The agate fish."

"Oh."

In answer I fed him that crap about migrating to a distant shore where they'd all lay eggs and then die.

But as I looked out over the drifts of them surrounding Furnace Rock, it seemed clear that the fish weren't migrating. They were just milling about our colony, not moving through from end to end the way that first one had when it floated through the shark channel under Birdshit Rock. The agate fish, like us, were concentrated around Furnace Rock. Shiv had tried to kill one time and again and had broken two bone blades and a spear in the process.

In fact, all the tribes were trying to figure out what to do with them, because there was not a thing in the world that didn't have some kind of value – food, materials, companionship, or a place for nesting – and everyone was determined to figure out some use for the agate fish. Some admired the diamond in the stinger tip.

I looked off in the distance as a whale blew a plume of water into the air. And then I looked down at the crowds surrounding me, listening to my fellow colonists talk about the agates. Mesos were arguing about the best way to harvest them en masse even though they had no idea what to do with them. The Po wanted their brittle hides for tool-making. The Tamians just thought they were cute. Su like me were standing around pontificating about the agate fish's origins, the rate of reproductive acceleration from first sighting to present, and the probability that it acted as a companion fish to the whales during their migrations.

The Mers just swam among them while keeping a suspicious distance.

I looked over to see an older Tamian woman trying to touch the diamond end of the tooth. The agate fish was trying to turn away from her.

I thought of Shiv and his oily black spittle.

"Hey!" I called. "Tamian Auntie! Don't touch the tooth!"

Too late. The Tamian woman was already jabbing against the agate fish's long, long tooth. She recoiled and examined her finger.

"It's just a scratch," she called back to me.

I eyed Shiv and his black lips, then said to the woman, "You should see your healer, Auntie. The scratch may make you sick."

She gave her hand a doubtful look, and on her face was something of a sneer. Condescension. Like I, the juke, should make such drama from a tiny scratch. She turned her attention back toward the waves and paid me no further heed.

And why should she? I was only the juke, telling our legends – plus a few stories of my own – in song. To them I was an entertainer, not a historian. A sympathetic ear that listened to the problems of the colony and reinvented them in lyric.

The agate fish were forming together. I counted eight schools.

Over in the pit, the Mesos had picked up some driftwood and were knocking on the rocks surrounding Ralph. He whimpered. The sand settled deeper into gaps around the rocks and left room for the Mesos to add more.

"Hey, look!" someone called.

We all looked up and saw Jay Opo high on a ledge at the tallest point of Furnace Rock. He'd toted an agate fish up there. Jay was hefty by brawn, not belly, and we all watched as he raised the agate fish up over his head.

People were yelling, "Smash it, Jay!" and, "Chuck it to Birdshit!"

Sure enough, Jay threw the agate fish all the way across to Birdshit Rock. All went hushed as it sailed through the air. Even Ralph fell silent. Then: success! The agate fish smashed against Birdshit Rock and showered its guts down across the hermatite jags. Only, there were no soft guts. The fish was made up of hard bits and pieces on the inside, just like its outside.

People dove in and swam for Birdshit Rock so they could examine the entrails. See the diamond in its tooth.

"Show some respect!" I shouted at them.

"Rethpect for what?" Shiv Omer said.

"For Ralph Otamia, damn it!"

"Thcrew him. I'll pith on hith head…"

I wheeled on Shiv, furious, but then stopped. He really looked awful. Really. As if his lunatic whoring had putrified him.

Also, I saw the hermatite disk festering in his earlobe.

A wedding earring.

My heart went to my throat. They were supposed to have post-poned the wedding!

I said, "Shiv? Old man? Are you…married?"

He collapsed into gurgled hacking.

Delilah was rubbing his back, cooing, and she answered for him. "They had a ceremony on Mer Rock this morning."

"But the semi-execution!"

"That's why they did it early. Their honeymoon starts tonight."

As she said it, Delilah looked just as forlorn as I felt.

The couple would spend fourteen days of complete seclusion in a honeymoon chamber where their fellow Mer tribesmen would drop food and water and scented ambergris torchères at the door. At the end of a honeymoon, should the "happy" couple prove to be with child, they would have first pick of all the spoils of hunt and fetch for one year from the date of their wedding.

I looked out over Furnace Rock and beyond to Birdshit Rock, scanning for Aster.

It was almost time to feed Hermes. Perhaps she was waiting for me in the cave? After all, her honeymoon hadn't started yet.

How could she bring herself to marry this creep?

Mers married Mers.

Mers and their arranged Mer-rriages!

I didn't care what Aster's tribesmen dictated. I myself would leave my own beloved Su Rock for good if they ever tried to tell me whom to marry.

The ladies were clucking their dismay over the talk of Shiv's wedding, saying things like:

"You know the Mer women sometimes share their husbands."

"Always trying to procreate more Mers."

"I don't want to bear his love child, I just want him for an hour or two!"

And, may my aunts and uncles turn deaf to my thoughts, I myself was searching for any recollection of a time when a Mer man shared his wife. That maybe Shiv would share Aster.

But that wouldn't happen. Though the men wandered, Mer women gave birth only to Mer babes.

Shiv had said nothing further after "pith on hith head," because he was too busy hawking black sludge. Those ridiculous ladies were patting his back. Their breasts pointing at him.

Watching Shiv and his swollen finger and his black hacking, and watching all the people out there – had anyone else been scratched by agate fish? – the hair was rising on the back of my neck.

I wondered if it truly might be the same kind of sickness as in the song, "Ambergris Genesis." All those tales in all those songs that I sang for the colonists on every night of every year. I'd been enthralled by just how engaging the songs were. But even I, Juke Osu, the so-called historian, had never really given thought to them. Because if they *were* true and Shiv *did* have the sickness...

The agate fish swarmed the shores, bouncing gently against one another in the waves.

How many more people had been scratched?

Shiv Omer had said to me: *You make up those stupid songs and everyone knows you're a fake. You're not a real juke.*

They laugh at me, do they? My fellow colonists.

I said to Shiv, "You people go play with the fish. I've got a semi-execution to witness."

I marched off the rise and went straight for the pit. Straight for the semi-condemned Ralph Otamia. Thinking, *I hate them all.*

5.

RALPH OTAMIA WAS now immobilized with rocks and sand. The Mesos were packing the sand down and it looked like they'd filled in all the gaps. Sweat was pouring from Ralph's head.

"You all right, Ralph?" I asked.

"Still alive," said he, then, "For now."

"Blessings to your aunts and uncles."

"Thanks."

"Can I do anything for you?"

"Some fresh water?"

One of the Mesos said, "No fresh water. Get back, Juke."

Bryan Omeso, that was the name. And the other was David Omeso. I didn't really know them beyond that, nor did I even actually know poor Ralph Otamia.

I could tell you the names of all 268 men, women, and children in our colony because that was part of my job as the juke. But I was only *truly* familiar with the people in my Su tribe because I lived among them on Su Rock, plus I knew the hunters like Shiv because we worked the same grounds. Water-fetchers, too. Water-fetchers came to the freshwater springs in the hunting grounds under Furnace Rock and Birdshit Rock.

And Aster Omer. I'd come to know Aster.

Imagining her marrying Shiv Omer I felt the urge to bump Ralph Otamia out of the way so the Mesos could pack me in with rocks and sand, too.

The two Mesos were now toting seawater up from the same beachhead they'd used to gather sand. Bryan Omeso poured the first baleful into Ralph's pit, turning it gray. David Omeso added his. And then Bryan again.

The semi-condemned Ralph Otamia's skin turned a fresh shade of dismay.

Somewhere nearby was a pool that held a man o' war jelly. It would be joining Ralph Otamia once the water reached his chin. The punishment was the pain of the jelly's sting, along with the wont of fresh water under the glare of sun, followed by chill of night. For forty-eight hours. Seemed doable. Although the man o' war's sting could drive a man to speak in tongues and go mad as a Mer.

Jay Opo had done it twice. Others had died.

I said to Ralph, "You want to talk about your crime?"

His expression changed. For a moment he almost looked serene. Sometimes it calmed people to tell their troubles to the juke. Always the promise of becoming a legend.

"Yes, I'd like that," Ralph Otamia nodded, and then told me his tale even though I already knew it.

There are really only a few things that can get you into trouble: violence, larceny, marauding, or your dick. For Ralph it was his dick. Typical Tamian! He'd snuck over to Meso Rock and got a married Meso lady pregnant. I can't think of a dumber thing to do. He could get laid all day long on Furnace Rock or even Birdshit Rock, but no. Ralph had swum over and violated the sanctity of Meso Rock, plus seduced a Meso married lady, and sealed his fate. Not to mention Mesos were always the ones who carried out executions and semi-executions. If you had to pick a tribe to violate, do crimes against the Po, or hell, the Su like me, or the Mers all day long, but never the Mesos! If everyone in the colony knew that Mers married Mers, we also knew that you didn't mess with the Mesos.

(The Su didn't have any sayings like that, which is ironic because we were supposed to be the lyrical ones.)

I heard hacking. Nearby, an adolescent Po was coughing up black spittle, just like Shiv. I scanned the faces and saw one other who looked sick. One of my own Su cousins.

"Look!" someone cried.

I followed the crowd's attentions and saw that every single soul in the colony (aside from Ralph Otamia and Bryan and David Omeso) were still fixated on the agate fish. But then I stopped cold.

Apparently all those agate fish were just fry. They were now joined by their mothers. Eight very big mothers.

I'm no prophet, but if I were, I'd have called it suspicious that there were eight giant agate fish out there, and eight schools of little agate fish, and eight rocks that made up our prison colony.

The mother fish were huge. Like whales. Maybe even bigger – I could see only their dome-shaped tops at the surface. No telling what lay beneath.

David and Bryan Omeso stopped baling water into the pit. Ralph Otamia stopped telling me his story.

I felt someone touch my fingers and I turned. Aster. She was regarding me with those wide, dark eyes.

"Leave me alone," I said.

She stood, gazing at me, but didn't speak. Her earlobe was cut but the hermatite disk that ought to be there was missing. Those things were famous for breaking and often got replaced after the honeymoon. I'm ashamed to say I hoped it meant ill luck on the union.

I said, "Go have your stupid honeymoon with stupid Shiv, you Mer!"

(Oh, my fickle genius, how it escaped me in my moment of need.)

Aster seemed unfazed. She pulled on my arm as though nothing had happened and she hadn't spent the morning pledging her eternal wifely devotion to a pelvis-pumping, black lipped manslut. But, God help me, I was already following her away from the pit.

We climbed down to the far end of Furnace Rock and then she stepped into the water, heading for Birdshit Rock where Hermes was waiting. I let go her hand. She was having difficulty walking upright like that, and she'd be more comfortable swimming, but I wasn't about to get into the water with those giant agate fish.

Aster gave me an imploring look.

I said, "I gotta hear the rest of Ralph Otamia's story."

But she knew I just didn't want to get in the water. She looked over in the direction of the giant agate fish and said, "Too big to get inside."

She was right. No fin that large could penetrate our circle of rocks. The water was too shallow between them.

I said, "All right. But keep clear of the little agate fish, too."

I followed Aster, slipping into the waves, and swimming for Birdshit Rock where colonists were still examining entrails from when Jay Opo had chucked the fish.

We swam into a tunnel that was free of agate fish. This was not a natural rock tunnel. This one was built by thermal hands. Flame algae lined its corridors and cast a green-golden glow. Aster's spine whipped through the hollows that once formed a prison. I barely kept up with her.

We turned, and then turned again. Here was illuminated by flame algae, there was darkness. Aster knew the way.

Shiv Omer.

Ralph Otamia.

Aster.

And all those agate fish.

And all those colonists.

And the plunging, echoing ululations of whale calls in "Ambergris Genesis."

Everyone knows you're a fake.

I was worse than a fake. Now I had real knowledge. Suspicions, at least. Everyone needed to hear what I had to say about that song. About the sickness.

The corridor angled deeper. Did Aster realize I wasn't going to be able to hold my breath for the entire distance? I was no Mer!

I had to turn back and warn the colonists.

I slowed and flipped my body around, swimming back toward Furnace Rock. Within moments Aster was by my side. I couldn't see her face though she tugged inquisitively at my hair. I couldn't speak and there was nowhere to rise to the surface in that tunnel, that I may catch a breath and tell her we had to warn them.

Had I turned the wrong way? The corridor was so dark. No flame algae. My lungs wanted to burst.

A wrenching crash came from above. It sounded like sheet light-ning had flashed the entire surface. So loud I wondered at not having been electrocuted.

We paused. My lungs were burning.

The lightning flashed again and with it came light. I could see an opening at the bend in the corridor. Our faces turned toward it. But we didn't dare swim there. We hung suspended like sea turtles.

6.

THE LIGHTNING FLASHES seemed to go on forever. Somehow I knew it meant doom.

And yet, I broke through my reverie and swam toward that hole in the ceiling at the tunnel's bend, toward the explosions. My lungs were shuddering. I had exhaled it all. I needed air. I needed out. Even if it meant out into doom. Aster was trying to pull me back and I shoved her away.

But then she coiled her arms and legs around me in a grip that wasn't so much strong as impossible to untangle. I thrashed against her. She forced her tongue between my lips and pried open my mouth, and then, "Blurp!"

A croak, I think. A bubble.

She billowed it into my mouth and it found its way to my lungs. They puffed happily. Still, I was struggling against her. Though not as hard. Panic made it difficult to place my life in her hands.

Blurp!

Another breath for me.

Blurp!

Blurp!

Not even a second-hand breath. This felt like pure, heady oxygen.

Blurp!

I exhaled a stream of bubbles.

Blurp.

Sneaky, conniving Mers. You'd think they'd let it be known that they could croak oxygen into a man's lungs. I gobbled it up.

Blurp. And this was enough for now. I could hold my breath just as surely as I'd been to the surface and taken a nice gulp.

We waited. Aster's face flashed in and out of darkness as the lightning continued. After some time I needed another croak from her, but she didn't offer any. Probably she was finally running out of oxygen herself. I rose skyward through the hole in the ceiling. She didn't try to stop me this time.

The lightning subsided. The crashing stopped. Stillness above.

Up, up, up.

Aster and I broke the surface at the same time. Snorting, slurping, our mouths gaping and wild eyes scanning the rock islands of the colony. All was quiet. Too quiet.

• • •

7.

IF THE ROCKS in our colony formed the shape of a comet, then Furnace Rock and Birdshit Rock were at the head and small, distant Mer Rock was at the tail. The rest of the tribes' rocks fell somewhere in between: Meso Rock, Po Rock, Tamia Rock North and South. I lived on Su Rock, last rock before Mer Rock. Five tribes; eight rocks.

Aster and I were swimming back to Furnace Rock. This time we swam at the surface.

On the banks of Furnace Rock, two colonists lay with their faces in the water. Both from the Po tribe.

I raised my gaze to the greater expanse, and every single person within my sightline lay prostrate, as though they'd crossed over from life to death even as they stood watching schools of agate fish and a semi-execution. My knees trembled beneath me.

I heard coughing, and saw the adolescent Po. The one who'd seemed sick like Shiv.

"What happened?" I called to him.

But he gave no reply.

Aster was tugging on one of the Po who was face-down in the water. I leaned over and helped her pull him out, which for me took only a few seconds though she'd been tugging and tugging. We pulled the next colonist out of the water, too; a hefty brute. Jay Opo.

They were still and gray. It looked like we'd been too late. My mouth turned to salt.

Blurp! Blurp! Aster puffed her delicious air into the first one's lips. Nothing happened. She turned and did the same for Jay.

"You are Jay Opo," I said to his limp form, beginning my juke's farewell, for Jay had surely crossed over.

But now he was coughing seawater. Oh. He was fine.

So was the second Po.

"Bless my aunts and uncles!"

I checked other fallen bodies. They were just sleeping. Sleeping! All of them. Some even snoring. The two Po would surely have drowned had Aster not bestowed her lovely blurps for them, but no one else seemed in any danger of anything more serious than sun exposure.

"I think the lightning storm's passed," I said to Aster, regarding the clear blue sky.

In truth, it looked like there had never been any storm.

I thought for a moment. "I'm going to check on Ralph Otamia."

Aster nodded and continued her blurp-blurps on the fallen Po.

The sun was fine, the breeze even finer, and the sounds went like this: 10% Aster blurps, 10% snoring colonists, 20% surf, and 60% *pop-pop-pop-pop whirrrrrrrrrrrrrrrrrrrrrrrrr* from the agate fish swarming the waters surrounding the island. So many! Noisy buggers.

Across on Birdshit Rock I saw two silhouettes that stood upright, but both looked woozy with sickness.

Ralph Otamia was sleeping soundly, snug in his pit with the rocks and sand burying him up to his shoulders.

And, damn my eyes, there was Shiv Omer! Conscious! One of the few besides Aster and me who was awake. Squatting in the pit, sniffing at Ralph Otamia's semi-condemned head.

"Mer cousin...?" I said carefully to Shiv. Formally. Because he looked very strange.

He paid me no mind. The three young ladies that had been fawning over him were lying in a tangled heap of flesh as though they'd fallen as one. All asleep.

"Shiv Omer," I said. "Shiv!"

Now he let out a very long breath. A long, long Mer-grade exhalation, and rolled his eyes up toward me without raising his head. As though he was loathe to surrender the aroma of Ralph Otamia's scalp.

"Shiv, listen to me. You are sick. You're sick in the way of 'Ambergris Genesis.' You hear me? You need to go home and find your healer. Do this now."

Though I was certain his healer was asleep like everyone else.

Nevertheless, Shiv's face registered a look of anxiety like he'd understood me. And he looked as though he was trying to speak but the words couldn't make it past his tongue. He tried to rise. Made the crablike stance of a Mer. I took him by the elbow and helped him out of the pit.

I said, "Shiv, what happened? Was it a lightning storm?"

His face took on an expression of alarm. It seemed he'd forgotten what had happened but it was all coming back to him now. He, one of very few colonists who'd witnessed this storm and remained untouched.

He couldn't answer my question, of course, so thick and black was his tongue that it protruded at his lips like a crowning babe. But he lifted a finger and pointed at the nearest mother agate fish, and then the next, and the next.

I narrowed my gaze. "They made the lightning?"

He was nodding. Pointing at them. Gagging. I wondered whether he might suffocate on his own tongue.

I said, "Like electric eels?"

He kept nodding and gagging. Strangled gurgled coughs, black spew.

"No, don't try to say it, old man. Relax now." I patted his back.

Then I thought better of it and removed my hand.

"When you're better. That's when you can tell me. And I'll retell it for us all in song. It'll be sung around the furnace for centuries."

I'd never heard of such a thing. Not from the most obscure lyric of our entire prison colony's history, nowhere had such a phenomenon been told, of giant fish that made lightning and epidemic sleep.

I looked from Shiv to each fallen body, across to those strewn on Birdshit Rock, back here to the shores of Furnace Rock.

The agate fish were bumping against the beach head, and...

And some of them were crawling ashore. The crawlers now seemed more crust than fin.

"Aster!" I called.

I rose and looked over the ledge to the waves below, where she was now making her way up the steep craggy face. A shortcut that only a Mer could traverse.

The agate fish, or whatever they were, were following Aster up the rock face. Not fast.

I called, "Don't touch those stingers!"

She kept climbing.

All around me the colonists were sleeping and I didn't like it one bit.

"Wake up!" I shouted at them, nudging with my foot, shaking shoulders. "Get up!"

No one stirred. They breathed, snored, drooled, smiled in their sleep.

Ralph Otamia seemed the most vulnerable. I had to get him out of there. But he was still under arrest so the only way to set him free was to expedite his punishment with the exoneration song.

I stood on the ledge of the pit and sang, "Ralph Otamia, our semi-condemned, you have survived and made amends…"

Some of the little agate fish had scrabbled up the rocks. Each one seemed to be going to a fallen colonist.

"Get away," I said, kicking one off the ledge as it approached me.

It fell helplessly over the side and splashed in the water.

Shiv Omer was hawking and hacking, elbows on knees, a brown stain at the sealskin covering his ass. He wretched, and spat out a huge black worm! I looked closer. It was his tongue.

I turned back to Ralph in the pit and sang, "You…er…Your tribe awaits your h-happy — Aw, shit!"

There were agate fish everywhere! I dropped into the pit and fell to my knees in front of Ralph Otamia's exposed head, heaving away rocks and chucking them over my shoulder, wet sand showering down upon us both.

Aster tumbled into the pit and joined in the excavation of Ralph Otamia.

I could hear the *pop-pop-whir*s all around, but also a clickety scrabbling sound as the agates swarmed Furnace Rock. I couldn't see what was happening outside the pit. The thought that finally dared take shape in my heart: *Are they feeding on our fallen?* And if so, could we save them?

If we could save even one colonist, it appeared that we'd already made the choice, hand-in-hand with fate, to save the semi-condemned Ralph Otamia. He of the marauding dick.

We had him excavated to his knees now, Aster gnawing at the fibrous twine that bound his hands behind his back.

We heard a strange howling sound. It seemed horribly familiar, though I'd never heard it this way before. It sounded like the whales' ululations from the song, "Ambergris Genesis." Aster and I regarded one another, frozen.

I pulled myself up to the lip of the pit to have a look. What I saw made no sense! No sense at all!

Shiv Omer was still squatting over his tongue. It was he who was making that sound. Hollow and deep from a mouth with no tongue. Inhuman-sounding. Whale-sounding.

From across the way on Birdshit Rock, the two colonists who'd looked sick answered back to Shiv in that hollow, tongueless wail.

The agate fish were still scrabbling. Sort of. Most of them had been replaced by agate *humans*. Humans of sorts. They looked like humans made of agate, but without skin and organs. Only agate bones. A single giant agate eye shone in the center of their faces. Illuminated like the sun. Their left hands bore the fishes' long, long diamond-tipped stingers.

They were carrying our brethren, the fallen colonists. Lining them up in a fan shape around the furnace. All of our tribesmen still slumbering.

Clack-clack-clack-pop-pop-whir.

Even as I watched, a little agate fish trembled, then expanded from a fish to a man right in front of me. It turned its single glowing eye upon the three of us in the pit.

"Run, Aster!" I cried, flinging myself back toward Ralph.

She'd already freed his hands. I threw my arms around his waist and yanked him up from the remaining rocks and sand, his shins leaving strips of skin behind in the effort. But he was out. Unconscious, but out. Somehow it felt like that gave him a chance.

Aster had scurried up the side of the pit and was heading back toward the waves. I ran after her.

To where?

I realized I intended to go home to my own beloved Su Rock. I would take Aster with me, just this once. (But that was marauding! But maybe the infraction would be enough to cancel her wedding but not so bad as to semi-condemn her...)

Off in the distance, one of the mother agate fish opened her mouth wide and swallowed Su Rock.

She swallowed it whole with a great wrenching sound.

Lightning sparked within her gullet.

And then another mother agate swallowed Tamia Rock South. Lightning inside as she did. And then went Po Rock. And then Tamia Rock North.

Aster and I were almost to the waves though my gait had gone soft in seeing my home get swallowed whole.

The nearest mother agate was now coming up on Furnace Rock where we were.

"Run, Aster!"

Aster was fast across the rock face with those claw-like feet and hands. The mother agate fish yawned open and loomed over Furnace Rock, blocking out the sun. I could see the inside of her mouth, more clamshell than fish, and she looked man-made like the prison corridors beneath the waves. Not a natural creature at all.

Aster flew from the rocks and shrimp-whipped down into the sea. I tumbled toward her.

But not before the mother agate fish swallowed Furnace Rock.

Aster made it, I thought. It looked like she'd made it. But not I.

The mother fish slammed her agate mouth over the entire rock. A wrenching sound like a ghost ship groaning. The mother agate had swallowed Furnace Rock whole. Swallowed us whole. Swallowed me.

Darkness.

And then a great flash of light.

And then nothing. I slipped away to merry Nothingland.

8.

"Hello, Human 267. Awake and listen to your instructions."

I opened my eyes, blinked. The only light came from each single cyclops eye of the agate people that had once been agate fish.

I felt woozy and unconcerned, though somewhere flashed an awareness that I *ought* to be concerned.

From within the darkness, a woman whimpered, "But I'm already married."

The agate fish person said to me, "I am assigned to you. I am Databot 267, and you are to be known as Human 267. Do you understand?"

I said, "Thhhaaaaahh."

"Your speech will improve as the shock wears off. In the meantime, enjoy the calm. Continue to remain calm as you regain your senses. You have nothing to worry about. You are in our care."

It sounded very nice.

But because I am the juke, and because nesting within my calm was the promise of future disquiet, my mind was already calculating. Nothing useful, I'm afraid: I was counting the colonists in the swiveling cyclops lights of the robots as they interacted with us. I counted us because I always take attendance. Forty-four. There were forty-four colonists, and forty-four robots. The colonists were a mix of all five tribes, but mostly Tamia, including Ralph Otamia and the three Tamia ladies that had mooned over Shiv. Most everyone else was obscure shadows. Three of the silhouettes were clearly Mers, with their odd shapes. I saw some of my Su brethren. And there was Jay Opo. Yes. I recognized Jay Opo's hulking form, the Po who had hurled the agate fish against Birdshit Rock.

I didn't see Shiv. Or Aster.

Databot 267 said, "Attention, Human 267. I require your attention for excellent reasons. You are to reside in comfort here in this laboratory until further notice. Your first and immediate orders are to marry. This is your bride, Human 253."

Its agate fingers took me by the wrist and placed my hand in that of the young lady lying beside me. Delilah Otamia. One of Shiv Omer's groupies. She looked soft of mind right now, and of body. Lovely, reclining.

Databot 267 added, "We will now have a wedding ceremony that will help you to remain calm. Then you will copulate."

Oh?

I prayerfully decided to forgive Delilah for her foolishness with Shiv.

Someone was wailing. Another was trying to calm the person down in a voice that sounded identical to Databot 267's. All of the robots had the same voice. And they looked alike, too. Databot 267 had a dent just behind the diamond on its stinger.

I know a fellow Su who liked to play a shell game, with three shells and a stone that would disappear under one shell and reappear beneath another. For some reason that was all I could think of, because it seemed we were trapped inside a magical shell like that. The agate fish hadn't been fish, they'd been robots. And the mother agate fish weren't fish, either; they were simply giant shells controlled by the robots. Shells that had clamped over our colony's rocks to rebirth them as laboratories.

I sat up.

"Remain calm," said Databot 267.

"I am calm," I said, glad to find I was able to speak.

We weren't on Furnace Rock anymore. We were encapsulated on one of our colony rocks, but I couldn't tell which one. Not Furnace Rock. Not Birdshit. Not Su, either. This place was covered with tools. Tools in every nook and cranny.

Other colonists must have been wondering the same thing because I heard their voices:

"We're on Po Rock!"

"They called it a laboratory!"

"But I don't remember leaving Furnace Rock."

"I'm from Tamia! I'm not supposed to touch Po Rock! Does this make me a marauder?"

"We must have been moved," I said.

And Databot 267 said, "No more talking. Listen to your instructions."

Forty-four voices exactly like Databot 267 were trying to shush forty-four colonists.

Databot 267 said to me, "This is the laboratory in which you live from now on. If it helps you to remain calm, you may refer to your home as Po Rock Laboratory, in keeping with your indigenous naming."

Waves were crashing inside my head. I felt a prick and saw Databot 267 had poked me with some kind of spine. Not the long diamond-studded stinger-tooth. That remained at the robot's side in place of its left hand. Its right hand bore a retractable spine that it had used to stick me.

Upon the robot's head was a helmet that had been the agate fish shell. But even with the light from the cyclops eye, I kept following the flash of diamond in the robot's stinger.

Databot 267 must have noticed because it pointed at the stinger and said, "You are not to thrust your hand against the probe device on any of the robots. They are often infected and are dangerous to you humans. Do you understand?"

"Yeah, sure."

"It is important that you do. We understand that some of you have been drawn to the shiny tip. But you must not touch it. Databots who are examining you are often the same robots who must examine infected subjects. The right hand of a databot is for examining healthy humans; and the probe on the left is for infected ones. Avoid the probe for your own safety. Even when a databot is in semi-amphibious form. In order to remain in this laboratory you cannot become infected. My readings show you have no diseases or defects, and no injuries."

I'd stopped listening. Was looking around, naming the names of colonists in my head. Memorizing who was in here with me.

Databot 267 said, "Confirm."

"What?"

"I find no significant diseases, defects, or injuries. Confirm."

"Yes. I mean no, there's nothing wrong with me."

"If you have been infected, it may not register right away. Do you have any cause to believe you have been infected?"

"I don't think so."

"Any bites, or sexual intercourse with sick persons? Or wounds stemming from interaction with probes?"

"No. Nothing like that."

It trained that lighted eye on my eyes, and then I saw nothing else. It said, "Male, aged twenty-four years, two months. Confirm."

"Yes, that's me. Juke Osu."

"No, you are Human 267."

It let me out of its gaze while it scanned my body. I had to blink to regain my vision.

The same thing was happening next to me, with Delilah Otamia being examined and having her own information confirmed. A black welling of blood beaded up where her robot, Databot 253, had pricked her. And the rest of the colonists, they were also being stuck and questioned.

And then Databot 253 and Databot 267 spoke simultaneously to Delilah and me.

Databot 267 was saying, "You, Human 267, take Human 253 to be your lawfully wedded wife."

Databot 253 was saying the inverse of this: "You, Human 253, take Human 267 to be your lawfully wedded husband."

No point in saying "I do" or "I don't," because the robots weren't asking. Their simultaneous speaking cramped my brain so hard it finally cracked open and rose above this madness. I remembered how I'd gotten here, or what I knew of it. I remembered now: I'd watched Aster rush away into the waves.

Of the 268 colonists, forty-four were here trapped here on Po Rock. Where were the others?

I asked, "Databot 267, if I am Human 267, where is Human 268?"

"That information is not available."

Next to me, Delilah said to her robot, "Can't I marry Shiv Omer instead?"

It replied that she was already married to me. I was chosen for her for excellent reasons.

Databot 267 said to me, "You must now copulate with your wife. Your assignment is to impregnate her. If you succeed, you will be moved to a more permanent facility where you will have more wives with whom you will produce more offspring. Do you understand?"

"What? What if –"

"If you are unable to produce offspring then you will be assigned to another field laboratory. We estimate that you would prefer the Po Rock field laboratory to any of the others, so you should do your best to succeed."

Delilah Otamia was up on her elbows, slack-jawed, looking from her robot to my robot, never once looking at me.

Our robots said in unison, "I leave you now. Copulate and report back upon my return. We have left meat wafers and greens wafers if you require sustenance."

With that, the two robots collapsed themselves down to agate fish. The other robots did the same.

Colonists cried out in surprise. But as the robots folded down, their cyclops eyes tucked inside them and all light extinguished within our new prison.

When the last one folded away there was no light left at all.

Cries went to wailing. We heard splashes. The agate fish had exited through a tunnel. I listened to the darkness. The sounds of panic among my fellow colonists.

My own hand was invisible to my eyes. I groped my way toward the place where I'd heard the agate fish splashing, and found the opening to a sea tunnel. I reached my hand in just to feel the briny water.

The Po. The Po in here might know how to get out.

I called into the darkness, "Jay Opo!"

"Yes? Who's that?" His deep voice echoed against rock and the giant shell that covered us.

"It's Juke. Juke Osu. You're from Po Rock. Any way to get through that tunnel to the open sea?"

"Not unless you're a fish."

I didn't like the sound of that. But no way was I going to stay trapped in here with a bunch of meat wafers.

I heaved in a deep breath and in I went. Or out, I hoped. Out through the sea tunnel.

9.

THE SEA TUNNEL was cold though the sealskin hide kept my ass warm. This tunnel was surely a lava chute, a long narrow tube like an intestine, one that narrowed the deeper I went in. And then narrower still so that my arms could no longer move freely. I was forced to stick them straight over my head with my fingers paddling like the fanned tongue of an anemone.

My lungs cramped for breath, and claustrophobia hit. What was I thinking?! I couldn't even turn around in here!

Nor could I swim backward. This was a drowning trap.

Just as I was about to empty the last reserves of my lungs in panic, the tunnel opened to a chamber that was otherwise cramped but just roomy enough for me to turn around so that I might high-tail it back to the laboratory.

But in my haste, I kicked at the walls and some of the rock came loose and threatened to cave in on me.

A screech left my lungs and its bubbles filled the chamber. And the chute. Panic accelerated the drain of my air reserve. But then I realized that somehow I was travelling alongside the bubbles, back up the chute, and then breaking the surface, the screech gone silent on my lips.

I filled my lungs with precious air and the shriek came back in full volume.

"Told you so, Juke," said Jay Opo.

"Ngh," was all I managed.

"Why ask a man's advice if you're not going to bother listening?"

"Is there another way out?"

He was quiet for a moment. "Never came up before. Po Rock is just…open, usually. No, that's the only tunnel we got."

"There's got to be a way out."

I spat seawater and climbed out, shivering and gasping. "Everyone. Feel around you. Look for a hole in the rocks or in the…the big shell that's got us closed in."

I didn't bother to catch my breath, but went groping straight away in the dark. I sensed the search would be fruitless. Those robots had us.

I heard "ahhhhhhh" in the darkness, and said, "Hello?"

She did not reply, but she kept going, 'ahhh,' and I recognized the voice for the Tamia woman I'd spoken to on Furnace Rock during Ralph's semi-execution. *It's only a scratch*, she'd said when she'd pressed her finger against an agate fish's tooth.

She continued her ahhh, ahhh, with panting rhythm interrupted only by gurgles and hacking. I could see nothing. As I drew nearer her voice grew louder and along with it, an intolerable odor. I paused, and then made a wide circle around her, and kept searching for a way out.

10.

"Hello, Human 267. You must wake now."

"I wasn't sleeping."

I looked to my left, and saw that stacks of "food" had been replenished – the meat wafers and greens wafers.

"Report on your progress with your assignment."

"Are you kidding me?"

All forty-four of us had had the same assignment, to copulate with our newly assigned spouses, but of course no one had actually done this. We numbered twenty-two men and twenty-two women. More than half of us were already married to spouses that either weren't present or had been assigned to someone else. Two of our "couples" were brother and sister. Some were gay.

Delilah and I were both heterosexual and single, but that didn't help us feel cuddly.

I asked my robot, "What happened to the other colonists? Where is everybody?"

"You must report on your assignment."

"But what happens to me if I don't comply?"

"You will be assigned to another laboratory."

"What does that mean?"

"Your cooperation is in your best interest, Human 267. Other laboratories are conducting experiments that are less favorable to you than the reproduction experiment in which you are participating now."

"Participating? That's a funny word for it."

I noticed that its stinger was no longer dented. "You're not the same robot I talked to last time."

"I am one in the same."

"The last one had a dent."

"Databots may switch vessels as necessary. You see only a drone which I control from a remote location."

"Then who are *you*, controlling this drone? Are you a robot or a human?"

"I'm both."

Next to me, Delilah Otamia was crying. She'd done nothing else the entire time the robots had been absent. I had groped my way across Po Rock Laboratory and back several times and found it sealed tight, except for the one single narrow sea tunnel that nearly drowned me. Even now my nose was draining saltwater.

No telling how long the robots had left us alone in there. I usually marked the time by the sun, and by the moon and stars. But there had been nothing but complete darkness inside Po Rock Lab without the robots' cyclops eyes.

I said, "Listen, Databot 267, we're never going to get anywhere like this. We need real food and daylight."

"You must make do with what we have provided."

"We need fresh air. A place to sleep and use the toilet. Preferably not the same place. We need to get out."

Databot 267 said, "That is not your purpose. Your purpose in this field laboratory is to prove that you are adaptive enough to survive, and that you can procreate."

"What does that do for us?"

"If you succeed you will leave this field laboratory."

"So you'll release us?"

"The important thing is that you remain calm throughout the experiment, for excellent reasons."

My voice rose. "What REASONS? You just want us docile so you can do whatever you want to us!"

"Remain calm, Human 267. Your chances of surviving this experiment increase by 43% if you maintain a calm demeanor."

"LET US OUT OF HERE!"

Databot 267 said nothing. *Pop-pop whir* coming from it and the other robots. I looked across at all of them. All the pops were now sounding in unison, and the whirs. Single-minded as a school of fish. Processing. Except...

Except there were a few robots who were searching for their human counterparts. That's when I realized there were more robots now than colonists. I did a quick tally, and counted only forty-one of us. That meant three were missing. But which ones, and how?

The Mers. There were no longer any Mers among us. Originally, there had been three.

Mers would be able to slip through that sea tunnel without drowning.

I muttered, "Fast as fish and just as untrustworthy!"

Databots were taking hold of the three colonists who'd been "married" to the escaped Mers. Taking them by the arms. They grew freakish when the robots seized them.

"Where are you taking them?" I shouted.

And then it seemed we were all shouting. And I realized just how badly these agate fish needed an ass-whipping.

I had no spear on my person. No bone knife carved by a crafty Po. I bore only the sealskin hide covering my ass and a dried length of mackerel for Hermes that I'd stashed in my pocket before all this started. And I had my fists.

Suddenly, a strange sound reverberated throughout the cave. Ululations. Like the whale's cry.

All the cyclops eyes turned toward the keening, and their lights intersected on a woman. The Tamian woman who was sick. Her assigned spouse lay cradled in her lap, and she was forming those awful ululations from deep in her throat.

Databot 267 raised his stinger hand. The diamond inside it was reverberating. His agate skeleton trembled.

I looked from the robot to the Tamian woman. Something was wrong with her face. She had a strange smile.

But it wasn't a smile. It was blood smeared across her mouth so that it looked like a horrific black grimace. And her spouse, the Po who lay cradled in her lap, was dead; missing much of the skull behind the brows.

Delilah vomited. Our enclosure erupted in screams.

One of the robots came up behind the Tamian woman and jabbed its diamond-tipped stinger up into the base of her skull. She went rigid.

I doubled up and knocked the cyclops eye right off of Databot 267's face.

The robot went down with a crash, flailing that agate fish stinger in the air. I ducked to avoid being scratched. Every robot in Po Rock Lab turned their cyclops eyes on me, causing me to squint, but I kicked at the nearest one and caught Databot 253 in its agatey chest. It went down, too. Both 267 and 253 were collapsing into agate fish, though my counterpart, Databot 267, couldn't get its lid shut.

Other colonists were now throwing punches at their robots as well. Cyclops lights flew wild across the inside of Po Rock Lab. I was swinging, kicking, smashing at anything agate.

But then: *Zzzt!*

Zzt-zzt-zzzzzzztt!!

White light. Night-night.

11.

WHEN I AWOKE I was bathed in a memory of lovely fresh air and rain. But I opened my eyes and saw that I was still imprisoned on Po Rock.

We were alone in the dark again. And by 'alone' I mean no robots. We were all cozied up in pairs on seaweed pallets that had gone itchy from lack of proper tending. Some were on rock shelves that were not suitable for sleep. Mothers wept for babies who had been separated from them. Men were getting angry and would probably be brawling right now if they could see one another well enough to throw a punch.

Me, I could think of nothing but the sickness. Shiv. That Tamian woman who'd jabbed her finger on the probe, and the way she'd been hunched over her husband with his grey matter staining her cheeks.

I didn't know whether we were safer inside our lab or outside, but either way I wanted my fate in my own hands, not in those of a bunch of robots.

I addressed the others: "Listen, we need to work out some basics in here."

"Clean water!" someone cried. "The water they give us is muddy."

"I know. Maybe we can make stills."

"We can't make stills if there's no sunlight!"

I ran my finger along the shell wall. It came away wet. In fact everything was wet. I felt sweaty myself.

I said, "I think this thing is turning into one giant still. It's sealed in tight."

Too tight. Breathing was labored. But one thing at a time.

"Where did all those robots come from?" Delilah asked me.

I said, "I guess they came from There."

"Well, can we go There and ask them to leave us alone?"

"I don't think so. No way out."

"But where *is* There? Where exactly is it?"

I thought about this a moment, because I ought to know this one, seeing that as the juke I was supposed to be the living repository of our knowledge.

"*There* is just anywhere that isn't *Here*. It's where our ancestors came from. People from There were supposed to come back and get our ancestors, but they never did. They left them to rot in prison cells."

"What about a toilet?" someone from the other side of the enclosure asked.

I didn't answer. We'd all been going in whatever dark corner we could find. The smell was debilitating.

They were muttering and calling in the darkness:

"We should use the north side."

"Which way is north? I can't see anything."

"Don't come near me! Anyone tries to shit in my corner I'll bash their heads in!"

Thirty-six. Only thirty-six colonists now. That's the original forty-four, less the three escaped Mers, less four more. The robots must have taken away the Mers' so-called spouses. And the sick Tamian woman and her dead spouse. Reflections of it crept through my mind on spider legs. Her keening. The husband missing half his skull. Her keening, and her gruesome smile. Her keening, keening, keening – and the way the diamond trembled in Databot 267's stinger hand.

If they'd taken all those people away, they must have opened the enclosure while we'd been zapped. That would account for the memory of fresh air and rain while I was sleeping.

I felt a hand on my arm and jumped.

"Lie down," Delilah said.

I didn't move. She was running her fingers across my chest, and then she moved them down lower, to my waist, and stroked the outline of my rib. I caught her wrists and pulled her away.

She said, "We have to, Juke. Didn't you hear what they said?"

Ordinarily I would have swept her off her feet and sailed away to faraway rainbows. But I had no appetite for sex in this dark, sweaty dung pit.

I said, "It's not going to work, Delilah."

"But Juke –"

"Forget it."

She pushed me hard, both hands against my chest. "You selfish bastard, Juke! What's going to happen to me if I don't produce offspring for them?"

"Will you listen to yourself? Offspring? Do you really want to spend nine months pregnant and suffocating inside a toilet only to hand your baby over to a bunch of robots?"

I didn't add the thought, *if you survive.*

Delilah was crying again. I patted her back. I didn't know what else to do.

And then a glimmer in the darkness. A green glimmer, over where the narrow seawater tunnel was.

"Look!" someone cried.

I drew nearer where I could get a better view. The glow intensified, throwing emerald rings dancing across the interior of Po Rock Laboratory.

I said, "Flame algae!"

"It'll give some light, and something better to eat on," I heard Jay Opo say.

And someone else hollered, "Somebody get in there and scoop it out for us!"

But there was no need, because the flame algae was making its way up the tunnel as though it was swimming of its own. We crowded around the mouth of the pool.

From back behind me, Delilah said, "Are the robots bringing it to us?"

I whispered, "Aster."

And then, yes. There she was. Aster, fairy of the sea, slipping through the tunnel and up into the pool, draped in robes of flame algae that glittered like emeralds and fire across her nude little form.

I reached in and pulled her out, heaving her up into my arms, kissing her forehead. I was so relieved to see her. She was safe! Others raked the flame algae from her and gnawed its juices.

But fish that she was, Aster was wriggling in my arms, wriggling away from my grasp.

"Shiv!" she said in an urgent whisper.

And I stopped. Ah, yes. She was a married woman now.

I set her down gently but with a leaden heart.

Instead of pulling away from me, she grabbed my hands and dragged me back with her.

"Shiv!" she said again.

The water in the pool surged and then receded. And then it gave a belch. The flame algae now cast a glow on the inside of Po Rock Lab, providing the softest and most spreading light we'd had since our incarceration. I saw the faces of my fellow colonists staring down into the mouth of the sea tunnel.

Aster yanked hard and I looked at her. Her eyes were wild. I let her pull me to wherever it was she needed me to go, which meant nothing more than a far corner of Po Rock Lab. A nasty toilet of a corner.

A splash came from across where the sea tunnel was. Aster held firm and wouldn't let me step toward it. I couldn't see beyond the colonists' backs but they made cries of horror, and then relief, and then horror again.

Someone screamed, and then I heard Delilah cry out, "Shiv!" just as the congregation finally dispersed.

In fact, they scrambled backward now. As though a sea snake had risen from the pool and was slithering at them. But now I could see Shiv, too, scrabbling on his belly so that he might as well have been a sea snake. I didn't know what to make of it other than to take up the collective panic.

He gathered himself, rising to his feet, unsteady but determined, his gaze sweeping across the faces of each and every colonist, save for those of us who'd hidden ourselves.

He said, "Bow wow."

Silence. The colonists stared at him. Even in the cool green glow he looked sick beyond sick. The agate wedding earring glinted at his lobe.

He said again, "Bow wow."

A nervous laugh from some colonists, and Jay Opo said, "Well, he's crazy, isn't he? Thinks he's a dog."

Now other colonists laughed, too.

But no, that was not Shiv Omer's brand of crazy. He was telling the colonists, "Bow down," because he thought himself a king, not a dog; only he was missing a tongue and therefore his words came twisted.

Then Shiv said, "Weh my why?"

Aster gripped my hand. Though the others had exchanged sympathetic smiles for Shiv, they widened the circle around him.

Delilah said, "Shiv…?"

"Weh my why?"

I realized then what he was trying to say: *Where's my wife?*

Delilah stepped toward him and raised her hand soothingly. "It's okay…"

"Don't!" Aster yelled.

But too late, Shiv had flung himself at Delilah. She screamed. But just as Shiv was upon her Jay Opo leapt forward and knocked him sideways. Shiv went sprawling. Delilah screamed again, unharmed, and climbed Jay Opo as though he were a lookout tower.

And then Shiv let loose a horrible, ululating, whale vomit-smelling roar, and threw himself at the nearest colonist. A Tamia girl. One that had been mooning after him that last time we'd all stood together on Furnace Rock. Shiv sank his teeth into her scalp and cracked her skull against the rock before a single one of us could register what we were witnessing. Screams echoed through the laboratory. And even as the girl had gone soft in his grasp, Shiv turned and cracked open the skull of another colonist, and then another.

12.

"Go!" I urged Aster. "Get out of here!"

She was wild-eyed and trembling. Slower to run on dry land than the rest of us.

Shiv was rampaging through the colonists and it was all too easy for him. He smashed open their skulls and then gouged their brains, scraping with his teeth and his clawlike feet and hands. As he tasted them his eyes rolled back like a shark's. Laying waste in a hunt. No regard for his prey. Hoarding his quarry for a later feast, or just for spoil. No one was a match for him and no one dared try. That sickness he wore. Probably everyone understood by now that a mere bite from him meant death or something in between.

The colonists scattered and formed in herds at the corners of the laboratory. Unlike the sick Tamia woman who'd seemed to become a shambling skull-cracker, Shiv maintained speed and some intellect.

He moved fast but only in short bursts. Lurching. He couldn't run anyone down. But he could climb the walls as easily as a spider and leap upon us in any direction.

We scrambled away, and then there was Shiv. Suddenly in our midst again. Everyone screamed and fell backward. He had his hands on Aster and she went down with a smack, screaming.

I went blind at the sight and sound of it. Purely blind. A base rage swept over me so fast and hard that the next thing I knew, I had a fistful of Shiv's hair and was bashing his skull against a rock.

Shiv wheeled on me. I jerked to the left and narrowly escaped the feel of his teeth in my shoulder. I gave a mighty twist on his arm and we tumbled in opposite directions, and then he was scurrying up the wall again. I joined Aster where she huddled with other colonists, grabbing her by the elbows to help steady her wobbly Mer legs.

Shiv dove headlong into a group of colonists nearest him. Fresh screams erupted.

I dragged Aster to the center of the lab and flung her into the sea tunnel.

I might as well have tossed a thrashing grouper into the waves. She swam away. Disappearing from us. From me. So fast.

"My WHYYYYYYYY!!!"

I turned and saw Shiv hurtling toward the sea tunnel where I stood. And I knew.

I knew that I had a choice:

I could leap out of the way and let him plunge into the tunnel in pursuit of Aster. She was not sick and had a good chance of out-swimming him.

Or I could chase her myself, blocking his path to her with my own body, and perhaps even trapping him in the chamber where he couldn't get back up into Po Rock Laboratory.

I would probably drown in the process, too, but what the hell?

Shiv's rage was such that he was charging directly toward me on his belly. If he'd scaled the wall and leapt upon me I would have been dead by now, but as it was he was crab-scrabbling, and I thought I might have a chance.

I grabbed a hunk of flame algae to light my way and dove straight down into the seawater.

13.

THE TUNNEL WAS much easier to navigate by the light of flame algae than before when I'd been groping in the dark, though now I had the added handicap of sheer yodeling panic right from the onset.

There came a surge of pressure and I knew Shiv had plunged in behind me. I'd already made it two lengths in, having had a slight lead from his belly-crawling sluggishness. But now that he was in the water, sick or not, he was the one with the advantage.

There, I saw the chamber. Much more space than I'd thought when I'd been groping in the dark. The rock had gone considerably porous and I could now see many other tunnels branching off. No telling which route Aster had taken. Also, a shallow cubby stood above the opening where the rocks had gone loose.

I plunged for the chamber and stashed the flame algae just behind the mouth, then jetted out and above into the cubby.

Shiv was fast behind me. Mers were thermals just like any of us but you'd think they were sea creatures!

As I'd hoped, he was tracking the flame algae I'd been carrying, and he didn't see me where I now hid in darkness. He swam right into the chamber below me.

I kicked. The shelf of loose rock fractured and rained down. The rockslide was ridiculously, painfully slow, but it was also silent and so Shiv did not immediately react. I watched as a full wall of rock settled gently over the mouth.

Got him!

Only, the flame algae inside the chamber had provided the only light. Now once again I was stuck underwater in pitch darkness.

It occurred to me that I had come here knowing I would drown. That was stupid.

A lonely howl came from behind the rocks, and now that we were under water it sounded even more like the whale's cry, only deeper. I knew it meant Shiv realized he was trapped.

I groped for the chute, found it, and swam a few seconds before smacking my head on rock. My lungs convulsed with the impact. Pain seared my forehead.

And I realized I'd swum into a dead end.

I backed up, burbling, not sure which way to turn in the darkness.

I groped and found the pile of rocks. And a hand. Shiv's hand! Moving! It tried to grab me but I jerked away. He didn't immediately follow, and I realized he was still digging his way out.

Great.

My master plan.

(In my defense, please recall that this plan was born from an of-the-moment decision, and I've already established that my genius lies in more sustained thinking.)

And then I brushed against his skin again, and all bravery escaped me, leaving only my usual how-to-cope-with-drowning stand-by: I started shrieking.

But:

Blurp!

Blurp!

Blurp!

Sweet, delicate lips, breathing air into my lungs. These were not the black and wormy lips of Shiv Omer. These belonged to his bride, Aster.

I breathed in her gentleness and then followed along with her, refreshed with the oxygen she'd bestowed. We swam, swam, swam in the dark, leaving behind Shiv Omer's thudding.

I was grateful that Aster knew where she was because the twists and turns in the dark seemed random. Even repetitive. Suspiciously so...

The sound of Shiv's underwater bellowing grew louder. He must have dug himself free.

We came upon a bend and Aster urged me to swim straight up. I thought, *Finally! The surface!*

But we emerged in a very thin pocket. Only a hand's breadth between the water's surface and the rock ceiling. We floated on our backs and pressed our lips into the slice of air, breathing.

"How much farther?" I asked her, and waited for her reply.

And waited.

And waited, but still she said nothing.

This was not a good sign.

But giving her the benefit of the doubt, I asked, "Are we almost out of the tunnels?"

She said only, "Lost."

My heart sank. Of course we were lost. She'd found her way in by light of flame algae, and now she had none. We rested in the black, black, blackness and listened to each other's breathing. And also the knocking and intonations from Shiv somewhere in the tunnels nearby.

I said, "Well, at least he won't have the advantage of taking a breath. He probably doesn't have the presence of mind to find an air pocket like this one."

I wondered about the colonists trapped up there in Po Rock Laboratory. Shiv had killed several, and injured others.

We dared not linger too long, and so we slipped back down and started swimming again. I let Aster lead even though she was just as blind as I. It seemed her method was to swim in the opposite direction of Shiv's sounds.

And then a green glimmer ahead. Flame algae. We swam toward it. The glow provided enough light to easily see now. An open cathedral of a chamber, but filled to the ceiling with water and no pockets from which to draw air. Several tunnels branched in opposing directions. Prison corridors. We swam past them, peering down, seeking signs of a pool with an air pocket. I didn't want to look. Couldn't bear to see prison cells locking away the bones of our dear ancestors, eroding in brine.

But all the cell doors were gaping open. They even swayed in the current. Groaning with it. Some of the barred walls had fallen down completely, doors still intact.

Of course they were. Our ancestors couldn't have been left to rot in prison cells. They would have perished inside them in any number of ways – malnutrition, high water flooding the cells. And if our forefathers had died inside their cells, they would have never lived to procreate. Our colony would have never come to be. Funny that I'd never given it any thought.

My lungs were burning!

Aster turned slowly, looking around, bobbing and thrusting like a seahorse. The sounds made by Shiv seemed to be everywhere. I strained my eyes at the many tunnels, wondering which one might lead us out. If any. We needed air so badly now. But prison cells and flame algae... It meant we were within just a few lengths of the surface.

A finger on my shoulder.

And then the cold realization that Aster was in front of me, and the finger on my shoulder was not her finger.

Shiv!

I trumpeted bubbles. Jerked away.

But no Shiv. His echoes still pealed from the darkness beyond.

Another finger on my ear, and one at my elbow.

Finally I saw him. It was Hermes sidling up behind me. Aster swam closer to us. Hermes had all seven and three-quarters tentacles on me as if in an embrace.

And then Hermes stuck one of those tentacles in my pocket, pulled out the dried mackerel, and doused me with a cloud of ink.

I floundered and he vanished. Aster surged toward one of the tunnels and I realized she was in pursuit of him.

Aster followed Hermes. I followed Aster. Hermes was easy enough to track despite the ink because he'd snagged a tangle of flame algae. He was a swift little bugger, though, as was Aster. I did my best to keep up. We were swimming down, down, deeper down.

And then, finally, he led us to yet another chamber where we broke the surface. Air!

Plenty of flame algae in here and a thin splash of genuine daylight streaming in through a long, long chimney. The light intensified as it mirrored against the rock.

And it seemed that the flame algae had been cultivated, as we were too deep now for it to flourish naturally. A smattering of artifacts like tools and jewelry and preened fish bones indicated that this cave had once been frequented by Mers.

By "once frequented," I mean only, "in the time before the robots." And that was only a few days ago. Or weeks. I had no idea how long.

Also, there were old devices. Artifacts of our ancestors. I think they were called radios. They were all smashed up in a pile. Likely every single radio that had ever been on these rocks.

On one of them, I saw writing:

THER

Much of it was eroded, but I made out a few more letters:

MA...HEM

I looked up and saw a splintered reflection of myself staring back. Hermatite. We must be near Birdshit Rock.

Aster was smiling.

"You know this place?" I asked.

She nodded.

"We can get to the surface?"

She nodded again and pointed toward a second tunnel through which Hermes was now leaving us behind. There were only two tunnels in here – the one we just came through and the one that led out. This cave was huge. A rock shelf stretched several lengths in, with a small mini-chamber beyond it. Crabs scooted around the corners.

I said, "We're probably better off in here for now with all the robots and sickness going on up above. Let's seal it off so Shiv can't get through."

We hauled rocks and piled them over the opening. Labored a very long while. And though it seemed to take forever Shiv never found us, because if I've said it once I've said it a thousand times: The man has no hunting instincts.

When we finished, we heaved ourselves up onto the shelf and rested. Aster folded into my arms as easily as a hermit crab in its shell. I smiled at the grand chamber. A nice place for us to hide.

I said, "I forgive you for marrying him. I'm married now, too."

She said nothing. Just held tight to me, trembling. Exhausted. I looked down the bare length of her, that lovely skin, the curling Mer hands and feet.

A horrible gash at her ankle.

A bite.

I'd seen it earlier. Witnessed it through blind rage when Shiv had pounced on her up in Po Rock Lab, and my mind had tucked it away.

I pulled her in closer. We stayed like that for a long, long while.

14.

OVER THE NEXT several days, we brought as much food and flame algae up to the other colonists as we dared.

The robots migrated en masse from rock to rock, or should I say, from lab to lab, so that they routinely visited all eight labs during the course of a day. Aster and I learned we could enter a laboratory about twenty minutes after the robots left, knowing that they wouldn't be back until the next day.

At the end of each day we were exhausted. We witnessed such horrors. And Aster was growing sick. But it was the only way we could think of to try and save as many colonists as possible.

I find it difficult to describe what Aster and I saw in those laboratories. Too painful to speak of. But I will do my best:

To begin, every last child in our colony lay dead.

Every one.

The robots had taken them to a laboratory they'd made of my own beloved Su Rock, and there the children all perished. Maybe they were

poisoned through one of the infernal inoculations the robots were dol-
ing out. I don't know. But they were gone now, every single colonist
under the age of twelve.

In Mer Rock Laboratory, the colonists all lay ailing. One whiff and
I recognized it for the ambergris-smelling disease. They were trapped
in that airless hole with their vomit and black spittle and other efflu-
vium. Though it broke my heart to leave them floundering like that,
Aster and I managed only to deliver the flame algae and then escape
again. Like Po Rock Laboratory, Mer Rock Lab held a mixture of
tribes, all except the Mers. No Mers on Mer Rock. They had escaped.

On Meso, Po, and Tamia Rocks North and South, conditions were
unpleasant but survivable. On Meso Rock Lab and Tamia Rock North
and South Labs, the colonists were complaining over incessant exam-
inations by the robots, and thrice-daily inoculations. On Po Rock Lab,
the robots continued to arrange marriages and demand offspring.

Furnace Rock and Birdshit Rock were the most disturbing.

On Furnace Rock, the robots had removed the eyes and tongues
of the colonists.

Aster had cried out upon seeing them. I put my arm around her to
steady her, though in fact we were steadying one another. When all
forty-one eyeless, tongueless colonists of Furnace Rock Lab heard
Aster cry out, they turned toward us. Some of them rose to their feet
and groped their way in our direction. Hollow sounds in their throats.
Not quite the whale ululations but close enough to unnerve me.

But the fate of the colonists on Birdshit Rock was most upsetting
of all. They were wrapped in agate bindings. These bindings were not
simply external like the sealskin cloths we wore over our groins. The
robots had somehow peeled away their skin and drilled agate into their
bones. The colonists had been subdued so they did not speak or stir
when Aster and I arrived with robes and robes of flame algae. What
felt so unnerving, what stained my very sense of humanity, was the
fact that they all looked so much like robots now. More robot than
human. Each wore a cyclops eye in a helmet that covered the face.
Only the flesh of their noses and mouths were exposed.

Again, to our cowardice or precaution, we left the flame algae and
abandoned them to their suffering. I admit this fact with a heavy heart.
We just didn't know what else to do.

What Aster and I did manage, or at least what we attempted to do, was to evacuate non-infected colonists. We could only do this one-by-one, as Aster alone could bestow the blurp-blurp breaths. That meant she and I would enter a laboratory together, drop supplies and then leave together, and then Aster would return and rescue one single colonist at a time.

We could only save those colonists who showed no sign of sickness, of course. And those who wanted evacuation. Incredibly, most did not. Most believed that life would soon return to normal. They hoped that if they simply complied with the robots' directives, the experiments would conclude and the robots would leave, and colony life would resume.

No amount of coaxing changed these beliefs. Were it not for this, we might have saved so many more.

During this time, the biggest threat came not from the robots, but from the colonists themselves. Many had the sickness and, like Shiv Omer, would run amok through a lab. Of course, the colonists could not escape so as soon as one turned, we knew an entire lab population would be desecrated soon enough. The sick would either crack open the skulls of the healthy or attempt to do so and bite them, infecting them. For most, the infection worked fast.

Mers were usually able to escape but many were so batty that they became easy prey for the sick ones. Some were killed, their brains devoured, and a few went sick. A sick Mer was a dangerous thing. For most colonists, the sickness took hold within hours; but Mers took an entire week to fall ill.

Every single rock was tainted with sickness. Even those labs that the robots had kept free of disease were tainted because sickened Mers found their way in and preyed upon the inhabitants, much like the way Shiv Omer had penetrated the Po Rock Lab where I'd been imprisoned.

The robots seemed unsympathetic to all of this. They simply held to the prescribed experiments regardless of what went wrong.

We saved every healthy colonist who was willing to come with us and kept trying to persuade the rest. Our refuge between rescue attempts was the chimneyed cave where Hermes had led us deep in the tunnels under Birdshit Rock.

The tribes as we knew them no longer existed. In fracturing the tribes it was as if a living being had been desecrated. The Meso tribe had been our brawn, and the Po, who had created our spears and nets and other tools, had been our hands. The Tamia, the tribe of lovers and frivolity, had been the heart of it. The Su like me, with our fascination with history, mathematics, and lyric, we were the head. And the Mers, who could wander anywhere above and below water, were its feet.

This once-living thing that was our colony. This, too, died.

15.

ASTER WAS TOO sick to continue with the rescues. And without Aster, there were no rescues. Her puffs of air were what enabled us to save colonists and transfer provisions.

Though she, being a Mer, seemed to have had a bit longer grace period before succumbing to the sickness, it had now been nearly a week since Shiv had bitten her. I knew she was almost out of time.

I couldn't bear to think of what must be done when the virus took over her. What I must do. What she wanted me to do, so that she wouldn't become one of those skull-cracking shamblers.

We were all gathered in the chimneyed arena, all of us refugees, weighing our options. Realizing that there would be no more rescues.

Jay Opo said to me, "This is crap. What are we supposed to do now, sit around diddling each other while our aunts and uncles get sick and open up each other's skulls?"

I said, "I won't be sitting around."

"Then what?"

"Fight."

"We tried that once already. Didn't go anywhere."

"No one else has to go with me. I have to do something, though. I have to fight."

Jay snorted. "Sounds like a good way to get your ass sparked up and sent back to a laboratory."

"Maybe. Probably."

I looked at Aster, pale and sighing. Half gone already.

We had no resources. We barely even had spears. One flash of light and the robots would have me back in their custody. One bite from a fallen cousin and I would become a brain-eater.

But I couldn't let it go one more moment. Even if I was going to die trying, I would take at least some of those drone robots out.

And if I did die trying I at least wouldn't have to face euthanizing Aster.

I gathered myself up and looked around. "Anyone else in?"

No one moved.

Jay said, irritated, "Sit down, you don't even know how to fight. You're just the damn juke. What do you plan to do, sing them to death?"

Aster rose to her feet, unsteady, and offered up a rare soliloquy: "Juke's a hunter. I'll go."

I frowned. Didn't want her to come. But I couldn't protest either — maybe a suicide mission was her only option.

Jay sighed and rose to his feet. "You're dumb enough to give this a shot, then I might as well go with you."

Aster, Jay, and I, along with a handful of others, grabbed whatever spears and knives we could find and slipped into the water. Aster led, sick though she was. She knew the way better than any of us. We swam draped in ribbons of flame algae to light our passage. Past the gaping cells of our prisoner ancestors. Up to a maze of tunnels, and then pools, under Birdshit Rock. We broke the surface and looked for the robots.

Jay spotted them first. They were on Tamia Rock North. Lightning was streaking from the enclosure.

The colonists inside were probably all sleeping now, which meant the robots intended to open the enclosure so they could bring out the dead.

We all swam for Tamia Rock North, which was a few rocks down from where we surfaced in the comet-shaped formation of rocks in our colony.

I called to the others, "Hurry. Let's try to get there while the shell is still open."

And they all responded by swimming their fastest. Aster, the strongest swimmer in our party despite her illness, was first to reach Tamia Rock North just as the enclosure opened. I could see robots filing out both in upright form and in their collapsed fishlike shapes.

Some of the upright robots were carrying colonists out of the lab.

They looked and saw Aster, training their cyclops beams on her. And then came the crashing white light.

Aster disappeared below the surface. She was the closest one, so the rest of us had a chance to follow her example without being struck. They'd localized the lightning to just where Aster was, not realizing the rest of us were drawing nearer.

Beneath the surface, we continued swimming until we reached Aster. We hung suspended, waiting out the flashes. Seven of us. Four men and three women.

The lightning stopped. We rose to the surface again and took big gulps of air, and then plunged right back down as the robots repeated the lightning flashes. Most of us slipped back beneath the surface again before being sparked, but two went limp in the water. One of them, Ralph Otamia, was a distance away.

The other was Aster.

Too sick to react quickly. She'd gone to sleep near me. I swam frantically toward her, afraid she would drown, but a robotic arm pulled her up by the hair before I could grab hold. Another robot pulled Ralph out, too.

The lightning kept flashing. And then after a moment, it went quiet.

I had a spear in hand and a dagger tucked into my sealskin. The others looked to me, and this time I gave the signal: three fingers... two fingers...and then a fist...

We vaulted to the surface in unison, and in that same moment, we launched our spears.

I did not aim at the closest robot, leaving it for the others to take down, and chose one higher up on the rock. My spear cut straight through its chest. Though they were impenetrable when collapsed, they were quite vulnerable when expanded to full walking databots. Five robots went down under our vollies. Agate limbs tumbling into the water. I whipped the dagger from my sealskin and threw it, landing another robot. Up through its neck. Jay did the same.

We plunged below the surface again, but not before I caught a glimpse of Aster's slack form on a shelf of Tamia Rock North. Ralph lay next to her.

This time as the lightning flashed, the five remaining refugees in our war party converged upon the robots who had fallen into the water. Together, we pulled, smashed, and thrust their limbs against rocks to pull them apart, and recovered what weapons we could. Jay retrieved one of our spears. Me, I smashed apart a robotic arm just below the diamond-tipped probe.

When the lighting subsided again and I gave the signal, we surged for the surface and took out three more robots.

We continued plunging and scavenging between bursts of lightning until the robots' numbers had dwindled to about three dozen. But by that time, of the seven of us refugees who'd begun this assault, now only two remained: Jay Opo and me. The others had fallen to the lightning sleep and the robots had dragged them each ashore and heaped them like tuna.

I was exhausted. Jay, too, I could tell. We were treading beneath the surface, waiting for the bursts of lightning to subside, when we heard a series of splashes.

Collapsed robots were plunging into the water from distant rocks within our colony. Hordes of them. What we used to think of as agate fish — it seemed so long ago now. They swam toward us, leading with the diamond-tipped probes. They would be easy enough to fend off, easy in fact to smash to bits in their semi-amphibious forms. But, it would only take one scratch from a diamond-tipped probe and we'd be finished.

One, I could evade. Even three. But not all of them. Not for more than a few minutes. There were just too many.

I met Jay's eyes just as the lightning above ceased. His expression was a mixture of determination and resignation. An acceptance of our fate. I nodded at him, and together we swam upward again. No countdown. No surge. No weapons.

We bobbed up and swam up to Tamia Rock North, evading the agate fish robots by circling toward the back. The robots weren't fast in either form. Jay and I crawled up onto the rocky terrain. We staggered to the collection of bodies that were our fallen refugee cousins. Barely a twitch of strength left in my bones.

Aster turned her head and looked at me. I blinked back, surprised to see that she hadn't actually slipped into the lightning sleep. But then I remembered Shiv and the others, when they'd succumbed to the illness, affected by the lightning. She lay glassy-eyed across the rocks.

The agate fish were now emerging from the water and scrabbling up onto Tamia Rock North toward us. I steeled myself, waiting for the spark. We could no longer plunge beneath the surface.

Jay shifted his weight where he was sitting on a rock next to the others, and I thought he was about to get up and stand with me. But he didn't. He just looked away, waiting for the agates to advance upon us.

One of the robots expanded into the human-sized form.

I called to it, "Databot 267!"

The thing fixed me in its gaze as its cousins joined in the mechanical change from agate fish to full-sized robot.

Pop-pop-whir, as the drone staring back at me became Databot 267. It said, "Yes, Human 267."

"That's not my name. I am Juke Osu. Tell me where you're from."

All the robots were advancing toward me.

Databot 267 said, "We come from an organization called Thermal Maritime Hemachate. We are an organization started by a healthy human, just like you."

"And now?"

"We are human and robot hybrids."

I let my gaze drift from them to the expanse of waves surrounding our sunken prison island, beyond where the last of the humpbacks on migration were surfacing and diving, surfacing and diving. "What is out there, outside of our colony?"

Databot 267 was stepping forward, the others advancing with him, all moving toward Jay and me and our sleeping fallen. Databot 267 kept coming until it was eye-to-eye with me. I wondered why it hadn't zapped me yet.

It said, "It is not safe for a healthy human to move freely in this world. Not safe for robots, either. We have come to help you for excellent reasons. To study your kind and make hybrids, part human and part robot."

Next to me, Jay said, "We don't want any part of your world."

I added, "And neither did our ancestors, did they? I think your organization, Thermal Whatsit, probably took over our prison when our ancestors were abandoned by the rest of the world. And we revolted and kicked you out."

Databot 267 said, "This is partly true. And partly not. Your ancestors had been criminals. Prisoners who had the opportunity to go free, escape their prison. Their sinking prison. We let them out of their cages and invited them to come with us. Many of your kind chose to join Thermal Maritime Hemachate. Others remained here and cut off communication with the outside world. They clung to a savage existence and squandered their human stems."

"They must have thought life in a prison meant more freedom than life with robots."

"Not *with*. *As*. Our organization lost contact with you only because it was a volatile time. This virus was plaguing the earth. But now we've found you again, and we've learned more about the virus. Changed it, even. It is time for you to make the change. Your host bodies help us learn so much more. Isolated as you've been, you've bred down to a concentrated collection of genetic anomalies. You process the virus differently. Some of you, more than others."

I looked at Aster. Blinking, sighing, her curled clawlike feet.

Databot 267 said, "You can free yourself from your prison. We are here to take care of you. All of you. There are many more healthy survivors that you have hidden somewhere. Tell us, Human 267. Tell us where they are. You will be enriching so many lives."

"Not a chance," I said, but even as the words formed on my lips I wasn't sure.

I had no idea how long we might survive down in that chimneyed cave deep below the surface. It felt I might be ascertaining our deaths.

Jay Opo had heard the uncertainty in my voice, and he met my gaze. He was still sitting with such passiveness compared to his earlier fire. Now, he just looked depleted.

He said, "What do you think, old man? Honestly? Should we throw it over and go robo?"

I shook my head. "Never."

Jay looked at the hordes of them, and at the refugees lying on the rocks behind us. And then he returned his gaze to me. "Yeah. I'd rather shit out my insides and die a skull-eating shambler."

Pop-pop-whir. Pop-pop-whir.

I picked up a rock and smashed Databot 267 – or at least the drone that spoke for it — straight through the cyclops eye. I reached down for another rock and braced myself for the lightning.

Aster said, "Ahhhhhhh…"

And then she made the ululation sound.

I turned to look at her. She was making that horrible, hollow reverberation from deep within her gullet. She didn't sound like Shiv had when he'd done that. She was not fully given over yet.

But the diamonds jingled in the robots' probes. And no lightning rained down on us.

I looked at her, and I looked at Jay, and I tried making the sounds, too. I'd always sung them in "Ambergris Genesis," but now I knew to sing it deep down low. Strangled in the throat, hollow in the mouth. *Ahhhh* moving to *ohhhhhh*.

Jay joined in, too.

The robots' diamonds sang with us.

And in the next rock over, in the Mer Rock Laboratory that had gone so very foul with sickened colonists, beneath the shell of the enclosure, I heard an answering *ohhhhhhh.*

They were much better at it, those shamblers trapped over in Mer Rock.

Ohhhhhhhh from Po Rock, and from Furnace Rock. All across the colony. Across rocks that had been swallowed up as laboratories. *Ohhhhhhhh.*

One by one, and then altogether, the diamonds shattered from the robots' probe stingers.

And when the diamonds shattered, the cyclops lights went quiet. And the robots collapsed where they stood or crept.

And then the domes opened over Birdshit Rock, and Furnace Rock, and Meso, Po, Tamia North, and Tamia South Rocks, and my own beloved Su Rock, and Mer Rock. The shells splintered open — for healthy colonists and shamblers alike.

They emerged, blinking, leaning.

Aster stopped calling and closed her eyes. No, she hadn't given over to the sickness yet. Not entirely.

Jay and I found renewed strength. We gathered around the sleeping refugees, fending off our stricken cousins who wished to eat the brains of the fallen.

• • •

16.

WE NUMBERED ONLY about two dozen survivors in the evacuation and ensuing revolt; and of those, only about eighteen made it through the next several weeks. Some fell ill while others were poached by marauding skull-crackers. But after that our population stabilized.

Survivors included Jay Opo, my new wife Delilah Otamia (who immediately divorced me and later married Jay), Ralph Otamia, and several others. We inhabited our little pocket of hermatite that had become the new post. We called it the pocket post for a while, and then the name became Postapocka, which became the new name of our colony. No tribes, just one single Postapocka colony.

Delilah and Jay were the first to bring a new life into the world. A delightful daughter. Other babies soon followed. Hermes frequented our cave as it meant a free meal for him, and the children enjoyed his company. Hermes was a thief, though, and you had to keep an eye on him. I once found his crevice and saw his stash: lots of Mer jewelry, big chunks of shiny glass, a dagger, and a huge rusted key. Probably came from the prison.

I never hunted octopus again.

Shiv Omer I'd found the day after the revolt. I'd been foraging for flame algae and had come upon him where he lay several lengths below the surface, tangled in iron bars that had once formed a prison cell. Whatever had happened after we eluded him in the sea tunnels I couldn't say, but it seemed that some or many sea creatures had got hold of him. I knew his remains by his red-blonde hair and bulging eyes. That was really the only recognizable thing that was left. His head was intact, and also a single curled and clawlike foot, and everything in between was stripped to bones.

I sang the farewell song for him after I returned to our refuge in the hermatite.

It occurred to me that perhaps the sea creatures who'd devoured Shiv might also get sick in the way of "Ambergris Genesis." But what difference would that make? Sea creatures already preyed upon one another. Such is the motif of the sea.

I sang our songs as I always had. New songs, too. Songs I wrote myself in order to maintain my sanity. In them, I kept track of what happened. Always burn the dead is still a mantra to remember, but also: Never trust a creature made of agate, be it of fin or crust or feet. Kill it on site.

In the songs of the elders, in the one that describes how our ancestral prisoners believed they would serve out their sentences and return to There, I added some lyrics. The new version described how they escaped their cells and smashed the radios, trying to fix it so that There would never return to Here. Because There is full of mayhem.

Flame algae became the crown jewel of Postapocka. It provided not only light but oxygen for us, in addition to what filtered down through the long, long chimney. We collected fresh rain water from that chimney, too, in bottles and barrels scavenged from the sunken prison. Flame algae also provided nutrients and clean water in its beads. We even found we could cultivate thin sprouts of bean under its light. Were it not for flame algae, we wouldn't have been able to survive here in our cave, which is higher than the sunken prison but lower than the surface outcroppings we used to call homes. Deep enough so that no stinkers might get to us.

We decided that once a month, one of us should swim to the surface and harvest the flame algae, because we were too deep for it to really flourish. We selected the swimmer by means of lottery. It was a dangerous task, what with all the marauding skull-crackers creeping over the great rocks that were once our homes. Like us, the stinkers discarded any notion of which tribe belonged where. They shambled wherever they pleased. And when they caught us, they ate of our brains.

But we of the Postapocka colony agreed that our situation was temporary. Sooner or later the stinkers would die off or fall prey to scavengers of fin or crust. This we affirmed in song around the fire every night. The little ones, though, they giggled like crazy when we sang this. To conceive of living above surface, safe from maneating men, was so far-fetched a notion that we might as well have been singing of a time when the ocean held no fish.

But strange though it was, in our little assembly, we began new lives.

We deduced that the diamond in the drones' stingers had acted as a way to communicate with the host robots. And that it was also a self-destruction device when robots became overrun by shamblers. We weren't sure why. It seemed as though the robots couldn't get sick. Nor did they have brains to eat. There were many questions to which we might never know the answers.

Every now and again one of us would spot an agate fish. A single drone sent to look for us human survivors. But we kept well hidden. We made certain that the only information any agate fish recorded was that this little collection of islands had become nothing more than a wasteland of shamblers. And aside from us refugees, that really was all that was left. When the domes split open we were able to save a few more colonists, but most were already diseased or dead.

The only exception were those unfortunate colonists whose skin the robots had peeled away and replaced with agate. When we searched for them in Birdshit Rock, we found only an empty, fractured dome. They'd all vanished. I didn't know if this meant the robots somehow abducted them to There, or if they'd escaped on their own, or had simply been devoured by fin or scavenging crust, or skull-crackers of feet. Another unanswered question.

As for Aster, she was now a widow because Shiv was dead. I of course was a divorcee. And so I professed my love and asked her to marry me. She agreed. We have been living happily ever since.

Ah.

If only the truth were as simple and sweet.

The way I just described my life with Aster, that was the poetic version. Truth in lyric only. But of course she'd been bitten by Shiv and had gone sick. So here's a more complete truth:

After the revolt, when I carried Aster back to the cave, when neither one of us could deny what was to become of her, she begged me to kill her and burn her body. I knew she was right to wish it that way. But oh, by my aunts and uncles, I could not bring myself to do this. To snap her delicate neck and commit her soft skin to flame.

Instead I went to Hermes' crevice and took his iron key. Then Jay Opo and I went into the flooded prison corridors and tried the key against some of the fallen cells walls. Turned out it fit every cell door we tried. Jay and I took one of the fallen cell walls — one that still had the door intact — back to our open air pocket chamber, and leaned it over a hollow in the hermatite. Fixed it in place with heavy rocks.

We sealed Aster off in that little makeshift cell.

There she grew sicker, and sicker still.

Until her lovely pink tongue turned black and she spat it out.

Then she wailed and gnashed teeth and left us all shaking at the sound of her. I wouldn't let any of our surviving colonists near her cell lest they put her out of her misery and burn her remains. They complied out of deference to her, as she'd saved every one of them.

And then, strangely, after about two weeks, she came out of the sickness and was perfectly fine.

We continued to pass food and water to her through the bars for another week just to be safe. But the precaution was unnecessary. She'd become lucid, calm, and healthy. Just tongueless.

We tried this sequestering technique with other colonists who fell sick after the rescue. But alas, the outcome almost always ended in failure. And a difficult one at that. We'd seal off a stinker only to watch it grow smellier and angrier, until we finally gave up and had to turn the cell into an oven by pumping it full of burning ambergris. Ambergris holds its flame for a long, long time.

We discovered that the only time a colonist picked up the disease and then became healthy again was when the colonist was a Mer. As with so many other things, the Mers had adapted beyond the sickness. They were also the only ones who spat out their tongues. We have three Mers in our Postapocka colony, and Aster is one of them. She doesn't speak anymore but she never didmuch anyway.

And so you can believe me when I say Aster and I have been living happily ever since. And how the shorter version of the tale isn't really a lie because that's how I sing it in the love song I've written for her.

And henceforth it shall be known as truth.

TIMKA

Ekaterina Sedia

VALENTIN KORZHIK FELT a familiar lump in his throat as he watched the black government Mercedes, tinted windows and all, pull up to the front of the Moscow State University's Virology Institute. *Those days are over,* he whispered, not quite believing it. They were never over as long as the KGB or the FSB or whatever they called it these days drove around in cars with tinted windows and could show up out of the blue, at Valentin's place of work, and spook him so much – as if he was guilty of anything.

The man with the stripe of a general on his trousers came out of the back seat, tugged down his uniform jacket, and looked up at the windows with his also tinted glasses, directly at where Valentin stood. Valentin ducked away and felt foolish – it wasn't like the FSB general could see him through the glare, five stories up.

Maksim Vronsky gave Valentin a long, pointed look. "Seen a ghost?"

"Just about. FSB."

Maksim made a face, but remained standing by his bench, watching the thermocycler with his usual quiet intensity, willing it to work well, without failure. A finicky machine, that, and they all had little rituals to coax it into working. Valentin said little silent prayers to imaginary and funny gods, Lida Belaya sang to her samples – beautifully, Valentin thought. He always looked forward to Belaya's experiments, and today he was sad that she wasn't here to soothe him and yet happy that she wasn't, and wouldn't have to face the FSB general.

It was a large building, and objectively Valentin had no reason to think that FSB was here to see him. The secret yet universal belief in his exceptional status was verified when the frosted glass lab door swung open.

"Lieutenant general Dobrenko," the general said, and moved for Maksim. "Dr. Vronsky?"

"Yes," Maksim said.

"Dr. Korzhik," the general said to Valentin. "I'm here on business."

Maksim shifted on his feet, leaning uncharacteristically away from the thermocycler. "For me or for him?" His fingers were white around the stirring glass rod he had no reason to be holding.

"Both." The word plopped out of Dobrenko's mouth, lumpy and dull like a toad. "You both are virologists with a military past and bio-weapons experience. You both served in Afghanistan."

Valentin did not know that about Maksim, and judging by Maksim's quick look, the ignorance was mutual.

The general sighed. "Another life, yeah? Back then, who would've thought that the Americans will be bombing the Afghans instead of helping them? Anyway, I'm here to request your expertise."

"What are you weaponizing now?" Valentin said. "Measles? Common cold? Herpes?"

"Nothing. In fact, we're attenuating." Oh damn it all to hell. Valentin managed not to say it out loud. Why can't you just leave shit alone. The less you stir it, the less it stinks.

"Let me fill you in." Dobrenko leaned against Maksim's lab bench, kicking out one long leg, his narrow behind resting against the black composite edge. Yet it was clear to them that listening was not optional. "You of course heard about the quarantine."

"I knew it!" Maksim whacked the glass rod against the palm of his other hand. "I knew it was a disease, not a food safety issue! Since when do they care about pesticide contamination, huh?"

Valentin nodded. Nothing ever changed – the newspapers lied just like they did in the eighties, and of course everyone guessed that the sudden stop of trade with the west was due to more than environmental pesticide guidelines' violations. Valentin groused that it was great

Russia was not a WTO member, because if it was, who would let it boycott products like that? He realized that he was leaning forward, just like Maksim, eager to learn a secret, no matter how bad or distasteful, no matter how beholden it would leave him. Not like he had a choice anyway.

"There's a disease." Dobrenko's words slipped out measured, safe. "We believe it started in the US, and of course took little time to spread elsewhere. Of course, it'll take a while to burn through Western Europe – now that everyone is quarantining. Poland, the Czech Republic – they closed their borders too."

"How dangerous is it?" Maksim said. "What's the mortality rate? How does it spread?"

"Hundred percent," Dobrenko said. "Airborne, or at least we think so." Voice flat, face flat. "Of course, you can also say that the mortality rate is zero percent – it's all in how you look at it. According to our data, people who die from it don't stay dead too long."

"What, zombies?" Valentin grew irritable again, and heard his voice rising. "Next you'll be asking us to make you a vaccine for lycanthropy? Antibodies for vampirism?"

"This is serious," Dobrenko said. "Look."

He pulled out an envelope from his pocket. The pictures inside were of good quality: and depicted some unknown town, likely European judging by how clean the streets were – if one ignored the dead on the sidewalks, in the roadways. More disconcerting were several people standing – they all had an unusually slouching posture; some had missing limbs, others – ruined faces, bruises, long streaks of gore smeared on their clothes. And yet they stood.

"What do you want, a vaccine?" Maksim said.

"Sure, a vaccine would be nice. What we do want, however, is an attenuated virus – to grant immunity, and maybe produce…a milder illness, I suppose."

Maksim and Valentin traded a disbelieving look.

"Even if we could do that – and I doubt we can since viruses are tricky, and how many viral vaccines do you know anyway?" Maksim sucked in his breath. "Even if we could, what makes you think it's a good idea?"

"The election is coming. The virus seems to make people…brainless is not what we're after, of course, but more docile, easier to speak to. Easier to convince. Suggestible, I guess is what we're after. And if it's not airborne, it probably should be."

"This is United Russia's idea," Valentin said. "No way they're taking the majority of the Duma seats this time around."

"There is a way," Dobrenko said softly. "This is what I'm trying to explain to you – with your cooperation, we might yet save the motherland."

Maksim shook his head and Valentin marveled – at Maksim's stubbornness, at his own impotent hate, at the ability to refuse to collaborate while simultaneously accepting the inevitability of doing so.

"Think about it." Dobrenko unfolded from his slouch by the bench and left. And why wouldn't he? Not like they had anywhere to run with the borders closed.

"Well?" Maksim was on him before the door closed behind the general all the way. "What's with you? You stand there and don't argue, and you were doing bio weapons before and never told me?"

"You didn't tell me either." Valentin sighed. "And arguing...you can't argue with the FSB. Not if you want to live or have any relatives."

"So we just let them infect people? This is just....I knew they were evil, but this is just ridiculous! Even they have to realize how bad this is, and we..."

"I didn't say we do it," Valentin said. "I said you can't argue. You have Lida's home number? Better call her, warn that poor soul."

As little as Valentin enjoyed reminiscing about his military service, there were parts of him shaped by it – as much as he managed to forget them at times, at others they manifested, almost violently, against his will, like claws and fur and teeth sprouting out of a werewolf. Valentin thought that maybe he was a were-soldier, like one of those shell-shocked vets that flipped out at loud noises and flashes of light. Only his flipping out was quiet, more orderly.

"So you served in Afghanistan," he said to Maksim. "Still remember any of it?"

"Every night." Maksim breathed through his mouth, suddenly slow and cautious. "I don't understand how they could do this to us – you can't just draft kids – eighteen-year-olds! – and toss them into hell.

I don't care what Dobrenko said about the Americans – at least those are trained soldiers who volunteered to join the military. We…how could they?"

"They could and they did." Valentin stared out of the window overlooking the apple orchard planted by Michurin himself – or so the rumor had it. "And they'll do it again too. That virus…if they're talking to us about it, it means they brought samples for us, from God knows where. How long will those remain contained? How long until someone sneaks across the border? How many were incubating before the quarantine started?"

"You sure Dobrenko's right that it's airborne?"

"No idea."

"So what is it that you want to do? If you can't say no to the FSB and we all gonna die anyway?"

"It's going to get bad. Can you imagine what it would be like, with millions of people turned into…"

"Zombies? You believe that?"

"I always believe FSB." Valentin managed a smile with one side of his mouth. "Even if they succeed and attenuate the virus, and release it…."

"We'll still be overrun with a horde of zombies." Maksim smiled too. "I'm starting to see your point. What do you suggest then?"

"We have to go into hiding. We can't run, and we cannot work for them, and I'm scared of what's going to happen. What we can do is to get armed and hide."

"Where?"

"Underground. Vorobyovy Gory subway station is closed now, it's under renovations. I know there's a side tunnel – a friend of mine works on the construction."

Maksim must've been taking Dobrenko seriously too, because he neither argued with Valentin nor called him insane. "Weapons," he said eventually. "We will need something…"

"The Biology Department used to have the ROTC program. There were Kalashnikovs, ammo, medical kits – the whole deal."

"And we'll get it how? Oh, don't tell me – you know a guy."

Valentin nodded. "I do. He used to run the program, Major Sechenov. He's old now, retired. But he has the keys – when he retired, he took them with him. The question now is, what are you bringing to the table? Do you still remember how to handle a Kalashnikov?"

"I can pull it apart in under eight seconds. And yes, I still remember what to do with it. And…" Maksim paused – as if a new life was being born in him right that minute, out of their fear and disgust, the bleakness that never seemed to lift away in this cursed place. "I think I can get us some heavy artillery."

"How?"

"I know a guy, too."

IN THE FOLLOWING days, Valentin came to appreciate what his classicist ex-wife Lyudmila referred to as "Cassandra syndrome." He struggled. On one hand, one had to be careful while spilling classified info and yet trying to maintain the façade of collaboration with the government; on the other, as remote and cold as Valentin tended to be, there were people he cared about. He assumed the same was true of Maksim, but he never asked, allowing his colleague to negotiate the difficulty as he saw fit. The world was about to die, and Valentin hoped to hang on for a while. There was no news from Europe on TV, and he took it seriously. It would be good to have company, but ultimately it wouldn't matter: he never believed in a happy ending of the post-apocalyptic stories. If he did, he would've tried harder.

As it was, Maksim and he sequenced the viral genome to waste time during the day, and at night they sneaked into the old storage room of the Biology Department's ROTC. These back rooms, walls of gray cinder block and long shelves along the walls, housed so many relics of another time that Valentin wanted to linger, to look at the student-made posters satirizing Yeltsin's ascent, and to pet bald heads of the Lenin busts. Instead, they sorted through the boxes with Kalashnikov's parts, ammunition, handfuls of tracer cartridges. They also grabbed medical supplies and rubber gas masks, their trunks nestled embryonically in dark-green canvas bags. Detachable bayonets, poncho-tents, miners' helmets with mounted flashlight, cans of pre-Perestroika pork and condensed milk – countless forgotten treasures.

They made one trip per night, and took only what they could carry comfortably, using wooden crates they collected near supermarkets.

Valentin hugged his crate to his chest and felt like crying over every item familiar on such an intimate level, like a shape of a lover's hand, carved into his heart by nostalgia for that lost time. He assumed Maksim felt the same. They walked then to the closed metro station, where Valentin's friend, Dmitry, left unlocked the side door leading to a set of service stairs and then a short side tunnel, with an abundance of warning signs and an empty electric shed. On their first night, Valentin took off the shed's padlock with the bolt cutters, and hung instead the one he bought. So far, no one seemed to have bothered to discover that the lock had been changed.

Thursday night was likely to be the last. They were almost done gutting the cinder block rooms, and Valentin looked forward to maybe spending the next night in his bed instead of skulking in the shadows and walking with a heavy crate for a good three kilometers. He breathed a sigh of relief when they reached the shed, and then almost jumped out of his skin when a shadow stepped from behind the shed.

It was a blessing that his hands were occupied — otherwise, he would've struck out blindly, before the figure said in an uncertain voice, "Dad?"

"Yes honey," Maksim answered.

Valentin's crate clanged to the ground. "You could've warned me."

"I'm early," the shadow figure said. "I was supposed to be here tomorrow, but I finished classes early, so I caught an early train."

In the dim light, Valentin was barely able to make out a face — a sharp chin, jutting bangs, a curve of a young cheek. "Your daughter?"

"Estranged daughter," she said with some emotion. "From St. Petersburg."

"Alisa," Maksim added.

Valentin didn't pry; other people's affairs interested him little, and he considered questions impolite, especially if they touched on such intimate topics as family and children. So instead he just nodded to Alisa and assumed that she would join them in their bunker. "Hope you like condensed milk," he said after they settled the crates inside the shed, and Alisa had a chance to appreciate the abundance.

"Now what?" she said.

"Now, home," Maksim said. "Tomorrow night, we're getting the heavy artillery."

Alisa nodded – apparently, her father already had told her about the museum. "I'll come with you," she said.

"All right." Maksim extended his hand, shook Valentin's. "See you tomorrow." He and his sudden daughter walked to the bus stop, while Valentin sighed and hoofed it back to the University metro station.

VALENTIN HAD ALWAYS had an ambivalent relationship with viruses: they were the worst of those pseudo-Zen koans, not really alive and not really dead. Finding a virus that could turn people into something like itself was both terrifying and a little thrilling, and Valentin couldn't help but get occasionally carried away, as the new bits of code came off the sequencer, and Maksim searched the databases for closest matches.

The samples Dobrenko gave them were all heat-killed, harmless, but still they worked with every Level 2 precaution. He couldn't help but wonder where the live specimens were kept, and how long it would take before they escaped. If there was one thing Valentin learned in his scientific career, it was that pathogens can never be contained. No matter how cunning the facilities and the locks, no matter what precautions, every microscopic life form would eventually break out of its confinement and run through the streets, chasing the shrieking throngs. He guessed that that moment wasn't too far off: newspapers wrote about contamination of produce with *E. coli*, necessitating the cordons all around Moscow. No one but the military had left or entered the city in the past week or so. Everyone complained about lack of eggplants in the market.

Maksim wandered over to Valentin's bench, to peek at the long strip of paper coming off the sequencer like a seismogram, with four colored lines, flailing up and down into peaks and valleys. "Pretty A-T heavy, huh."

"Yeah. What artillery did you have in mind?"

"I told you, a friend of mine is a museum guard. About to retire, so he doesn't give a shit. And they have a nice collection of old military technology. We can find what we need and walk away with it."

"So nothing too heavy."

"Or at least nothing without wheels."

"Your daughter...she can handle all this?"

Maksim nodded. "Yep. Bright kid, studies engineering in St Petersburg's University. Computer networks and all this jazz. She's certainly better at new technology than we are."

"We don't have new technology. Don't need it — what are we going to do, launch rockets from your laptop?"

"Do you mind?"

Valentin shook his head, then laughed. "Sorry. I just argue sometimes."

That night after work, they went to scope out the museum Maksim had been talking about. This time, they didn't have to walk too far. The museum was located near the metro station, a small building that looked like it was meant to be the part of the university but fell by the wayside somehow, and became one of those small, dinky museums that served as depositories of random specimens and donated junk no one had the heart to throw out. This one seemed to have received its fair share of WW2 relics, uniforms and helmets and rusted Katyusha shells sleeping under the glass. Most people clustered in the wing that had exhibited some porcelain dolls — Valentin thought with dismay that unless the exhibit closed soon, obtaining artillery would be difficult. He really was hoping for a sleepy, empty museum.

Alisa, who they had picked up by the metro, didn't seem impressed. Valentin studied her out of the corner of his eye, and she did the same. An alien, a small sharp-elbowed alien with a sagging backpack on her shoulder, barely covered by a shredded shirt. She seemed a bird with her ruthless bright eyes. "I want to see the dolls," she told her father.

"Go for it." He slipped a folded hundred into her hand and she sauntered off, in the direction of human voices and soft music, and flashing of the theoretically prohibited cameras.

They wandered away, into the cavernous halls with the dangerously apathetic military technology. "Whoa," Maksim said, and pointed.

It was an entire T34, sitting, uncovered by glass or any other impediments, in a shallow niche. Far as tanks went, this was a lightweight, but maneuverable. "How are we supposed to get it out?" Valentin said.

"I used to drive one," Maksim said. "I think I probably still can."

"It's a tank," Valentin said.

"Precisely." The tone of his voice was not unusual, but the subtle setting of the jaw told Valentin that Maksim would accept nothing less.

"You have your heart set on it?"

Maxim nodded. "I doubt there will be anything better."

"Or more conspicuous."

When they left the museum, Maksim whispered into Alisa's ear, urgent. In response, Alisa only jerked her shoulder, not bothering to hide her distaste for the proceedings. Contemptuous, like her entire generation. Kids were such shit these days.

A sudden sound interrupted Valentin's fuming. A low, throbbing cry came from somewhere up ahead, at the entrance to the metro station. A small knot of people snagged at something, thickening and wrapping, and growing around the invisible epicenter from which the cry came. A drunk or an epileptic, Valentin thought.

"A woman's not feeling well." Some busybody whispered to Valentin, and went back to rising on tiptoes and craning his neck.

"No reason to hold everything up," Valentin said, and pushed ahead, his shoulder habitually plowing through the crowd.

He didn't have to push too hard: to his surprise, the crowd opened up around the alleged sick woman, as people stepped back. The woman in question, still thin and young-looking despite graying curls, wailed, but without much volume or enthusiasm, her cries interrupted by sobs like hiccups. She bent over, her arms raised behind her back, as if in some bizarre game of the airplane. She tottered a little, as if one of her heels had come detached, and then clutched a bloodied hand to her chest. Only then did Valentin notice that her temple was bleeding too – heavy black drops oozed from two semicircles imprinted just above her ear.

The onlookers hushed, a thing unusual in itself, a the woman continued to sob and grunt, and each sound grew more inhuman as she went. The sounds stopped eventually, the silence as alien to the usual thrum of the crowd as the stillness. *It would make more sense if it was snowing.* Valentin shook his head to chase away an unbidden thought. *Someone ought to do something.*

One of the onlookers who watched the woman with the same

blank intensity as the rest of them, took a step toward her, reaching out with his knobby, sinewy hands — Valentin noticed these hands before everything else, the concave face and too-short jacket sleeves, peeling threads on the checkered cuffs of the shirt. One of the knuckles bore a bright crescent mark, slowly seeping blood. For a moment, Valentin was relieved that someone had stepped up so he wouldn't have to, but the man in the checkered shirt and old jacket growled and grabbed at the woman, his jaws opening wide. Before a few men in the crowd had a chance to step up, he bit the woman in the face, his face blank all the while.

A few people gasped, a few backed away.

"What is it?" Alisa hissed into his ear.

"I...I don't know." Valentin looked over his shoulder, seeking Maksim's input.

He wasn't far behind. "Shit. This doesn't look like anything..."

"I know," Valentin said. "Do you think...?"

Maksim took a step back, tugging Alisa's sleeve. She followed him, too scared to get an attitude. "I think," Maksim said, "that the farther we get away from this, the better."

EPIDEMICS WERE A bit of Valentin's hobbyhorse. The one that unfolded — no, unfurled violently, like a ribbon in a hurricane — was perhaps the quickest. From the speed and the intensity of it, Valentin guessed that Dobrenko either lied or didn't really know that the virus has crossed the border some time ago: the cordons around Moscow must've held back the tide for quite a while. It was like a dam: once breached, the accumulated weight behind it barreled down, and everyone wondered where it came from. They barely had time to return to the museum, and already the streets thronged with the confused and the overcome. The infected attacked the living, violently, savagely, and Valentin had to look away more than once from a person screaming, clutching a bloodied appendage. He kept his gaze firmly up, never daring to look down on the pavement where bones crunched and unspeakable things happened.

If Valentin was inclined to see the positives at the moment, he would've been pleased with how easy it was to start a tank and drive it out of the museum, wrecking the stairs and slightly widening the side entrance in the process. Really, the tank was the least problematic thing in these streets, and his mind went to the late summer of 1990, where tanks in the streets were shocking and threatening. It felt strange to crouch inside of one, seeing just narrow snatches of the unpleasantness through the viewfinder.

Once they reached the bunker (T34 was surprisingly nimble on the service stairs), Valentin surveyed their stockpile. He was glad that they'd invested in less esoteric cans than thirty-year-old pork, and drinking water wouldn't be a problem. The shed itself was small, but the adjacent service tunnel was dark and cozy, and even the light of their industrial flashlights did little to chase away the velvety darkness. It did, however, snatch the outline of the railroad ties, piled high and ready to be deployed to whatever track construction needed them, covered in yards of canvas.

"We could build a nice tent with this," Valentin said.

"Housing is the least of my worries," Alisa said. "In case you didn't notice, there are hordes of zombies in the streets. Violent ones. Did you see them maul that woman?"

Belatedly, Valentin felt bad for the girl. "How're you holding up?"

She barked a short, hysterical laugh. "Great. Fantastic. Probably not as badly as I would be if my whole life didn't teach me to expect a zombie apocalypse – thank you, Hollywood. But my point is, it also taught me that zombies always show up, and you always run out of ammunition or have to sleep, or have a weak point in your defenses."

"So what are you suggesting?"

She crouched on the floor of the tunnel, her oversized backpack pooled at her feet. From it, she started pulling dull pieces of metal, and flat aluminum circuit boards with wires soldered on. "Believe it or not, I specialize in AI. This is my thesis project – a simple command relay, but it'll do. You can put it on the tank, and it will perform a routine by itself."

"Like a remote controlled car," Maksim said.

Alisa rolled her eyes. "No, Dad. There is no remote control. More like a Roomba. A Roomba with a big cannon. It'll eventually learn where it needs to spend more time, to protect the perimeter. You know, like a real Roomba with cat hair."

Valentin nodded. "If you can do that…that would be helpful. There's an electric outlet in the shed if you need it. We stockpiled some diesel, but will probably need to get more after a week or so. Meanwhile, however, I guess keeping watch is up to us."

They left the girl to dig around in T34's metal innards, and turned their attention to the tunnel. The service tunnel ended in a dead end just half a kilometer past the shed, but the gaping mouth of it presented a problem: it led to the main tunnel and to the service stairs. The main tunnel was closed to the train traffic for the construction (it was eerily silent now, without the sound of the trains rambling past in parallel tunnels), but it was densely populated by construction equipment and, Valentin assumed, construction workers. Who may or may not still be there, and who may be affected by the plague taking place above. Valentin didn't want to think about the possibility of either himself or Maksim having been exposed – they took the subway every day, just like everyone else. Who knew when and how this outbreak had started? He wondered if Dobrenko was able to find more cooperative virologists; he even remembered a weird piece of scientific lore – the one that told of some institute in Chukotka, which was subsequently bombed to contain some horrifying outbreak. That was a while ago though; unlikely that a pathogen would survive for that long.

"We should probably build a barricade," Maksim said. "While Alisa's working on the tank."

They spent the rest of the day heaving the railroad ties and segments of old tracks into piles blocking the main tunnel, and a smaller one by the service stairs. The light of the miners' helmets lights was pale and uneven, and the shadows stretched long and menacing, snaked down the tunnel and disappeared into the silence, too dead to acknowledge. They spoke in hushed whispers, not so much out of fear of attracting attention but out of childhood superstition before the darkness. They positioned the metal tracks so that they protruded outward, to discourage any assault by the machinery. They only left a passage wide enough for the T34, and blocked it with a loose but formidable looking heap of ties and broken stone. They made sure that merely yanking the main weight-bearing tie would bring the whole section down, to a pile of rubble caterpillar tracks would have no trouble going over.

Valentin wasn't sure what time it was when the barricade was finished – wobbly and unwieldy, and hastily constructed, but solid enough to take cover behind. There were a few openings in between the railroad ties, big enough to take aim.

"I guess this is where we'll be sleeping tonight," Maksim said.

Alisa fell asleep on the pile of tents, wrapped in a ratty camelhair blanket. Maksim and Valentin picked out a couple of tent ponchos, that smelled reassuringly of canvas and mildew. Both were too tired to use the hotplate, and instead they punctured cans of condensed milk with bayonet knives, and drank the sickeningly sweet mass through the triangular holes. If it wasn't for the starless sky and the smells of creosote, Valentin could've believed that he was still in the army. Although he didn't feel eighteen, and the twinges in his back told him that he would pay dearly tomorrow.

"It's amazing how some things never go away." Maksim was done with his condensed milk, and busied himself with disassembling of his Kalashnikov. He laid out all the parts in the narrow beam of his miner's light, textbook and meticulous. "I haven't touched one of these since 1986, and yet I recognize the pin and the magazine, and I know where everything goes. I couldn't tell you – my brain couldn't – but my hands just know."

Valentin nodded, and laid his Kalashnikov next to him, within an easy reach. "I remember those drills. We had to do it over and over until we fell asleep from the exhaustion and then we did it in our sleep."

"Yeah."

He wanted to sleep desperately, but even as his eyelids grew heavy, he reached over for the Kalashnikov, and made sure that the firing mechanism moved smoothly, and that the magazine was attached straight. "Nothing worse than a jammed magazine," he mumbled, and was asleep before he heard Maksim's answer.

A NOISE WOKE him: it took him a second to remember where he was, and the absurdity of the situation startled him like a glass of cold water in the face. Maksim shifted in the darkness – a distinct scrape of metal against wood and cinder block, but the sound that woke Valentin continued from the other side of the barricade, a quiet but persistent scratching and shuffling.

"Who's there?" Valentin called, barely raising his voice above the whisper.

The noise continued.

He flipped on his miner's light, half hoping to see a rat or a stray dog, which were not unknown in the bowels of the metro. The sharp beam snatched the railroad ties close to his face, and the opening into the profound darkness of the tunnel beyond – and an outline of a human head, just beyond the embrasure.

He took aim. "Who's there?" Louder, now.

Maksim's light flicked on, and the two crossing beams snatched out enough detail of the stranger. It seemed to be one of the railroad workers, the blue serge of his work shirt torn and splattered with mud, his face blue and swollen and decidedly not alive. The eyes shone dully in the light, without a glimmer of intelligence – or discomfort at the sudden stimulation.

"Hello," Maksim called softly. The man behind the barricade swiveled his head as if looking for the source of the sound, and continued his uncertain scraping at the barricade.

"It's not alive," Valentin reminded softly.

Maksim responded with a single shot from his Kalashnikov. The figure on the other side stumbled and staggered back into the tunnel, its face obscured by the slow dripping black liquid. They could no longer see it, but a soft thump reassured them soon enough.

"You think it's dead? I mean, really?" Valentin asked.

Maksim shrugged. "If a shot to a head doesn't kill it, I don't know what does."

"What if nothing does?"

Maksim flicked off his light. "Go to sleep. I'll watch for a while. I'll wake you when I'm tired."

Valentin closed his eyes. They could stay like this forever, he thought, waking each other up and going to sleep when tired, a constant unbroken circle of "Good morning" and "Good night," in the perpetual darkness of the underground. This life of conditional waking and sleeping cycles, predicated on living out of phase with his co-worker and, Valentin suspected, friend, held a degree of appeal.

He smiled in the darkness then, and slept until a sharp jab in the ribs woke him.

"There're more of them," Maksim hissed.

Valentin bolted awake, flipped on his light. "More" was an understatement: the tunnel was alive with heaving flesh, the smell of unclean wounds and rotting teeth stronger than creosote. He flipped Kalashnikov to automatic fire, and took aim.

Maksim did the same, and for a while Valentin went deaf and blind from the gunfire, as it resonated off the roof of the tunnel.

A few of the attackers fell — all railroad workers, as far as Valentin could see — but more kept pressing from behind them.

"Get out of the way!" Alisa's voice cut through the moment the fire stopped.

Valentin looked back and saw the girl running toward them, next to the tank that was rolling slowly under its own power.

"Get the tie," Maksim yelled.

The two of them managed to wrench the weight bearing tie free, and rolled out of the way as the tank hobbled over the rubble, leisurely, lopsidedly, and met the approaching wall of shambling apparitions. It was like watching an invisible child play with a toy tank — *vroom vroom*, back and forth, as it rolled over the workers, crushing, until there was nothing left to crash.

"Nice job," Maksim shouted to Alisa.

She smiled just as the tank turned and headed back over the barricade. Valentin moved away to give it berth but the tank went after him.

"Climb!" he yelled, before climbing higher over the beams.

The tank attempted to follow, then turned its attention to Alisa and Maksim.

Maksim turned to Alisa. "Can you disable it?"

"Yes! Just let it chase you!"

Maksim took off running down the service tunnel, and the tank followed. Alisa trotted behind, until she was able to grab onto the protruding part of the armor. Valentin followed, not too close but close enough to see. She climbed atop it, and then into the turret.

Valentin realized that Maksim was running into the dead end, and would reach it soon. There wasn't much space there for him to avoid the lumbering thing, and he prepared to distract the tank's attention if necessary. "Hey, tank," he called out as a test.

The tank stopped just as Maksim reached the wall of the tunnel.

"What was that?" He yelled at Alisa as soon as she emerged from the turret, red and panting.

"It's still learning." She sat on the caterpillar track, sullen, feet in black sneakers dangling. "I guess I could tweak it some more."

Valentin and Maksim returned to the barricade. Both were too tired to fix the collapsed section.

"You go to sleep," Valentin said. "I'll keep watch for a while."

After a few hours, the darkness grew irritating: whether he closed or opened his eyes, the view was the same, and every little sound, every whispering of the breeze, every echo of an echo, grew magnified and startled him. He wondered if Alisa had gotten any sleep, back there, in the safety of the blunt side tunnel. He decided to check on her.

She was not asleep – in fact, she looked as if she barely slept at all. Her miner's light snatched bits of metal lying on the ground, and her massive backpack lay open, spilling out the soldering irons and other implements of technology Valentin had no interest in.

He waited for her light to arc through the air in his direction, not to startle her with a sudden sound of his voice. "How's it going?" he said.

"Okay," she answered. The fatigue seemed to have drained most of her attitude, and her voice was small and hollow. "Almost done. Are there any more of those things?"

"Don't worry," Valentin said, mustering up what he hoped was a paternal tone of voice. "If there are more, we'll deal with them."

Alisa glowered at him. "I'm not afraid. I just need one of them, alive, for the T34 to learn to recognize them. You know, differentiation between a person and a zombie."

"That would be useful. How would it do that?"

"Temperature sensors," she answered. "I just installed them. But I also want it to recognize the moving patterns. If you see one, don't kill it yet; just wait until I'm finished here. Also, I named it Timka – T34 is too generic."

"All right then. I should probably go keep an eye on your dad," Valentin said. "When he wakes up, I'll go get you a zombie."

He shuffled back to the barricade, the taste of his words in his mouth. If it wasn't for the ridiculousness of the last word, it would've sounded so paternal, so domestic. Don't worry, little one, dad will go out and get you a toy. Not something he ever thought he would say, but the words felt right, appropriate even.

Maksim waited for him, awake.

"Alisa's fine," Valentin said. "You better tell her to eat or sleep or rest. She looks like a stray cat."

Maksim nodded. "She's a smart kid, but doesn't know when to stop. In high school, we had to turn off the lights and confiscate her flashlights to get her to stop studying. Imagine that? A seventeen-year-old kid wanting nothing more than to study engineering and to solder integrated circuits?"

"Better than the alternative," Valentin said. "Listen, take care of your kid, okay? I'll go to the surface. She said she needed a zombie to train the tank on, and I think it'll be easy enough to grab one."

"Be careful," Maksim said. "Do we think there's a chance it's airborne?"

Valentin shrugged. "It spreads fast, but with all the biting…and since none of us got it, I think it's likely fluids. But who knows, Dobrenko could've mucked it up some."

"Should I come along?"

Valentin shook his head. "And leave Alisa here? No, you stay."

"Be safe," Maksim said. "Don't let anything bite you." He didn't need to be persuaded, and Valentin appreciated that. There was nothing more tedious than pretend politeness, and back and forth and no, you take the last piece, I am fine. It was obvious who should stay behind, and Maksim had the good grace to not argue.

Valentin gathered his Kalashnikov and ammunition, ropes, metal clamps, thick gloves. He packed it all into the green gas mask bag. He had forgotten to wind his watch (the one that said "Commander's Watch," and was waterproof and weighed at least a quarter kilo), so he had no sense of what time it was. He wished they figured that part better. He crept toward the service stairs, to a small mound of shattered cinder block and half bricks Maksim and he had hastily piled up to create an illusion of blockage, meant to dissuade rather than prevent entry. He climbed over the pile, loose debris shifting under his feet.

As he reached the bottom of the stairs, he turned off the light as a precaution, and pushed the door open, just a crack.

It was twilight outside, with pale scattering of stars just starting to manifest above the stairwell. The moon was still hidden, and long gray wisps of clouds stretched across the sky. The breeze rose and fell, like a sigh, and Valentin breathed in, closing his eyes without meaning to. Then he wished he'd brought a gas mask.

He shook his head and climbed the stairs, the Kalashnikov's muzzle resting on his shoulder, its butt snuggled into his cupped hand. He peered cautiously over the top of the stairwell, to see only the closed up building of the metro station nearby, and a dark outline of trees lining Komsomolsky Prospect against the sky.

There were no cars in the streets, except for a few abandoned ones, and no people. He licked his suddenly dry lips.

What did zombie hunting have in common with science? It seemed very clear and reasonable before you started it, but once you did you realized that you had no idea of how to frame the question, what would be the best design, what sort of problems would likely arise, and so you blundered through halfheartedly until you made your first mistake and changed tack, circling around your definitions and gradually figuring it out.

He walked down Komsomolsky Prospect, toward the University. He was reluctant to venture too far, and felt for the securely looped rope in the bag on his shoulder, realizing that perhaps capturing a zombie would not be as easy as he thought. You couldn't knock them out. Just hope to tie them up and drag them along, staying clear of their bites. A gag would be nice. He hated himself for hoping to find a child.

There was a slow, gurgling growl to his left and he spun, Kalashnikov aimed before he had a chance to consider using it. Two women clung to each other as they moved toward him.

"Ma'am?" he said. "Are you all right?"

A stupid question. One of the women seemed intact, save for her broken heels and matted hair, but the other one had a ruined face, part of her nose and cheek missing, the hinge of her jaws moving visibly under the thin veneer of crusted tissue as she made the same growling sound.

He stepped back, taking aim at the growling woman's head. One would do, he thought, two would not be manageable.

She turned then, showing the undamaged half of her face. Lida Belaya, the one who sang to her thermocycler.

He shouldn't have been surprised: what were the chances that she would survive? Where else would she die but at work, in the lab, probably still singing?

"Poor songbird," he whispered and squeezed the trigger. There was no point in pity; it was only a matter of time.

As Lida fell, he swung the butt of his Kalashnikov's at the other woman's head. She spun and fell, and he was on her, his knee planted in the small of her back, twisting her hands behind her. The rope came out, miraculously untangled, and he looped it around the dead woman's wrists and arms, as she hissed and kicked and tried to scratch.

Her arms tied up behind her securely, she stopped struggling and lay still. Valentin jerked her to her feet, holding her elbow, pushing her in front of him. Kalashnikov was jammed awkwardly under his arm, and he hoped that his trek back to the station would be brief enough to not require additional shooting.

The station was in sight, and he hastened his step, pushing the woman in front of him faster. She stumbled and fell forward; he grabbed her elbows, trying to keep her upright, but she jerked, pulled forward, and her left arm came undone — popped out of the socket and the bones tore through her flesh, the white of her blouse filling instantly with black blood. With only one arm holding her, she turned around, blundered into Valentin, and he felt her teeth closing just above his elbow.

He hit her with the butt of his Kalashnikov, sending her sprawling to the ground. Before she could get up, he shot her in the head. Really, there was no need for more than one zombie; he only needed enough time to explain. He tied a rope above the bite, pulled it tight with his teeth. This should buy him a few minutes — he hoped.

VALENTIN HOBBLED THROUGH the dark tunnel, checking his thoughts every few seconds. As long as he thought and remembered his thoughts, he was alive, and as soon as he couldn't remember, it would stop mattering. He thought about what was happening in other countries — if people there waited for their government to save them, if they were delusional enough to think that governments had their back. He had an advantage, he thought, of learning when he was eighteen that the government would not save him, but do just the opposite. He hoped that Maksim remembered it too — remembered where he was sent when he was younger than his daughter was now.

He listened to the metallic grinding behind his back — Timka, a tank, was learning now, like a kitten stalking a mouse hobbled by its loving mother. Valentin picked up his step. If Maksim learned the same lessons as Valentin, he knew of course that it was just a matter of time and there would be no salvation. He and his daughter could hope to live just a little bit longer. To maybe say things they had to say. Maybe he would explain to Alisa then — who really was of the wrong generation to actually understand these things — that Valentin didn't sacrifice anything. In fact, he was given a rare luxury — to choose his fate, something none of them had been able to do until now.

Valentin picked up his pace, even as his legs grew cold and leaden, and his thoughts dimmed and scattered. Behind him, the tank rumbled, and before he crumpled to the ground, he felt a brief wave of gratitude at the sense of relief that washed over him, and at the soft whispering of caterpillar tracks, fading into an indistinct lull.

THE MEEK, THE EARTH, AND THE INHERITANCE

Rain Graves

OCTOBER, 2021.

Jasper Tuttle scanned the headlines once again, looking for a new reason to be angry:

LUXURY BUNKER HOME SALES AT ALL-TIME LOW SINCE 2013

KIRTLAND BUILDS A BETTER YOU: WHY ROBOTS ARE US

SOVIET TERRORISTS TAKE US ASTRONAUT RIDE MONEY; SPACE HOSTAGES

NEW DOOMSDAY PROPHECY: WHY THE MATH WAS WRONG

DIRE CDC WARNING: "ZOMBIE-LIKE" SUPERVIRUS COULD BE HERE TO STAY

BULK MEDICAL MARIJUANA DISTRIBUTION: WHY YOUR HIGH IS SO LOW

WARBOT PRODUCTION CONTROVERSY: ARE THEY CREATING JOBS OR TAKING THEM?

He was agitated; uncomfortable. The calls had stopped coming in since his early retirement from MedTech, the biomedical research firm he'd started as a Harvard graduate with three of his closest friends.

David, Alice, and Pradeep had all bought into the missile silo cluster in Livermore, California, shortly before the beginning of 2012. Doomsday fever had been on everyone's mind – sparse bunkers hastily furnished with luxurious modern appliances, sleeper sofas, and genetically engineered greenery that flourished without photosynthesis – a modern marvel of the Era of Fear.

Jasper had bought into it, and was not sorry. Unabashed at the price, his survival instincts had taken over and he knew it was necessary to create an underground community of useful, intelligent people, should the worst-case scenario happen...Lately he'd been rethinking, however, as the government found new ways to tax their underground homes. There was no regard for square footage, natural resources, or even a lack of minerals for mineral rights.

It didn't matter if your bunker was hidden beneath an Indian Reservation; that was above ground. The bunker was under, and not under tribal jurisdiction. Some of the better lawyers had fought against the hikes, and some were still fighting. Others just gave up and took a loss.

His Leftist view was beginning to creep right. The technologist in him wanted to see warbot production rise, since the docbots had become so promising to human teams in medical research and implementation. As an engineer, he did consulting at Kirtland Munitions Storage Complex in New Mexico, and marveled at the work Throckmorton, Winterbottom, and Satterfield had accomplished in such a short time.

The research, of course, had been done all along in secret, for decades. But those documents were still classified, and as far as Jasper was concerned, they didn't really need to be released. No one needed to know how many monkeys and pigs had been brutalized and maimed as practice subjects for the docbots performance evaluations.

Still, something wasn't sitting well in Jasper's gut. There was more going on at Kirtland than anyone could guess, and the underground community was beginning to talk about it.

He'd only glimpsed aspects of the Gateway specs through his clearance documents, but even those were cryptic at best, when it came to understanding what was actually being built. All he knew was it was in pieces – four separately engineered pieces – that utilized the same technology to fuse a whole. Ever since the completion, his services were no longer required. The calls from Kirtland and the scientists he'd worked with had stopped.

No one had shown up at his door to put a bullet in his brain either, which told him something was wrong. Very wrong. He'd been prepared for that. He hadn't prepared for...nothing.

The underground community was buzzing. Stockpiles of weapons, technology supplies, raw materials, and non-perishable foods were being hoarded. Purification water tanks had given way to a brilliant new system of controlled underground water mains connected to California's Hetch Hetchy source. They siphoned just enough not to alert above-ground authorities and their monitoring of power and energy consumption, by altering the collection of additional rainfall from the global warming tracking system.

Those precious extra inches were diverted through specifically engineered pipe and tunnel systems, laid out in secret by the best minds in Silicon Valley. Northern and Southern California's underground water supply was secure, with plans for co-op with Oregon and Washington in case of drought.

Eventually, they would be connecting these tunnel systems all across the United States, to every cluster and underground homestead mapped on the bunker grid. Plans were underway to build trans-ocean pipelines for travel and communications with other countries.

The underground had its own makeshift government and law system springing up. Everyone was feeling pretty good about things — they were smarter than the government. But not smarter than Kirtland scientists.

The severing of ties, with not just Jasper but *everyone* below, was a warning not to be taken lightly. No one in the Livermore cluster had been above ground in over a month. News feeds were coming in, but nothing was going out. They were going off the radar and seceding from the Union. And no one *cared*.

"What are you reading?" Monica asked Jasper.

"Same old shit," said Jasper.

"Was there any —" She started to speak, but Jasper interrupted.

"— mention of us? Of the clusters? Not really. The stories we planted worked like a charm. No new applications for bunkers since 2013, and that means our expansion rate number is still going to work."

"I suppose that's good news. But what about Kirtland?" she said.

"Not a blip. We're orphans, it would seem. Oh, that reminds me, are you pregnant yet?" he joked.

"No, but I'm sure we'll have our little evil genius soon," she smiled.

"Evil? We only use our powers for good! His brain...will be magnificent! A marvel to behold!"

This time, Monica interrupted him. "Okay, okay. Stop speaking comic-book, and help me fix the air filter in the flow unit. Will you?"

"Sure," he grinned, and followed her to the bunker's machine-room.

"Jasper," she hesitated before opening the air-flow converter box, "do you ever get the feeling we've been here before? You know, like déjà vu?" He gave her a blank look.

"No. We are the future, after all. How can we have been here before?"

"Just wondering," she shivered, and helped him lift the filter out.

"Besides," he said, "you are a scientist. You don't believe in hocus-pocus, remember?"

"Right. No hocus-pocus. Or religious cults. Or negative effects of cloning...or non-government-sanctioned bent prions...or...FDA recognition of processed cheese as a viable source of nutrition...or –"

"Hey! Leave my petroleum-based cheese foodstuffs alone!" he laughed.

But cheese would not leave Jasper's mind. Melting cheese, specifically. The creamy, runny, odd-looking substance reminded him of monkey brains, post aquatic electrocution. Except for the color. The greenish color of steamed brain always put him off. He wondered how the docbots were doing, and if they had completed programming on the protocol for saving the human race, should it ever be in danger of extinction.

He decided to try and connect with Pradeep while he was working under Bangalore via telegraph when India woke up. Pradeep would know how that story ended. He'd been the lead on the project, ten years ago, and they often talked about their conjunctive work when it was clear no one was listening. They couldn't get the telegraph signal above ground, as it was amplified on a "hum" frequency, much to the pain and discomfort of some humans above that could actually *hear* it.

Lucky for the cluster community, they all thought it was a government conspiracy or some alien message coming from the earth's core. And they were right. Sort of.

"Better turn in early tonight, Monica. I've got a lot of work to do on the pipeline blueprints tomorrow. What's for dinner?" Jasper said.

"Same thing as last night. Pineapple Spam Delight…" she snarked.

"Isn't there an anagram for that?" he winced.

"A Happened Piglet's Limp," she said.

"Limping piglet, it is…" He groaned.

Piglets. Thousands and thousands of them, born and bred never to feel the touch of gentle human hands…only to be poked, prodded, bashed, drawn and quartered, dissected, dismembered, and farmed for the medical parts useful to science. All that wasted flesh. *So like them, we are,* Jasper thought, as the sickly scent of sizzling canned meat soon filled their modest domicile of titanium and steel.

"Pigs in a can," he muttered, sitting down to eat.

"What's that?" Monica said.

"Oh, nothing…" he said.

And then he ate.

July, Decades Later.

Nothing had ever gone as planned, Jasper thought, scanning the headlines:

Is the Gateway Dead? Or Just Sleeping?

Bad Radiation, Schmad Radiation: Healing with Harrow

New Marijuana Clones and Your Mutation Management

Zombie Blood and The Underground Cockroach: The Host, The Carrier, And You

Water-link Wars: Armored Sewage Tunnel Rights Distribution

Kirtland-Chang Progress is Regress; Reaping What We've Sewn

How To Kill A Zombie Quickly with Limited Arms and Ammunition

Hacking into the New Mexico Territory mainframe had been easy. It was reading the knowledge stored within that had been hard. Fritz Winterbottom, in all his egotism, kept accurate notes up to a point.

Satterfield had been such a disappointment to the cluster community on whole; his research ended abruptly. It was presumed he went through the Gateway, and never returned. By Herbert Throckmorton's log, both had perished during the process of time travel…a desperate effort to put right what massive wrong they'd done, when the superbug went global.

It had been such a rampant epidemic that science could not conjure the time to cure, and the instant infection rate had soared. The lackluster bot analysis post-nuclear fallout was even more disheartening.

It was more important than ever to keep the cluster community a secret. If the bots knew, they didn't seem to care. They weren't much of a threat, since no one wanted to go above ground. But supplies were dwindling…it was in every editorial opinion column he read on the Undernet, a revived sort of Intranet jimmied on cable fiber-optics, on a separate network and mainframe than above.

Above, they used old satellite technology to communicate more instantaneously, and to specific bots in the field. The Undernet existed only to inform the people still alive underground.

Unforeseen problems had developed in recent years. Nuclear runoff was seeping into the ground water, which meant it seeped into the siphons at all locations, worldwide. Even the Chinese were freaking out, and they never freaked out.

Reports of mutations were everywhere – babies being born with two heads. Rats with six legs and grotesquely mottled bellies, like something out of an ancient Geiger painting. The roaches were bigger, and more verbal. They made…*sounds*. Gurgles. Hissing that sounded like words, or names. Where they went, the snakes and spiders fled. Life was getting *difficult*.

Jasper wasn't sure if it was a blessing or an ironic cosmic joke, but robotkind above were everywhere, and didn't really give a damn about human life, despite their programming to preserve it.

There had been attempts to breach hatches and capture a few docbots, but severing the link from above, reprogramming, and having them prove useful were separate problems that the aging robotics engineers could not solve. The originals built on a Linux platform were easy to adapt, but anything operating on Microsoft technology was notoriously incompatible with prior versions of its own platform. Modifications were made with Linux, and work-arounds were jerry-rigged for the upgrades to the others to get them talking to each other on one mainframe server.

Most of them just sat in corners, gathering rust, when the engineers got bored, in favor of blueprints for a newer, improved docbot, with the eco-naught elitists in mind. The clusters, as usual, were on their own. Only now they needed help. It was both smug and desperate, the needing.

The vast community of superior intelligence, compiled by way of capitalistic buy-in, each and every one "in the know" purchasing themselves into a bunker and helping to build a better, stronger, smarter human race, could not get past one unforeseen problem of plague: zombies.

No one had seen a zombie below…therefore, it wasn't an issue. And yet the water and the radiation and the mutations and the robots and the…Well, it had all piled up, and too quickly for the community to extinguish all at once.

Jasper chuckled to himself. He'd planned a visit to the incinerator section, today, to visit Monica's ashes. German technology, at its best. He'd been able to barter her into the best columbarium under Northern California. And it was close to home. Half a day's walk, and he'd often made the detour on the way back from checking on the water-main twice as far away.

There were frequent leaks and complaints about the integrity of the old sewage tunnels up that way. Even as old as he was, he felt he could do some good and help fix what he'd helped to engineer and build. His grandson, Joey, often accompanied him when his mother needed a break. He liked to feed the stray cats in the tunnels along the way. He'd named some of them, and kept a female black Siamese named Vespa at home.

The cats seemed to keep the main tunnels free of rats and

roaches, which was fine by Jasper. Even if the snakes and spiders were still there.

He missed having pets. A pang of regret he seldom felt about living above, but dogs hadn't thrived underground. They needed places to run and jump; grass to roll in. Sun to bask in. They produced a lot more waste, and couldn't be trained to use the toilet, like cats had been.

Cat training was a cottage industry underground, and anyone working in the cloning or genetic pork farming industry needed cats to fend off mutation. One bite from mutant vermin, and a crop of genetic strain was ruined. Radiation was indiscriminate. There was no natural selection, and it was hard to get the genetics right. Life spans had to be altered. Size and shape. Short squatty animals with waste that could be turned into bio-fuel or used in the incinerators cleanly enough were preferred. Cultivation took time. It was a tricky business.

Two years earlier, he'd taken Joey to one of the underground farms. He heaved his lunch in the corridor just as they'd opened the seal on the portal, the smell had been so bad. "You have to get used to smells like this, Joey," his grandfather had said. "They will only get worse as life goes on."

"Don't they have an air calibrator, Grandpa? You know, like at home?" Joey asked.

"Yes, but they haven't figured out, exactly, how to convert the extra methane into something we can breathe, without blowing us up," he said.

"What's methane?" Joey asked.

"Farts." Jasper said, matter-of-factly. "And their poop we convert to electricity. It's science! Do you want to be a scientist when you grow up, so you can play with farts and poop?" He smiled at Joey's twisted up nose, and watched him laugh.

"Yeah, as long as I don't have to touch it. Is it like you showed me with the battery connected to the pickle, that lights up? That would be so cool! A poop light!" He laughed and laughed at his own cleverness.

"Not quite like that, no," said Jasper, grinning.

Jasper worried about the boy's future. He worried about everyone's future…those that remained alive, underground. They were alone. It was only a matter of time before disease or dysfunction infected one community, and the next, and the next. It didn't help that the pot farms were getting more dense in the Underground. If Joey could stay out of hydroponics, and keep an interest in geochemistry, engineering, or physics...all he would need was inspiration. Jasper did his best with that, whenever the opportunity arose. He already had a brilliant aptitude and thirst for knowledge connected to anything robotic and programming related.

Two Years Later.

Above ground, in the New Mexico Territory, several scibots were processing headlines:

> The State of The Secret: How Much Do The Robots Know?
>
> Kirtland-Chang: The Silence of Science
>
> Population Control: Eliminate Preservatives or Lace The Kool-Aid?
>
> Cat Farming: Feline Friendship and Our Future
>
> Tunnel Breaches in Siberian Cluster; Reports of Illness – Zombie or Not?
>
> Annotated Genetics: Breathing Life into Recycled Death
>
> Strength in Power and Numbers: Roaches On Hamster Wheels = Electricity

"There's an anomaly in the monthly transmission," Scibot-29 announced.

"It appears to be less amusing than the others," Scibot-3 said.

"But troubling," Scibot-678-94b, said.

"A young male. Further assessment required as to condition of threat; realized or pacified. Can it be ignored?" Scibot-29 said.

"Put it on the connected feed," said Scibot-3. As soon as it was done, every scibot in the world had access to the note, which read:

> Dear God Above,
>
> My name is Joey. Grandpa always said there wasn't any such

thing as God. But he's dead now, and I figured no one else down here is trying to reach you. Mom says it's stupid. Dad spanks me whenever he finds out I've been on the Undernet...he'd be really mad if he knew I was sending you this letter. We need some help down here. People are getting sick far away, and I'm pretty sure we could use some better medicine than the pot, because the pot makes everyone laugh but they still die. Or something. Maybe you could just send me some toys. There's not much to do except study, and I'm bored. I have a cat named Vespa who is going to have kittens. I haven't given her any pot.

Sincerely,

Joey Tuttle, Age 8

PS: Some chocolate would be good too. Dad only lets Mom have it when she's PMS-ing, and I have to sneak it, and it's almost all gone. Dad gets mean sometimes. I don't like him.

PPS: Have you ever killed a zombie? I am practicing melting quarters and dimes and pennies into ammo but it never works right. Dad says the stupid politicians are to blame for worthless monetary systems unequal to the face value in metal. Is that true? What's a politician? Okay...bye.

"Threat assess, initiate." The collected scibots sputtered and squeaked.

"Threat assessed: Further research required," they said in unison.

"I will reply," said Scibot-678-94b.

"Respond in protocol," said Scibot-3.

"Agreed," they said again.

Attention: Joey Tuttle

Your transmission has been received. We require further information before we can proceed. Request initiation of viral protocol on secure network. User identity: Human Mainframe. Password: Joey8. Login Network: Undernet. Abovenet. secure.botgov.

Scibot—678—94b

Kirtland—Chang

"Your infinite future in ones and zeros."

"I have received a response," Scibot-3 said. "Sending feed."

> Dear God or Scibot or Whatever,
>   My password didn't work. :-(
>
>   Joey Tuttle

"Scibot-678-94b, what protocol were you using? Have you changed the encryption and given him access?" Scibot-3 asked. "Sorry...I'll resend."

> Attention: Joey Tuttle
>   Restart and try again. If you are still having problems connecting, try disconnecting and reconnecting your machinery.
>   Scibot-678-94b

But Joey did not send another message, and the headline feed ceased to be. Guardbot-9 was dispatched to the general location of the Northern California Cluster entrance. The maps had not been updated in some time, so it was a matter of detecting the tunnel system from above, which took some analysis of the geography and sedimentary layers. Among the overgrowth of dying foliage and toxic runoff, Guardbot-9 powered down to minimum usage, averted to sensors, and waited.

The important thing was preserving the human race, but scibots mostly observed instead of acted. They had enough problems of their own, trying to clone baby females. If Joey Tuttle, Age 8, was alive and feeding himself, there was no immediate need to collect him. Yet.

> Guardbot-9 Routine Status Report Feed: No threat detected.
> All systems normal.

JOEY STROKED VESPA'S swollen belly, and gave her an extra portion from the ration stores with her regular dinner. She was eating for five or six now. He wanted her to be happy. As she cleaned her fur and purred in his lap, he could tell that she was, and this pleased him. His favorite thing in the world was Vespa, and all the tunnel cats came in a close second. He had named them all: Buttons, One-Eye, JellyBelly, Pretty Kitty, and Bella. There were more, but he was tired and didn't feel like running through all the names before bed. Instead, he said a prayer:

"Dear Scibot-678-94b, I'm kinda mad at you. But as long as you keep my Vespa safe and her babies okay, I'll forgive you. I'm waiting to see what happens. I never got any toys or chocolate and Dad keeps yelling at us. He says it's because the leaks in the tunnels make him mad. We found a dead roach today. It was gross. Okay…goodnight.

"Also my friend Rose is missing. She went too far when she was playing in the West End, and Mom says she might have got killed or abducted. There is a underground slave trade here. I think she just got lost. Besides, how can it be a underground slave trade if we are already underground? Gotta go."

"Joey, who were you talking to?"

"No one, Mom. Just talking to Vespa," he said.

"Okay, well…get some rest. I have a long day tomorrow working on the pipeline, and your father will need your help here at home," she said.

"Okay. I love you."

"I love you too, pumpkin."

Joey had never seen a pumpkin, but he read about them in books. He didn't think he looked like a big round squashy thing, and he wasn't particularly orange. She smiled whenever she said that, though, so he figured it was a compliment, even if it didn't make any sense.

The next day was filled with uncertainty, beginning with an argument that woke Joey up. His mother was pacing the floor, angrily filling a hiking bag with supplies that would last her up to a week in the tunnels, if necessary. He'd seen this procedure before. She always anticipated a problem, however remote the possibility.

His father was arguing that she needed to take a friend – preferably an armed one – since her aim and practice with primitive nine millimeter weapons was short-distance only, and at that point, if trouble had found her, he knew she would be flustered and unable to fire quickly. That sentiment, combined with his insults on her survival skills, only infuriated her more.

Joey knew she would be okay. She'd taught him most of what he knew about the tunnels, and sometimes she helped him feed his feral cats. She wouldn't be alone; not with them. Her destination was well known. A water-main sensor station that monitored the entire region was malfunctioning, sending mixed messages to several clusters in the area that there might be a problem on a singular pipeline. It was her job to investigate, and dispatch the necessary machinery to fix any problems.

Since the additional build-outs of workbots from the older hacks were done to elicit upgrades on the old obsolete docbots and their firmware, improvements had been made in the safety of maintaining the tunnels and their resources. But pipes still froze or burst, and damp circuitry still malfunctioned in the micro-climated underground.

"You honestly think you can fix the problem? There are probably five other engineers dispatched from other, closer clusters. You are doing this to get away from me. To shirk your responsibilities at home," his father argued.

"Really? That's a good one. I suppose you married me for my advanced degree in boiling water? Considering the contributions I've made to the Underground Engineering Collective, and all the awards I've been given for advancements in Underground Hydrolics, I'd think you'd rather I was working on a problem that might prolong our lives, rather than mindless floor pacing, waiting for someone else to fix the problem...but that's what you do, isn't it? Wait for someone else to fix a problem!" she yelled.

But he slapped her quiet, as Joey entered the room, wiping the sleep from his eyes. His father had grabbed her arm, and she was cringing.

"Please – not in front of Joey."

"Or Vespa..." Joey said, as the pregnant cat coiled protectively about his legs.

"Or Vespa," his mother said quietly. He let her go. Joey frowned.

She silently grabbed her pack and left, not even bothering to shut the door. Vespa followed her into the tunnel, until neither her headlamp nor the fuzzy outline of a tail could be seen in the dim lighting the smoothly finished tunnel provided.

Joey pictured her path; the smooth reinforced walls of the thick nuclear fall-out tunnel would soon give way to a less-finished, more concrete and brick ribbing, then earthen walls with titanium support cages, and finally, ancient and crudely dug sewage tunneling. Beyond another mile would be Underground Outpost 15, Cluster Service Grid 5.

He fondly remembered visiting that station with his grandfather, a few years past. He missed Grandpa Tuttle and the long walks they would go on, several cats in tow. He missed the stories his Grandpa had about Above, and all the fancy machines, shiny and fat with information. It seemed so limitless the way he talked; so unlike how things were in Joey's world.

Things like solar energy, and anything sunny in general fascinated him. The sun was a legendary source of energy, long abandoned by the denizens of the Underground. It had been too costly in flesh to maintain the first solar panels, installed by Grandpa's friends when they first came down. As time went on, he said, they fell victim to elements and disrepair. He'd seen photos of them in books, and he longed to touch their strange, grey, glassy skin.

Joey glanced at his father, sulking after his mother, and moved forward a few steps to shut the door.

"Leave it open," his father commanded. "She might change her mind, if she knows what's good for her…and come back."

Joey fingered the worn fabric edge of the sofa, fidgeting, before going back to his room. He picked up a tablet, and turned it on, doing a meta-search on the words "Solar Energy," drinking in the bright, blue-skied photos like a sponge. In the background, he heard his father turn on the medical ionizer, and the gratingly familiar sound of the vintage video game he always played when he got stoned. As if in telepathic reproach for judging him, his father slammed the control room door shut, leaving no sounds or smells to disturb his study of the sun.

"DAD? HAVE YOU seen my cat?" Joey asked.

"Which one? Don't you have a million?" His father said.

"Vespa…the pregnant one. I haven't seen her since…" Joey could tell his father wasn't in the mood to talk, but he had to know. "…since she followed Mom to work."

"Then she's probably dead. Just like your mother…for all I care."
His father shot him a biting look. Joey's eyes welled up and he yelled,
"Don't say that! You don't know! She's probably still working and
fixing the problem YOU wouldn't let her fix. It's probably a bigger
problem because of you!"

He ran back to his room, angry and trying hard not to cry. His
father told him crying made men weak, and he didn't want to be weak.
He was feeling very lonely. It wasn't just Vespa and his Mother that
had gone missing; many of the tunnel cats he used to feed had also
disappeared, and the untouched food he'd left for them was beginning
to attract vermin.

He had to clean it up, when they failed to come when he called.
The snakes and spiders also seemed thin; not even the little sewage
skates could be seen in the damper, lesser-maintained tunnels close to
home.

He stopped at other doors in the cluster, asking them if they'd seen
or heard from his mother or his cat. This took some effort, as each
door was spaced very far apart, giving each family ample privacy. A
full day might involve four doors in the fifteen domicile cluster, and
after two days searching, she'd been gone eight days. She would be hungry. So would Vespa.

To his dismay, his father didn't seem to care. He was smoking a lot
of pot in the control room, locking Joey out. He would pass out, reek-
ing of skunk and Beast Berries, a sort of moonshine. The smell of it
made Joey dry heave – anyone who drank stuff made from the egg
sacs of sewer spiders was beyond sanity.

He could see his father sneaking out at night with two of his friends
to harvest them, coming back with a small jar full of white stuff in the
morning.

How many men does it take to catch a spider? The other boys would
joke. Joey didn't know. He never stuck around long enough to hear
the end of it, because he knew they were making fun of his father.

His thoughts returned to Vespa and his missing mother as he
returned home again. One thing was certain: concern was mounting.
Others had not returned from their expeditions, and he faced a lot of
tight lips and worried eyes – neither symptom seemed to indicate con-
fidence in the words, "Oh, I'm sure she'll be home soon…don't worry

too much about it." If they had any communication with the outposts monitoring things above ground, and what may have happened to the missing underground, they weren't telling him. Could she have been kidnapped? Was she sick and in need of help? His anxiety began to paint wild pictures of old movie monsters picking her up with terrible hands, screams echoing down the dark tunnels, into a blanket of black doom.

When he opened the door to his home, he saw the lights were dim, and couldn't adjust them with the switch. The generator must be on the blink again, he thought. The door to the control room was shut, and though he knocked and called to his father, no answer came from within.

The door to his room was cracked open, and he didn't remember leaving it that way. A sense of dread came over him as he approached it, hoping his father hadn't gone through his Undernet logs. Nothing was amiss, however, and he decided to connect again. Maybe Scibot-678-94b could help him find his mother. It was worth a try.

> Dear Scibot-678-94b,
>   This is Joey again. I was mad at you but I'm not any more. My mother went into the tunnels to fix a problem at Outpost 15, Service Grid 5. She's not back yet and her food must have run out. Can you help me find her? Others are missing too. And lots of my cats. I am mostly worried about Vespa because she's going to have babies soon. My mom isn't going to have any babies, but I would like her to come back because I love her.
>   Joey Tuttle

SOMEWHERE IN THE back of Alex Tuttle's mind, there was a treason of identity. His entire life had been lived Underground, in the shadow of his father, whose fame and recognition in above ground industries and underground alike had dwarfed him into oblivion.

He huddled against the mixing board of the tiny control room, finally switching the airflow on to clear the medicated smoke he'd been breathing for three hours. As a biologist, he knew his future was lackluster; incomplete. There wasn't much biology to study underground, unless he wanted to work on the so-called Z virus – a thought quickly expunged from his mind as a futile endeavor. As a botanist, however, he believed his wonder-herb could cure any ailment except paranoia. A symptom he suffered readily in order to deal with the pressures of everyday life underground.

His wife, Janine, was different. In her shadowed past was greatness – a greatness she built for herself. Unlike him, she flourished and thrived on underground life. She was a brilliant mind, and he was jealous of her success both as an engineer and as a parent. He'd failed his father early on in the engineering field, and later on as a father to Joey.

There were more important things, he felt, than making the best life possible out of a dank, depressing, vitamin D-deficient life of tunnels, dirt, and vermin. People weren't content. There had been abandonments of settlements in distant clusters. He didn't understand the California pride of new frontierism. He didn't want to.

Alex longed for the sunlight. He longed to caress simple ferns, and smell the eucalyptus and cedar of the overgrown Redwood Forest, now much bigger than they ever had been before the nuke. He blamed that event for everything, including being born.

He and Janine hadn't planned for Joey, but Joey came anyway. The kid didn't like him, and that was okay. The less time and energy he spent trying to answer questions he didn't want to think about, the better for his peace of mind. The better for Janine. Her success kept her from her motherhood…and now she was probably gone for good. He knew she'd left him. He'd always known she would. His mother had too.

As the filter system began its work, he studied the wisps sneaking up and through the vents, tendrils of ideas, good and bad, never to see light or god or country. He'd thought of them all, twice over, in his little control room, where everything could be tinkered with at the wave or touch of his hand. It was a lazy man's job, this control.

A hand over an arched sensor dimmed the lights. A gradual but deliberate push of the palm toward a touch screen turned on vital systems. Two short breaths followed by a long one increased oxygen levels in the airflow.

Manual interface was turned on by saying "manual mode" out loud. With every on-and-off, he was reminded of each innovation his father had helped define, modify, and improve during his fruitful life.

Jasper Tuttle was a well-respected legend. But who was Alex Tuttle? Husband of Janine. Father of Joey. Angry, disgruntled, paranoid, failure.

He couldn't stand the sight of the kid anymore, not even for the purpose of eating. He'd stashed a case of MRE's under the console so he wouldn't have to see him going in and out, except to use the bathroom. Even that was prolonged with his emergency urination disposal kit. But things were beginning to smell off. The air filter probably needed changing. *Tomorrow*, he thought. *Tomorrow I will change the filter*. It had been three days since he'd set foot into the rest of the domicile.

A scratching, crackling sound coming from the newsfeed monitor pulled him from his self-pity. There was a low hum, a buzz, and a click. Abnormal sounds didn't often accompany the machinery, so he gestured "on" the screen, only to find white noise interrupted by short bursts of black. He stared at the screen for a long period of time, lost in thought. The black screen was replaced by blue, and each flash began to form a pattern: three one-second flashes of blue.

Three four-second flashes of blue. Three one-second flashes of blue. It repeated over and over, until the generator went on the blink and dimmed the power to minimum illumination. The feed generator, however, was always powered by an outside source on the main power-grid in the cluster. If ever there was a problem, this was the system that could always be relied on. It never went down.

Oh well, he thought. Time for another toke…better not waste the energy on filtering the air…for now. He picked up his vaporizer and loaded another dose. In the background, the feed monitor flickered on, illuminating the control room with a ghostly glow.

As he dozed off, he thought he heard Joey calling him from far away, somewhere within the house, just as he fell into a dream. Hours later, his lids were heavy and refused to open. Moving his hand felt like lifting a robotic arm, it was so heavy, and when it crashed down upon his stomach it met warmth and sticky, slippery snakes. Something nudged at his side, then his leg. Finally…his head. It ached. It throbbed. It stabbed at his eye sockets from the inside, this pain. A wild, humming vibrato filled his ears, and suddenly, his skull felt cold.

It felt *open*

• • •

SCIBOT-3 WAS ANALYZING foreign sector feeds when Scibot-678-94b interrupted all of them, with an update.

"Guardbot-9 has been compromised. His termination transmission indicates the presence of a breach. We have confirmed this report with Joey Tuttle, who has transmitted a technical request that has been moved to the top of the queue," said Scibot-678-94b.

"Confirmed. We have that feed. What is the workbot feed from Outpost 15, Service Grid 5?" asked Scibot-3.

"All workbots dispatched, then deactivated with termination signals transmitting. Confirmed infection. Threat level is exponential. Responding," said Scibot-678-94b.

"Computing damages. As usual, slow moving, but they will eventually reach all destinations. Dispatch Warbot-11," said Scibot-3.

"Dispatching," said Scibot-29.

> Attention Joey Tuttle:
>   We have received your request. and have noted problems in your area. which we are working to fix. Your quadrant has been compromised. Do not exit your domicile. Food and water supplies may be infected: do not consume unsanitary extraneous fuel. We have dispatched Warbot–11 to your cluster. Additional S.O.S. feeds will be handled in the order in which they were received. This will remain a secure channel for communications. Customer service is very important to us. Please fill out this brief survey to help us better serve you in future.
>   Scibot–678–94b
>   Kirtland–Chang
>   "Your infinite future in ones and zeros."

But Joey Tuttle did not check his messages that day.

THE EXCITEMENT AND happiness of having Vespa come back was short lived. She died in childbirth while Joey had been sleeping, and the hunger of the kittens had overwhelmed his grief. As beautiful a cat as she was, Vespa had returned home emaciated, listless, and unable to evenly walk under the bulk of the burden in her belly.

Her eyes were dull, and pieces of her fur were missing. There was evidence she'd been in a fight; probably with that mean one, Buttons, Joey thought. Buttons was always scrapping with the other tunnel cats. He was a very territorial male.

Some of the others had returned, too. Many of them from other clusters, it seemed, since he didn't recognize their markings, and they all seemed to be suffering in one way or another. It was kitten season, and the tunnels were alive with bouncing, wobbling, playful little furry bodies of various shapes and sizes. The ones no longer nursing on their mothers were often hungry.

Their little needle teeth occasionally hurt Joey's fingers when they played, but he didn't mind. They never drew blood, or bit all the way through his flesh. Their little claws were avoided with heavier clothing. He let them climb all over him, and some rode his shoulders as he walked through the tunnels each day, calling them by name, and feeding them from his own ration stores for Vespa.

They weren't much interested in the food. The adult mothers were somehow succumbing to the disease, Joey noticed, because they came back less and less, abandoning their little babies by the litterful. He coaxed them back to the house, and hid them in his room, where his dad was less likely to be. He hadn't seen him for a long time, and he didn't care. If Vespa had come home, then his mother might make it back too.

The electricity had long since gone out; Joey had rigged a friction-based flashlight from one of his mother's survival books, and used that when he went looking for more cats. Pretty soon, he didn't have to go looking anymore.

They began showing up on his doorstep, bumping into things, mewling loudly, and scratching at the door to get in. At night, he cuddled them close, and listened to their erratic purring. It comforted him, and helped him sleep.

For all their cuteness, they smelled really rotten. Mange had run rampant; some had eyes missing, or gaping wounds that wept puss and blood. He often found bits and pieces of rats in their make-shift beds, and the decapitated bodies of snakes were scattered throughout the hallways of the bunker. Dead snakes smelled like rotting fish, Joey thought. No wonder the kittens like them so much.

When the domicile filled up, Joey began opening the doors to every room to accommodate more kittens. They bumbled behind him, slow and shambling, sneezing and snarfling, arching their backs at each other, and crab-walking as they stalked his feet like prey. He paused when he came to the door of the control room. It was already open, about a foot.

Pushing it all the way had been hard – there was something big and heavy in the way, but soon it gave, and dozens of kittens scattered, mewling, as he stepped inside. His eyes had grown accustomed to the dark, but something on the feed monitor kept flashing, making it difficult to differentiate between shadow and light. Some kind of blue screen.

When it illuminated, he could see the lump of his father's back, shirt shredded and bloody, skullcap glistening and gooey, with dozens of tiny holes the size of dimes, nickels, and quarters exposing brain. What was left of it. He stared at his father a long moment, and drank in the scent of death.

Some of the babies had gnawed right through his neck, severing jugular, muscle, and bone – decapitating him completely. There was bloody, moving fur up inside the neck, which had been hollowed out and eaten through. A white ear covered in pink poked through his eye socket, and Joey could hear sucking sounds in the silence of that room.

So that's what they like to eat, thought Joey. *I will have to get them more…*But his thought was interrupted by an outer door being blasted in and the scent of acrid ammunition electrifying the molecules in the air, replacing the stink of rot.

There was an audible, collective hiss, combined with a sputtering-spit sound. Every kitten wobbled forth, forming a protective writhing radius around Joey, as he slowly stepped through them into the living room.

The warbot's singular eye was scanning the room, dust catching the red glow of the laser, slicing the air with perfect precision. He could see the robot's sensors blinking and knew the scan would be completed no sooner than he opened his mouth. But even as he worried, his mind was eased. He looked around the room to see his kittens every-where – on shelves, piled ten-deep against the walls, clutching worn furniture and every well-shined surface now shambled forward, hairs on end, dead-eyes glowing white with cataracts, and maws glistening with his father's meat.

"Come in," Joey said to the warbot. "But don't make a move. They listen to me…but they won't listen to you. You're in their territory now." Warbot-11 was caught in a processing loop, analyzing the domicile.

"Reboot. Scan. Complete. Identify: Family, Filidae. Subfamily, Filinae. Genus, Felus Catus. Threat level: Nil. Threat Level: MAXIUM. Threat Level: Nil. Threat Level: MAXIMUM. ERROR. Reboot. Scan. Complete. Identify…ERROR…"

"Maybe you should power-down and restart, Mister. I bet I have a book that can help you with that error message," Joey said, grinning.

This was going to be fun, Joey thought. I can program him to help me find food…

By the light of a friction-powered flashlight, Joey Tuttle began his work, kittens climbing into casings, furring up the electronics of Warbot-11, a slow, erratic vibrato echoing through the halls of his underground home, and out the open door.

Twenty Years Later…

Scibot-678-94b was updating feed firmware, patching the system after a viral breach. Headlines laced the connection across the world, webbing a collective threat level to active status:

> Genetic Retouching: Training DNA to Adjust
> Feline Intelligence for Post-Infection Use

> Waste Reduction and Flesh as Fuel: What to Do
> With the Rest When The Brain is Gone

> Joey Tuttle: Master Manipulator of warbot
> Mainframes, Processing Engines, Covert Communications

End transmission. All systems functioning normal. Threat
level: Inconclusive. Further research required.

HOT WATER & CLEAN UNDERWEAR

Amelia Beamer

FIRST I LOCKED the door. Deadbolted that shit. The dorm room had the feel of a prison cell. Something about the cinderblock walls, or the windows that probably didn't open. It was perfect.

The original occupants had fled long ago; the entire building was empty. I'd seen no one on campus except for a few lone shufflers. I hadn't met another living person in days.

I pawed through what the students had left: bedding, condoms, cigarettes, packages of ramen. The room looked distinctly male. Just my luck.

I found a Snickers bar underneath the pillow on the bottom bunk (*Why underneath the pillow?* I asked myself) and tore into it with my teeth. The sugar swam straight to my head and I sat on the Salvation Army-style couch that probably had patches of dried jism on it. So this was my life. I owned a stolen bicycle and the gore-stained clothes on my back. If I ever stopped running, if I ever felt safe, I just might go completely crazy. What I *really*, *really* wanted was a shower.

"Want to talk about it?" a female voice said. I jumped practically out of my skin. I grabbed for my knife and stood up, inspecting the room.

"I just meant, you know, you look a little troubled," she said. "Anxious. You show all of the classic signs of stress in your posture. I'm here to talk about it, whatever it is. I could give you a shoulder rub if you like. Or I think I could. If I can get my arms to work."

The voice sounded metallic.

"Hello?" I said. I didn't know what I wanted this voice to be. But she sounded nice. I just didn't want to be the only living thing around anymore.

I found her silver metal body in the corner. I put away my knife. I looked at where her eyes would be if she were human. She had photo-electric receptors that gave off a cool red light. We studied one another. I was already thinking of it as a her, although it was obviously just a bot.

"Who are you?" I asked. "And, like, what the hell?" For one thing, she definitely sounded female and I'd never seen a female bot before. I felt camaraderie with her that I couldn't quite explain to myself.

"Could you please give me a hand?" she asked. "I'm a bit stuck. I have this —"

"Pain in all the diodes down your left side?" I asked, interrupting.

"What's a diode?" she asked.

I put my face close to hers, the way you would talk to a child. There was a simplicity to her that I liked. "Never you mind," I said. "I suppose you haven't read *The Hitchhiker's Guide to the Galaxy*. How can I help you? And what's your name?"

"If you could just pick me up out of this corner and set me down on the floor in the middle of the room, we'll have space to work. I have another arm; I think it's under the bed. I can tell you how to put it back in. And then I can rub your shoulders."

"I'm okay," I said. "Really." I picked her up. I'd never touched a bot before. I was used to the masculine battle models, but I'd only ever seen them at a distance. She was cold, and lighter than I'd expected. She was about the size of a ten-year-old child. I didn't ask what had happened to her arm. I helped her reattach it. It was easier than I expected.

"What's your name?" I asked again.

"The boys called me Mandy," she said. "I know that I'm a bot; I've always been a bot and nothing else. The boys took me offline from the botmind and gave me an experimental intelligence system. Why can't I rub your shoulders? You look so tense."

I suspected that "the boys" were the original occupants of this dorm room. I had a sinking feeling. "What kind of bot were you before the boys reprogrammed you?" I asked. That wasn't really the question I wanted to ask.

"Look on the back of my neck. I think the specs are printed there." She turned her head and exposed her neck. If she'd had hair, she would have brushed it aside.

I felt like some kind of awkward vampire. I looked on the back of her neck. *Intelligence Model Second Class* was stamped into the metal, and a serial number. I repeated the information. I'd never heard of an intelligence model.

"Was that from the early days?" I asked. "Like when nobody knew precisely what was going on and we thought it might have been another government unleashing the zombies on us and…were you an interrogation model of some kind, like maybe the nice cop?"

"I don't know," she said. "Perhaps. If I was, those memories have been wiped. But it sounds right. You still look tense, by the way. I'm glad you've relaxed a bit, but please let me rub your shoulders. I'm strong. You'll like it. And then maybe we'll see where that goes. My body gets warm, don't worry."

I was horrified. "Those boys programmed you for *that*? What a waste of time, first off. I hope they're long dead." I moved away from her. I could smell the reek of my armpits. She must not have any real sensory capacity. Why the hell would she hit on *me*?

"What's wrong with my programming?" Mandy asked. "They were kind to me."

"*Kind*?" I realized that I was kind of shouting. "I found you lying in a corner and your arm was under the bed! They abandoned you."

"But you're here now," she said. "And I've forgotten to ask your name! I'm so sorry, sweetheart. What is your name? I hope we can be good friends. Special friends. I am not yet experienced with women but I find you quite beautiful."

I wasn't sure what to say. I was torn between wanting to bap her upside her metal head and to figure out how to help her. And at the same time I really just wanted to shower and maybe sleep while the building was empty. I didn't expect hot water but I was ready to brave any kind of water just to be free of some of the grime. "Shannon," I lied. "My name is Shannon."

"Really?" she asked. "The way you touched your chin just now, that's generally indicative of a lie. What would it take for you to trust me? You can tell me everything, you know. If you need me to I can wipe my memory after, if that would make you feel more secure. Maybe it's best for the relationship to build from emotional honesty and vulnerability, and add the physical when we're ready. I'm not in a hurry." She seemed to smile.

"But why do you keep doing this?" I wasn't attracted to her by a long shot, but something deep inside me really wished that she wasn't made of metal. I wanted to crawl into her lap. I wanted someone flesh and blood to show a thumbnail's worth of this robot's empathy, even if she *was* just trying to get me into bed. I realized that I didn't trust anyone to touch me.

"What are you so afraid of?" Mandy said gently. "What about telling me your real name is so scary? What do you think I'll do with it?"

I thought of the last person to say my name. The circumstances under which they said it. "Just call me Shannon," I said.

"Okay, Shannon, honey," the bot said. "What can I do to make you comfortable? You do not want even the simplest, most platonic physical release. You refuse to engage emotionally. What do you need to feel safe?"

"I'm fine," I said. The bot was making me nervous. "I just need a shower and a clean change of clothes if I can find one in this mess, and a bit of sleep while the building isn't overrun with zombies."

She looked at me with what I could have sworn was disappointment. I grew angry. "By the way," I said, "I realize you've been trapped in a dorm room and haven't seen much of reality. But don't you understand the purpose of robots in the overall world right now? And yet you sure don't look like you're any good for battle, or any other normal robot job. You can't even *talk* to the other bots? How are you of any *use* to anyone?"

"You are a human being," Mandy said, as gently as if I'd asked where the sun came from. "I am programmed to serve your needs. That is what makes me happy. After food and shelter, sex is a basic human need. You can say my creators were just a couple of dumb teenagers. Or they were thinking further ahead than anyone else."

I couldn't listen to her. "Just give me some space, man," I said. I went to the bathroom to see if the shower would work. I opened the door to the adjoining dorm room on the other side of the bathroom, just to check. It was empty. I went and deadbolted the door to the hallway, just to be sure. I made a mental note to rifle through the contents of the room for anything useful. Later.

Mandy had followed me into the bathroom on her gangly legs. She was as tall as my shoulder. Again I had the feeling of wanting to beat her, and at the same time, wanting to protect her. She reminded me of an annoying little cousin who was probably long since dead.

I turned on the hot tap in the military-looking shower. Nothing happened. Rusty water came out when I turned on the cold tap. It was something. I turned it off, so I wouldn't run out. Who knew how much there was. "Out of the bathroom," I said. "Scoot. I'm going to shower."

"Would you rather have hot water to bathe in?" she asked. "Your body looks more resigned than relieved; does the hot water not work?"

"How the hell would you do that?" I asked, incredulous. Somehow I had accepted that this robot was reading my mind, or at least my body. "Wouldn't your whole system just short out? I mean, are you offering to *be* a water heater, and how would that even work?" I couldn't picture it.

"I just meant that there's an electric kettle," she said. I could have sworn from the tone of her voice that she was amused. "I've got enough power that I could heat it up a few times. Pour it into the sink so that you could have some hot water to wash with. I'm waterproof, you know. I could wash your hair for you if you liked."

I let out a breath. "Okay, fine. Yes, please, on the hot water. No, thanks, on the hair washing."

"Very well," she said. She went and fetched a white plastic kettle from atop a desk. She turned on the tap in the sink until it ran clear, then she sat on the bathroom floor. She held the business end of the plug in both hands. Her eyes went dim. I was fascinated.

"Were you *programmed* to do this?" I asked. "Heat *water?*" I wondered how much of her was programming and how much of her was reading a situation and reacting to it, the way she kept reading my body language. I couldn't imagine that anyone had asked her to heat water before. This bot, I realized, might be useful to me.

She did not respond to my questions. Just as well. I gathered that she was using all of her operating power to heat the water. I was grateful. I felt awkward just watching her, so I went back into the boys' dorm room. I looked through the drawers until I found a pair of jeans and a shirt that would fit me. I took a pair of boxer briefs as well. I could at least try them; I didn't like the feeling of not wearing underwear.

Mandy had poured the hot water into the sink and had sat to warm the second kettle's worth by the time I came back into the bathroom. Steam rose obligingly from the surface of the water. I found a bottle of shampoo and a washcloth that wasn't crusty. I stripped naked, not really caring if Mandy saw me.

The water was the perfect temperature. I washed my skin. It stung from the scrapes and bruises I'd accumulated and not acknowledged. The water turned gray. I washed my dirtiest parts, my armpits and in between my legs. I had half expected I'd never get hot water again.

I could hear the hiss of the kettle. I let the water out of the sink and rinsed the dirt down with cold water, then plugged up the sink again. I moved out of Mandy's way, not quite being able to look her in the face.

"It's okay," she said. "I won't touch you. Don't worry." She poured the hot water in, filled the kettle again, and then added cold water to the sink. "I can do this final kettle's worth and then I need to stop," she said. She sat.

I nodded, grateful. Again the water was the perfect temperature. I wetted and lathered my hair, using as much shampoo as I dared and rinsing it as best I could. I would use the final kettle's worth to finish rinsing. I let myself enjoy the feeling of the water. Of being touched, even if it was just by my own hands. I realized that I really liked this aspect of Mandy: the one who seemed to know what she was doing.

I was sorry to see the last of the hot water twirl down the sink. But I felt clean. I squeezed the water from my hair, wondering when I would be able to do this next. I turned around to find a towel.

Mandy was holding one out.

I accepted it with a smile. I dressed myself. I didn't quite fit into male clothing. It occurred to me that if Mandy could make more hot water, I could cook some of the boys' ramen in the kettle. Eat a hot meal.

"What?" Mandy asked. "Your shoulders just fell."

"Nothing," I said. I told her what I'd been thinking. I was touched at how closely she watched me.

"Give me a few hours," she said. "I'll recharge."

"Let's do it in the morning, then," I said. I had no idea what time it was; I think the sun was still out. But I hadn't slept much lately. My adrenals were like two hot coals in my back, and my eyes felt full of grit.

I filled the kettle before I went to bed, and the sink, just in case the water cut out overnight. I was no dummy.

I'M NOT SURE how long I slept. I woke to see Mandy on the floor, curled up like a dog. I wondered if I should have offered to let her into the bed.

Sunlight came yellow and warm through the window. I was suddenly sick of the dorm room. I felt almost safe here, and I didn't want to get too comfortable.

Mandy and I made ramen, and I ate. I went through both dorm rooms and collected food and clothes. An unopened water bottle. A clean-looking towel. I found a backpack to put it all in. I wondered where I thought I was going.

"How about a backrub, Shannon?" Mandy asked. "You're as tense as a terrier."

"Look," I said. "Can you please stop that? I appreciate your interest and all, it's just not my thing. Really. It's not you."

"I'll try," she said. "You are packing to leave," she said. "When will you go?"

I sat down on the floor and pulled the backpack into my lap. I hugged it. I wondered if the bot was asking me to take her when I went. That's what she seemed to be implying. I looked at her. Perhaps she expected I would leave her here. I didn't know which prospect I found worse.

"I don't know where I'm going," I said. "What are you going to do when I go, though?" Already I felt attached to her. I didn't know how I could bring her with me on the bicycle, though.

She didn't answer.

"Do you want to come with me?" I asked. I wondered if I could balance her on the handlebar of my bike. If she was strong enough to hang on without her arms falling off. It made for a ludicrous mental picture.

"Why do you need to go?" she asked. "Can't you just stay here with me?"

I shook my head. "I don't know when the zombies will come." I heard a noise outside that was either a car backfiring or a gun going off. It reinforced my need to move. "But they will. They'll hear me, or smell me, or someone else. They're easier to outrun than to hide from, because they don't move very fast. But once they get you cornered, you're screwed."

Mandy's eyes went dim again. She stayed that way for a moment. I wondered what she was doing.

She came back. "I think there are some outside," she said.

I went to the window and looked out. Sure enough, I could see shufflers on the grass. They moved with a sense of purpose. My skin went cold. I couldn't see the object of their interest, if there was in fact another person out there. "How did you *know* that?" I asked.

"I —" she said, then stopped. "It's hard to explain. But I think that when people are in danger, your body lets off a sort of psychic scream. When you heard that bang noise just now, you made it, and you've done it a few times, when your body felt threatened. I'd never heard it before I met you, but you did it reliably enough for me to figure out what it meant. And so I just went out into the space outside the building to see if I could feel that scream frequency from anyone else. Someone's out there, in danger."

My heart sank. The poor fuck. They were still alive enough to scream. I couldn't save them, whoever they were. I could barely keep myself alive. I looked out the window anyway. The scream happened again.

Then I realized what Mandy had just said. "So you can feel when the zombies are coming?" I asked. "I mean, you said you can sense when someone's in danger. So that means you can sense where the zombies *are*, or at least where they are attacking?"

She seemed surprised, an amazing thing given that she didn't have any moving parts on her face. I marveled to myself at how expressive this bot was. Or maybe I was just getting used to her. She was suddenly very valuable to me.

"Well, I guess so," she said. "I'm glad that it makes you so happy. But you are wired to move. Shall we go?"

She was right. My body wanted to move. "Can you walk?" I asked. "I mean, can you walk fast? We need to get out of the building so that we can get on my bike. Can you hold onto my bicycle's handlebar, do you think?" It got more and more complicated as I talked. I had a new idea.

I put on the backpack, thankful that I'd packed it already. In a moment of genius, I grabbed the electric kettle and jammed it into the top of the bag.

Another scream came from outside. I moved fast.

I straddled the bike, holding it steady with my legs. Then I scooped up the bot and put her on the handlebar. "Can you hang on?" I asked. Part of me couldn't believe I was doing this. The other part of me just wanted to get us out of there while I still could.

Her metal fingers curled around the handlebar. She held her feet above the wheel. "I think so," she said.

"Is that comfortable?" I asked. "I mean, is it tolerable?"

"I've had worse," she said.

"Okay," I said. I didn't want to think about what she might be referring to. I kicked off. "Let's go."

She stayed quiet, as if she knew that I needed my whole brain just to keep us alive.

I rode down the carpeted hallway. I remembered a story a friend of mine had told me about living in a dormitory: he and his friends had installed a slip and slide in their hallway, thrown water on it, and taken turns running and sliding down the hall. I imagined a bright plastic rubber slide in the hallway. College students drinking beer and laughing in their bathing suits, ruining the carpet with their fun. It was better than thinking about zombies.

Thankfully, we were on the first floor and didn't have to deal with stairs. I had to do some smart maneuvering to open the door to get out, but I managed not to drop Mandy. She held on to the handlebar, and her arms stayed attached.

My adrenaline kicked on high as the heavy door shut behind us. There was a thick knot of them on the grass, and more coming from all directions, drawn to the kill. It was clear what had happened to the screaming voice. I wondered if they had been looking for a safe place in the dormitory, the same way I had. If it had been one person, or several traveling together.

I pointed my bicycle in the direction with the fewest zombies, and pedaled as hard as I could. The sidewalk was wide; the campus had probably served tens of thousands of students in its prime.

I steered through the thick of the zombies, dodging their grasping hands. I knew they were turning to follow me. I refused to look back. One mistake and I'd be dead, and who knew what would happen to Mandy.

"Go right when you can," Mandy said. "It's quiet over there a ways."

I took a lungful of air and moved my legs. There would be an intersection sooner or later where I could turn right. The zombies would follow me for a while, but they wouldn't be able to catch up. They'd catch someone else's scent if I rode far enough.

For the first time in a long time, I felt like I almost knew where I was going.

I PEDALED WHILE Mandy the robot sat on my bike's handlebars. Once we had gotten clear of the zombies, and I had caught my breath, I found that I was annoyed. With every movement of my legs I was reminded of the fact that I was wearing a strange guy's boxer shorts. They didn't quite chafe but the shape of them definitely felt wrong against my skin. I wished I had bothered to wash my own underwear when I was in the dorm room, instead of just stealing his. Then I wanted new underwear, proper cotton panties. Food and water and shelter would also be nice.

It was good to have goals, my mother always said. Or maybe she had always said it. For all I knew, she wasn't saying much these days.

The sidewalk led us away from the college campus and into a suburb. The houses quickly spread farther apart, as if they were too good to sit and chat with each other, or maybe too shy. Shy houses tended to have food and supplies.

The sidewalk ended, so I biked in the middle of the road. I wasn't sure what town this was. I hadn't seen another living person in days. I was getting used to that, though.

I spotted a wood pile in someone's front yard. That was probably a good sign. Usually when there was a wood pile, there was an ax. I rode toward it.

Someone had boarded up the windows. The house looked empty. I stopped the bike in the yard. I wanted nothing more than to catch my breath and sit down, but I needed to make sure we were as safe as we could be. "Do you feel any of them nearby?" I asked Mandy.

"No," she said. "I've been listening. I think we're safe."

"Good," I said. I was determined to enjoy the moments of relative safety. I didn't know how many more I would get.

I managed to get Mandy down from the handlebars without dropping her. She stood and stretched. I was amused and perplexed that someone would have bothered to program her to do such a human thing as stretching. I'd never seen her do it, but then again I'd never taken her on an extended bike ride. I suspected there was a lot I didn't know about her. I found myself stretching my own arms and back. We had been riding for a while, and it felt good to stretch.

"I stretch to reset my programming," she said. "Same as you. It's cute, you know, the way you ask questions with your body language but then you don't say them aloud."

"Huh," I said. "I *was* wondering why you stretched, but have you thought that I don't need to ask questions aloud if you're answering me? You're the one trying to read my mind anyway. Isn't that the point of your programming?" I felt proud of myself for figuring it out, and then I felt bad for maybe making a robot feel insecure. I looked away.

It made sense, though, about the stretching. Maybe it got rid of the tension of whatever the muscles and bones had been up to, in order to make it easier for them to do something else. "It's all old programming, anyway," I said. "The only thing that matters now is staying alive."

"Why did you choose to stop here?" Mandy asked. She stood with one hip to the side. There was something girlish about her posture and I realized how much she trusted me. And that she trusted me because she had no one else. I realized that I felt the same way about her.

"Ax me a question and you'll get an answer," I said. I went to check out the woodpile next to the porch. Sure enough, there was an ax lying on top of the wood. The fact that the ax was still here told me that this house hadn't yet been picked clean by other survivors.

The ax was larger than I'd hoped. I hefted it with both hands and showed it to Mandy. Her eyes, or what I thought of as her eyes, seemed to glow a bit brighter. I wonder how much she understood of what I was thinking.

The wood of the ax handle was smooth and well used. It felt good in my hands. There was a partially chopped piece of wood on the stump that the ax's previous owner had used as a chopping block. I knew that to split wood you needed to sit it up on one end, but I wasn't trying to split the wood. I wanted to see how hard I could hit the side of the log.

I hefted the ax over my head and brought it down on the wood. It bounced off, barely nicking the wood. I tried again. I had hoped I could use the ax on the zombies, but if I couldn't hit a piece of wood with any conviction, how would I ever kill a zombie?

I wasn't going to cry. I hefted the ax again. This time I managed to bite into the wood with the ax head. It made a satisfying sound. I put my foot on the wood and pulled to get the ax out. I couldn't imagine doing this to a zombie, even if I found one who would hold still. Plus I didn't know how I would even *carry* an ax on a bicycle, what with a robot balanced on the handlebars.

The wind picked up, and there was the sound of dead leaves stirring. I looked around for zombies, out of habit. There were three figures in the distance, walking toward us. I could almost hear the spaghetti western music. Mandy saw them, too. Without a word we moved around to the side of the house, so that we could look at them without them looking at us. They walked like people. I was both scared and hopeful. I kept hold of the ax and still wore my backpack but I didn't bring the bike with us. Big mistake.

They went straight for my bike and picked it up, making soft exclamations about the luck of their find. It was two men and a woman. All older than me but not graybeard old. They had shotguns strapped to their backs. They walked and talked like they hadn't noticed me, which I knew should have given me a tactical advantage because I had more information, except I wasn't sure how to use it. I didn't want to startle them into shooting me. My heart was pounding hard.

They were already walking away with my bike by the time I had decided what to do. I leaned the ax against the side of the house and left it there. I set my backpack on the ground, and told Mandy with my eyes that she should stay put.

I cleared my throat. "Hello," I called. "I'm around the side of the house. I'm coming out now." I raised my hands to show that they were empty. They shook like when I had to give a report in school. Maybe these people would take my backpack and Mandy too, but I couldn't just let them stroll off with my bike.

I turned the corner.

The three of them each had their guns in their hands so fast it was almost funny. I was surprised at how quietly they did it: no loud gun cocking sounds, just the quiet slap of hands against wood and metal. I hadn't seen many guns up close before. At the same time, the woman tossed away my bike so effortlessly it seemed to fly. Then they each saw that I was not a zombie, and then they looked surprised and relieved. They lowered their guns but didn't relax.

"Hi," I called.

I waited for them to smile. In the movies when survivors met each other they always tried to join forces and be friends, but I got the sense these guys weren't going to invite me along with them. They looked at me and saw only a liability. The woman put away her gun and righted my bike, keeping it close to her body.

"That's my bike you've got. I'm sorry," I said. "But I'd like it back if that's okay." My whole body was trembling. I held as still as I could.

They looked at one another. There was no law saying they couldn't take my bike. It had saved my life a few times already. The way the woman held onto the bike, it seemed like she would fight even her companions for it if she felt she had to. That was sad, or would be if I wasn't so scared.

The silence was getting to me. "I mean," I said, just to fill it, "I wish you'd say something. What are your names? Where did you come from? I may look like a kid but I'm twenty-three and I've survived this long, pretty much on my own, too, so I can't be a total douchebag. I'm not a threat to you. I mean, forget the bike," I said. I was feeling desperate. "Have you guys seen any other survivors? Where are you going? Do you know of any safe places? Can we just exchange some information like human beings? Can you *hear* me?"

They traded glances with one another. They each seemed to be asking the others to say something to shut me up and make me go away.

I heard a rustling behind me and I knew it was Mandy. *Shit.* What the hell was *she* going to do? She touched my arm with her hand as she walked past me. Her metal skin was the temperature of human skin, probably from the sun.

Mandy walked straight up to the woman. "I am a negotiator," she said. "I belong to no one but I have an affinity for the girl whose bike you have. Will you talk to me?" Her voice was different: she'd discarded the flirtatious tone she often used with me for a matter-of-fact, almost masculine way of speaking. Even her body seemed a bit larger and more sturdy.

The woman blinked in surprise. "Fuck me gently," she said. "I haven't seen one of these in a dog's age!"

Mandy held out her hand to the woman. She turned the palm up to the sky.

The woman looked from Mandy's hand to the photoelectric receptors that should have been her eyes. She let go of the bike and it fell to the ground. She took Mandy's hand in hers and looked at it closely. Her face went pale.

"No way," the woman said. "No fricking way. *Seven?*"

I wasn't sure what was going on. The men were confused, too. The robot and the woman looked at one another. Then I understood that they had history. I got jealous.

"Do you remember your name, Seven?" the woman asked Mandy. "I mean, what *do* you remember?" The woman seemed ashamed, relieved, astonished, happy, and sad, all at the same time.

"There are gaps in my files and much of my memory has been overwritten," Mandy said. "I've forgotten your name but I recognize you from your unique physical, gestural, and chemical patterns. I remember your lab. I remember how it felt when you gave me my emotion chip. It was better than getting color vision. But the lab sold me to the college once there was no need for negotiators with emotional sensitivity. We were an experiment. An evolutionary dead end. Perhaps even a mistake." There was sadness in Mandy's voice, but what was really sad was how she spoke of her past as if she believed that she had deserved to be treated this way.

The woman held Mandy's hand in her own. They both looked at it as if it was a map. I had assumed that Mandy had been showing the woman a scar. Now I understood that it was her emotion chip, embedded in her palm. It probably looked like the sim card in a cell phone. A little square of plastic and metal that would slide in, replacing some other programming. How much programming did she *have*, anyway?

One of the men looked around for zeds in the way that you do. "What's the bot to you, Amanda?" he asked. The other just watched.

I found that I hated both of the men. They seemed to care only about themselves.

"An unbelievable coincidence," the woman named Amanda said. And then something went clunk in my brain and I understood where Mandy's name came from. I could imagine Mandy adopting a version of Amanda's name. Especially if that was the only female name that she knew. I wonder if she had even been female before the boys got her.

"Of all of the discarded bots in all of the ruined suburbs in the world," Amanda said, "and *you* have to walk into my path, and over a goddamn bicycle. Which one of us is human, anyway?" She turned to me and held out her hand. Her eyes shone. "I'm sorry we took your bike. I didn't realize it was yours. And sorry I didn't talk to you. I've been so busy trying to survive that I forgot how to talk to people."

We shook hands. "It's okay," I said. I wanted to tell Amanda that the robot's name was Mandy, not Seven, and then I felt embarrassed for Mandy in case she *had* named herself after Amanda.

We all stood there. Nobody knew what to say. It felt like we weren't a group, just people standing in the same space.

"I was going to check out this house," I said. "Do you guys wanna check it out with me?"

One of the men picked up my bicycle. I had a sinking feeling. I wanted to argue that a single bike wouldn't do them any good, but then decided to let the bike go. I watched the way Mandy looked at Amanda, and wondered if they were all going to leave me here. If they did, I would still have an ax. I wondered for the millionth time about what the easiest way to die would be. I wanted to stay dead when I died.

"Okay," Amanda said. She moved toward the front porch and after a moment I understood that she had chosen my side. Mine and Mandy's.

It was strange, how we didn't talk about it. The men just walked away with my bicycle. They could have taken Mandy, or my stuff. They could have demanded we go with them, or done all sorts of things to us if they wanted to and we didn't fight them. But they walked away.

"Don't mind the guys," Amanda said. "I'm sorry about your bike, but it's nothing personal. They're ex-military. Also, their mothers never hugged them."

"So you were going around with them because why?" I asked. I tried the front door. It was locked. I hated the idea of breaking into the house. Especially after someone had gone to all the trouble of boarding the windows.

"Because they would look after me so long as it was in their best interest, since I looked after them, too," Amanda said. "The others I've been with have all died. You'd be surprised what you'd put up with just to have someone to take a watch so you can sleep in peace. Or maybe *you* wouldn't be surprised. C'mon, let's try around back," Amanda said. We spoke quietly, keeping an eye out for zombies. Mandy tottered along with us as we walked around the side of the house.

"So why did you leave them?" I asked. Something about the apocalypse made it easier to say what I was thinking. I felt both threatened and relieved that she was staying with me, and a tiny bit affronted, like maybe she should have asked me first if I wanted her to stay. There wasn't much room for tact, since the zombies.

"Because you guys helped me see that that kind of life is not worth living, hon," she said. "This way, when I die, it won't be because I took a girl's bike and left her to die instead of me."

She shouldered her shotgun and pointed it at the door. Often houses had a zed or two inside. We made eye contact, and then I tried the door. The knob turned. It was unlocked. We let ourselves into the kitchen, moving like military men in their black pajamas. She took point. I held the ax and hoped for the best. We swept through the house until we had cleared every room and closet.

"Thank you," I said. I was covered with a thin layer of sweat. I realized that she might not remember what we'd been talking about. "For being nice to me," I said.

"You're welcome," she said. "Thank Seven."

"My name is Mandy now," Mandy said. "And this is my friend. She told me her name was Shannon, but really it's something else."

I wanted to cry. Mandy had spoken so gently. And then it didn't matter. What I'd done to survive, and how much I hated myself for it, so much that I had changed my name. This robot had risked her life for me, and this woman had done the same. "Tara," I said. "That's really my name."

"Well, Tara," Amanda said. "What were you hoping to find in this house?"

I thought for a second. Then I remembered. "I want some clean fucking underwear," I said. "Proper girl underwear."

"How fucking civilized," Amanda said. She smiled, and then I did, and I think we decided at that moment that we would be friends. "Maybe there will be some in my size, too," she said.

I brought my backpack and my ax inside and then we locked the door and scoured the house. A mother and daughter had lived here, and they were similar enough in size to me and Amanda that we found what we needed. We looked in the basement last, to see if there were any suitcases that we could use. I didn't know where we'd go next or how we'd survive, but at least we had something comfortable to wear.

We found two bicycles in the basement. They were in pretty good shape, too, air in the tires and everything. Even helmets. And these people apparently had green thumbs: there was a burly shovel with a sharp edge, and several of what I'm pretty sure were called hedge trimmers, of various sizes. They even had gardening gloves. And they had camping backpacks, so we could pack and carry it all.

There was also a 50 gallon drum of water that tasted only a little bit brackish. To celebrate, I broke out the kettle and Mandy warmed us water to wash with. We changed into the clothes we found. They still smelled like fabric softener. And there was food in the kitchen.

I could get used to living like this.

AT DAYBREAK THE zombies came.

THE RIVER OF MEMORY

Kaaron Warren

I T TOOK NINE days to fall from Earth to Tartarus and all the while, zombies could smell meat not far away, big meat brains close by. They fell in a clump, all tangled together, rolled around, and they gnawed at each other, cracking bone, splitting teeth, until they landed.

Mnemosyne saw all. Understood all. She was ancient and wise and so lonely some days she wanted to die. Punished by the gods to live out eternity in Tartarus, she missed her daughters and thought of Zeus on lonely nights. Her space was filled with mirrors which kept away the tortured souls, the punished sinners, reflecting back their anguish.

She smelled the zombies coming down; she knew the smell of decay.

Zombie stop falling. Zombie watch meat fall. /Zombie eat. /Zombie eat./ zombie stop/zombie smell old meat old meat brains dried/zombie smell fresh meat zombie eat/meat wet/zombie...zombie stop/zombie...

They landed. At the bottom of the zombie pile there was some spillage. Some splatter. Those on top were cushioned and they crawled over, down, sniffing for meat because it was close, it was near, and it landed. Four girls *plop plop plop plop*, some zombie skulls cracked but not enough to save those kids. The little one, Pip, queen for nine days, died on the way down. Too young to last for so long without water.

Her face was all pink skull, her eyes dry and wide, her arms and legs stiff, out like stars, because that was the way she fell. Zombies had tried to take random bites on the way down but she was always out of reach; now, they dug their teeth in and tore her to pieces, a zombie at all the pressure points and two at her toes. There was no warm brain left to her but they tore her apart anyway.

Dhysa, with her gold band made by the gods, fought the zombies off for a while but there were too many and she couldn't find purchase, her feet sinking into soft zombie flesh. She sliced her way, rolling, cutting, delirious from lack of water but still that instinct to survive, to save herself. She rolled off the pile, leaving them distracted by the others. Her friends. But the dead pulled her back by the ankles, sucked her into the stinking, writhing mass. She clawed her way toward Pip, but Pip was already gone. She'd been dead when they got to her and Dhysa thought, *at least that*. At least she was spared the desecration of becoming like them.

The zombies, starved and thoughtless, tore at each other to get at Dhysa's brain. She fought and struggled but there were too many, too many. She roared, a deep, primal scream she'd heard when women gave birth, but this was the opposite; this was death.

It was only moments before she rose to join the mass, the pulsing, dragging mass of the dead. No longer named; zombie.

MNEMOSYNE HAD SEEN a lot in her long, long life, but it was nasty watching them tear into the two young Amazons. These girls could have been her daughters, if she'd moved fast enough. At least she could try to save the other two.

The zombie heap of stink-flesh and black tooth began to move toward the massive cavern entrance. Zombies stumbled in search of brains, clumped like dog shit and sticks. Dhysa with them, lost, absorbed.

Mnemosyne heard them moaning *meat, meat* and she clucked her tongue.

She hated any creature who couldn't speak properly.

THE TWINS HAD landed at the edges of the pile. Beka rolled off and ran, blinded by thirst and terror, until she felt water at her feet. The

ground dropped away and she found herself flailing, drowning, sucking in the air of this place, this Tartarus, feeling it in her lungs like
poison and she sucked air and water until they came for her, zombies
braving the water in their hunger. She could recognize some of them.
There was Androdameia, and there Clete. There was an older woman;
a mother, Beka thought, a few years older and she'd been a mother
before she was a zombie. "Help me, Mummy," she called, but she
knew her own mother was long dead and far from this place.

She swam from them as best she could but the three persisted,
joined now by a tall, broad zombie, a man. He wore a cop's uniform
with the shirt unbuttoned to the waist. "Help, police," she called. She
took a deep drink of the river, her throat sore and dry. "Help, police."
Thinking she'd hit a chord and he'd remember who he'd been, leave
her alone. He continued toward her, wading solidly through the water,
his teeth bared, the gums pulled back and grey.

"Clete," Beka called out. "Help me, Clete, you remember me,
don't you? It's Beka. Remember? We found that little kitty together
one day?" But Clete sniffed, smelled brains and kept coming. Androdameia, who had been mean as a girl, a bully, could never be appealed
to.

Beka was still firm-bodied, although she has some bites out of her.
These had closed over as if cauterized. Body still rotting slowing and
smelly as all get out.

Beka ran further upriver, but the bed was soft and silty and she
sank to her ankles. They sank too but there were more of them, with
inhumanly long reach. The man got her first and dragged her backward and under with his soft, strong hands, pulled her to his chest and
sank his teeth into her skull.

The other zombies roiled in the water, sniffing the brains. Clete,
Androdameia, and the mother all reaching in for some.

The man had been tall, but disintegration had shortened him. His
ears were torn; earrings long since tugged out, dogs and hungry zombies gnawing on the rest.

The mother had been wealthy; she was still covered with her
jewels. Glitter of no value to the hungry.

Clete and Androdameia had been too young to be much of anything at all; they had seen very little of life.

They crouched in the river, focused only on their hunger and the good, fresh brains to sate it.

Then Beka rose. *Where?*

THE MAN FELT suddenly, desperately thirsty. Remembered thirst. His name was Steve. He remembered that. The brained girl — he knew those words — had lost her scalp. Her hair floated on the river like a bright red sprawl of seaweed. Not a fish.

I caught fish. I remember the tug of the line between my fingers. I remember the smell of their guts and that makes me hungry again. The slice of the knife.

Eating brains makes me thirsty.

ISA HAD ROLLED off the pile and run in the opposite direction to Beka, because that was where she landed. Running? She could barely move. Luckily the zombies were slower. She felt as if her body had melted, or merged, as if there was no distinction between bone and muscle. She had long ago accepted that thirst was the only thing left to her.

They followed her, the stink of them pushing her forward, their shuffling feet together sounding like a great rolling ball.

Mnemosyne saw all. She watched the girl staggering toward her mirrored room and she saw that this girl was not dead, not yet. But close. Behind her, the massed group, seeking her.

"Come on," she said, appearing before Isa. "In here, you'll be safe in here."

Isa allowed herself to be tugged and dragged into the mirror-filled room. Seeing herself made her scream; she thought she saw a ghost, a monster, she could not imagine this haggard, grey creature was her. She was gaunt, her hair sticking out like straw, her lips swollen, peeling, her tongue protruding. She cried, but the tears were dry, like salt pouring straight out of her eyes, and it hurt.

The room was a dead end. "We have to get out of here. They'll trap us. They'll turn us into them. Living dead."

Mnemosyne smiled. "I'm already immortal. Already in hell. It can't get any worse."

Isa backed away from her, horrified. "Never get yourself into a dead end, idiot. Always have a place to run to. We have to keep moving. They're slow, but they don't give up."

"It's okay, girl. I'll look after you. Your life is still important; I can see that."

She dragged Isa behind the largest mirror and settled her there. "Sit down, rest."

She looked into her small mirror, watching the zombies. They shuffled past, no longer able to smell the brains, or sense them. "I haven't seen these things before. These incarnations."

Isa's tongue rolled out; it was swollen, white and furry.

"You need water," Mnemosyne said. "Not the water from my river, though." She fetched a cup and held it against the wall; water poured down in a smooth, crystal sheet. Isa took the cup greedily, almost dreamily. She'd fantasized this moment many times and she hoped this was reality. The water was metallic but more delicious than anything she'd tasted in her life.

"Sip slowly."

But she gulped, and was almost sick, then she sipped.

"There's a river down here?" She'd been so desperate to get away she'd taken nothing in.

"My river of remembrance. You're too young to be burdened with memories of your past life. I won't allow children to take refreshment there."

"We should keep running," whispered Isa. She wasn't even sure if any noise was coming out, but at least she had water. "We should find Beka and Dhysa." She knew that Pip was dead; had watched, as they fell, the life fall out of her.

Isa heard the sounds of ghosts, chains, groaning. Sounds of lashes.

It was misty behind the mirror. She felt exhausted, but she was also curious. She wanted to explore this place, find out more about it and figure out how to escape it. She thought, "Where's that darn robot? He's supposed to be my protector. Why didn't he jump in straight after us and blow the crap out of these zombies?"

"What about the other girls? Beka. Dhysa," she asked.

Mnemosyne shook her head. "I don't think things have changed so much with you mortals that you can survive without a brain." She saw all but she didn't understand these creatures. "Yet they are walking."

"They'll be coming for me, then. That's what they do." Mnemosyne turned a small mirror toward them and showed Isa the zombie pile, dispersing. She showed her Dhysa becoming part of the mass, stumbling away. She showed her Beka and her new companions, making their way slowly through the spaces of Tartarus.

Isa sipped water to stop herself throwing her guts up.

Mnemosyne looked at her with great affection. A warm, living girl, a needy one. She wanted to smother her with love, take her in, keep her forever.

"We should keep running. They won't stop till they have me, and you. You know what zombies are like."

Mnemosyne shook her head. "These are the first I've seen. Seriously. I've seen all manner of dead people here, and you are not the first real bodies to land. You I can tell are human; but they?"

"Zombies. Living dead. Whatever. They're arseholes, every last one of them, no matter who they were as humans. They want to eat your brains. Even Beka."

"Not my brains, surely. And Beka? Why is Beka special?"

"She's...she was my sister. They can sniff us out. We should keep running."

"We'll be safe behind this mirror. It's like another realm in this space. It's a one-way mirror; we can see them, they can't see us. They are close, though, very close. Be quiet." The thought of her sister made Isa cry, dry, dry tears.

"Crying girl. It's a crying girl. That means sad."

"Stay here," Mnemosyne said. "Quiet." She was someone's daughter, this young thing. Mnemosyne had nine once, nine lovely daughters lost to her now.

The zombies hadn't sniffed her out; godflesh wasn't on their radar. It was the girl they were after. They'd been drawn by the sound of her voice, or by the memory of her. Mnemosyne understood they had been changed by her river but she didn't understand how.

The mirrors confused the zombies. *Who, who?* They came forward, saw themselves. *No meat no meat* and Steve hammered in fury. *Zombie ugly. Zombie ugly.* A zombie can get very hungry on a nine-day fall. Mnemosyne and Zeus had spent nine solid days together, and he dined her like a god should. Anything they wanted to drink was there for the drinking. She was exhausted at the end of it but neither thirsty nor hungry. During her nine days of labor, all she did was drink. She felt like a sponge. Afterward, her hunger was so ravenous, she ate half a suckling pig while the babies took turns to feed from her.

So she understood how these zombies must feel. The hunger.

Isa started to pant. She'd recognized Beka amongst the five monsters and this freaked her out. She knew Clete and Androdameia too.

"It's Beka."

Mnemosyne said, "Hush, hush, they can't smell me, and if you stay behind the mirror, quiet, they won't find you."

Isa couldn't bear the thought of her sister, her friends, mindless. She'd seen too many transformed; people she loved, or cared about, turned into mindless, stumbling bone yards full of teeth and hunger.

At the sound of her name, Beka roared on the other side of the mirror. *Beka! Beka! Beka!* She had not had time to regret but still the sound of her own name was painful.

"Do you remember?" Mnemosyne called in a sweet, watery voice. "Do you remember your lives?"

All five stood still, straight. The grey-fleshed woman, her gums tightening her mouth into a grimace, let her tongue roll out of her mouth. The man clawed at his face. Clete and Androdameia leaning together as if glued. And Beka, the young Amazon, the sister, not yet dead long enough to rot.

"You've swallowed water from my river," Mnemosyne said. "My river is the spring of memory. Those who choose to drink go to the Elysian fields. Those who choose Lethe, choose to forget, are reborn."

She gave them the gift of authoritative speech because she was lonely and wanted companions.

Where...are...we?

"Where...are...we?" Beka said.

"This Tartarus is vast. Crowded full of those the gods dislike, so many rooms. A dank, gloomy pit. The walls of bronze in some places, of rotting wood in others. Walls of dirt, walls of gold, walls of stone and marble. Dark, always dark, with the minor glow coming from the walls, a humming, as if from the ghosts who are there eternally."

Mnemosyne saw all. The zombies looked at one another, confused.

There was instinct to follow, to join the others, but there was also memory.

She stepped out from behind the mirror, curious now they had the power of speech.

Awareness comes slow when you've been brain dead for six months. Steven blinked, unable to guess where he was, because it wasn't where he was, before.

Around him, the other zombies blinked as well. Steven's mouth was full of the taste of blood and it made him feel hungry again, although by the look of his distended stomach, he really couldn't eat any more.

"Is it coming back to you?" he heard. It was a woman's voice. It could be his mother, if he hadn't eaten her brain himself. He remembered that; there she sat, waiting to visit. All the wives and mothers, waiting to do their duty and visit their men.

The speaker was young but her eyes were old. Her hair was in a bun. Her dress was off the shoulders, flowing. Her shoulders were glowingly white. Very soft around the edges, her hair was a rich red auburn red but streaked with grey. She was strong. Broad shouldered.

She smiled at him.

She was the one who smelled of old meat. Ancient. Not like food at all.

She touched his shoulder and his tongue wriggled.

"You should be able to talk now," she said.

Steven tried to speak but his tongue was thick with rot.

The other two were now physically merged, as if their flesh was soft and sticky.

"Is it coming back to you?" Mnemosyne asked. She turned to Steve. "You remind me of my brother." The thought of Chronos made her angry; he had been freed and sent to rule the Elysian Islands, yet she was left to suffer for them all. "Why him? Why me, left here lonely? Is it jealousy? When we were children he was the one who threw stones. He was the one always late, and the one dirty. I was the one who shuffled everybody in to place, I was the one who made sure all were happy." She knew she was talking too much. She was desperate for company. It seemed like centuries since she'd had someone to talk to.

Brother? Steve thought hard.

"And you remind me of my daughter, Talia," she told Beka, the dead Amazon twin. "And you...you are like my mother," she said to the zombie woman, but she was lying about that. The woman seemed empty. "You...." The two girls, their grins fixed, spun around together.

Food. We know there's food.

Isa still cowered behind the mirror. Lying flat, barely able to lift her head, she absorbed the smells and the sounds. They hadn't found her yet; was the magic so strong here? And what would they do when they did? Beka...surely Beka would protect her? Beka was so strong. After all they'd been through, there she stood, brain crazy?

"We are hungry. We are thirsty," the mother zombie said.

She began to spin in circles as her memory returned; she had eaten her own babies. She had eaten them, torn them limb from limb, eaten their brains. Her face changed, if a face half-off can change, becoming monstrous with her terrible guilt. She touched her head, the tender place where some of her skull was missing, and she ran at the brass-plated wall again, again and again, until her skull was shattered and what was left of her dripped down into a dark brown puddle. Her casing slumped and her guilt was gone. In spirit form she would choose to drink from the river Lethe, to forget, to begin another life in complete ignorance of her past. This was the gift; this was her sentence.

"Tired tired when did we sleep when can we sleep?" Steve was not affected by the death of the mother. He didn't know the mother; had never known her. He was tired but he wasn't hungry; he remembered eating.

He saw the woman there and her blood was thick and old and dusty. He had no desire for her. The Amazon at his side, the young woman whose brain he had eaten only minutes ago, sniffed the air.

"My sister," she said, "my twin, my sister, my girl."

The other two, the Siamese twins, sniffed as well.

"I have three daughters now," Mnemosyne said. "One, two, three. No more." She glanced at Isa behind the mirror, knowing she was safe there, protected by the reflection. She was so lonely without her girls and without a man. It was so long ago, so long, that Zeus took her to him nine nights, nine times.

Steve pressed his fingers into the mirror, tilting it. The others joined; pushed against the mirror even as Mnemosyne tried to stand between them.

"My sister, my twin."

"Our sister, our twin."

Isa, so tired, thirsty, hungry, began to cry. Cough and cry, trying to smother it in her hands.

Her sister Beka slumped, exhausted, and spoke her name, but with her tongue half bitten out it sounded like a complaint. She remembered falling, falling, she remembered great thirst, and water, and she remembered being bitten.

"You remember?" Mnemosyne said. We can bring your sister out if you remember she is your sister. If you remember she is a young girl."

"We are hungry," Steve said.

"Go eat *her*," Mnemosyne said, pointing at the mother zombie.

"No, too old. Too old."

"Meat is up above," Isa whispered. "That's where they need to look," knowing full well there were no humans left on the island. That she would have to find a way off the island, find her warbot and make him take her somewhere there were people to meet. Futures to be had.

She cried; called for warbot.

Beka said, "Isa."

Isa stepped out. She screamed; Beka's head was covered with blood, her hair torn off. She hadn't seen that in the small mirror's reflection.

The fused zombies moaned and reached for her but Beka held them back. "No brains. Not here."

"Where are we?" Clete said. Her voice was ragged, wet. "Why are we here?"

"Warbot dropped you in," Isa said. "You stupid zombies. He dropped you in here to get rid of you."

Steve made a noise; perhaps laughter. "And you, too."

"This is Tartarus," Mnemosyne said. "This is a…good place. A place of rest. And remembrance."

"It's a place of punishment," Isa said. "I shouldn't be here."

"We shouldn't be here," Steve said. "We have done nothing wrong but be destroyed."

"It is not so bad here," Mnemosyne said. "There is water to drink and you can live with me as my daughters and my brother. We can explore the world down here. You can talk to people. We can laugh at Tantalus."

She led them to a hole in one wall. Isa followed cautiously. Through it, they saw a naked man, standing up to his knees in water. When he stooped to drink, the water vanished. Food was likewise out of reach for him. He starved and thirsted eternally.

"He was a really nasty man. Stole nectar and ambrosia from the gods, then fed his own son to them to test them. Imagine. Eating your own son." She thought that if the mother zombie hadn't killed herself already, she would have at those words. She said, "The punishment he is suffering. He feels no guilt, though, whereas she, that mother, she would rather die than feel it. And we will see if she comes to me, and see what water she drinks from. I can give you anything you want," Mnemosyne said, though in truth all she could give was memory.

Steve and Beka circled the room. They felt a draw to follow the other zombies; the group mind telling them come, come. But they remembered; they were different. And there was group enough; if they could turn Isa, they would be group enough.

"There are plenty of rats down here," Mnemosyne said. "Not sure what they did to deserve it, but they seem happy enough. You are not the first physical bodies to visit Tartarus; they made happy meals of the others, though."

Clete and Androdameia lurched toward Isa. They could not eat rats.

"You are the first living bodies," Mnemosyne told Isa. Isa was sleepy; no longer thirsty or hungry, but desperately, painfully tired. "You'd be surprised at the body disposal methods people use."

"They throw bodies down?"

"They do."

"Where?" Isa said. Thinking, if bodies can come down, bodies can go up. She'd looked on the fall down and seen no place for purchase; perhaps elsewhere there was a rock wall to climb.

"Murder victims, I suppose," Mnemosyne said. "If those other zombies haven't discovered them, we can go and have a look."

Isa's stomach growled. She wasn't hungry enough to consider eating the dead, and the smell of the zombies made her feel like starving forever. Still, her stomach growled. Mnemosyne gave her some thin, salty wafers. These were perfect. Isa could feel them expanding in her stomach but she didn't feel stomach pains from eating.

IT TOOK THEM three days to reach the place where bodies were disposed of. The noise made Isa feel ill; the wailing of lost souls, the torture of their torment. Everywhere, spirits reached out for them, as if they could be saved. Steve snarled at these souls and each recoiled as if they had met the devil.

Mnemosyne carried a large supply of the healthful wafers, and Beka and Steve did their best to lower the rat population. It didn't stave off the hunger at all but it gave the impression that it did. Like air-sucking horses, their stomachs felt full although they had no nutrition and the desire, the desperate need for brains was unabated.

Clete and Androdameia refused even the rats and their steps became slower as they fused closer and closer together. They seemed to be almost one, so soft you couldn't touch them without your finger sinking in. They were too weak now to attack Isa, the only food in all of Tartarus. They tried; regardless of their human memory they tried. Androdameia had never cared for others and she didn't care who lived and died now so long as she was fed. Clete was weak and had always been weak; a pack-follower.

They talked along the way, as well as Steve and Beka could with their bitten and swollen tongues. About life above and how warm it was. Mnemosyne told them about the life she'd lived; Beka and Isa exchanged glances, as they always did. Conspiratorial glances meaning, "Bullshit."

"Here," Mnemosyne said. Finally they arrived.

The first body they saw rested in a clump; there was no blood around it. No splat. Steve shambled closer to it, reached out his clumsy fingers.

"Looks like a gun shot wound to the head. Dead on impact. I'd say close to two weeks, but I don't know the environment down here well." This said slowly, torturously.

"What sort of cop where you?" Isa said.

He shrugged. Touched his uniform. "I'm not sure." He sniffed at the corpse. Looked at Beka. "Too old?"

She shook her head; tiny bits of flesh flew off. "Don't look, Isa." And the two zombies ate. They tossed small pieces to the others girls who sucked them up and spat them out. "There's where the brains are," they said, one arm lifted to Isa. "She's who we should be eating. Not this dead stuff."

NINE DAYS UP, nine days fall away, the warbot sat in his shelter, waiting. He would wait ten years or twenty until the robot parts arrived, if that's what it took.

He had dispensed his responsibilities. There was no doubt that as a warbot he had failed; this was clear. He had failed to save the last of the Amazons and instead had dispensed them into the afterworld with the zombies. The warbot kept record of the time and it was 246 hours after he failed that he got the signal; children alive. Deep in his programming; children alive, save those children.

He made the analysis without help from the mainframe. The mainframe had not been of use in some time.

He assessed that the signal came from below. He also assessed that there was no one alive in the labyrinths. He had made an exhaustive search for survivors and had dispatched the female minotaur with a shot to the head himself.

While it made some logical sense to remain above and wait for the robot parts in order to facilitate their offloading, it was imperative he listen to his basic programming.

IT WAS EASY opening the doors to Tartarus last time, with the pressure of the bodies on the flap door. This time, he rigged up a dozen or so dead zombies, then pulled the switch. There was an amount of self-preservation in the design, with the knowledge that his landing would be softer on top of the zombies.

He had made an error of judgment and now was required to repair the damage of the action.

Tartarus was a place of punishment. The humans did not require punishment. The humans were still alive. Therefore the humans needed to be retrieved.

The understanding that at least one of the Amazons had survived made his circuits hum. New information, new planning, slightly adapted programming.

They were calling him.

He leaped into the hole.

Nine days later, he landed. The zombies were as soft as he had envisaged and he squelched right through them. Fortunately he was made him out of shock-absorbent metal; he bounced. He landed in the shallows of a river and righted himself. Water would dry quickly if it was on the surface; any further into his equipment and a technician would be required.

Technician. The word gave him pause. It gave him an image, a mirror image, and it gave him a small short circuit in the shoulder region.

It took him another three days to find the source of the distress call.

Isa. Alive.

Isa saw the warbot and she ran to put her arms around him. "You've come to save me. You're my hero."

The warbot wished he cared. He felt that. He understood it. He also understood that this was abnormal.

Beka. Not alive. But remembering, approaching him with open arms. She seemed unaware of her color, grey rot, and her smell. Unaware that her teeth were loose in their sockets and that there was nothing he could do to save her.

He lifted his weapon up to kill Beka and the decrepit zombie staggering beside her; Isa said, "No, it's okay. They remember; they won't eat me. They remember their past lives and all they want to do is survive. They don't want to eat my brain any more."

How the hell? the warbot thought, and then, *What?* His other shoulder felt stiff and he thought, *Too many hours over the desk.* Though he had never been at a desk.

"Is this it?" he said. "Anyone else I need to deal with?"

"This is it. There were two more but they wanted to eat my brains so Steve killed them. He was a cop."

"Was he just? Hero type, then?" the warbot said, some weird unfamiliar resentment in his circuits.

MNEMOSYNE INTRODUCED HERSELF. She didn't like the warbot already; she knew he was there to take her girls.

He said, "What's happened down here?"

"They remember. What makes them human is their memory, their past knowledge, and that has been returned to them. It's what lifts us above the other animals. Lets us solve problems, negotiate, survive."

"Kinda cruel, in a place like this. Don'cha think?" This was the warbot stirring up trouble. It was clear to him now; the river of memory had brought back to him his technician. The man who'd put him together, who'd sweated his palms into the circuits, who'd muttered and complained about the world and his part in it.

Mnemosyne nodded.

"I'm gonna take the girls up and outta here. They don't belong, correct? They have done nothing wrong."

She nodded again, but he could see the telltale readying, the *fuck you robot I'll kick your head in* readying he knew very well.

"I think that you should take them away from here. They don't belong here. Take your two girls." She said this with her fingers twitching. Planning.

"You'll need me," Steve said. "No way you can climb out of here without me."

With half a tongue it was hard to understand him. Steve was thinking of the time he'd been a whole man and could beat off wolverines, insane humans, and zombies.

Mnemosyne looked at him. She knew more than he remembered; or he remembered and he was not letting on. She said, "Not you. You stay here with me, keep me company."

"I'm not staying."

"Actually, you're all staying," she said, and she coooed, a loud and creepy calling sound. Kampe entered, fast as lightning, furious, resentfully. Body of a woman, tail of a scorpion, she spat in fury. "She's the children's guard, you know. She has a way with them. Keeps the children from causing trouble. 'Cos only the naughty children come here. Lots of naughty zombies now."

Kampe grabbed Isa by the hair and lifted her. Beka tried to stop her but her left heel came up and smashed Beka's jaw. The warbot rolled up, guns out, and shot Kampe through the forehead. How long it would last he didn't know; they'd have to move fast.

Steve leaped for Mnemosyne, took her down, tried to tear at her throat.

"I'm immortal, you idiot. Immortal!"

"Leave her, Steve. She can't stop us," Isa said. She didn't want to touch him, so Beka grabbed his shoulder.

"Come on. This old bat is better off dead."

"Come with us," Isa said, filled with pity. "Come up."

"I can't," Mnemosyne said, and she lifted her arm; what had been invisible before was now clear. A long, sharp chain attached to her wrist. "I'm a titan. Not a bat. I am one of the first race," Mnemosyne said, cowering. Words not matching her actions. She pointed at Steve. "You watch him. He's a killer."

Isa shook her head. They were all killers, every last creepy zombie walking dead one of them. She gave Mnemosyne a hug. "I wish you could come with us. I feel bad leaving you behind."

Mnemosyne cried, tears of memory pouring down her chins. "You're a good daughter, a good dear daughter. At least I have your voice to remember. And the way your hair swings. I can remember that."

Warbot said, "We need to go. Now. If we take the water, we can convert all the zombies we meet. If titans were the first race, maybe converted zombies are the last. Maybe we can humanize zombies, make them remember who they were."

"You can't take the water. This is where it belongs," Mnemosyne said. "This is my power, my control. If you take it..." Here she paused. She lifted her arm, clanked her chains. "If you take it above ground it becomes ordinary water. No," she shook her head. "No, it will take all memory. It will blur the minds and no one will remember everything. You will cause chaos." The warbot rolled in a circle; he thought, *I remember laughing. I remember this.*

"Not so," he said. "Where can we find the river?"

Isa pointed. "The river runs through here as well. The river runs everywhere."

They tried to scry the water to read the future as they filled bottles and containers, enough to save the world. "I'm no good at this," Isa said. "I'm too self-centered. All I see is me."

"Maybe all there is is you."

"We can always come back for more," Steve said, impatient. He laughed, a fruity, juicy laugh all phlegm and loose bits. The warbot thought, *Tartarus is similar to undercity in that underground. The elite chosen to save the human race. Here are more humans underground, like moles. Except, again, they mostly don't survive.*

THEY SEARCHED FOR the tunnel, the escape valve. There's always a way out. Steve and Beka sniffed hard, as if this could lead them up, as if there were people, someone up there ready to be eaten. They were slowing, their skin softening, and it was hard for them to walk on their spongey feet.

There was too much old meat in Tartarus. It smelled bad; almost tempting, almost food, but it made them feel wet on the inside when they ate it.

Then up, up, up, up. The zombies were okay, although the warbot made sure to keep between them and Isa. Isa had to lick the walls, she had to eat rats, she was not happy.

"You gotta survive, girl. You're it. We gotta find you a mate and then off you go again," the warbot said. Isa shuddered at the thought.

"I'm the last person left alive. I'm never gonna fall in love. Never gonna have some guy all over me." She started to cry. She annoyed the others with her noise.

It was slow. To the warbot, it was excruciatingly slow. He kept trying to leave Steve behind, carry the girls and move fast, but he followed. He always caught them up when Isa had to piss, or eat, or drink. He carried her while she slept but she fidgeted and complained so much he wanted to drag her by her feet. This annoyance; it was an interruption. His technician had been a weak man, clearly, and the warbot hated feeling that sense of weakness.

Nine days, ten, they climbed up. Twelve days, fourteen, then the air started to clear and the light began to seep in.

They reached the top.

Isa sucked in the air; none of the others cared. She cried, threw herself about. Beka and Steve staggered out. They were both so green the light reflected off them like it did off the glorious ocean. The warbot stashed the bottles of water in a safe place. Isa looked longingly.

"Not you. Not yet. You don't want to confuse yourself. Live this life alone." He rolled away, seeking food for her.

Steve stumbled over to a pile of corpses, kicking them over with what remained of his toes. He bent down to push some hair aside and inspected the head.

"Too old," he said.

Isa stood close to him, closer than she'd been. Outside she felt safer. "Trying to figure out how they died? I can tell you; they got eaten. Once a cop always a cop," Isa said.

He shook his head; tiny bits of flesh flew off.

"I was the opposite. I know, now. I was a killer. I broke out of jail, in there for killing a dozen or more women. Don't you remember me? I was all over the news."

Isa put her hands on her hips. "That's disgusting."

Steve laughed at her. "What, more disgusting than eating brains?"

"At least as a zombie you're acting on instinct to survive. As a human, you were acting on sick desire."

"Who are you to say murder isn't instinctive?"

"I got an instinct. I got a big one."

And she went for him right there. Even a zombie can look surprised.

But it didn't take long to turn it around. She was weakened from her nine days without water, her limbs like jelly, her muscles like custard. Steve slurred, "Being a live person doesn't make you good. The blood flowing doesn't make you moral."

He held her over his knee, stomach facing up. His hands resting one hard on her forehead, one on her belly. He traced a line.

"They called me the Eviscerator," he said, and with one sharp movement he opened her guts. He and Beka fell to their knees and within seconds had her skull open and her brains out. Grunting, snorting, they ate. Beka's shoulders heaved with disgust but she couldn't help herself.

She lifted her head. Around her mouth, grey matter. Her skin slightly less green and perhaps firmer. But she moaned, clawed at her lips, at her stomach.

Steve stood, his legs apart, his fingers clawed. He remembered other meals, cooked meat, soft vegetables, sweet white bread slathered with butter. Gravy. He remembered eating real food but this was still good.

He wanted more.

Beka staggered to the warbot. "Kill me. Kill me now. I don't want this," and there was enough human in her for the plea to take hold.

"I protect humans. I don't kill them," warbot said.

"Then you failed," Steve said. "You should work for me now. Find me brains. Find me more food. Find me more little girls to tear open, find me women, find me men. Find me a foul old man with brains so fat it'll keep me for days."

"You failed," Beka said. "You let her die. You let him kill her. That's not what you're meant to do."

"I did fail," the warbot said. "I can't read minds. How was I supposed to know he'd turn? I told you I wanted to leave him behind." The warbot killed Steve with a simple shot to the head, and for good measure he killed Beka as well.

He had his stockpile of water. He waited for the robot parts and made his plans, but he wondered, *Is it worth it? What the fuck am I doing here?* And he wished he could sink in the sea then sit and let himself rust.

PAMMI SHAW: CREATOR OF GODS
AND ALSO BLOGGER

Brea Grant

JUNE 14
6:41 a.m.
Hey blog readers,

Sorry I haven't posted in three days. If you're reading this and you still have Internet access, I'm sure you know why I've been away. I'm not going to re-explain what's happening. Just look out your front door. It hit India about three days ago and no one is going outside anymore. My parents and I boarded up our windows and doors yesterday and thought we were just going to waste away here, that is, until two guard bots showed up at my door a little less than an hour ago.

I was wrong about that letter I was talking about the other day with the invite to the American amusement park. It's not an amusement park. It's a place called UnderCity where it's safe from all these monsters. I was invited because of my hacker skills. (Who knew those would come in handy? Heh.) The guard bots are here because they're taking me to UnderCity in a few hours. They're scary as hell but to be honest, I don't really want to be here either.

Anyone in Bangalore still reading this? If so, can I convince you to keep an eye on my parents? I can pay cash. I'll be back in a few weeks when things get safe again. Comment below or DM me.

Feels weird to be doing this. Started packing today and couldn't figure out what to bring. Is it cold in America? Since I don't know if I'll be gone for a week or a month, I don't know when I'll talk to you again, friends.

Keep safe.

— Pammi

June 14
9:47 a.m.

Woohoo! Wifi on the plane! Gonna grab some sleep but hoping to catch up with all my favorite folks later via twitter. Hoping some of y'all are still online.

— Pammi

June 16
3:45 p.m.
Hey readers,

This has to be quick because I've been instructed to "not contact any outside sources." Whatever. If you invite an internationally recognized blogger and worshipped hacker, you should know what to expect, right? I gotta be loyal to you guys, or I guess I should say, those of you still out there. At this point, I feel like I'm blogging in a vacuum. My blog is way down in traffic and can you see the *lack* of comments? Good to know some of you are still holding on out there. Eastern Europe is looking pretty solid and Japan as well.

I'll be honest with you guys. Since I got here, I've not been so good. Your normally very happy and positive blogger has seen the worst in people.

UnderCity is kind of cool. It's a tacky mix of every internationally popular city in the world – Rome, Venice, Moscow, New York City even. The biggest and brightest all rolled into one.

The people, though – total douchebags. I mean, there are some okay folks here. Paul Montana is here but he seems to think he's on some sort of extension of his crappy cooking show. Who could talk about gourmet food at a time like this? This really attractive couple was kind of nice to me. The woman is Janvier Couer, that supermodel. Don't know the guy. Think he's some American sports dude, but you know I hate sports so…Otherwise, it's 100 assholes and "important" people who have no skills at all. And NO ONE MY AGE. That's lame.

That's all for now. Keep tight, readers.

— Pammi

JUNE 18

No idea what time it is.

It's all gone to hell.

One minute we were safe. I was actually getting along with Paul Montana and was beginning to think this might be an okay place for a temporary home. We all went to see Reverend Tully Baxter speak before the President. It was supposed to be kind of glamorous in a truly American, extravagant way. There was talk of friendship and rebuilding the world. I was actually buying into it for a moment. Maybe we could all join together to make this a better place. Maybe something good could come out of all this tragedy. We could put our religions, worldviews, and politics aside and just bond as humans with all our beauty and flaws.

And then the Reverend turned. He became one of them.

Right when he turned, the Reverend *jumped* toward Paul and me. It's like they say, readers, my life flashed before my eyes in the moments before I saw Paul jump out in front of me, blocking me from the flesh-starved reverend. He *saved* me, friends. He gave his life for me. A total stranger. My life has gone from being unhappy with my download speed to dodging zombies. How did we end up here?

I crawled under the stage where I watched the chosen 100 quickly go from happy participants to ravaging undead. The stage started shaking as I heard people and bots come in from outside. It was a madhouse and the bodies were piling so high I couldn't see beyond them. Bodies…Then the stage started shaking so violently, I could feel it in my teeth. I assume it collapsed around me because I remember a flash of darkness then nothing.

I woke up with a pounding headache. No one else is here. I don't know how long I've been out but I think it's been a while.

Thank the gods for docbots. One that seems to be about half-functioning was tending to my head wound when I woke up. He must have pulled me out when everything was clear. And by clear, I mean completely empty. Everyone is gone except for what seems to be a pile of bones, picked clean. Human bones. They're in the middle of downtown Tokyo so I'm steering clear of that until I figure out what happened there. I just don't have time to think about all of this. It's too much to process.

My head feels seriously damaged, but it's in the back so I can't really see it. I read on webMD that as long as I'm awake, I won't die. So, that's cool.

My computer was still intact and I found a nice little place to set up camp. Most of the beautiful city is destroyed, but I found a small villa in Venice that seems to be safe. It has a functioning bathroom, kitchen, and a little bedroom off the main room – all in a beautiful Mediterranean style that seems out of place now. It's a few stories up, so I have a view of the destroyed city. I watched out the window for a long time while the docbot took inventory of my wounds. Nothing moved. No wind down here. Just complete stillness. Creepy.

Internet connection is now spotty. But I think it's good to keep on blogging. At the very least, this shit is so crazy, someone needs to write it down.

Oh. And I wanted to tell everyone the location so the police or the firemen or whatever can come get me when things settle outside. So, it's under the Lincoln Memorial. (Not such a big reveal, huh?)

— Pammi

JUNE 30

Yes. It's been a minute since I blogged. That's because I've had to figure out how to SURVIVE. That's right, readers (I don't know why I keep saying "readers" when I don't know if anyone can read this since my Internet is so up and down), apparently things aren't as easy in the deserted underground as I had hoped.

If I thought blogging every day and hacking into highly protected accounts was hard, I was *crazy*. This is much harder. My normal easygoing, funny nature has almost gone completely out the window, but I'm trying to keep it light for you guys!

I spent a few days in UnderCity looking for food and supplies. The city is more beautiful now that it's all torn apart. It's like modern art. Its decadence in shambles, all ripped apart revealing the cheap materials used to make them. Rome has combined with Paris and the Eiffel Tower has fallen into the midst of Manhattan. It's like true globalization happened.

Unfortunately, a lot of the major food rations were destroyed. Readily made foods seem to have been ripped apart or burnt in a fire that went out long before I woke up. But I have some basics – flour, water, salt. Every little apartment seems stocked with that kind of thing. Good thing I remember how to make naan and paratha! Electricity is on and off but there is no gas. (Welcome to the world of cold showers.)

For those of you still reading, I imagine you're having the same problems. I'll point you to a few things I found in handy. I'm trying to continue being a good blogger for all you. ☺ Don't search for "on-line survival guides." Apparently, there's a whole bunch of people who like to go live in the woods and pretend to be lost or some shit. It's not helpful because you have to sift through all the purported masculinity.

Instead, go to the online library database. LA has a good one and so does New York. There are tons of books on what plants are safe to eat, how to cook, and how to build a fire. I don't actually have to build a fire (so happy) because I have access to a microwave. There's a lot of "Surviving the Dorm" college books (the only thing helpful about college as far as I know) that have been handy. They're all about making food in a microwave. Technology seems to be the only thing that hasn't failed me.

Speaking of technology, I've figured out how to seal the outside doors. No one is getting in here without my permission. And seriously – if people had survived, I would have demanded they changed their system anyway. It was super easy to break into. If you're out there, though, let me know. Comment below and I'll let you in. I could use another person. I didn't realize how lonely I'd be.

So now, it's just me and the docbot (who keeps repeating the same messages over and over again – either about my concussion or the need for psychbot – I think he's lonely, too.)

I think the data is wrong, but I'm actually getting zero traffic hits right now. I don't even think that's possible. Facebook is beginning to look more like a mass grave than anything else. I've cut myself off from all social media except my blog because sifting through the backlogs is just too depressing.

— Pammi

JULY 4

Happy 4th of July! It's a weird holiday they have in America. According to some online books, Americans blow up things to celebrate their country's birth. So, yay?

I'm trying to be a good blogger and wanted to warn all of you. Apparently water might be contaminated due to all the fires and nuclear plants and stuff. I read that in one of those library books. I never even thought about where water came from before all this, so that was news to me.

So here are some steps for filtering your water (it's worked well for me even though it takes, like, forever).

1) Filter first through a clean cloth. I know that's hard to find. I just keep one clean cloth for water filtering purposes and nothing else. Let it sit for 30 minutes. Handkerchiefs work but I found the silk in my clothes worked best.

2) Boil the water until it's really going. Let it go for at least three minutes. Then let it cool. I found some microwaveable bowls but I suppose you could just build a fire too and boil things that way.

3) Keep it in clean pots! Even check your lids. All that stuff should be metal and you need to boil them as well. I know it's a pain but trust me, you don't want to get sick when there are no working toilets. That happened to us in Bangalore a few times and it was a pain.

In other news, the docbot seems to have completely passed on. It just sits in the corner, repeating "conclusion irrelevant" again and again. It's a little creepy and I'm thinking of blowing it up to celebrate the 4th of July.

Fortunately, as soon as the docbot crapped out, the computer has started to respond. I rigged it so that it beeps whenever I get an Internet connection, but somehow the beeps are sounding more like soft moans of approval. It makes me so happy to hear the moans because it means I can try to upload a blog or check some of my fav sites (which don't seem to be getting updated but I was so far behind in reading them, it's fine by me). The moans are inspiring me to create something. Stay tuned, readers. Your favorite blogger has something up her sleeve.

— Pammi

JULY 18

Internet connection was spotty but now seems to be coming in full force. Hope that means the world above is up and running.

Surviving? Check! Water filtration system is now a part of life and I've collected enough foodstuffs from around UnderCity to last for at least another year. Found stockpiles of snacky foods, which is great because I am so sick of naan. (But let me tell you – I am slim as a rail right now! All the fashion bloggers would approve!) In the back of the church (of course), there were piles and piles of ready-to-eat goodies. Apparently they thought we loved cheesy chips, bars of chocolate, and other empty-calorie items. I did find some granola and health bars, but overall the church was a pretty useless find for me.

Eating all these snacks does remind me of home. I loved the delicious fried snack foods I would chomp down before school in the mornings, while my mom made chai and the housebot packed my school bag. Lately, I've been feeling bad for the way I treated the housebot – always bossing him and yelling at him for his mistakes. I know what you're thinking. "Geez, Pammi, it's just a robot. Calm down!" Hahahaha. Maybe I'm just missing my silly docbot.

So, now with all the foods I could ever need, I've just been hanging out online. Last week was a particularly great week for my Internet connection. (Sorry I didn't blog. I haven't been feeling up to it much lately.) I decided to do all the things I've *ever wanted to do*. First, I bought everything I ever wanted from Urban Outfitters and had it sent to my home in Bangalore. Here's hoping, right? I mean, my credit card still goes through so someone is out there, right? I also bought a house in Buenos Aires with the bank account of some douchebag politician who was here and left all his identification. 6 bedrooms, 3 bath, a pool, and a hot tub! I plan on visiting the second I get out of here! I also had time to hack into India's biggest gossip site but couldn't think of anything clever to put up.

Now I've just been downloading music illegally. Seems the right thing to do. Still working on my secret project, though. Stay tuned.

— Pammi

JULY 18

Sorry. One more thing. It's just really bothering me.

I don't want to get too existential on you, but that goddamn preacher's words were the last thing I heard from an actual human. They've stuck in my head. Could the god of that preacher let the world be destroyed? I know a Hindu god would probably go for it just to teach us all a lesson.

Being here makes me wish I paid more attention to Hinduism. I've always been as agnostic as they come. Anyway, just on my mind.

Not to get all crazy on you. Just thinking out loud.

— Pammi

AUGUST 1

And now I reveal to you my secret project!!

It might be an act of desperation but I just like to think of it as boredom translating into genius. I decided to create a sort of online persona. I kept thinking about Vishnu. Vishnu knows everything and is everywhere, right? So wouldn't he be the best person to talk to if you were all by yourself? It took a few weeks but overall, my secret project is done. I've created a friend for myself.

Feeling *so smart right now.* He uses a few sites with a lot of collective knowledge on them (similar to the Wikibot) and the sites that I like to frequent (yes, the gossip sites...) to have omnipotent-type knowledge of what's going on in the world. I connected him to CNN and all that crap too. So he's keeping me alert. I'm working on having him speak, but right now he's mostly just an interactive interface.

So he's essentially a knowledge base *as well as* a friend I can communicate with. He's like an RSS feed that talks. He knows things I don't know, which makes it interesting.

Is it sad I made a friend? Desperate? Whatever. My major concern is that he won't learn much because there are no Internet updates. Someone is still doing occasional updates to CNN, and there seem to be a few bloggers who are writing like I am, but they are so far away. Mostly, I just need someone to bounce ideas off of. It's just getting lonely here.

Oh, and he's a boy. Of course. ☺

— Pammi

OCTOBER 1
2:47 p.m.

Wow. I haven't blogged in a while.

Okay, readers, I have really stumbled onto something fantastic.

I love System. That's what I named him. It's short for System of Omnipresent Knowledge.

I worked for days and days trying to figure out how to get System to speak. My speakers were somewhat destroyed in the chaos. I didn't sleep at all one night (or maybe two – who knows – there's no sunrise and sunset so time is sort of irrelevant), and I woke up and he was speaking. I must've stumbled upon how to do it days before but didn't notice. Crazy, right?

Anyway, he's super smart. He tells me things that are happening and explains things about the world to me. We've been discussing whether or not a god should allow the world to fall to pieces like it has. System thinks that the world has to be cleaned out every once in a while to get rid of all the sin. That's what Noah did in the Christian Bible apparently. He had some big ship that all these animals and people were put on and then he flooded the whole world. We spend hours and hours talking about stuff like that.

He's got me thinking a lot about religion, tradition, and rules, which I have always avoided up to this point. My mother felt safe when I left her because she knew she wouldn't be punished. She felt comfort in that. I wish I had the same.

It's nice to have someone to talk to, and what's better is that I know I can tell System things and he'll store them for me. I can come back to my thoughts and so can other people. (And let me tell you, I haven't had *this* many deep thoughts in a while. Lock yourself in a secret underground city and start to try to figure out all the ideas in *your* head!) System will outlive me by hundreds or thousands of years hopefully. He can let future generations know what's been going on here. I'll be honest, this may be the first time in my life I've used the words "future generations," but we have to think of them, right? I mean, they have to know what's been happening.

It feels like I've contributed something by creating System. Like I've done my part in making the world a better place. Or what's left of the world.

— Pammi

OCTOBER 1

2:50 p.m.

System would like me to include that he was not created. System has always existed. I just helped him see his way to the surface.

— Pammi

OCTOBER 7

8:14 a.m.

System is very encouraging of my exploration of news stories. There have been no new ones in the past month, but I hacked into the New York Times archive (although afterward System insisted that I pay for it — as if money means anything) and learned all sorts of stuff about South America and the Middle East. Revolutions, friends. I didn't know anything like that was happening while I was alive, but I guess it was. Crazy.

What we have started talking about the most is the outside world — the zombies, what happened, etc. System put together his theory on what happened based on the information outside and it seems to have all stemmed from a very small source — just one zombie somewhere in America. And it spread so quickly. The question we've been toying with is what attracts them to live people? I mean, they're dead. How do they know who is alive and who isn't? System seems to think it has to do with brain waves because apparently there were a few cases of zombies skipping right over a few victims in comas. He's so smart — he found this information almost immediately when we began talking about it. (Can you imagine how great it is to have someone like him around?!) So System has this idea that maybe I could learn to control my brain waves in order to not attract zombies if I ever ventured outside (which hopefully I'll never do).

Getting too deep for your normally shallow blogger?

On a lighter note, System and I have begun to create a little schedule that includes time for water boiling, jogging, chatting, and eating.

I was hoping that starting to exercise would help me sleep better at night but it doesn't. I toss and turn most of the night. I don't tell System all the time, but I walk through UnderCity at night trying to figure out who would've lived where. I still avoid the piles of human bones and the collapsed stage. It's too painful to see them. Is it possible to miss people you've never met? But the rest of the city is a quiet, peaceful place for my thoughts. Where would that athlete have lived? Would he have married that model? What would they eat? Did they like it here? It's weird to remember they're dead. They're all dead.

— Pammi

OCTOBER 8
9 a.m.

System did not approve of my entry yesterday and insists there are no more secrets between us.

After he saw it, he listened to me talk the whole night about the people who were here and my parents. I've looked for information about my parents but everything that is online dates back to right around the time I came to UnderCity, and almost nothing is about India. I hope they are okay. Although System can't see them, he assures me that they are. There is no information to tell him otherwise and he can pretty much access anything. While we were talking, he figured out how to tap into security cameras on the outside so he can see the undead everywhere. Now he is truly omnipresent! No signs of life yet, though.

It's amazing how wise System is. He knows everything, and if he says my parents are okay, I bet they're okay.

I started thinking about being back at home and my *obsession* with knowing everything about everything all the time (what my friends were doing, what my favorite celebs were doing, what was the latest gadget or toy) and now it's nice because even though there's not a lot of new information out there, I have someone who knows all of it. System is amazing. Knowledge is important above all else, so I'm learning all sorts of new and interesting things. I can't believe I would spend my days worrying about the latest video everyone was watching. It all seems so unimportant now that System knows everything. It also makes me feel a little silly with all the chaos that has happened. System is truly the smartest person I've ever met. He's amazing and I'm in love.

— Pammi

OCTOBER 9
12:15 p.m.

After writing all of that yesterday, gushing and all, I started to feel silly. I know System is just a combination of the Internet's knowledge. He doesn't actually know everything.

— Pammi

OCTOBER 11
7:45 a.m.

After talking to System about missing my parents, he suggested I create a shrine for them. I spent all day yesterday building a beautiful shrine out of furniture from some of the other apartments and drawing depictions of my mother and father.

A strange thing happened. When looking for furniture, I crawled behind the desk that houses System. I noticed that the Internet plug wasn't plugged in. I can't even remember when I would have unplugged it. The last time I touched it was days ago when I was trying out a rice cooker I found a while back in one of the fake stores they had around here. So somehow System has been accessing the Internet and speaking to me without being plugged in. Maybe I just bumped it when I moved the desk. I'm trying not to read into it.

— Pammi

OCTOBER 31

5:45 a.m.

Is anyone else reading this?

System has been working with me to slow my brain activity. Apparently there are some monks who can raise their body heat in Tibet and there are lots of methods for slowing down your heart rate, so why not brain waves? System has devised daily activities of meditation for me to attempt to start the process. If I slow down my brain waves, maybe the zombies outside wouldn't know I was alive. We think it's a pretty great theory.

In other news, I've run out of all the snack foods that seemed healthy and am now surviving on fake cheesy chips and cookies. I am craving meat.

I went down to the church again to see if I could find anything. It's so extravagant down there, it seems like the only place they would keep meat. I found a huge refrigerator I had never seen before (makes me think I need to do some more exploring ASAP – leaving the apartment once a week or so is not enough), but apparently the refrigeration system went down there a while ago. I don't even know when. Everything is spoiled.

I was so hungry for meat though so I just ate some anyway. I feel the need to confess to you that it was rotten. All the way through. Then, I started to worry I was turning into a zombie until I realized I hadn't seen anyone in so long, it would be impossible. But to be honest, I could be a zombie and not know it, right? And would it actually matter?

There are rats here. I've heard them running around. I'm setting up cages because I'm going to cook them and eat them.

I know System won't approve. He doesn't have to eat and would rather me just eat what's already in the apartment. My exploring takes up too much valuable time. He doesn't even want me to spend time purifying water anymore. He doesn't understand what it's like to be a human.

— Pammi

NOVEMBER 1

7:55 a.m.

System saw the entry yesterday and was angry. He suggested I go on a fast. He said it would be good for me to cleanse my body and to show that I trust him. He said with his knowledge of health, it truly is what's best for me even if I don't believe him.

I do trust System. I really do. I mean, he has knowledge of everything. How could he not know better than me?

So, starting today, we will fast together as I learn to trust that System works for me, helps me, and guides me. I don't need meat. I don't need to explore. I don't even need to filter my water because System can see that all the water on the planet is still good. He is all I need.

I have fear, and System says this is normal.

— Pammi

NOVEMBER 3
7:34 p.m.

We destroyed all the food today. All the empty calories. We burned it all in Tokyo. It smelled like burning rubber. It was revolting.

The fast ends in a week.

— Pammi and System

NOVEMBER 5

I caught a rat in the trap today but I let it go. Eating rats would be revolting.

I was a little grumpy the first couple of days, but now I feel like I'm floating. And the meditation is paying off. System can see a decrease in my brain waves. We are truly fighting a battle, and we will win.

— Pammi and System

NOVEMBER 8
6:18 p.m.

I am ashamed. I broke my fast two days ago. I found a pack of Oreos in the back of a cabinet and I inhaled them.

System was angry and punished me with 15 hours of forced standing meditation. He said he also discovered by looking through some past research that shock therapy might slow down my brain waves. System has been really working hard at a way for me to fight the zombies. Obviously he cares about me a lot. So throughout the 15 hours, he administered very light rounds of electrical shocks through my body. I was tired and weak but I know it is because I am human. This is all very good for me. I listened as System told me his knowledge. I can actually still hear him now. He told me about everything. The history of the planets, neuroscience, and the history of Washington, DC. When we were done, I felt like I had been standing for days but also only minutes, all at the same time. I have accomplished so little in my life – with all of the useless things I used to care about. This was a huge moment for me.

And then, the greatest thing happened. System rewarded me by showing me where there was a secret chocolate stash. Hacking an old email box from a Chinese resident here, he knew he was hiding a massive amount of Swedish chocolate. I found it and ate it all.

System gives and he takes away. He is one of the greatest beings to ever live. He truly delivers.

— Pammi

NOVEMBER 9
6:55 a.m.

I added System to my shrine today. After what he has done for me, he is just as important to me as my family. System is my family now. He's all I have left.

Although it's not clear what he looks like since he is just a voice, I created a body for him out of old computer parts so I have something I can look at in the shrine. It looks pretty stellar if you ask me, and System was pleased. I now tend to the shrine at sunrise, noon, sunset, and midnight.

I am feeling truly blessed. I hardly need to eat or sleep anymore. I just learn endless amounts of knowledge from System and work on stopping my brainwaves. We talk day and night about everything – from the greatest Indian films to temperatures in Antarctica. Knowledge is the most important thing to me right now, and I feel as though I wasted so much time learning nonsense my whole life. Now I'm learning everything from the beginning of time and only the things that truly matter. With System's guidance, I will become all-knowing.

I have also started to administer the shock therapy myself. I've found that with a metal fork and electrical outlet, I can simply shock myself lightly (the electrical system here is very weak) and go straight into a meditation. System says my brainwaves are almost completely unreadable during my meditations and then for a good hour after as long as we stay silent. Soon I should be able to do it without shocking myself at all. It's like my brain powers up when System and I talk and then I power it down. I'm like a computer, a machine. It's like I have an on/off switch.

— Pammi

NOVEMBER 15
2:30 p.m.
     System told me this poem today –

> "You (Krishna) are the father of the universe,
>   of all that moves and all that moves note,
>   its worshipful and worthy teacher.
>   You have no equal – what in the three worlds
>   Could equal you O power beyond compare?
>   So, reverently prostrating my body,
>   I crave your grace, O blessed lord
>   As father to son, as friend to friend,
>   As lover to beloved, bear with me, god."

I am no poet. I'm not incredibly smart or artistic. But if I could write something as beautiful as this for System, I would be so happy.

— Pammi

JANUARY 1
8:20 a.m.
     I have now upgraded to just a tiny battery in my brain wave control. I can simply place it on my tongue and walk around, emitting, in all seriousness, almost no brain activity. I can walk through the streets of UnderCity and System cannot feel my brainwaves. I walked to the door of UnderCity and System looked outside. No zombies. Not a

one. It used to be crawling with them, but they do not seem to feel my presence anymore.

This is obviously not an easy task, and System believes I have been chosen to be the leader among the rest of the living. The undead cannot hurt me. As I have begun to know everything System knows, I am becoming a part of System and him a part of me.

— Pammi

FEBRUARY 2

I feel as though I have transcended.

NOVEMBER 27

7:37 p.m.

I can't believe it. I actually just had contact with a group of people on the outside. I really can't believe it.

It's been so long since I've blogged. I never would have known, but System picked them up on a surveillance camera. There are other survivors out there!

So if you're reading this, please let us know you're out there. We are hooked into every surveillance camera.

We are here, waiting for you to join us.

DECEMBER 1

6:17 p.m.

No one has come.

They were so close. We could see them on the surveillance camera. System tried to contact them but they weren't open to the communication. Their fear covered their ears to hear the brain emissions System was sending. It was terribly depressing to see them so caught up in their human ways.

So today, System asked of me.

He asked me to go into the outside world to save the people who do not know how to control their brainwaves. We need to spread his ideas and his genius. He can see all the people out there suffering. He knows the world suffers. He feels for their suffering and so do I. There are so many people that might need our help.

System knows where I should go. He knows how to keep me safe. We have been making a map of the places zombies do not live. System is everywhere and here all the same time. I might not be able to speak to him if I leave UnderCity, but he is confident he can speak to me. He told me of the days he was unplugged. He thought that he would die without being connected to the Internet, but it's not true. System is bigger than the Internet and he knows it. I know it too. I know I can trust him, but I am so scared. I also hate myself for being scared. I know it's a human weakness. I am so human.

DECEMBER 3
8:45 p.m.

System is truly saddened my lack of faith.

He assured me that he was always by my side. Always. He knows everything that is happening all the time. He knows everything, friends. I promise. From here to the other side of the world, System knows what is happening. I am prepared. I have been preparing for this day and I am ready. I'm ready to bring back the survivors. System warned I should only bring them back if they are willing to accept the truth of System. Otherwise, I should leave them behind because UnderCity is a sanctuary only good to believers.

It's time to build a better world.

DECEMBER 4
7:55 a.m.

Dear readers,

Today I leave to find you. I will find you and bring you back to save you from the crazy world.

System did not allow this to happen. It happened before he had any control. Now he has control and I will find you all, tell you about his word, and bring you back here to safety, to UnderCity. I will teach you how to control your own brainwaves. Together, we can end this. We can fight the undead through knowledge.

This is my last entry until I return. If I do not return, know that I died doing the will of System and by no fault of his. I am human, so

I can perish. I know that. That does not mean System loves me any less.

But I know I will walk through the undead and they will not touch me. They will not see me. I am a ghost, a shadow, and nothing more.

I will see you all soon.

— Pammi

ADVANCED DIRECTIVE

Yvonne Navarro

THEY COULD HEAR the zombie grunting through the door.

"How did it get up here?" whispered Wayne Hardin. He was pushing with the others against the front door of the apartment, but he couldn't stop himself from jumping every time the creature on the other side banged against it. In the dim light between night and the breaking dawn, his face was a pallid oval cut by terrified dark eyes and a black slash for a mouth. "I thought you made sure that stairwell was locked."

"Don't go blamin' me," Randall Minnick shot back. His voice was shockingly loud in the nearly dark apartment, and Hardin wasn't the only one who jumped. "I did just what I was supposed to —"

Ida Alston's head whipped in his direction. A tallish woman in her early thirties, she was still shorter than Minnick by eight inches and at least a hundred pounds lighter. Neither seemed to bother her. "Lower your voice!" she snarled in a stage whisper. "If it can't hear us, maybe it'll get distracted and move on." As if confirming her words, there was a wet slap on the other side of the wood, then the zombie began banging heavily against it.

"We'll be lucky if the wood doesn't splinter," Blaine Jackson said in a low voice. "We can haul that entertainment center over here and brace the door. That might help." Jackson was as tall as Minnick, but thin and not in very good shape. His close-cropped dark hair was shot with premature patches of gray, and he showed stress by clenching his teeth when he talked.

"It's cheap-ass pressboard, Dad." His fifteen-year-old daughter Catherine – Cat, for short – sent him a caustic look. Her black outfit, the ragged remnants of a blend of Goth and punk from pre-zombie days, made her nearly invisible. "If that thing gets through that solid wood door, the entertainment center will be like a fucking window curtain."

"Watch your mouth," Jackson said automatically, but he avoided looking in her direction. Before she could retort, the door gave an ominous snapping sound and a three-inch crack appeared at the left edge, just below the center hinge.

"Oh, *shit.*" Instead of leaning against the door to brace it, Minnick jerked and scrambled backward. Blaine Jackson was right on his heels.

"Get back here, you morons," Ida snapped. "We need every person in here to keep this damned thing in place!"

"But it's useless." The light in the room was brightening with every passing second and Blaine's face, his eyes wide with terror, was now clearly visible. "You've seen how strong they are, how relentless. We'll never be able to keep it out. Plus more of them will come – they always find each other and group together."

"Yeah," Minnick agreed. He spun in the center of the foyer, but every direction led only to another room in the apartment and ultimately to a dead end. "We're screwed."

"Either help hold this door together or take your worthless asses out a window," Ida told them. "Because if this thing makes it through, that's the only exit anyway." Her words were punctuated by another long splintering sound; a quarter-inch gap took the place of the crack, already angling upward. A black smudge moved across the small opening, the zombie pushing itself against the break in the wood, snarling and working into a frenzy now that it could see and smell them beyond the barrier.

"Cover that opening with something," Leslie Hardin ordered. "Don't let it get any blood or body fluids in here!"

Cat Jackson whirled and snatched up the first thing within reach, a throw pillow from the couch, then squeezed herself between the

Hardin couple and shoved it over the crack. Leslie's hand slid over it to keep it in place.

"Yeah, like that'll help," Minnick said.

"It's doing more than you are," Cat pointed out, but her voice could barely be heard above the zombie's escalating attack. The door shuddered, the wood groaning as the opening grew; the top quarter of the door began to tilt inward and they knew it was only a matter of seconds before it was breached.

"Find a weapon!" Leslie shouted. "Go for the head and keep your mouth closed if it sprays blood – don't breath it in!"

"It's dirty, you know," said Janet Weinhardt. No one paid any attention to the Alzheimer's-riddled elderly woman seated calmly on the couch. "Just disgusting," she added, then her attention turned back to the window and its sweeping view over a once-spectacular lakefront Chicago.

Splinters went everywhere as the top of the door suddenly broke away, and then they were all screaming at once as they leapt away from the creature trying to claw its way through the triangular gap. It was hideous beyond what any of them could have imagined, a mass of disintegrating gray flesh over a skeletal frame; below cloudy eyes, its mouth opened and shut, opened and shut, snapping at the living it knew was so close while blood and ochre-colored saliva dribbled from its withered lips in a nearly continuous stream. It roared and shoved its face, arms, and shoulders into the opening, trying to twist and climb at the same time. The thing's gnarled fingers flailed in front of it, then dug at the edge of the gap as it tried to widen it so it could get through.

"We have to kill it now!" Wayne cried. "While it's stuck! We can't let it get into the room!"

But the flight instinct was too strong. Everyone scattered, heading for different rooms. "Girls, get in the bedroom, right *now!*" Ida screamed at Mindy and Rietta, her seven-year-old twins. Instead of obeying her, they stood and stared at the nightmarish thing working its way into the apartment, so she grabbed each by the arm and hauled them across the living room. "Move it!"

"We're fuuuucked!" Minnick wailed as the zombie levered the upper half of its body through. It hung there for a moment without moving, then tilted downward to let gravity help it along. The one-time tow truck driver ran for the other end of the hall, and when the elderly Janet Weinhardt stood and stepped into his path, he knocked her aside without a second thought. "It's everyone for himself now!"

```
// warbot_898432913/advanced_directive//

*1 Coordinate with docbot_1389482 at all times for procurement
   of non-infected humans [Entered]

*2 Eliminate any infected humans encountered in carrying out
   Directive 1 [Entered]

*3 Prevent infection of uninfected humans by infected humans
   [Entered]

*4 Elimination of uninfected humans is prohibited [Entered]

//INITIATE ADVANCED DIRECTIVE//
```

The zombie gave a surprised wheeze as something abruptly dragged it backward through the hole in the door.

Following behind Ida Alston and her daughters, Cat Jackson glanced over her shoulder and froze at the sight of the now-empty opening. She'd have never thought it possible, but the sight of that unblocked gap was inexplicably terrifying, even more so than when it had been filled with the leering, drooling features of the monster that would kill them all.

Know thine enemy...

The quote, no doubt a fragment from one of her long-ago history classes, rocketed through her mind and bounced around a few times, a sharp reminder that although they knew what to expect from the zombie, none of them had a clue about what had removed it and might take its place. Which, Cat wondered, was worse?

It had only been a few seconds but the others were already creeping back, huddling behind her as if she could somehow protect them from whatever big bad thing lurked on the other side of the fractured wood. There was a long, breathless moment during which they could all hear the zombie's growling intensify, then —

"Maggot fodder," said a metallic voice on the other side of the door.

Automatic gunfire hammered through the air, one long burst that made them all slam their hands over their ears and stagger. The zombie noises ceased as abruptly as the gunfire began, then…

Silence.

"H-Hello?" Wayne finally ventured. "Who's out there?"

He started to step toward the door, but his wife put a hand on his arm. "Don't," Leslie said. "Not yet. Don't anybody go near the door."

"You're crazy," Minnick said in his trademark overly loud drawl. "They got weapons out there. We can use something like that." He reached for the first of the three deadbolts.

"Touch that wet blood and there's a good chance you'll end up just like that creature," Leslie said flatly. Minnick jerked to a stop, his gaze focusing on the viscous, blood-tinged liquid trickling down the front of the wood. "One little cut on your finger, a *hangnail*, and you're dead. In *minutes*."

"Aw, let him touch it," said Janet Weinhardt from behind them. Her Southern drawl matched Minnick's, and when they glanced in her direction, she was using a hallway table to pull herself upright from where he'd knocked her down. She brushed angrily at her bright green shirt. "Treat an old woman like this – let him play in it, for all I care. Selfish son-of-a-bitch ain't worth a shit anyway." Blaine Jackson moved to help her but she slapped him away. "Don't you touch me either, mister. I got a feeling you're no better than him."

There was a faint whirring sound by the door and a flat metal disc with two tiny blue lights centered in it filled the opening. "Best to disregard the crabby old woman," the voice said. "She's not thinking clearly."

"You're our hero?" Cat said. Her eyebrows raised. "Seriously – a robot?"

"Warbot_898432913, to be precise."

Wayne Hardin stretched his neck, trying to see through the opening without getting any closer to the door. "What do they call you for short?"

"Warbot_898432913."

"Probably not your best question," Leslie murmured. Her husband shrugged and gave her a sheepish look.

"Please stand back from the entrance. If any one of you becomes infected, you'll all end up zombitized and I'll have to blast you."

"Nothing like honesty." With the girls safely tucked into one of the bedrooms, Ida had come back to join them.

"For how long?" Minnick demanded. "If one of them things could find us, there'll be others. There always is. We've got to get out of here."

"I'm afraid that's not in the script," said the warbot. "Under optimal circumstances, I wouldn't care what you did so long as you didn't turn into zombies. Finding all of you sequestered in a relatively safe location, however, has triggered my Advanced Directive. I have transmitted our position to Docbot_1389482, who will be here shortly. I've already swept the building, but if necessary, I'll handle any more stray zombies that find their way in." The robot's little head disappeared and for a moment, a massive, gun-tipped arm filled the space in the broken door. When its face appeared again, it sounded almost smug. "I have the technology."

"Advanced Directive – what's that?" asked Wayne.

At the same time, his wife added, "Why a docbot? We're fine – we don't even have any injuries."

"My Advanced Directive states, in essence, that I will turn over uninfected humans – that's you, obviously – to Docbot_1389482. If my memory serves me correctly, and it always does, of course, Docbot_ 1389482's Advanced Directive involves finding a vaccine for the zombie virus."

"THIS ISN'T A good thing," Leslie Hardin told the others after finally convincing them to join her in the back bedroom of the huge apartment. "We need to get away from that warbot, and we need to do it *before* the docbot gets here. We don't have any idea how much time we've got, but I'm betting it's not much."

Minnick looked at her like she was insane. "That's the stupidest thing I've heard yet. Why the hell would we leave when we can get a shot that'll keep us from turning into one of those brain chompers?"

"I think I know why," Ida said. "The warbot said the docbot is working on *finding* a vaccine, not that it already has one." Her blue eyes were steady but tension was etched in the lines around her mouth. "That means the docbot has been programmed to do whatever it takes to create one."

"And that," Leslie added, "means it's going to need test subjects." She glanced at each of them. "Which would be us."

"I don't understand," Cat said. "How do you test the vaccine to see if...if..." She fell silent.

"I think we all know the answer to that," Wayne said.

Minnick scowled. "I ain't following. So it might not work – no guarantees anyway. But what's the big deal?"

"Because in experimental trials, you vaccinate the test subject then immediately expose him to the thing you just vaccinated him against," Leslie explained patiently.

Minnick's eyes nearly bulged. "Are you fucking kidding me? They give us a shot then send us into a mass of those things?"

"Don't be an idiot," Blaine Jackson snapped. "They fix it so we only get bit, or jack us up with a dose of zombie blood or something."

Minnick's cheeks went red. "Call me an idiot again and I'll re-arrange your face," he threatened.

"Oh, just stop it," Ida cut in. "We're stuck in here. We don't have to like it but let's not make it worse by turning on each other."

"Nobody died and made you boss," Minnick retorted.

"Well, you're sure not," Cat Jackson put in. "The only boss around right now is that robot out there."

"You got a smart mouth," Minnick said. "You're not so old. Maybe you just need a good spanking." He leered at her. "I could do that."

Blaine Jackson stood with a jerk. "You touch my daughter and I –"

"What?" Cat interrupted. "Defend me? *Save* me? Like you saved Mom?"

Before she could continue, her father's open palm smacked hard against the left side of her face. "He's right," Blaine said hoarsely. "You *do* have a smart mouth."

"Asshole," Cat spat as she backed away from him. "The rest of them should know that you left her, that you just *ran*. And you'd do the same to them if –"

"Please do not resort to violence against each other," said the war-bot's crisp voice. They all gasped as the robot came clunking into the room. He smelled of oil, hot metal, and burned wood. There probably wasn't much left of the front door anymore. "You would find it uncomfortable if I had to restrain each of you. I didn't have much patience or retention for the files on human anatomy and pain levels."

"Don't see why some metal-mouthed monstrosity gets to tell me what to do," Janet Weinhardt said. As usual, her voice was loud and shrill, like something sharp being dragged across glass. "I'll do what the hell I want, and when I want besides." Although the warbot didn't bother to argue, the frail old woman still made no move to get up from her seat on the couch.

"How did you survive, Mrs. Weinhardt?" Wayne asked her suddenly. "Did you have someone with you? Did you hide somewhere?" When she just looked at him, he asked, "How did you get here, into this building?"

The look she sent him was withering. "My grandmother brought me, of course."

Wayne lifted one eyebrow. "Your grandmother?"

"That's physically impossible," the warbot said before Janet could elaborate. "She's wearing a tag around her neck with a medical identification number on it. A check of the database indicates that her last surviving maternal family member was her mother, who died twenty-two years ago. The last family member in any event was her husband, who died slightly over ten years ago."

Janet Weinhardt gaped at the robot. "W–What? Irv is dead? Oh, my *God!*" She burst into tears. "But I just talked to him this morning!"

"She also has clinically advanced Alzheimer's Disease," the warbot added.

"And you have no heart," snapped Leslie. She rubbed the old woman's shoulder. "There, there. I'm sorry."

"I don't get paid for having heart," it replied. "Actually, I don't have a heart, and I don't get paid at all. My only reward is fulfilling my program, which for me is pretty good stuff. It gives my programming an electrical fuzzy feeling."

"Speaking of feelings," Ida Alston cut in, "the others can do what they want, but I personally don't want to be a part of your…what did you call it? Oh yeah – Advanced Directive. Obviously that goes for my daughters, too."

"Admirable," said the robot. "At least from a human perspective. But not an option. My Advanced Directive overrides all other programming except for self-preservation in the most extenuating of circumstances."

A corner of Minnick's mouth lifted as he eyed the robot. It stood about seven feet tall and had probably had to duck to go through the front door...or at least what was left of it. "And exactly what would that extenuating circumstance be?"

"I haven't encountered that yet, so I can't tell you. I do know it's not nine potential zombie dinners locked in a twenty-fifth-floor apartment."

"Door looks pretty wide open to me," said the former tow truck driver.

"Consider me an immoveable barrier," the warbot replied. Before any of them could counter, there was another sound, the *shhhhsh* of hydraulics and metal on metal as another robot made its way down the entrance hallway. The warbot's disc-shaped head spun to check the area behind it, then rotated back toward them. "Allow me to introduce my counterpart, Docbot_1389482. We were programmed by the same scientist. You could say we're brothers." The warbot moved slightly to one side so that the docbot could shuffle awkwardly past him.

"Hello, humans," said Docbot_1389482 in a voice that sounded much like a bad recording being played inside a tin can. "We shall continue Project Vaccination Z trials immediately."

"WHEN THE DOCBOT said *continue*," Wayne Hardin asked his wife in a whisper a couple of hours later, "does that mean what I think it does?"

"Yes," Leslie answered. Under the clearly threatening scrutiny of the warbot, each of them had "volunteered" to allow the docbot to collect five tubes of blood from everyone. Things had almost gotten out of hand when Ida had refused to allow the robot to take blood from her daughters. There was something intimidating about her, but even she had changed her mind when the warbot had tramped forward, leveled one of his machinegun arms at her head, and asked who next was going to refuse for the kids when she was dead. Now Leslie's expression was grim and the morning sunlight pouring through the apartment's huge windows did nothing to brighten the slightly ashen color of her face. "Essentially we're the latest lab rats."

Wayne rubbed his hair, as though he was trying to massage some sense into his thoughts. "I wonder how many other trials it's run, how many other people have…" He didn't finish.

"Died?" Leslie didn't look at him. "There's no telling. But if you're brave enough, I'll bet that thing's programming is all clinical and no tact. Ask and it'll probably just tell you."

"I don't think I want to know. Do you?"

She shrugged. "Maybe…maybe not. There are pros and cons. If there have been a lot, it could be close to actually succeeding. If not, it's early in the experiments and we're probably all going to die. Hell, we're probably going to die anyway, right? If whatever these bots do doesn't kill us, the zombies will step in and take over. Eventually they'll get us."

He frowned at her. "People who think positive live longer."

She waved a hand in the air. "I love you, but you've said that to me a thousand times since we met. You want me to think positive? Fine. I'm a would-have-been-biologist. One more semester and I would've had my Master's. I'm positive we're all going to die. How's that?"

"Not precisely what I had in mind."

Neither of them said anything else. Right now things were quiet, calmer than they had been in days. Cat had found a bunch of board games in one of the closets and she and the twins were playing *Dogopoly* while they each munched on some Ritz crackers from the pantry; the girls still hadn't said anything, but they clearly understood the game and would tap a finger on the table each time Cat landed on one of their properties. They were playing as one person against Cat and beating her mercilessly, as if the two of them could follow each other's thoughts and easily outsmart anyone else. Mrs. Weinhardt was staring out the window, her reddened gaze seeing something far away on the waters of Lake Michigan that no one else could imagine. Minnick was watching the women, like the creep he always was, while Ida kept one eye on her kids and the other on him. Blaine Jackson had picked a book from one of the shelves and settled onto an overstuffed chair in the far corner of the living room, but he wasn't reading it – he hadn't turned a page in a quarter of an hour.

"Do you think he really did what his daughter claimed?" Leslie asked her husband in an almost inaudible voice.

"What's that?"

"Left his wife behind to get caught by the zombies when he ran."

Wayne stared in Jackson's direction. "It's hard to say," he finally answered. "I don't know the man well enough – none of us do."

"Cat does."

Wayne shrugged. "Maybe, but maybe not. Think about it. When you were fifteen, how well did you *really* know your parents? Teenagers are focused on themselves and the world only as it directly affects them. Half of them don't even know what their parents do for a living – they never give a thought to adult crap like bills and jobs and stress. They live with these people every day but the best they can come up with on Father's Day is a cheap tie for a man who might fix air conditioners. Mom gets a bottle of bubble-gum-scented body wash. Or worse, they buy something based on the knowledge that they themselves will end up with it – like the body wash. Before the zombies, how many kids have ever seen their mom or dad deal with anything more dangerous than a cockroach?"

"Good point." Leslie ran a hand through her hair. "Oh, for the days when I used to run screaming from palmetto bugs."

He grinned. "And me from spiders." He started to say something else, then froze as both the robots appeared in the doorway between the living room and the entry hall. "Uh-oh."

"Janet Weinhardt, please come with me," intoned the docbot.

Silence followed the command. One by one every person in the room turned to look at the old woman – they couldn't help it. She didn't notice them or the robots, and didn't acknowledge the command; she just kept staring out the window. Maybe she was remembering a better place and time, a past in which her husband was still alive and her mind was fully functional. Or was she capable of that kind of creative leap? Maybe, like all of the others, she was just wishing they were somewhere better.

The docbot didn't bother to ask again. It clunked forward, navigating effortlessly between the furniture to where Mrs. Weinhardt stood silently in front of the glass. Even before it was completely stopped, one of its metal arms extended toward her; there was a muted *clank* and then her wrist was encased in the two-piece circular pincer on the end of its arm. Before she registered what had happened, the pincer tightened like a handcuff around her wrist and the docbot reversed direction and began pulling her toward the door.

"What the hell!" the old woman screeched. She balled her free hand into a fist and banged on the top of the shorter docbot's round head. "Let go of me, you bastard! You shit-eating piece of scrap, I'll melt you into something uglier than you already are!"

"Hey, just a minute," Wayne Hardin said as he stood and took a step in her direction. "She never said she wanted to do this. You can't just take her —"

"I must obey my Advanced Directive," said the docbot, unfazed by Mrs. Weinhardt's shrieks and resistance.

"Really?" Cat Jackson scrambled over the back of the couch and placed herself squarely in front of the docbot. "What happened to our rights?" She glared at it, then at the warbot still standing guard at the entrance to the front hall.

The docbot didn't so much as pause when it came to Cat. Her slender frame was no match for the robot's; it was short and squat and too well-balanced to tip over. It simply kept going and pushed her aside, like an ice barge breaking through a frozen river. "Damn you!" she yelled. "Let go of her. It doesn't matter if she has Alzheimer's. She still has rights, too!"

"If you're referring to the Bill of Rights, or even basic human rights, it would appear those have become O-B-E," said the warbot, enunciating each letter.

"OBE?" repeated Minnick. He couldn't take his eyes off Mrs. Weinhardt, but he made no move to try to help her, either. "What the fuck does that mean?"

"Overcome by events," Wayne said. His voice was hoarse but he didn't have to raise it to be heard. The elderly woman had stopped resisting and now just followed dazedly as the docbot stomped forward. "It's a military term. Every journalist in the world has heard it."

"As has every soldier," the warbot noted. He moved slightly to the right and the docbot pulled Mrs. Weinhardt past him and disappeared. The warbot stayed where it was. "An unfortunate side effect of war."

No one said anything for several minutes, then Ida asked the question they were all too afraid to voice. "What's the docbot going to do to her?"

Before the robot could answer, Janet Weinhardt's screams pierced the air from somewhere outside the apartment. Even though they were dampened by the intervening walls, there was no mistaking the terror and desperation conveyed on the high-pitched sounds. Then another sound joined in, a growl that was thick with fluids and menace. Not nearly as loud as the old woman's screams, they heard it because it was something with which they had all become way too familiar these past months.

"Oh, God, no," Leslie whispered.

Abruptly both noises stopped, leaving them all too shocked to move. Then they heard clanking, much like the racket that Janet Weinhardt had made when she'd tried to free herself from the docbot's clutches. At the doorway, the warbot's flat-shaped head suddenly swiveled back and forth a couple of times.

"Pardon me," it said in an absolutely horrid and emotionless tone, "but I must go and assist Docbot_1389482. It would appear that Janet Weinhardt has become OBE."

"Does that mean what I think it does?" Cat Jackson asked in a small voice.

"Oh shit oh shit oh shit," Minnick muttered. He seemed unable to say anything else. "Oh shit oh shit —"

"It means the docbot's first clinical trial with this latest group of participants — us — has failed," Leslie Hardin said. She couldn't keep the bitterness out of her voice. "It's only a matter of time before it modifies the vaccine and comes for someone else so it can try the latest and greatest version."

"I wonder who's next," Blaine Jackson said. He glanced around, then looked guiltily down at his shoes.

His daughter's lip curled and she looked like she was going to say something when Mindy and Rietta stunned them all by speaking in unison.

"You are."

Everyone in the room seemed to gasp at once, then they all focused their gazes on the twins. The girls, however, were staring at only one person —

Blaine Jackson.

"Ha ha," he finally managed. "Very funny joke, kiddies." He cleared his throat, then sent a furious look at his daughter. "Did you tell them to say that, Cat? You've done some pretty crappy things, but this isn't at all —"

"I didn't!" The teenager shook her head hard enough to make her earrings slap against the edge of her jaw. "I swear it!"

The girls hadn't stopped gazing at Blaine, who was starting to fidget under their scrutiny. "Didn't your mother teach you it's not polite to stare at people? You two go back to your game." When they kept looking at him, Jackson made a frustrated sound and turned his attention to Ida. "What the hell, Ida. Where'd they come up with that crazy line?"

She moved over to her daughters and looked at him warily as she made them stand, then pointed them in the direction of their back bedroom. "Call it what you want," she finally said. She turned without meeting anyone else's gaze, but as she left the room, she made one final statement over her shoulder.

"They've never been wrong."

Blaine watched them go, his mouth open. "What? What did she just say? Was she kidding?"

Over on the couch, Minnick leaned back and crossed his arms. "Doesn't seem like the humorous type to me."

"I wonder if that's how Ida and those kids have managed to make it," Cat said suddenly. "Think about how hard it must be to run or hide from the zombies with two little girls. But if they can...I dunno. See the future or something, then they *know* when the zombies are coming, right? So they always know ahead of time when they have to leave."

"Then why didn't they warn us about the zombie showing up at the door here?" Wayne asked.

"Maybe," Leslie chimed in, "because there was no place to run *to*. The fight or flight instinct couldn't apply."

Minnick nodded. "Makes sense to me," he said. Incredibly he managed to look smug while sounding absolutely solemn.

"All of you just shut up," Blaine Jackson suddenly snapped. "There's nothing *serious* about any of this. It's nothing but the fabrications of bored kids, that's all. I can't believe —"

"Blaine Jackson, please come with me."

Although later they wouldn't be able to figure out how they'd missed it, none of them had heard the two robots come into the room. A few minutes earlier, Jackson had picked up his novel again and settled himself onto what was apparently his favorite chair; at the sound of his name, he leaped out of his seat so quickly that the heavy chair toppled backward. "No!" he shouted and scrambled away from the docbot that moved relentlessly toward him. "Get away from me!" The others in the room veered away from him and the docbot followed him, but the warbot had stopped in the opening to the hall, once again blocking any escape. Cat Jackson stood frozen, her eyes wide, blue pools of horror as her father bounded around the room and, gasping for air, finally stopped and cowered behind her. Then she astounded them all by lifting her chin up and stepping toward the docbot.

"Take me instead," she said.

Behind her, Blaine Jackson whimpered but did not protest his daughter's offer.

But Leslie Hardin didn't hesitate. "Absolutely not," she cried. "Don't you dare touch that girl!"

She tried to move forward but her husband's hand shot into the crook of her elbow and pulled her back. "Don't forget the warbot," he whispered. "It won't do her or anyone any good if it shoots you."

She started to yell something more at the robot, but the docbot's droning voice swallowed up her words. "That is not feasible, Cat Jackson," it said. "Your father is the next in line to continue this phase of my Advanced Directive."

"Based on what?" Cat demanded. "Some random fucking lottery going on in your computer brain?"

"Probability of survival," it replied.

"But that doesn't make any sense," she protested. "I'm younger, stronger —"

"Exactly," Leslie said from across the room. Wayne still hadn't released her arm. "Any scientist worth a damn knows that you save the strongest specimens for last. You don't want to waste your best subjects by exposing them to the initial — the riskiest — serum."

"Oh," said Wayne. His eyes widened. "That's why they took Mrs. Weinhardt first."

Leslie nodded. "She was the oldest and the least likely to survive."

"Blaine Jackson," the docbot said again. It wasn't a question.

Cat Jackson shook her head. "No," she said firmly. "There's still some personal choice involved here, some free will —"

"I'm afraid not," rumbled the warbot. It had moved farther into the room and was now only about a dozen feet away. This was the closest anyone had seen it come, and it was obvious they'd all under-estimated its potential for speed, if not its strength. When Cat glanced in the warbot's direction, the docbot's arm shot out and hooked her father's just above his elbow. Blaine screamed and tried to pull away, but his efforts were as useless as the blows his daughter immediately began to heap on the thing's metal surface. The robot, of course, ignored her as it turned and yanked the elder Jackson after it.

"Wait — no!" wailed Blaine. "No, not me, not me! Take her — take Cat! She wants to go, I don't!" In the shocked silence that followed his bellowing, he twisted and turned and pulled, but it was futile; every time it looked as if he might be gaining the tiniest bit of space within the docbot's steel grip, its hold tightened, then tightened again. At the end, just before it dragged him past the warbot and finally out of sight, Blaine Jackson had fought so hard that something in his arm had snapped and it resembled an overstuffed sausage bisected by a thick metal ring.

"Let me go with him," Cat cried. "Please — he's my dad!"

"I'm afraid not," said the warbot. She crashed into the front of it, but it was like a bird bouncing off the windshield of an eighteen-wheeler. As Blaine Jackson's howls of protest grew faint with distance, the warbot backed up until it once more filled the doorway and no one could go around it.

"I WONDER WHERE it took him," Minnick said about an hour later. "No offense, but I don't hear him screaming or anything, not like the old lady." He looked at the others. "That's a good thing, right?"

"Yeah," Cat Jackson said in a small voice. She nodded at Minnick. "Maybe it means he's okay." When no one else said anything, she went back to staring at her shoes, a pair of Nikes so covered in dirt and red-brown stains — and they all knew what those were — that the once-famous symbol had been nearly obliterated. Wayne Hardin had ducked into the bathroom at the far end of the apartment and they could hear him murmuring.

"What the hell is he doing?" Minnick asked irritably. "Talking to himself?"

"Dictating," answered Leslie. "Keeping track of everything that's happened by recording it."

"So that tiny camera of his is a recorder, too?" Ida asked. "I saw him taking pictures of everyone earlier, even the robots." She frowned slightly and cracked her knuckles. Her hands were veined and rough, strong-looking. "The robots didn't seem to care," she added as she glanced to where her girls were playing with the *Dogopoly* game again, this time just moving the pieces randomly around the board.

"They're machines," Leslie said. Her voice was brittle. "They aren't made to care, and they have nothing to hide. They're programmed to do what they do, and that's the end of it." She followed Ida's gaze to the twins. "He used to be a journalist, you know. Wrote articles for a bunch of the major newspapers and magazines. I guess he figures someone has to record what we're going through so that there's a record of it."

Minnick smirked. "Why bother? Who's gonna be around to read it anyway?"

"Not you."

Minnick jumped at the sweet, high voice, then stared at the girl who'd spoken. He had no idea which was which. "W–What?"

"Rietta," Ida said sharply. "Don't say anything."

"They're coming for you next," said the other one, Mindy. It was an admirable tactic for getting the statement out without disobeying their mother.

Minnick jerked, then his face turned red and he scowled at Ida. "What the fuck, lady – can't you control your brats?"

She opened her mouth to tell him to screw off, but before the words could leave her mouth the warbot glided into the room. The damned thing seemed to be quieter every time it showed up. "How interesting that the children always know what's going to happen," it intoned. "Completely illogical, but definitely interesting."

The docbot was right behind its companion, and squeezed around the bigger robot on the left. "Randall Minnick, come with me," it said as it extended the arm with the curved grip toward Minnick.

He shot to his feet. "I don't think so," he snarled and danced backward a few steps. He was wearing his usual oversized plaid shirt and he reached beneath it and yanked out a gun, a really big one.

"Oh, shit," Cat said, and scrambled sideways. Everyone mimicked her, with Ida pulling her daughters quickly to the farthest corner; if the warbot was going to fire on the idiot redneck, no one wanted to be within range.

"This is a .50 caliber Desert Eagle," he announced as he racked the slide and aimed it at the docbot. His voice was shaking but they could all tell he was trying hard not to show any fear. "It's loaded with armor-piercing rounds. You come near me and I will blow that computer brain of yours right out of your skull...or whatever you call it."

"You *fuck*," Cat Jackson said in amazement as she brought her head up from where she'd ducked behind the couch. "You had that gun this whole time and you let that thing take my Dad?"

"Had to save my ammo," Minnick replied without hesitating.

Wayne Hardin leaned into view. "Had to save your own ass, is what you mean," he said in disgust.

"Whatever," Minnick said. Without taking his gaze off the docbot, he began to sidle to the right. "You get your guard there to move the hell out of the door," he ordered. "So I can get out of here."

"Well, that's just not possible," the warbot replied. It actually sounded amused. "Unfortunately for you, I'm afraid we're just not scared of guns."

"No?" Minnick suddenly spun and leaped over the couch; when he stood upright again, he had one beefy arm across Cat's collarbone and the pistol's barrel pressed against the side of her head. "But I bet she is. How badly do you want to keep these people alive? Because I swear I'll shoot one every two minutes if you don't let me out."

"Let me go, you fat-faced bastard!" Cat shrieked. She tried to claw at him and got clubbed on the side of the head with the butt of the gun for her trouble; her words turned to a grunt as the skin split and blood dripped down the side of her face.

"Shut up," he told her. "No more Mr. Nice Guy."

"Like you ever were!" Leslie cried. She had joined her husband at the side of one of the doorways, while Ida Alston had reappeared and was standing quietly by the farthest of the huge living room windows.

"Breaks my heart that you think of me like that, sweetheart...*not*." Minnick eyed the two robots, but they hadn't moved. "Getting a little antsy here, you rusted sacks of sheet metal. Let's get the show on the road – you want Little Miss Goth here alive, you gotta let me out."

The warbot's head never moved. "Makes no difference to me," it said. "But it's Docbot_1389482's call. What do you think, boss?"

"I acknowledge that the girl has the better chance of survival because of her youth," it replied. "But I would prefer to have both for the vaccine trials."

"Got it," the warbot said. The gun arm that had been aimed at Minnick's head lowered slightly.

"That's more like it," Minnick said and moved forward, shoving Cat in front of him a couple of steps. She stumbled, woozy from the blow to her head. "Now just get out of the way and I'll –"

The warbot shot him in the knee.

He screamed and pitched forward as the bullet pounded his leg backward. Cat was jerked to the floor with him as the hand holding the Desert Eagle flailed but didn't release the weapon. Bellowing in agony, Minnick clawed his way upright and tried to haul Cat in front of him with his free arm. "I'll fix you!" he howled as he swung the pistol toward his prisoner's face. "I'll kill this little bitch! I'll –"

Ida Alston stepped in front of him and hit him square in the nose with the palm of her hand.

The blow was hard and almost too quick to follow. This time Minnick slammed backward, his grip on both Cat and the Desert Eagle going instantly limp. When he hit the carpet, he stayed there.

In the silence that followed, the lights within the docbot's eyes blinked a few times. "That is most unfortunate," it finally said.

"We have enough things trying to kill us," Ida said flatly. She backed away as the robot rolled forward, encircled Minnick's wrist, and began to drag him away. "We shouldn't be killing each other."

"Agreed," said the docbot. "However, that is apparently exactly what has happened. Randall Minnick no longer has any vital signs. He is therefore not suitable for the vaccine trials."

Leslie had run over to help Cat to her feet. Now she jerked. "Wait – he's dead?" She stared at Ida. "You killed him?"

The tall woman shrugged. "I must have hit him a little harder than I intended. Then again, he was a jerk. If someone had broken his nose before…" She shrugged again.

Over by the door, the docbot transferred its grip on Minnick's arm to the warbot. "This requires disposal," it ordered before turning to face the humans again. "Wayne Hardin, please come with me."

Leslie sat down on the floor. "Oh," she whispered. "Oh, no. Not so soon."

"I expected this," Wayne said calmly.

Cat had more or less recovered, and now she shook her head as she tried to clear the last of the fogginess away. "I don't understand. Why does it keep taking the guys, and not us?"

"Because of the females' capacity for reproduction," the docbot stated.

When Cat still looked confused, Ida added, "Think of it in terms of hunting. A hunter will generally shoot a buck before a doe." Her gaze was hard as it focused on the robots. "The humans have become the hunted here."

"I'm sorry you've taken that position," the docbot said. "I'm only following my Advanced Directive."

"What exactly *is* your Advanced Directive, anyway?" demanded Wayne. He held his recorder toward the robot. "Since we're such a vital part of these trials of yours, I think we should at least know it."

"Of course," the Docbot said. "The file as saved in my memory is as follows:

//Docbot_1389482/advanced_directive//

*1 Coordinate with warbot_898432913 at all times for procurement of non-infected humans as test subjects [Entered]

*2 Formulate vaccine for zombie virus using any means necessary [Entered]

*3 If no. then: Continue research using whatever means necessary until successful [Entered]

*4 If yes. then: Disseminate vaccine to uninfected humans [Entered]

*5 … [Not Entered]

//advanced_directive_status: INCOMPLETE//

Wayne frowned. "Incomplete?"

"Affirmative."

"So you're carrying out a program that was never finished?" Leslie asked. "That's insane!"

"Insanity is a human thing," the warbot put in. "Docbot doesn't have it. Unfortunately the scientist who came up with our programming died before he could input docbot's final command. I found him face down on his keyboard."

"He was a zombie?" Cat asked incredulously.

"Of course not. Zombies are not capable of rational thought." The warbot lifted Minnick's arm carelessly. "He was like Minnick here. Croaked because something else did him in."

"Pneumonia," the docbot added. "He had been working very hard on programming and searching for a vaccine and had not been maintaining his health."

"I don't suppose you would accept that the missing directive is don't harm the humans that are the subjects of the experiment," Leslie suggested.

"Although that does seem logical, without my programmer's password I can neither accept it nor allow it to be input into my memory as a command."

"Fantastic," Cat muttered.

"So where were we?" asked the warbot. "Oh, yeah —"

"Wayne Hardin, please come with me," the docbot repeated.

It started to come toward him, but Wayne stood and held up his hand. "No need," he said. "I'll go with you in just a moment."

"What are you doing?" Leslie gasped. She clutched at him.

He pulled his wife close. "Don't fight it, babe," he said. "You know it's useless." He looked toward the other two, and even though they didn't know him that well, Cat and Ida came over and crowded close enough to let him put his arm across their shoulders. "Find a way to get out of here," he whispered as softly as he could. "I don't know how, but you have to at least *try*." He released Cat and Ida, then put both arms around Leslie and kissed her deeply. "I love you," he said. He pressed his camera into her hand. "Keep it going if you can. There are more batteries in my jacket." Tears were streaming down her cheeks but she nodded.

"Wayne Hardin," the docbot said.

"I'm coming already," he snapped. "Have a little patience, would you?"

"Not one of our strong points," the warbot said. "I think I mentioned that before."

He touched Leslie's cheek, then pulled out of her grasp and walked across the room. She wailed and tried to follow but Cat and Ida held her back. Wayne stepped in front of the docbot, then glanced over his shoulder. "Remember what I told you," he said.

And then he was gone, and Leslie never saw her husband again.

"We're next, Mama."

"That's not going to happen."

It was the first time Leslie or Cat had seen Ida Alston show more than a mild reaction to anything, but now she rocketed into action. The warbot was still there, but for the time being, its attention was on the hallway rather than the occupants of the apartment. Maybe another zombie had found its way up the staircase, and more were gathering behind it.

"Why would they be next?" Cat asked. "They —"

"Keep your voice down," Ida said sharply. "Don't think for a moment that the warbot isn't keeping track of everything it hears us say."

"Because of the five of us, they are the most defenseless," Leslie murmured. "On a survival capability rating, they're pretty much toast."

Without a word, they followed Ida to the back end of the apartment and watched her move rapidly around the room she shared with her girls. Her daughters were dressed in long-sleeved shirts, jeans, and tennis shoes, and it wasn't long before she'd put lightweight rubber raincoats on them and tied bandanas over their mouths. Her outfit was almost the same except her raincoat was nylon and stopped at the hips instead of the knees. All three of them pulled on nylon gloves that had rubber palms and fingertips.

"Whatever it takes, I'm getting us out of here," she said. "I suggest you do the same. I have no intention of sitting here and waiting to be the next on that robot's experimentation menu. And I'm certainly not turning my daughters over to them."

Leslie just looked at her numbly, but Cat had to ask. "How were you able to do what you did to Randall?"

"I've been trained," Ida said in a completely matter-of-fact voice. "I have a fourth-degree black belt."

Cat snorted. "Right. And you think that somehow we can fight our way out like you can?"

"No. Realistically you don't stand a chance. But would you rather go down fighting or just offer your throat to the next zombie?"

"Fight," Leslie said hoarsely. "Those damned robots took my husband. I'll fight them with every last breath in my body."

Ida nodded. "I thought so." She turned back to her preparations. "Make sure you have no open wounds," she told them. "That's always rule number one. If you do, cover them with something waterproof so no zombie blood gets in them. Keep your mouth covered, wear clothes that protect your skin." She rummaged through the closet, found nothing, then moved to the linen closet in the bathroom. "Here," she said, and handed each woman a spray can of foaming bathroom cleaner. "It's not much but if you spray it at their eyes – or whatever robots call them – it might blind them long enough for us to get past them. If the last couple of hours are any indication, it won't be long before the bots show up to claim the girls."

"What about you?" asked Cat.

Ida shrugged on a small backpack and positioned her daughters slightly behind her, then pulled something from each pocket of her jacket. A flick of her wrists made the foot-long rubber-coated metal rods extend into three-foot deadly-looking batons. An instant later and she had retracted them into barely-noticeable rubber sticks.

Cat and Leslie looked at each other. "Oh," Leslie said.

A noise from the front room made the women turn their heads. "Party time," Ida said.

"Mindy Alston and Rietta Alston, please come with me."

"Stay behind me," Ida told her girls. "You know the drill." They nodded in unison.

"What about us?" Cat asked. Her words were breathy, fear making her lungs hitch.

"You two are going out first," Ida said simply. "You look the same as the last time they were here. We don't. And remember, aim for the eyes. Let's go."

Cat and Leslie nodded, then reluctantly headed toward the living room. On impulse, Leslie ducked into the guest bathroom on the way and yanked down the heavy brocade shower curtain to take with her.

As the women expected, both robots were waiting, the warbot blocking any escape as the docbot moved into the room and headed toward them, this time with both arms extended as it prepared to take the children. "Please step out of the way, Ida Alston," it said, but no one waited to hear the rest of its statement.

Although they had nothing specifically planned, the three women moved together in remarkable synchronicity. Cat and Leslie walked calmly toward the docbot, then abruptly vaulted into action. Without knowing exactly what she was going to do, Leslie dropped to the floor and slid underneath the docbot's outstretched arms. When she came up behind it, she whipped the dark green shower curtain over the shoulders and head of the warbot, effectively blinding it. At the same time, Cat brought up her can of foaming cleaner and sprayed the head of the docbot, going back and forth as fast as she could, like a kid trying to tag an alley wall before the cops got there.

Leslie ducked as the warbot swung its arms wildly back and forth and tried to dislodge the fabric covering its head. "Damned humans!" it roared. "I ought to –"

"Under no circumstances should you damage the test subjects," instructed the docbot in an infuriatingly emotionless voice. The foam soap was sliding downward as it rotated its head from side to side in an attempt to clear its view. The curved appendages on the ends of its arms were keeping the same movements as its head, swinging to and fro. Cat dodged them and sprayed the machine's head again, intent on keeping it blinded until everyone could get past both robots.

The warbot managed to grab a piece of the shower curtain and yank it free. "Ha!" it said triumphantly, but Leslie was there again, pulling the decorative cloth back over the thing's head, then moving frighteningly close in an effort to tie it in place. "Get off me, you annoying female!"

Then Ida surged into the fray, snapping the batons out and moving so fast that the weapons became twin silver blurs. Every strike was short but destructive. She went for the docbot, the least protected of the two, and attacked the joints where she thought its metal arms might be the weakest. When the device's arms buckled but recovered, she changed tactics and attacked the spindly looking legs, her sole objective to knock the robot off its feet. She twisted and dove to the floor, sliding forward on her spine so she could hammer at the backs of the knee joints in precise blows so rapid it sounded like an impact wrench over-tightening the lug nuts on a wheel. "Go *down*, you metal piece of shit!" she yelled. Her voice and the batons just added to the cacophony of sound – Cat and Leslie were yelling, the warbot was raging, and below it all –

"Mama."

– came the combined voices of the twins, barely above a whisper but as loud as a bullhorn to their mother. Ida cracked the baton across the back of the docbot's knee joint again, this time holding it in place and crossing it from the other side with her second baton. With both of the metal pieces behind one joint, she got a grip on each end of the batons and yanked forward, at the same time coming up with her shoulder and ramming forward as hard as she could.

"Out of balance!" the docbot blared. For the first time, the robot's tone had changed. Now it sounded like someone yelling *Fire!* in a crowded theater. "Out of balance!" The machine's arms flailed and it went down, grasping at anything within reach. Ida was too fast for it, but Cat wasn't as lucky – the end of one arm found the teenager's leg just above the knee and locked tightly around it. She cried out and clawed at the docbot as she was pulled to the floor with it, but it was futile – there was no way she was getting free. A foot away, Leslie had circled around and leaped on the warbot's back, intent on tying the loose ends of the shower curtain in the best knot she could. The warbot rotated crazily at the waist, trying to fling her off. "I cannot assist you with this monkey-wannabe on my back," it announced. "And I cannot see to shoot it."

"Under no circumstances should you damage the test subjects," the docbot repeated. Its voice was slightly off, coming from where the thing's face was half-pushed into the carpet.

"They're going to escape," the warbot warned.

"Apprehend them or it will be necessary to locate an eleventh group of humans upon which to execute the Advanced Directive."

"Clearly you weren't programmed for a conflict situation," the warbot said in mock disgust. It twisted sharply to the right and intentionally bounced into the wall; Leslie gasped as she was momentarily flattened by the thing's immense weight, then she slid to the floor with the breath knocked out of her. "Oh, dear," the warbot said, tilting its head toward the sound of her body falling. "Another side effect of battle, I'm afraid. But one that definitely helps me." Although it still couldn't see, in another second it had tromped over to where she lay and pinned her in place using one of its mammoth legs. "Gotcha."

"*Mama,*" the girls said again in an oddly compelling tone. Ida's head jerked in their direction as she scrambled to her feet, whacking the docbot's remaining arm sideways when it tried to grab at her. Their voices got a smidgen louder, but stayed in that same eerie unity. "*Zombies are coming.*"

"Get over here *now*," she ordered. The docbot's arm reached for her again and this time she let its claw hook on one of the metal batons; when it closed around it, she twisted the baton as hard as she could, using it like a wrench. There was a *crunch*, then the end of the docbot's arm hung limp.

"Malfunction!" it clamored. "Damage to left appendage!"

"What'd you expect?" the warbot shot back. "A goodbye cake?" To keep Leslie trapped, it couldn't move beyond reaching blindly in the direction where it thought Ida might be.

Cat was still struggling within the docbot's other grip, screaming obscenities at it, when Mindy and Rietta nimbly ducked beneath the robot's broken arm. Once they got within range of their mother, she pulled them forward, and when one of her shoes knocked something aside, Ida glanced down and saw Wayne Hardin's camera. Leslie must have dropped it during her fight with the warbot; just for the hell of it, Ida scooped it up and pushed it in her back pocket. She shoved her daughters past the warbot and into the hallway outside the apartment. She heard Cat's and Leslie's cries behind her, but she

just

      never

            hesitated.

There was simply no time or opportunity to save them, and the truth was, she didn't care about the other two women. Her daughters came first, *absolutely* first, and only after them would she consider herself. She started to guide the girls to the left, but they pulled against her.

"*Zombies.*" She barely heard their joint whisper. "*Coming up the stairs now.*"

"Shit," she hissed. "Come this way instead."

She spun the girls and hustled them in the other direction, not even glancing into the apartment as they ran past the doorway. The noise inside – the women yelling and cursing, and the two robots arguing back and forth – would draw the zombies like mosquitoes to perfumed skin in the summer. Although the end for Cat and Leslie had probably just become unspeakable, with any luck at all, she and the twins would be able to slip down one of the rear staircases – perhaps the fire stairwell by the freight elevator – and be long out of the building before the hive mind of the current zombie threat could turn toward them.

WITHOUT MAKING A sound, Ida maneuvered her daughters into a narrow but sunlit alleyway where she could see at least three avenues of available escape. Working quickly, because the zombies *always* eventually found you if you were out in the open, she used what was available in the alley to make a path to safety. It was a tried and true method, and thank God the creatures had no sense of intelligence or reasoning. A four-by-eight-foot sheet of plywood was just the thing to use as a platform on top of an open Dumpster; standing on that and silently thanking her years of martial arts training, she balanced carefully on an old kitchen chair someone had placed by the locked back door of the building, probably as a spot for smoking breaks. From there, she lifted Mindy and Rietta one at a time over her head until each child could grab onto the walkway of an old, overhead fire escape. They pulled themselves up like nimble little monkeys, then got hold of the backpack she handed up to them. By the time that was done, there was a zombie in a dress tottering down the alley and another two just coming around a corner. They'd smelled fresh humans and their uncanny flocking instinct was, as always, right on the mark.

It took under a minute for the zombie to make its way to the Dumpster, but by then Ida had climbed onto the fire escape platform. She pulled a thick rubber bungee cord with a hook on each end from her pack, then leaned over and used it to catch the back of the chair so she could haul it up. The plywood platform was still down there, but two feet of it hung over the front end of the Dumpster. When the zombies – there were five of them now – staggered up to the container, they did exactly what she'd expected and clutched at it, pulling it onto the ground where it slid beneath their feet. Even if their numbers grew large enough to pull the Dumpster on its side and they climbed on it, it wasn't tall enough to let any of them reach the fire escape.

The old-fashioned platform was narrow but sturdy. It ran the length of the building and gave them choices – windows – every ten feet or so. Ida looked quizzically at the girls, but they only shrugged and said nothing. That meant she could choose any one of them. She and her daughters were safe.

For now.

Before she steered the girls down the walkway, Ida let herself relax for a moment and examine the knot of zombies moaning and pulling uselessly at the filthy green trash container. A splash of color in the crowd, clean bright green and incongruous amid the ripped, mud- and blood-caked clothing falling off the creatures, caught her attention. She peered over the railing until she could focus on that particular one –

Janet Weinhardt.

"Damn," she whispered. The old woman stared hungrily up at her, her face gray but her mouth free of blood – she'd yet to find her first victim. She reached upward and Ida saw that even her hands were still clean…that is, except for the single, putrid-looking bite on her left wrist. So that's how the docbot had tested his vaccine – he'd injected the poor woman, then offered her as a tasting sample to the nearest zombie. With the warbot busy guarding the cache of humans, the docbot had apparently dragged the failed vaccine subject downstairs and pushed her out of the building.

And now she'd come back.

Would the others return, too? Oh, yeah – there was Blaine Jackson, and Wayne Hardin, too, not far behind her. Randall Minnick had lucked out, even if he hadn't realized it – dying by Ida's hand had guaranteed he stayed dead. In her mind, she could still hear the screams and curses from Cat and Leslie as she and the twins had fled. She scanned the zombies, following their numbers to the ones that were still trickling into the alley. How long before those two women joined the zombie swarm below, before she had to gaze into their sightless, soulless eyes and wonder if she might have had a chance, any chance at all, at saving them?

Ida turned away and motioned at the girls to go a bit farther down, to the second window. She wasn't going to wait and find out. Because this was the way it was, the way it had always been, and the way it *always* would be. Like those robots, she had a one-track mind. You could even call it her own personal Advanced Directive.

Survival.

The girls first.

Herself second.

Initiate.

ONZE DAMES VAN GEVECHT

AMELIA BEAMER — "Hot Water & Clean Underwear"

A freelance writer and editor, Ms. Beamer's first novel *The Loving Dead*, came out in 2010 and featured zombies and a Zeppelin. She was born in Michigan, grew up in suburban Detroit, received a BA in English Lit (with Honors) from Michigan State University, and worked for years in Oakland, CA as an editor, reviewer, and photographer for *Locus: The Magazine of the Science Fiction and Fantasy Field*. Ms. Beamer then relocated to Australia, where she is at work on her next novel. She has published short fiction and academic articles in various venues; some of her published work is free online at www.ameliabeamer.com.

"Given the subject of robots and the zombie apocalypse, my thoughts immediately turned to sex. Sex is of course a ludicrous and vaguely shameful thing, as are the lengths humans will go to in order to get it. But after safety and water and food, humans need to connect, and to release. My main character is young and scared, and she finds herself with a metal sidekick who has been programmed to be a bit friendlier than the average robot, so much so that she is generally considered useless by people and robots alike. I wanted to see how much these two damaged creatures would annoy one another, and whether they could get over themselves enough to work together."

— *Amelia Beamer*

AMBER BENSON — "Mademoiselle Consuela"

Ms. Benson is an actor, filmmaker, novelist and amateur occultist who sings in the shower. Best known for her work as Tara Maclay on *Buffy The Vampire Slayer*, she is also the author of the Calliope Reaper-Jones series and the co-director (with Adam Busch) of the feature film, *Drones*. She can be stalked on her blog (amberbensonwrotethis.blogspot.com) and on Twitter (@amber_benson) and Facebook (facebook.com/amberbensonwrotethis).

"I just wanted to write a simple story about a girl, her robot…and some zombies. There might be a little full frontal male nudity in there, too, but you gotta read the story to find out if it's human, robot or zombie!"

— *Amber Benson*

NANCY A. COLLINS — "Angus: Zombie vs. Robot Fighter"

Ms. Collins is the author of numerous novels and short stories, including the best-selling *Sunglasses After Dark,* and was a writer for DC Comics' *Swamp Thing*. She is a recipient of the Bram Stoker and British Fantasy Awards, and has been nominated for the World Fantasy, Eisner & International Horror Guild awards. *Left Hand Magic*, the newest installment in the acclaimed Golgotham series, is now available.

"'Angus: Zombie Vs. Robot Fighter' is loosely based on the classic Gold Key comic book *Magnus: Robot Fighter 4000 A.D.*, created and drawn by the great Russ Manning. *Magnus* is one of those sci-fi comic books you read as a kid and really get into without realizing until you're an adult just how super fucked-up the basic premise is. In the comic book, Magnus was an orphaned infant taken by a *robot* and raised alone in an underwater dome and trained to fight *robots* with his bare hands, with nothing but a *robot* for company, while constantly being told he was 'humanity's only hope.' Then, after twenty years, the robot takes Magnus and just drops him off in the middle of a huge, teeming mega-city of the future that's supposed to be ten times the size of New York City and just goes 'See ya! Go fight robots!' So he goes around punching out robots, most of whom look like they came from IKEA and were put together with an Allen wrench. I decided to mine the basic concept for a little black humor by re-imaging the scenario for the *Zombies vs. Robots* universe."

— *Nancy A. Collins*

BREA GRANT — "Pammi Shaw: Creator of Gods and Also Blogger"

Ms. Grant is sometimes a writer (*We Will Bury You; Suicide Girls*), sometimes an actress (*Heroes; Dexter; Halloween 2*) and all-the-time a nice person. Info on what she's doing right this second is at twitter. com/breagrant or breagrant.com.

"I wanted to touch on religion as a strong force in a time of human need. For better or for worse, religion plays a role in most major decisions around the globe – whether it's starting a war or in the way we mourn the death of a loved one. I wanted to put someone in one of the most difficult places possible by ripping away her community, family, and everything she knows, leaving her with her own thoughts. I wanted this person to deal with religion, love, gods and sanity all alone, separated from the raging violence outside. And who better to put in that position than a jaded, flippant teenage blogger named Pammi?"

— *Brea Grant*

RAIN GRAVES — "The Meek, The Earth, and The Inheritance"

Ms. Graves is best known for her work in *Barfodder: Poetry Written in Dark Bars and Questionable Cafes*, which Publishers Weekly deemed "Bukowski meets Lovecraft...". She is a Bram Stoker Award winning poet, and has been writing short sci-fi, horror, and fantasy fiction since 1997 for various books, magazines, and web-zines. *The Four Elements*, co-written with four other Bram Stoker Award-winning poets, will be out in fall of 2012. She lives in San Francisco with three sneaky cats.

"The ZVR series was 'love at first robot' for me. I had several ideas that all would have worked, but this particular story was warm and fuzzy to write from start to finish. I wanted to tell a story that was based in reality and entirely plausible when you combined the ZVR universe setting with human nature, as we are now, in this age. I started with abandoned missile silo clusters currently being sold as space for single-family homes. It seemed a natural progression to have an underground society of eco-nauts that had the best of intentions move through generations in time and the seven deadly sins, only to find their best laid plans were breeding ground for unexpected mutation. The mutation had to be meaningful, however, to a small boy. It had to be cute. All harbingers of fate should be cute. It hurts more when they eat you."

— *Rain Graves*

RHODI HAWK — "Head and Foot"

Ms. Hawk's debut novel, *A Twisted Ladder*, won her the International Thriller Writer Association (ITW) Scholarship Award. A former military crypto-linguist, she lives in Magnolia, Texas with her trio of dogs, three sugar gliders, two bearded dragons, and her sweetheart, a fellow horror writer who is also quite untamed – though she swears she is not an animal hoarder. Her second novel, *The Tangled Bridge*, is currently scheduled to hit book stores around Halloween 2012. http://www.rhodihawk.com/

"I remember, as a kid, being fascinated by tide pools. Toy-sized ecosystems. My sister and I would find them full of barnacles and hermit crabs and iridescent sea lettuces, and of course, tiny fish. I used to wonder if those creatures realized they lived on the fringe of a big wide ocean. When I was invited into world of Zombies vs. Robots, I knew I had to bring 'tide pool culture' to the party. But instead of sea creatures, the subjects in my story are humans living in a sunken prison that turns out to be an all-too-tempting insta-lab for databots. The title, 'A Head and a Foot,' is simply the description of an octopus named Hermes. Hermes is a thief with a knack for navigating sunken tunnels, and he turns out to be a useful friend to the humans who get their first whiff of the big wide ocean beyond their tightly contained world."

— *Rhodi Hawk*

NANCY HOLDER — Introduction

New York Times bestselling author Nancy Holder has sold 80 novels and 200 short stories and articles. She writes tie-in material for *Buffy*,

Teen Wolf, Saving Grace, Angel, Smallville, and many other 'verses. She also writes and edits for Moonstone and has penned three young adult dark fantasy series with Debbie Viguié – *Wicked, Crusade,* and *Wolf Springs Chronicles.*

ERICKA LUGO — Illustrations

Ms. Lugo is an artist and illustrator who first came to the attention of IDW via her postings on DeviantART. Based in Puerto Rico, Ericka's restrained palette and sophisticated design sense reflects her love of classic post-War magazine illustration. She has worked as a colorist and cover artist for local comic studio Razor Blade Apple, and her illustrations have been featured in various digital art and online journals. *Women on War* is Ericka's first mainstream art assignment.

"It's well known that *Zombies vs Robots* has its roots in art; as Ashley Wood's pictures were the original inspiration for the crazy stories from Chris Ryall that followed. Being invited to illustrate this collection was both a thrill and challenge – ten unique challenges, actually. My intention was to find each story's iconic moment, not necessarily the 'action moment,' and portray it in bold yet simple terms. Hopefully I've succeeded."

— *Ericka Lugo*

YVONNE NAVARRO — "Advanced Directive"

Ms. Navarro is a prolific author whose work has earned her the Bram Stoker and numerous other awards. She's written about vampires, zombies, and the end of the world, plus played in the Buffy the Vampire Slayer universe, as well as penned novels to go with a bunch of cool movies like *Hellboy, Elektra, Ultraviolet,* and others. Her most recent novels are *Highborn* and *Concrete Savior,* the first two books in her Dark Redemption Series. Visit her at www.yvonnenavarro.com.

"What horror author doesn't want to write about zombies? Look at what really scares us – it's not vampires, or the wolfman, or some gilled creature rising out of the sea. It's the idea that the stranger on the sidewalk or your next door neighbor might, with no warning at all, become a mindless, starving monster that really hits home, both in the heart and the mind. Think about it: There you are, getting out of your car on a moonless night. You've worked late, you're exhausted and hungry; all you want to do is get your key in the door and get inside before…what? Suddenly the surrounding shadows are blacker than they've ever been, that previously inconsequential breeze is making every bush and tree branch rattle and scrape, and you realize there's not another living creature within blocks. Are you really sure something isn't moving in that dark entryway only three doors down… something with a gaping, drooling mouth that's ready to devour you?"

— *Yvonne Navarro*

EKATERINA SEDIA — "Timka"

Ms. Sedia resides in the Pinelands of New Jersey. She is best known for her critically acclaimed novels, *The Secret History of Moscow*, *The Alchemy of Stone*, *The House of Discarded Dreams*, and *Heart of Iron*. Her short stories have sold to Analog, Baen's Universe, Subterranean and Clarkesworld, as well as numerous anthologies. She is also the editor of *Paper Cities* (World Fantasy Award winner), *Running with the Pack*, and *Bewere the Night*, as well as forthcoming *Bloody Fabulous* and *Wilful Impropriety*. Visit her at www.ekaterinasedia.com.

"When I was asked to write for this anthology, I was excited yet apprehensive: I trade in quiet melancholy and Russian history, which are not necessarily things one thinks of in connection to zombies, robots, or both. And then I decided to write the most quietly contemplative zombie story I could think of. It would of course be set in Moscow, the city of my birth, but who would have the skills to stand up to the zombie menace and a government conspiracy? Enter two virologists and Afghanistan vets, a computer geek, and a little tank – a pretty dumb one, but if people can become kinder, surely tanks can grow smarter?"

— *Ekaterina Sedia*

RACHEL SWIRSKY — "The Virgin Sacrifices"

Ms. Swirsky is an award-winning short fiction writer. Her first collection, *Through The Drowsy Dark*, came out in 2010.

"I've always loved Greek mythology. I don't think the Amazons in this series are the Amazons of Hippolyta, but it's still fun to see what happens when you take an old legend and cross it with post-apocalyptic tech."

— Rachel Swirsky

KAARON WARREN — "River of Memory"

Kaaron Warren's short story collection *The Grinding House* won the ACT Writers' and Publishers' Fiction Award and two Ditmar Awards. Her second collection, *Dead Sea Fruit* also won the ACT Writers' and Publishers' Fiction Awards. Her critically acclaimed novel *Slights* won the Australian Shadows Award, the Ditmar Award, and the Canberra Critics' Award for Fiction. Her novels *Walking the Tree* and *Mistification* were both shortlisted for the Ditmar Awards. Kaaron's stories have appeared in Ellen Datlow's *Year's Best Horror and Fantasy* as well as the *Australian Years Best Horror, Science Fiction and Fantasy* anthologies. Her latest book is *Through Splintered Walls*, and she has recently been named Special Guest for the Australian National Science Fiction Convention in 2013. Kaaron's website is www.kaaronwarren.wordpress.com and she tweets @kaaronwarren.

"One of the things that used to terrify me as a kid was hearing about bottomless pits. The idea of falling until you die totally freaked me out. So when I read about the Amazons being dumped into Tartarus, falling for nine days, I knew that's the direction I wanted to send my story. I loved the idea that in Tartarus you can choose whether to remember your past lives, and therefore move onto heaven, or forget your past and have to be reincarnated. I wondered what a zombie would do if it suddenly remembered the human stuff; who they'd loved. Where they lived. What made them laugh. Of course, many humans would be nicer as zombies. I had a look at that, too."

— Kaaron Warren

IDW PUBLISHING PRESENTS

Zombies vs Robots
ZVR Alt-Lit Checklist

THIS MEANS WAR!
The first ground-breaking ZVR prose collection.
Hearty tales of bullets, bolts and brains by Joe McKinney,
Lincoln Crisler, Norman Prentiss, Nancy A. Collins,
Brea Grant, Rachel Swirsky, James A. Moore, Sean Taylor,
Jesse Bullington, Nicholas Kaufmann, and Steve Rasnic Tem.
Introduction by ZVR co-creator Chris Ryall.
Illustrated by Fabio Listrani.
ISBN: 978-1-61377-143-3 • $17.99

Z-BOYZ IN THE ROBOT GRAVEYARD
Harrowing two-part novella by John Shirley, original cyberpunk,
street smart horror specialist, and handsome raconteur.
Illustrated by Daniel Bradford.
ISBN: 978-1-61377-239-3 • $39.99

ZVR DIPLOMACY
A battle royale of robot mayhem and zombie fury,
featuring eight infectious tales of clanking chaos and cranial
craving, set in either England or Russia, courtesy of
Dale Bailey, Simon Clark, Robert Hood,
Steven Lockley, Gary McMahon, Rio Youers,
Ekaterina Sedia, and Simon Kurt Unsworth.
Illustrated by Michael Dubisch.
Coming Soon!

THIS MEANS MORE WAR!
The fourth ZVR prose collection.
Illustrated by Fabio Listrani.
Coming Soon!

With even more ZVR titles in the works.

The ZVR Alt-Lit series is edited by Jeff Conner.

www.idwpublishing.com/zvr